COLLATERAL DAMAGE

Eileen Nauman a.k.a. Lindsay McKenna

D1452807

Blue Turtle Publishing

Collateral Damage
First edition 2023
Original Copyright © 2015, R. Eileen Nauman
ISBN: 978-1-951236-45-8, Print Edition

Excerpt from *No Quarter*
Original Copyright © 2015, R. Eileen Nauman

This edition is published by arrangement with Blue Turtle Publishing Company.

Dear Readers,

Welcome to my latest romantic military suspense series: SHADOW TEAM!

Ex-SEAL Cal Sinclaire is going to marry Sky Lambert, and everything seems to be a dream come true for them until a shocking event occurs. Sky disappears on the day before her wedding. Anguished, Cal calls on his old SEAL team friends, together with a Master Chief at the SEAL units, to try to find Sky. No one has any idea who did it or why. They have no evidence to go on to locate her. She could be anywhere in the world, and his SEAL team dives into finding microscopic clues to her possible whereabouts. Come hell or high water, they will find her…or else.

Sky's whole world implodes as she slowly regains consciousness and finds herself bound, gagged and blindfolded after being heavily drugged. She has no idea who has done this to her, where she is or where they are taking her. Her heart cries out for Cal, for all they've gone through over the years, and for finally being able to admit their binding love to one another. WHO has done this to her? All the years in Witness Protection, hiding at the ends of the Earth from a crazed Russian man who wanted her for his own, whether she wanted to be his or not. She was rid of him, killed earlier in the Peruvian jungle. Her dreams are destroyed, and Sky sees no way out—not realizing she is collateral damage.

Dedication

To all the readers who love romantic military suspense!

CHAPTER 1

June 1

C AL SINCLAIR DIDN'T have the heart to interrupt Sky Lambert, the woman he was going to marry in two weeks' time. He halted near the cedar stairs to their master bedroom on the second floor of his Virginia home he'd built himself over a seven-year period. The cabin sat on a hill surrounded by Douglas fir, oak, maple, elm, and beech trees. There, in the alcove where the bay windows looked out over the pristine meadow below, he watched Sky sitting and drawing with her pastel chalk set on her easel.

Weeks ago, she'd discovered all his drafting tools and accessories he used to build his two-story cedar home down in the basement. Cal smiled a little, wrapping his arms across his chest, watching her intently. The morning sunlight poured through the cathedral windows that stretched skyward on the eastern side of their bedroom. He loved this woman who had stolen his heart and fed his soul like the sunlight drifting silently through the bedroom. They had both lost so much in the past, and Cal felt incredibly grateful it was behind them. He enjoyed watching Sky choose certain pastel colors and apply them to the paper attached to the easel, capturing the beauty of the meadow and stream beyond the bay windows.

His mouth twitched as he remembered looking for Sky and finding her rooting around with eager curiosity through every drawer and shelf in the basement. Along one wall, he'd placed all his sketched drawings, some in ink, some in pencil, and others in pastel chalks, that he'd imagined his dream home would someday look like. It had been a seven-year vision spanning five years when he was in the SEALs, and two years with Shield Security in Alexandria, Virginia. Any time between missions had been spent building it. Sky had discovered the colorful box of chalk and had been transformed into an excited child, finding sixty pastels, touching them as if they were precious jewels. She carried his easel, the paper, and chalks up to her favorite place, the bay windows that overlooked the meadow and stream north of where the house sat.

Cal's heart opened powerfully as he watched Sky working intently, her blond brows drawn down in concentration, trying to capture the meadow where deer crossed it daily at dawn and dusk. Sky had a special connection with the dark green velvet settee that sat facing those windows. After he'd brought her home from Cusco, Peru, from that hellish challenge to get her out of there alive, Sky had settled in with him on Valentine's Day. And over the past months, he'd watched her make his home her home. It was something Cal had wanted desperately for Sky because her childhood had been a nightmare existence. Now she was at peace. He could see it in her oval face, the way her incredible, turquoise-colored eyes shined with happiness. Sky WAS happy. Hell, so was he. He loved her. And for whatever reason unknown to him, she loved him just as fiercely in return.

Rousing himself, Cal deliberately made enough noise to catch Sky's attention. He'd been a Navy SEAL and could walk silently with the best of them. Only, it scared the hell out of Sky to be walked up behind and she didn't hear him approaching her. Cal knew it was because of her past, when Vladimir Alexandrov, the other foster child in the Zimmerman family where she lived, had hunted her like the sadistic sexual predator he was. At seventeen, Vlad had trapped Sky in her bedroom and nearly raped her. He'd stalked her for a year previous to that, and it had made her a frightened shadow in the family. Frowning, Cal tucked her terrifying past away. He saw Sky turn, surprise in her expression.

"Cal! I thought you were going into the hardware store?" She halted her progress, pink chalk between her fingers.

"I am," he murmured, allowing his arms to fall to his side as he moved from the stair landing toward her. "Got breakfast going. Interested?" and he grinned as he saw the colorful chalk dust all over her hands, some sprinkled down the front of her bright yellow tee that lovingly outlined her body. A body he never would tire of making love to.

Groaning, Sky looked at her watch. "Oh, crap," she muttered, "I'm sorry, I lost track of time." And then she gave him a childlike grin. "I got carried away," and she pointed to her large chalk drawing on the easel.

Cal wandered over. "Hmmm," he said, lifting his index finger and gently removing a purple smudge on the tip of her nose, "you've really attacked this project," and he held up his finger that now was purple with the chalk dust. He heard Sky's husky laugh, going straight to his lower body. Cal thought about scooping her up into his arms and carrying her over to their unmade king-sized bed and taking her slowly, pleasing her once more.

"Well," Sky said wryly, setting the chalk in the tray, "I get lost in the drawing." Giving him an apologetic look, she picked up the damp cloth sitting on her easel and quickly wiped off her fingers, the colors smearing across them.

"Is breakfast ready?" she asked.

"Almost," Cal murmured. Looking across her shoulder, he studied her efforts. "Nice. You've captured the morning shadows across the meadow really well."

Groaning, Sky said, "You're just saying that Cal." She launched herself against him, curling her arms around his broad, thick shoulders. "Because you say nicest things about my struggling amateur efforts," she whispered against his mouth. "And you have nothing but praise for my poor attempts."

Her whole body went from simmer to boil as his arms swept around her, his mouth opening, curving, and hungrily taking hers. A soft moan of satisfaction caught in her slender throat as she felt his large hands move sinuously from her shoulders, down across her long spine and cup her cheeks, embracing her against him. Sky smiled as she broke the kiss, feeling his erection pressing strongly against his Levi's. "I thought you got enough earlier?" she teased. They had left Cusco, Peru months earlier and Sky had found herself nearly insatiable for him, unable to get enough of Cal in every way. She saw the glint in his narrowing gold-brown eyes. She knew that look. The more gold she saw in his eyes, the more turned on, the more he desired her.

Grunting, Cal reluctantly released her. "I will NEVER get enough of you, Sweetheart," and he placed a swift kiss across her wet, smiling lips that he could drown in forever. And that was exactly what was going to happen: he was going to marry Sky in two weeks, on June sixteenth, in Coronado, the SEAL training center, with San Diego right across the bay. She would be his forever.

Sky eased away, slipping her fingers into his large, calloused hand. "I'm hungry, too, and I need some physical fuel to run on." She gave Cal a wicked, teasing look. "Fuel? You know? For us mere mortals who aren't godlike SEALs, Supermen in disguise? You must take pity upon me," and Sky pulled him along toward the stairs that would lead to the the kitchen and living room below.

Cal preened silently beneath her praise. Yeah, he used to be a SEAL and yeah, they all thought of themselves as impervious to normal human complaints and weakness. He liked that Sky saw him in that way. It made him feel good about himself. "Okay," he offered grudgingly, releasing her hand and allowing her to go down the stairs first, "I'll bow to your need for food."

Sky gave him a merry look, skipping down the gold and red cedar stairs. Cal had hand-shaped every one of them. This gorgeous house, that could easily be on the front page of Architecture Magazine, had been patiently created. "What are you making for us?"

Cal watched Sky move gracefully over to the black granite island, snooping around for clues. She filled out a pair of jeans like no other woman he'd ever seen. As a SEAL, he'd had as many women as he wanted, but she was the prize and perfect for him. Sky was tall, graceful, and hot. The way her hips swayed made his aching lower body feel scalded and needy. The woman could incite a riot, Cal decided darkly, with that sweet movement of hers. Sky wasn't built lush and curvy. She was slender, reminding him of a willow being orchestrated by some invisible breeze. Her hands were long and spare. She had small breasts that pressed sweetly, teasingly, against her yellow tee she wore to perfection. Best of all, Sky's once short blond hair was now being allowed to grow. The wheat, caramel and gold strands gleamed, almost touching below her delicate ears as she moved across a slat of sunlight beaming silently through the room.

"I'm making pancakes with walnuts and dried cranberries in them. Interested?" he baited, moving around the island to the Wolf stove against the north wall. Behind the appliance, Cal had fashioned, ground and polished large, thin pieces of flagstone as a backsplash. The colors reminded him of Sky's short, streaked blond hair. She never dyed her hair, and he found it amazing that the colors he'd chosen so long ago for the backsplash contained the same colors of gold, caramel, and burnt sienna found in the strands of her hair.

"Mmmm," Sky sighed, "my favorite." She poured them coffee and handed him a bright red ceramic mug. "How can I help?"

He pulled out a black leather stool from the the island counter for her. "Sit down, look beautiful, and keep me company."

Sky set the mug on the island and then stood on tiptoe because Cal was six foot five inches tall to her five foot seven inches of height. She gave him a quick kiss. "Okay, SEAL god, go to work. I'm starving!"

Chuckling, Cal moved around the island and got serious about making them pancakes. "I wonder why you're always starved," he said, slanting a teasing glance across his shoulder as he poured the batter into an awaiting hot iron skillet.

Sky pouted playfully and then sipped her coffee. "Well, you woke me up out of a perfectly wonderful, deep sleep earlier this morning, for starters."

He grinned. "Couldn't help myself, Sweetheart. You're candy and I just can't keep my hands off you." He flipped the cakes expertly with a spatula. "Besides," Cal growled, giving her a baiting look, "as I recall, you rather enjoyed it. What? Three orgasms? Oh, wait… I think you had four?"

"You're jealous because you can only have one at a time."

He chuckled. "Yeah, that's me, all right." Cal gave her a mocking look, "But I had very willing and hungry company this morning. I don't recall you being a shrinking violet or telling me no."

Sky colored over his gritty words, seeing that primal look linger in Cal's eyes. "I swear, Sinclair, you could turn a rock on with just that steamy look you give me."

He placed the hot cakes on a platter and then brought them over to her. He slid them slowly across the island and into Sky's awaiting hands. "Sweet, you're no common rock. You're volcanic lava waiting and bubbling just below the surface. It just took the right man to inspire you, was all."

Groaning, Sky took the pancakes. "Stop with the sex talk, Cal, or I swear, I'm going to jump you here and now on this island." Sky had never experienced it with another man. Not that she'd had that many, but all Cal had to do was drop into that gritty tone, and her body responded hotly and without apology to him, much to her amazement. Both agreed they were highly sexed people who enjoyed it often. Nothing wrong with that!

Chuckling, Cal said, "You love sex just as much as I do," he challenged, pouring more batter into the skillet. He heard Sky snort. The pleasant clink of silverware against the plate told Cal she was enjoying the pancakes after buttering them and pouring maple syrup on the stack. When Sky had come out of Peru with him, she'd been terribly underweight. Now, months under his roof with his cooking, she'd regained every pound she'd lost. She looked filled out and beautiful to Cal, no longer a skeleton with skin stretched across her bones. He frowned, glad to be out of Peru. He hated that Sky had been forced to run and hide in South America to avoid being discovered by Vlad Alexandrov. She had found a job down there as a helicopter pilot and was flying for the Helping Hands Charity. When he'd finally found her, Cal was shocked at how thin, how ethereal and fragile she looked. He'd made it his personal mission to get Sky eating more food, and happy.

"Well?" he called over his shoulder. "Good?"

"Mmmmm."

Cal grinned and checked her out. Sky was sitting with half the pancakes gone, a bulge in her cheek, unable to talk. His heart opened fiercely with love for her. For the first time in her twenty-nine years of life, she was happy. Cal felt a tunnel of joy flowing through his heart. She was always the serious adult that life had demanded of her, and now, he was privileged to see those walls she'd lived behind all her life dissolve and her child-like joy shine through. The difference in Sky now versus years earlier that he'd known her was heart-stopping to him. Cal felt like he was watching a woman who had run and hid most of her life begin to unfold for the first time, because she was finally safe. With Vlad Alexandrov killed by an Army Special Forces Sergeant Mace Killmer in Peru, he could no longer hunt her down. His torments and threats wouldn't ever need to trouble her again. Vlad had talked of marrying her, that she would be the mother of his children, by force if necessary. Sky thought he was insane but could not escape him at age sixteen. She loved her foster parents, the Zimmerman's, but was afraid to tell them of Vlad's continued harassment for fear of causing them trouble and being removed from their home. He was dead now, and she was free.

"...Really ...delicious, Cal..."

"Good to hear." He flipped his cakes onto a plate and turned off the stove. Joining her at the island, he pulled over the butter and the maple syrup. "You want more?" Sky had gobbled down all three of the cakes, her appetite hearty. He appreciated a woman who could really enjoy food and eat, instead of always worrying about calories.

"No," Sky protested, holding up her hand. "I'm stuffed, Sinclair. No more," and she wiped her mouth with the red linen napkin.

Cal buttered his pancakes, absorbing her nearness next to him. They often ate breakfast here, but sometimes, he would surprise Sky with a breakfast tray and present it to her in their bed. "I don't want you losing weight again," he growled.

"If I gain one more pound, I'll be in trouble with that wedding gown," she warned him pertly, poking him in his muscular upper arm.

"I can hardly wait to see you in it," and Cal gave her an evil look. "Though you won't be wearing it it very long."

Sky laughed and carried her plate and flatware over to the sink, washing them off. "You'll see it the day Dylan McCoy walks me down the aisle at Coronado."

"Lauren Parker says it's beautiful," he taunted, pouring syrup over his cakes.

Scowling, Sky rested her hips against the counter, staring at him. Lauren was an ex-Marine Corps sniper who now worked for Shield Security with Cal. "There's no WAY she's giving you ANY intel on my wedding dress. The groom is not supposed to see it until the wedding." She shook her finger at him. "It's bad luck if you see it beforehand, Cal. I know you're black ops, and I wouldn't put it past you to get sneaky, pick the lock on the wedding shop in Alexandria, find my dress and look at it just to satisfy your own burning curiosity."

"Guilty" Cal jested. He saw Sky's face suddenly fall. Anxiety filled her eyes.

Cal cringed. He'd been teasing her, but she'd taken him seriously. "I have NOT done that, Sky. I promised you I wouldn't see it before you walk down the aisle. Okay?" Sky's face was so readable. He saw the mutinous look she gave him.

"Really? You haven't seen it, Cal?"

"Honest," he muttered, holding up his right hand, "Boy Scouts honor."

"You were NEVER a Boy Scout, Sinclair."

"True," he admitted, devoting his attention to the pancakes. "But I have NOT seen your dress." Cal pinned her with what he hoped was a sincere look, "Nor will I try to see it beforehand. I believe in old sayings. There's no way I'm cursing our marriage, so stop worrying. Okay?"

Cal was rather superstitious, sometimes. Sky found out many SEALs had a talisman they carried in their gear to ensure their luck would continue to hold out in the field on their dangerous, deadly missions. It was their protective charm. Cal, to this day, carried a pretty much hairless rabbit's foot on him. He felt it was his good luck charm and never left on a mission without carrying it in his gear. "Okay," she said, coming back and joining him at the island. "So? Your boss wants you down at Shield HQ at 1300 today? Big meeting there with all his employees?"

"Yeah, Driscoll's got several missions coming up all at once, and he needs me there to help in planning."

Sky moved her hand along Cal's shoulder. The red polo shirt he wore fit him like a delicious second skin and she felt her fingertips tingle as his muscles reacted instantly to her grazing touch. "You're his top mission specialist."

"Me and Lauren Parker are," he corrected. "We have to show up for all the briefings."

Sky knew Cal usually did all black ops planning for Shield, along with several other men and women. He worked on a part time basis, three days a week. Sometimes, he brought the work to his office here at home. "I was talking with Lauren yesterday over lunch. She said Jack had hired in another security contractor."

"Yes," Cal said, finishing off his pancakes, "we'll meet them today."

"Jack's business is growing fast," Sky murmured. She took his empty plate and walked it over to the kitchen's double sink.

Cal nodded. "With the way the world's going, everyone who can afford good security is more than willing to pay for it. Which is why he's hiring."

"Is it a woman?" Sky asked. Half of Jack's company was composed of ex-military women.

"Dunno," Cal murmured, sipping his coffee, watching her walk toward him. "I'll find out at the meeting." Her blond hair, in another six months, would touch to her shoulders. Sky said she wanted it to grow long and be feminine. He was all for that, but she'd been an Army Medevac pilot and short hair was a helluva lot easier to deal with when wearing a helmet during flights than long hair. Cal was glad Sky was done with the military. Now, she could look forward to a happy life with him. Very few people knew about Sky's prior life. It wasn't something she wanted to discuss with hardly anyone except himself and her best friend, Lauren. Those two were thicker than thieves and Cal was glad Sky had such a loyal woman friend after arriving home with him.

Sky slid onto her stool and pulled over her mug. "Tomorrow, Lauren's coming up and the last sewing adjustments on my gown are supposed to be done late in the afternoon."

"Lauren being a sniper? She'll eyeball that fitting just fine for you." The woman sniper vet had become Sky's closest confidant and friend. Because Sky had been on the run and trying to hide from Vlad Alexandrov, she hadn't been able to make friends. She was never in any one place long enough to make those important connections. Now? She could.

Laughing softly, Sky said, "For sure. She's driving the seamstress into a nervous breakdown, but I really want the gown to fit me well."

Raising his eyebrow, Cal growled, "Sweetheart, anything you wear looks beautiful on you." Cal knew there was going to be a wedding videographer and photographer at their wedding. Lauren had been behind that idea, and he could have strangled the red-haired sniper for the suggestions at the time. Cal wasn't eager to be photographed or on film. It came from his SEAL background to remain hidden and remain in the shadows. But one look into Sky's unearthly colored azure eyes, and Cal caved in on her request to have their wedding videotaped. Sky had never really had a family. Now, she had a cosmic family cobbled together between his SEAL team buddies and Lauren, who was a positive addition to Sky's life. They were close, girlfriends who often went hiking or had lunch together usually at least once a week. Cal was glad because he'd seen Sky begin to let down her guard and start to shed that old self of hiding and wariness that had overrun her life in order for her to survive and remain hidden from Vlad.

"I know," Sky groused, "but I want this PERFECT, Cal. I'm only getting married once, and," she gave him and tender look and sighed, "someday, if we have children, I want to be able to pull out the video and the photo album and show them how happy we were on that day."

His heart squeezed with fresh emotions. Cal had discovered that since living with Sky, it was impossible to keep his SEAL, non-readable facial expressions in place. He loved her, he wanted her happy and as a result, he'd become vulnerable for the first time in his life. His own childhood was a train wreck, too. Somehow, Sky's husky voice, the emotions so clearly etched in her expression, just unlocked him like a safe. Every day, Cal felt emotions. Most of them good. Some bad, like when he remembered that he'd almost lost Sky in Peru. He still had the intense SEAL focus and was able to put his feelings aside, when necessary. Around Sky, Cal was discovering daily he wanted to feel the happiness she gave him by simply sharing her life with him. He had never envisioned being happy. That word just didn't exist in his world. *Until Sky. Until now.*

Cal reached over, grazing her flushed cheek with his knuckles. "I want you happy, Sky. And we'll be sure to have our wedding videotaped and you'll have all the photos you've ever wanted. Okay?"

She gave him a grateful look. "Thank you… it means a lot to me, Cal."

Setting his mug aside, he stood up and eased Sky's cup out of her hand. "Come here," Cal rasped, picking her up easily into his arms and carrying her into the huge living room. He brought her to the chocolate leather sofa and sat down in one corner of it, sliding Sky across his lap so that she could snuggle up against him. She rested her head on his shoulder, her hand sliding in a caress across his broad chest. "Tell me about what you just said," Cal urged, wrapping his hand across her hip, his other arm around her shoulders, holding her close. He craved these intimate moments with Sky. He could tell by the darkness in her eyes that she was upset about something. As a SEAL, he was damn near psychic at times, his intuition so finely honed by nearly ten years of constantly being out in danger.

She rolled her head a little so she could meet and hold his warm gaze. "What? About the video and photo album?" Sky caressed the thick column of his neck, watched his eyes turn more golden, more intent like the apex predator he was.

"No," Cal rasped, caressing her cheek. "You mentioned children. You've never talked about wanting a family before, Sky."

Her mother was a drug addict and accidentally had gotten pregnant with Sky. The father was a druggie as well, selling meth and cocaine for the Italian mafia in Trenton, New Jersey, where she'd been born. Sky had been an unwanted accessory to their drug dealing business, basically abused by her father and ignored and left unprotected by her mother. At sixteen, Sky had run away, been caught by the police, and placed into state care. She'd been lucky for the first time in her life, given to foster parents Jack and Marielle Zimmerman, who taught her about family, love, values and respect. Cal wondered if Sky was opening up, dreaming, and wanting children of her own. He watched her expression closely and saw her struggling to put what she felt into words.

"Well," she began, her voice low and fraught with feelings, "I've been thinking about that, Cal." Sky gave him a concerned look. "But—"

"But what?" Cal purposely kept his voice gentle because Sky could pick up in heartbeat if he was upset. She was like a thoroughbred, super sensitive to everything and everyone around her. In truth, Cal admitted, Sky's all terrain radar awareness of people and environment was what had kept her alive, kept her one step ahead of hunter Vlad Alexandrov, who had relentlessly pursued her to finish what he'd started: to rape her, control her, marry and force her to carry his children. And the bastard would have done it—and almost had—in Peru.

"Well," Sky began, moving her finger nervously across his polo shirt, "how do you feel about children, Cal?" She bit down on her lower lip, studying him beneath her long, blond lashes. "Your father beat the hell out of you growing up. He was a drunk. And you protected Chad and Tracey, your siblings, from him. I can't imagine, with that kind of experience, that you'd really want to have a family?" and she earnestly searched his darkening gaze for reaction.

"You were born into a cesspool, Sky," Cal growled. "Your mother abandoned you, never protected you from your father who used to knock the shit out of you whenever he felt like it. Your experience with family is no different than mine: they both sucked."

Squirming, Sky flattened out her hand across his chest. "I know." She sighed and then offered him a soft smile. Picking up his hand, she pressed it against her belly, her hand over his. "But sometimes, when we make love, Cal, especially afterward, when you hold me, I wonder…"

Moving his hand gently across her rounded belly, Cal said, "You wonder what it would be like to carry my baby?" He always used a condom, never wanting to father an illegitimate child.

"Yes." Sky released a nervous sigh and rushed on, "Because I love you, Cal. I never knew what love was until we met. I know I ran for two years from you before you finally found me again, but I was scared. Jack and Marielle Zimmerman showed me what a real family COULD be. THEY loved me, Cal. I had a year and a half with them, despite Vlad being there. And I discovered what love really was. I guess…," and Sky nervously moved some golden strands of hair off her brow, "I guess that because I love you, I've been fantasizing about what it would be like to have your child," and she peered up at him, holding his narrowed gaze.

Cal's long, calloused fingers spanned her belly, gently massaging the area, the look on his face thoughtful. "How long have you been feeling this way?" he asked her, his hand stilling over her abdomen.

Shrugging her shoulders, Sky admitted, "About two months… Why?"

The hard line of his mouth softened. "Because, it was about that time, after we'd made love one morning and I was holding you as dawn was coming, that I wondered what it would be like to start a family with you."

Gasping, Sky's eyes widened as she stared up at him. "Truly, Cal? You're not kidding me, are you?"

Cal felt bad. He constantly teased Sky. And sometimes, she didn't know if he was teasing or being serious. He felt her tense, felt her joy and then her trepidation. He gathered her closer, his mouth grazing her lips. "Truly." And he heard Sky give a little shriek of joy, her arms sliding around his neck, her lush lips searching against his mouth. Groaning, Cal drowned in the heat and hungry movement of her beneath him. Felt her quiver with possibility. Felt her hope. Finally, he eased Sky away from him. Her eyes shone with a luster that totaled his heart and suffused him with a happiness he never thought could exist between two people. It bubbled up and embraced him.

"Then," Sky whispered, her voice trembling, "maybe we could think of starting a family?"

"Right after we're married," Cal promiser her thickly. They'd both been born out of wedlock. *Unwanted and abandoned.*

Sky felt tears burn in her eyes and she struggled to push them away. "Then... you're okay with this, Cal? Really okay? You're not teasing me? Right?"

He chuckled, the sound rumbling through his chest as he held Sky gently in his arms. "Really okay, Sweetheart. I'm dead serious about this, and I'm not teasing at all." And then his smile dissolved, and he became somber. Leaning down, he pressed a soft kiss against her wrinkled brow. "Because I love you, Sky, there's an urge in me to want to have children by you. They'll be beautiful, like you, Sweetheart. And more important," Cal rasped, kissing her closed eyes, "they'll be welcomed with opened arms by both of us into this world." He brushed her mouth with his lips, tasting the salt of her tears drifting silently down her cheeks. "We've come a long way together," he told her gruffly. "We were brave enough to reach out, despite our pasts, to love one another. And because of it, we're getting rewarded for that courage."

Sky slowly opened her eyes, tears beaded on her lashes as she stared warmly up at Cal's hard, weathered face. He was a man of powerful emotions, so often hidden, unavailable. But right now, Sky saw the raw love shining in his eyes for her alone. Reaching up, her fingers sliding against the hard line of his jaw, she whispered, "I want your baby, Cal. I want to feel her or him in my belly. Because that baby will have been created out of the love we hold for one another..."

CHAPTER 2

June 1

THE PHONE RANG. Sky made a noise of frustration at being interrupted, frowned, and wiped off her chalk-dusted hands. She quickly picked up her cell. The late afternoon sun had shifted, giving the pristine meadow and lazy creek flowing through it a different quality of light she was trying to capture. Without much success, Sky noted. As she saw the call was from Cal, her frustration dissolved. He was probably done with his day at Shield Security and letting her know he was on his way home to her.

"Hi," she said, a little breathless.

"Hey," Cal said, "thought I'd give you a call. You still working with your drawing?"

Sky plopped down on the bed and smiled. "How did you know?" Cal's sixth sense always impressed her.

"Just a guess," he drawled. "I'm bringing home a friend of ours. What do you have planned in the way of food for tonight's dinner?"

"A friend?" She heard a smile in Cal's deep voice. "Lauren? Is she coming for dinner?" She was going to visit tomorrow and help her with the last fitting of her wedding dress.

"No. Someone else."

Sky said, "I pulled some venison steaks out earlier. Why?"

"How many?"

She smiled. "Lots, Sinclair. You have a growing boy's appetite as I recall."

He laughed. "You are going to be very happy to see. And he's starving for some good, red meat."

Frowning, Sky said, "A man that I know?"

"Yeah. Alex Kazak was just hired by Jack Driscoll. He's now officially onboard as one of our security contractors."

Gasping, Sky leaped to her feet. "Alex? Alex is HERE? But... he was in the hospital in San Diego!" Her heart took off and joy tunneled through her. Alex Kazak, an ex-Spetsnaz Ukrainian black ops soldier, had worked with Vladimir Alexandrov's Russian Mafia team in Cusco. All the memories of that horrible time came rushing back to Sky. Almost four months ago, she'd been captured by Vlad's hardened ex-Spetsnaz soldiers. If not for Alex, who was a trained combat medic, she and Cal would have died. He'd turned on his feared Russian boss, helping her and Cal to escape and make it to safety. And not without peril to himself. Alex had been wounded in the leg by Cal as part of their escape plan to fool the Russians and send them in the opposite direction of their escape. Once Vlad Alexandrov found out Alex had lost Sky, he'd beaten the medic nearly to death. An American Army Special Forces three-man team had found Alex when they entered the village and saved his life. Later, Cal had pulled a lot of governmental strings, with Jack Driscoll's help, and gotten the twenty-nine-year-old Ukraine-born soldier to the US, to Balboa Naval Hospital, where he'd been recovering.

Sky owed Alex her life. He'd been kind, gentle, and protective of her while Vlad was raging at him and trying to get past him in order to rape her. She'd fallen ill with malaria for three days in that Indian village in the Highlands of Peru, after her capture by Vlad. Alex Kazak and the other Ukrainian medic, Nik Morozov, had cared for her, getting her through it.

"Yeah, he's here," Call said. "Shocked me at first, but he's going to be a good addition to our security team. I invited Alex to stay a few days with us. We'll give him one of the guest bedrooms. You okay with that?"

"Okay? I'm fine with it! How is he doing?"

"Well, I'm looking at him right now and he's a bit on the thin side, which is why he's wanting some good, red meat. Otherwise, he's the same ole Ukrainian boy we met in Peru."

The amusement in Cal's voice made Sky smile. "How long before you're home?" Sky glanced at her watch. It was four p.m.

"Another hour. Lauren and I have one briefing to go," Cal said.

"I'll have a huge meal waiting for you and Alex. I can hardly wait to see him in person!"

Sky heard Cal pull the black SUV into the garage of their home. Still wearing an apron, Sky rushed down the stairs to meet them. When Alex emerged from the car, she called his name, hurrying in his direction, her arms open to the tall combat medic. At six foot five inches tall, Alex looked much thinner to her. But he'd been sustaining on hospital food and through several surgeries at Balboa Hospital in the last three months. His black hair was still military short, but it was the glint in his large, intelligent hazel eyes that made Sky smile.

"Alex!" she cried, throwing herself into the Ukrainian's opening arms. He was a farm boy, he had told her proudly one time, showing her his big, calloused hands. And Sky remembered his large hands, work worn and oddly beautiful to look at when she was a captive. Alex was a man of the land and had traded in his plowshare for becoming a black ops soldier in the Russian army. His face was square, his nose broken several times. It was his broad, unlined brow, the dancing deviltry in his eyes, and that boyish grin that made tears rush to Sky's eyes as he gently leaned down and hugged her very carefully, aware of his height and strength against her diminutive size. For being a giant, Alex was a gentle bear of a man.

"Sky," Alex said, his deep voice choked with emotion, "you look well, my friend."

A sob caught in Sky's throat as she squeezed the medic as hard as she could. "Alex... I'm so glad you're here!"

Cal smiled as he sauntered around the SUV, watching them embrace one another. He owed Alex everything. If not for his intervention and his care of Sky while she went through that hell with another bout of malaria, Cal knew they'd never have gotten out of that Indian village alive.

Sky laughed, delighted, as Alex set her back down on her feet and carefully released her. Looking up at him, she saw he was dressed casually, in Levi's and a dark blue plaid cowboy shirt. He was even wearing a pair of highly polished black ranch boots. "Look at you," she said, "you look like a cowboy, Alex."

Cal slid his arm around Sky. She had a spot of white flour on her cheek. She liked to cook, but was messy, but he didn't care. "He can walk without a limp," Cal noted, grinning over at him.

Alex had the good grace to blush. "True. Three surgeries later." And then he teased, "You did not have to shoot me so well in the leg, Sinclair."

Cal grinned. "You said a through and through, Alex. I did what you asked." As part of their plan for escape, Alex had asked Cal to shoot him in the calf. That way, it would appear the American shot him, rescued Sky, and escaped because he'd been wounded. The Russian team had bought the story.

Sky sighed and leaned up and kissed Cal on the cheek. "This is just the best of surprises."

"Hope you didn't mind if I invited Alex up here to stay with us for a few days?"

Sky beamed at Alex, who was really quite shy despite his bulk and size. "I'm GLAD you're here, Alex. And we love having you! How on earth did you hook up with Jack and his security company?"

"Come on," Cal murmured, pointing toward the stairs and door leading up to the first floor, "let's go inside. Alex will tell you everything." He clicked his fob and the garage door slowly shut, making it darker within the area. A light automatically snapped on as he led Sky to the stairs.

Alex followed them into the massive cedar home. His eyes widened as he absorbed the floor plan. "This is a beautiful home," he murmured in awe. He ran a knowing hand over a cedar post, noting how smooth it felt beneath his exploring fingers.

Cal saw the kitchen was, indeed, close to becoming a certifiable disaster in the making. Sky had flour strewn across the black granite counter, several bowls in a row, and was halfway through making a huge salad for all of them. "I built this house over a seven-year period. It was a labor of love." he told Alex. "Have a seat," and Cal gestured to the stools at one side of the island. "Want a beer?"

"That sounds good," Alex agreed, sitting down. He folded his hands and smiled as he watched Cal and Sky work together in the kitchen. Cal opened a bottle of beer and slid it across the island to him. "So," Alex murmured, holding up the cold bottle, "a toast to your coming marriage?"

Sky washed her hands and dried them off. She let Cal take over in the kitchen. "Thank you. You're going to be able to make our wedding, aren't you Alex? We truly would love to have you there with us." She opened another beer, handed it to Cal, and took one for herself. They raised them in a toast.

Taking an appreciative swig of the beer, the bubbles dancing on his tongue, Alex said, "I will be there if I'm not out on a mission assignment. I promise."

"You and half of SEAL Team Three," Sky noted wryly. She worked around Cal and placed three plates on the island. They had a formal dining room, but they tended not to use it. The delicious smells originating from the kitchen, the warmth and coziness of the area was something Sky cherished. She'd never had it growing up and appreciated it so much more now. Taking off her apron, she set it aside.

"And many of Mr. Driscoll's people will be at your wedding, as well," Alex noted. He moved his hands off the island so that Sky could set up the three plates for dinner.

"Did you meet Lauren yet?" Sky wondered, adding flatware and red linen napkins to the place setting. "She's going to be my maid of honor. And she's helping me with my wedding dress fittings." Halting, Sky added, "And she'll be coming up here tomorrow! I have my last dress fitting in the late afternoon." She saw some of Alex's joviality disappear.

Cal called over his shoulder as he finished making the salad, "Lauren and Alex didn't exactly hit it off at the meeting. She hated him on sight," and he chuckled.

"What?" Sky eyed Alex, whose cheeks turned a dull red. He wouldn't look at her. Instead, Alex stared at the beer bottle and slowly moved it around between his massive hands. "Alex? Lauren is one of my best friends. Didn't she know you saved our lives?"

Shrugging his massive shoulders, Alex said, "I do not really know, Sky."

Sky sat down next to Alex, watching Cal quickly clean up her mess and get everything militarily organized once more. The man was a perfectionist and her heart opened wide with a fierce love for him. "What happened between you two, then?" she demanded. She saw Alex's hazel eyes darken and he bashfully shrugged.

"I do not really know. We just… I guess you would say… did not hit it off?" He gave her an apologetic look. "Since the US has given my sister Kira and I a path to earn our green card, we are on our way to becoming American citizens. I have been trying to learn and understand your American slang."

"Good luck on that one," Cal called, laughing. "We got more slang per square inch than any other country on Earth. We make 'em up as we go."

Chuckling, Alex nodded and drank more of his beer, savoring it.

"Alex," Sky chided, poking his forearm with her index finger, "tell me about Lauren."

Sighing, he said, "Not much to tell. Mr. Driscoll introduced me to his team members in the briefing room earlier this afternoon."

"He's the first Ukrainian to be hired by Jack," Cal added, dropping diced tomatoes into the salad. He brought the large wooden bowl over to the island and set it down. Giving Sky a look, he added, "Everyone welcomed him except Lauren. She refused to shake his hand."

"Wow," Sky murmured, "that's not like her at all…."

Alex shrugged. "She is beautiful. I have never seen red hair the color of hers. And her eyes remind me of emeralds I have seen in the Columbian Mines of South America."

Cal gave Sky an amused look. "I think Alex has fallen head over heels for Lauren."

"Wait," Alex protested, "what does head over heels mean? I see this in English, and it is a very odd movement of a body if I try to visualize it."

Sky squelched a smile and reached out and patted Alex's arm. "Slang for you have fallen hopelessly in love with Lauren." She instantly saw his frown disappear. His chiseled mouth, the softest part of his hardened, weathered face, moved into a hopeful, crooked smile.

"Ah, I see. Well, yes, I was very drawn to her but," he shrugged, "I do not love her."

"No," Cal said drily, eyeing him, "but you're sure as hell were in lust with her."

"Ohhhhh," Sky murmured, nodding, "now I understand."

Alex gave her a confused look. "Understand what, Sky? Why does she hate me?"

"I'm sure Lauren picked up on your interest in her," Sky tried to explain. She opened her hands. "Alex, you probably came on too strong to her. She's very sensitive. She's a sniper. She picks up on subtleties most of us miss."

"But," he sputtered, defensive, "I said NOTHING to her. I did not get a chance. She refused to come over and greet me as everyone else did. So, I went over and offered my hand in friendship to her because we are now part of the same team. But she turned and walked away."

Frowning, Sky gave Cal a concerned look as he put salad in each of the bowls. "That's not like Lauren, at all."

"No," Cal said, "but Alex wasn't exactly subtle that he liked her, either." Eyeing his friend, Cal said, "You don't stare at a woman like a slavering wolf, Alex. It puts a woman on the defensive. Lauren probably felt threatened by your obvious stare that had bedroom written all over it."

Sky rolled her eyes. "You're so crass sometimes, Sinclair."

Alex blushed. "But… Lauren is beautiful. She reminds me of a Valkyrie."

Cal snickered and retrieved three bottles of salad dressing from the fridge and placed them in front of them. "Even Valkyries don't like to be stared at like they're meat on a slab, Kazak."

Sky saw how crushed Alex looked. "Er, Alex, you can't chase someone like Lauren. She'd pick up on your intentions in a heartbeat. She's very independent. She picks the man she wants and lets him know it. Not the other way around."

"Does Lauren have someone special in her life? Is that why she was angry with me staring at her?"

Cal sat down next to Sky. "Lauren's single. No man in her life right now, Alex. Dig in," he told them.

"I must learn how a man lets an American woman know he is interested in her, then," Alex decided, wolfing down the salad without apology.

Sky saw how underweight Alex really was. He was a tall man, well-muscled but not muscle bound. The camaraderie between him and Cal was that of good friends glad to see one another again. "What if you two get assigned to the same mission?" Sky wondered out loud. "If you two are uncomfortable with one another, that won't work out at all. It's a distraction that could get both of you killed."

Cal slid his hand across her thigh and patted it. "They'll work it out if that happens," he reassured her. "They're professionals."

"But," Sky protested, "you don't need the battle of the sexes out on an op where you have to rely and trust one another."

"Give her time," Cal counseled her gently. "Eventually, they'll make peace with one another."

Making an unhappy sound, Sky said, "But Lauren's coming up here tomorrow…" And Alex was here for a visit. Did Lauren know he was up here with them? Would she be upset about that?

Cal shook his head. "You're SUCH a worrywart, Ms. Lambert. Look at us. When I met you, I fell head over heels in love with you. And just like Lauren, you didn't want ANYTHING to do with me. As a matter of fact, you ran as soon as you could, away from me. It took me two years to pick up your trail and finally find you down in Peru."

Alex's black brows rose in surprise. "You did not like this good man?" he asked her in disbelief.

Sky snorted. "It's a long story, Alex. I was running from Vlad Alexandrov. I had been put into the Witness Protection program. When I was transferred to a forward operating base near the Pakistan border, all I wanted to do was be a medevac pilot and fly my Black Hawk." Sky gave Cal a warm look. "I didn't expect Cal to come busting into my well-ordered life."

"Why?" Alex wondered.

"Because I wasn't looking for a relationship," Sky told him. She watched Alex pile more salad into his emptied bowl. It felt good to offer him good food and friendship.

"But," Alex said, pouring Italian dressing on his salad, "your heart decides who you love. Not your head."

"Oh," Cal murmured, giving Sky a wicked look, "the little head gets involved in the process, too."

Sky punched him in the ribs with her elbow. "Cal! We're eating."

Alex grinned. So, did Cal. Like two little boys caught red-handed.

Feeling heat in her cheeks, Sky thought she would never outgrow men's coarseness when it came to sex and women, and not necessarily in that order. "Look," she told Alex in a patient voice, "I was running scared from Vlad Alexandrov. Plus, Cal wanted to jump my bones."

Frowning, Alex cocked his head, running around the words in his head. "Is that slang?"

"Yes," Cal murmured. "It means you want to take a woman to bed."

"Is it another slang for rape?"

"No, no," Sky said quickly. "It's slang for a man wanting to take a woman to bed, is all."

"Sex on the brain," Cal explained. "Well, sex on the big and little brain."

"Cal!" Sky gave him a warning glare. "Enough! I want to have a nice dinner conversation, not this frat house boys club crap…"

"Okay," Cal said, chastised. He looked around Sky and told Alex, "we'll have beers in the basement after dinner. We'll play some pool and I'll talk about this slang thing later, okay?" And then Cal brushed Sky's flushed cheek, seeing she was genuinely upset. In some ways, she was so innocent. And he loved her fiercely for it. Her turquoise eyes grew warm when he stroked her cheek. "I'm sorry," he told her, meaning it. "We'll keep the rest of our conversations above the belt."

"Thank you," she muttered defiantly. "I feel like I'm in a teenage boy's locker room." She saw Alex grin. So did Cal.

They were hopeless.

"Well," Alex said, catching Sky's gaze, "I think Lauren is a very beautiful woman. I am happy to hear she has no man presently in her life. That is good for me."

Groaning, Sky said, "Alex, don't make the mistake of chasing Lauren. She's one tough lady and doesn't take crap from anyone. Especially men."

"Mr. Driscoll was very proud of Lauren," Alex pointed out, finishing off his second bowl of salad. "She is their chief sniper. She's served in Iraq and Afghanistan with Special Forces and SEAL teams on many ops." His eyes sparkled with challenge. "I prefer a strong woman like her. She knows her own mind. She knows who she is. I have great respect for women, anyway. But a strong woman? Well, that catches MY attention."

Cal slid off the stool and gathered up the empty salad bowls, taking them to the sink. He pulled on two oven mitts and opened the oven. Over his shoulder, he said to Alex," Lauren studied Krav Maga over in Israel. Did you know that?"

"No. That is impressive. I have always wanted training in that Israeli fighting method."

Cal pulled out the venison steaks and sat the dish on a trivet on the island. "Ask her to teach you. Lauren is one of Driscoll's instructors at Shield. She usually teaches the finer points of sniper shooting, but I'm sure she'd like to knock you on your ass and knock some respect into your head regarding her," and he gave the Ukrainian a wolfish grin that spoke volumes.

Alex laughed heartily. He watched as Cal brought over five baked potatoes, added a bowl of sour cream along with cut up scallions in another dish, and crumbled bacon and shredded cheddar cheese on platters, as well. "In Spetsnaz, we have woman warriors, too. But," and Alex gave Sky a smile, "none as beautiful as red haired Lauren. She is truly a prize worthy of being captured."

Groaning, Sky cautioned Alex, "You don't capture a woman you like. Capture is the wrong word. You're mixing words up here."

English was not his first language and Alex nodded. "What word should I use, Sky? I want her to not feel threatened by me."

Her heart went out to Alex. He was hopelessly smitten with Lauren. Only Lauren didn't want anything to do with him. Sky knew Alex was tall, rather awkward, somewhat shy and a bumbler. He was being dropped into American culture, of which he knew nothing. And from her perspective, Lauren probably thought Alex was little more than a bull in a china shop. "Alex, if you like a woman in Ukraine what word translates?"

"Ah," he murmured, "well, it depends." He eagerly took three venison steaks and settled them on his plate along with two huge Idaho baked potatoes. "If I was in love with this woman, I would woo her. I would sing to her old Ukrainian love ballads. I would take her for walks at my side and we would talk of many things. I would want to hear what makes her smile. What makes her laugh? I would ask her what is important to her life? I would want to show her that I am a big, strong man. And that I can care for her. Protecting her."

Sky took one steak. "I guess there's a huge difference between Ukraine and America when it comes to courting a woman you love."

Cal snorted. "Just a little." He chuckled. "Somehow, I don't think Lauren would appreciate love ballads."

Giving them a good-natured smile, Alex shrugged and cut into the thick steak. "Then, you two can help me court Lauren properly. Teach me American ways that she prefers."

Groaning, Sky eyed Cal. He grinned. She recognized that evil grin. The hunter stalking his prey. Giving him a warning look, she muttered, "Lauren is NOT meat on the hoof, Cal. Don't you DARE go that direction with her! She's my best friend."

"No worries," Cal soothed her, sliding a few blond hairs behind her delicate ear. "Lauren is like a sister you never had. I get that." He peered around her to look at Alex, who was wolfing down the first venison steak. The medic was starved. Of course, Navy hospital food wasn't at the top tier, either. "I'll instruct Alex on how to court Lauren properly. Okay? With respect. Treating her like the equal she is to any male."

Sky gave him a mutinous look. "You'd better, Sinclair, or you're answering to me." She watched his mouth draw into a faint smile as he slathered sour cream into his steaming baked potato. "Remember how kind you were to me at Camp Nichols? I never felt like you were stalking me. I honestly looked forward to talking with you when you'd suddenly show up out of the blue."

Nodding, Cal said between bites, "Sweetheart, trust me. I'm not throwing your best friend to this Ukraine black wolf. Okay?" And then his voice lowered to a gritty growl. "I was stalking you, Sky. But you never realized it. Us black ops types can be damned subtle when we want to be," and Cal gave her a wicked smile.

Sky shook her head. "Now, the truth comes out," she griped, the corners of her mouth curving upward. "Seriously? You WERE stalking me like the wolf in sheep's clothing you are?"

Cal tried to appear humble. "I fell so damned hard for you at first sight, Sweetheart. But I could tell you were jumpy and nervous about men. So, I went into stealth mode with you. I got you to trust me just a little, to let down those shields you were hiding behind." He shared a warm smile with Sky. "And it worked. When I kissed you in the hospital after you'd been shot, that sealed our fate with one another. You knew it and so did I."

Sighing, Sky nodded. Alex was listening politely even though he was eating nonstop. "You're right. That one kiss... wow... I never forgot it, Cal."

Cal slid his hand across her shoulders, giving Sky a quick kiss on the temple. "I won't, either. That one kiss kept me going until I finally found you in Peru."

"You're SUCH a gloater, Sinclair." Because he was a wonderful kisser. Even now, Sky could feel her lower body tightening with anticipation. She saw the glint in Cal's eyes, knew that tonight, he was going to love her. Her lower body flexed with anticipation. Hunger flooded her. Sky swore that Cal was the most sensual, sexual man in the world. And she could hardly wait to move into his arms tonight, be one with him again, feel his maleness, his power and his tenderness that he always shared with her.

Cal shrugged. "Not gloating. I just knew you were the woman for me, was all. And I'm not the type to give up, even if you ran from me. I could tell by the way you kissed me back in the hospital that you liked me one helluva lot, Sweetheart. And based upon that kiss, I wasn't about to let you get away."

Alex smiled. "Then, you must teach me your techniques, Cal, because I want to use them to lure beautiful Lauren into my arms."

Groaning, Sky shook her head. "Men," she muttered, getting up. She chose the smallest bake potato left on the plate. "You two are truly hopeless..."

CHAPTER 3

June 2

"WHAT DO YOU think?" Sky ask Lauren as she slowly turned around, showing off her wedding dress. The seamstress stood nearby, angst written in her face. Lauren was in her usual black t-shirt, jungle colored green Camo pants and black, polished combat boots. Her red hair was a lush cascade around her proud, drawn back shoulders as she critically examined the white satin sheath dress.

Lauren's green eyes narrowed, and she put up her hand, asking Sky to stop. Her long, slender fingers nudged a few of the blue and pink beads across the top of the bodice. "Hmmm, okay. They just jostled out of position was all," she murmured, smiling up at Sky.

"So? Is it okay?" Sky worriedly touched the slender sides of the satin sheath. It was a simple design, the pink and blue beading across the top enhancing the color of her turquoise eyes. She saw Lauren step back, finger on her chin, critically giving the dress a final inspection.

"Perfect, Sky. You look gorgeous. Cal is going to think he died and went to heaven," and she gave a husky laugh, a wicked look glimmering in her emerald eyes.

Sky saw the seamstress give her a look of utter relief, eyes rolling heavenward, silently thanking someone in prayer. Lauren was hell on wheels when it came to details. After all, as a sniper, details could either keep people alive or get them killed. Lauren's oval face and high cheekbones gave her eyes a slight tilt. To Sky, her friend looked exotic, one of a kind. Lauren dropped her hand and nodded to the seamstress, thanking her for all her hard work and efforts.

The seamstress beamed, hands clasped to her bosom, absorbing her sincere praise.

"So?" Lauren baited. "Let's have a mid-afternoon appetizer together. Your favorite place?"

"You got a deal," Sky murmured, stepping off the dais, running her hands lovingly down the satin fabric. She felt elegant in the dress; like a fairy tale princess come to life. Cal certainly treated her like a queen, no question. "Give me ten minutes to get changed?"

Lauren hooked a thumb across her shoulder. "I'll wait for you out in my Jeep. I'll check my emails and texts."

Sky nodded, following the seamstress into the large dressing room. "Meet you there," she called over her shoulder. It amazed Sky that even though Lauren was wearing military combat boots, she couldn't hear her walk across the shining pine floor of the boutique. Did they teach all black ops people how to walk silently? They had to, Sky decided.

At three p.m., the best restaurant in Alexandria was fairly emptied of lunch patrons. Sky sat in a brown leather booth across from Lauren. Her friend had stretched out her long legs, her boots hanging off the end of the bench seat. The music was quieter, and for that she was grateful. Lauren was drumming her fingers on the wooden table in thought.

"What are you thinking about?" Sky asked, sipping her coffee.

"Oh," Lauren groused, "the surprise of seeing Kazak at your place earlier. He's the LAST person I ever expected to see at your home."

"Mmm," Sky said.

Lauren sipped her black coffee, scowling. "I think Jack is making a mistake opening up our company to foreign black ops nationals."

"Maybe there's a need for them? People want a contractor in more than just the USA. And they want to hire someone who knows that country's language and customs?"

"I guess." Lauren grumped. She pushed some of her thick red hair off her shoulder. "He was SUCH a horse's ass at that meeting yesterday. He was slobbering over me like I was a prize hunk of meat to be eaten."

Sky quelled her smile at being right about Alex's staring at Lauren. "Do you know why he's our friend, Lauren?"

"No," she said, her mouth moving into a grimace. "I can't even begin to imagine how you all met."

The waitress arrived with their order of deep-fried artichoke hearts with ranch dressing. Lauren sat up, gleefully grabbing an artichoke heart and dipping it in the dressing. Sky proceeded to tell her why Alex was so important to her and Cal. When she finished with the explanation, Lauren's face had grudgingly softened just a tad.

"He's a better operator than I thought."

"He's also a good person," Sky said.

"Jack said he was a trained combat corpsman. That's something we can always use in our ranks during a mission."

"He fought and protected me from Vlad." Lauren knew that Vlad had hounded her since she was sixteen years old, and almost raped her at age seventeen.

"Well," she snorted, "for that, I can honestly and sincerely thank him."

"Give Alex a chance? Remember? He's from Ukraine. His family has run a wheat farm for a hundred years, many generations. All of a sudden, he's been dropped into the U.S., an alien world to him." Sky smiled a little, hoping that Lauren would ease up on her assessment of Alex. She didn't look happy. And Lauren wasn't one to hold her bile inside herself. Sky knew she'd come out of a rough childhood like herself. But Lauren wore those defensive shields like medals. Most people thought she had a massive chip on her shoulder. Lauren let few people into her personal world, beyond those formidable walls she would allow no one to scale. Sky was grateful to be one of the few who had earned entry to soft-hearted Lauren.

"I just hate being stared at," Lauren muttered, wiping her fingers on a napkin.

"Especially by a man."

Lauren stared at her for a moment. "You know a lot about my private life?"

"We're more alike than you realize." Sky shrugged. "It's just a sense around you, Lauren. I've known you long enough, seen you in enough situations to know you're not comfortable around most men." She lowered her voice and added gently, "It was probably a man who stole or broke your trust a long time ago, and that's why males, in general, are a threat to you, even now. Because of that event or time in your life, you don't trust them. And with good reason."

Her nostrils flared and she considered Sky's gentle assessment. "If it was anyone but you saying those things, I'd deny it," Lauren grumped. "This is not where I wanted our conversation to go today. We're celebrating you getting married to Cal."

"We're friends, Lauren. Friends trust one another with their deepest, darkest secrets. And God knows, you and I carry enough of them."

"Yeah, well mine are so far beyond dark and deep I don't ever want to think about them again. Much less discuss them."

Sky felt Lauren's fragile vulnerability even though she was growling at her like the alpha female wolf she certainly was in her military world. Lauren was one of the best at what she did as a sniper. But her defensiveness was screaming at Sky. She knew that look in Lauren's green eyes, saw it in the way her full mouth thinned, as if trying to protect herself from whatever else she might say. People got prickly when others got near a truth within them that they wanted to hide.

"I know the gentle, medical side of Alex," Sky offered her quietly. "When he came in last night and we got to talking, Cal and I realized he'd stared at you, and that it made you uncomfortable. I explained to him how it makes a woman feel threatened; as if the male is stalking her."

"Yeah, and then the guy had the balls to come over and offer me his hand after I refused to go over and welcome him to the team. What was he thinking? Oh, wait. Men think between their legs first, right? It's the little brain that runs them since they don't have one in their head. Well, that's where Kazak was at with me all day yesterday. It was painful for me. I felt like a target."

"This morning? When you came over to pick me up? And you met him in the kitchen? Did you notice he treated you very differently this time?" Sky lowered her head, catching Lauren's dark look.

"He was much better," Lauren muttered defiantly. "But I can FEEL him, Sky. I'm a sniper. I feel everything times ten," and she shrugged. "He's too interested in me, and I have absolutely no interest in him. Ever."

"Maybe because he's drawn to you? You can't hang a man on a yardarm for liking you. Can you?"

"Yes," Lauren said, lifting her head and scowling, "I sure as hell can. A man that looks at me like that wants to screw me, that's it. Nothing else but sex on his little, tiny brain. I'm so SICK of those looks, I could vomit, Sky." Lauren pushed her fingers through her long, slightly wavy hair, giving her a look of utter frustration. "This Patriarchal bullshit has to go. Women are not here to service men. We're human beings. I demand to be treated as a human, not a sex toy to be screwed and then thrown away afterwards."

"I totally agree with you. You're cursed with being beautiful. Men are going to look at you. You've got to know that."

"I wish I was dog ugly, to tell you the truth. As a sniper, the rifle doesn't care what the hell I look like. All it cares about is I know how to treat it so I can blow the bastard in my scope away."

Sky felt her heart cringe for Lauren. She exuded a toughness she'd seen in other women who had been very badly damaged by a man. She recognized it because of her own childhood. "Have you ever been in love, Lauren?"

"No. I don't believe it will ever exist for me, Sky. I'm not trusting enough of men to let it develop that far."

"But you and Cal are friends. He's a man."

"He doesn't lust after me, either," she noted, raising one eyebrow. "He's so madly in love with you, he doesn't see anyone else but YOU."

Sky's heart opened powerfully. "I never thought I'd ever fall in love either, Lauren. Not until Cal stepped unexpectedly into my life."

"You got lucky," Lauren said, her voice low with feeling. She reached out and patted Sky's hand on the table. "And you know what? I can't think of two people who deserve happiness more than you two."

"Might rub off on you," Sky teased, giving her a warm look of understanding.

"I'm twenty-nine," Lauren said. "My two relationships with boys when I was in high school cured me of ever thinking that way. I don't mind working with men who respect me, but I'll be damned if I will be regarded as a sex object or be objectified by the rest of the men in the world. I won't tolerate it."

"I was twenty-seven when I met Cal the first time." Sky saw Lauren look sad for a moment, which wasn't like her. Normally, she kept her game face in place, rarely allowing anyone to know how she really felt beneath the armor she wore so well. "I'm probably overstepping my bounds here," Sky began hesitantly, "and I know you'll tell me to back off if I have, but Lauren, you're a GOOD person. When you're not out on a mission, you give your time to the Humane Society. You help train security dogs for Jack's company. And you work hard with the Marines in the Toys for Tots program during Christmas time. You give a lot of yourself to charity and helping others whether they're two-legged or four-legged."

"I like serving," Lauren conceded, all the bluster gone out of her voice. Resting her elbow on the table, she said, "Look, my foster father sexually abused me from the time I could remember. I fought back when I was old enough." Her mouth became a slash. "When I was ten, he came after me in the kitchen one time, to screw me. I took a skillet and hit him in the head, and it killed him."

Sky's mouth dropped open. She stared disbelievingly at Lauren. "Oh, my God... oh, Lauren... I-I'm so sorry for you...," and she was. Sky knew that aching loneliness of no one to protect her against her druggie father who beat her, but he had never sexually molested her. Still, Sky understood the pain Lauren carried within her.

"Don't be sorry," Lauren muttered, frowning. "Keep this to yourself?"

Sky's eyes widened. "Yes, of course. Were you put into legal jeopardy?"

"No. My foster mother, who was cowed by the bastard, told the police what happened. I was never punished for it."

"Then what happened to you? I'm sure the state wouldn't allow you to stay in that family?"

Lauren shrugged. "I was glad to go. After that, I became a real handful. I was angry. I fought. I rebelled. I was out of control. So, I went through six different foster homes until I turned eighteen."

"You had a right to be angry because of how you were abused."

Her mouth tightened, eyes growing hard. "Now you know why I don't trust men. I can pick up, like radar, on a man who wants sex with me, in a millisecond. And maybe, in a sick sort of way, that all-terrain radar I developed as a very young child has served me well out on ops. I can sense things long before anyone else can, so there's a positive side to it, I guess."

"You're like Cal in that regard. Sometimes, he's scary. He's so psychic. He says he isn't, but I swear, he senses like an animal does out in the wild."

"That's about right," Lauren said with a short laugh. "We've been reduced to our animal, limbic, primal self. If nothing else, people like us know how to survive and read subtleties most others will never sense or see in another person or situation unit it's too late."

Sky hurt for Lauren. What she'd just revealed told her so much about the way she was presently. "Maybe, over time? Give Alex a second chance? He does like you. And yes, he says you're beautiful, which you are. You can't damn him for that, Lauren. He's a good person. Cal thinks the world of him, and he doesn't give that kind of respect to another operator unless he's earned it."

"Yeah, that's what Cal told me privately later when I left the room after refusing to shake Kazak's hand."

"Have you thought what might happen if you two get thrown together on an op?"

Grimacing, Lauren growled, "That will NEVER happen. It wouldn't be pretty."

June 2

THE JUNE WIND blew cool and chilly, which was unusual for a summer day. Yerik Alexandrov knelt in front of his son's gray tombstone, thinking it was because of climate change. He carefully placed the dozen white roses into a permanent gray vase that sat nearby. Lifting his eyes, he felt tears burning in them. Vlad's face stared back at him. Below, in Russian, was, "Here lies my beloved son, Vladimir Alexandrov. Rest in Peace." Below that in smaller black engraved letters was, "Beloved son of Darya and Yerik Alexandrov."

His heart was so torn that Yerik knew he would never be the same after hearing Vlad had been murdered in Peru four months earlier. The wind blew in a gust, rustling the white roses. He looked up, hot tears running down his face, soaking into his blond and gray trimmed beard. Yerik had so many grand plans for Vlad. His son was a strapping six foot five inches tall with blond hair and green eyes, just like himself. He'd taken strongly after him in every way. If only... oh, God, if only he hadn't been killed in Peru! Pressing his hand against his black topcoat where his heart lay, Yerik sobbed openly. He had never cried as much as he did now. When Darya died giving birth to Vlad, he thought he'd cried more than was humanly possible. Now, with his strong, brave son gone, he'd cried his soul away in a river of unending tears that rose in him at the most inopportune moments.

He slowly struggled to his feet. At forty-nine years old, Yerik sometimes felt like he was in his seventies. Today was one of those days. He came to see his son every week, to speak to him, to tell him about what was going on. Resting his hand on the top of the smooth, gray granite, Yerik whispered, "I promise you, my son, I am going to find Sky Lambert." He patted the gravestone as if he were patting Vlad's cheek.

Turning, Yerik stood on top of a small knoll in the cemetery outside Brooklyn. The island of Manhattan stood glittering in the distance. This was his turf. As the Russian Mafia leader, he should feel pride. Since Vlad's death, he'd felt nothing but pulverizing grief. But now, rage was rising in him, and he swore on Vlad's grave to fulfill his son's dream.

Grimly, he pushed his hand across his beard and noted his two bodyguards standing nearby, looking around for any threat. As a mafia chief, his life was always at risk. His men were ex-Spetsnaz black ops. Oleg, who was six-foot one inch tall with black hair and blue eyes, stood a few feet away. Beneath his long black wool coat was an assault rifle. To his left was Pyotr, six foot three inches tall, two hundred pounds of mean muscle. He was further down the hill, carefully watching for any unusual movements. His driver, Vadim, a blond-haired blue-eyed operator, stood watching around him as well. These men were the blackest of the black ops. They were killers who enjoyed killing. And they had sworn their loyalty and their lives to him.

Moving down the hill, Oleg joined him at his side.

"There is a call from your source," he said quietly. "He said it was about that woman, Sky Lambert."

Yerik's eyes lit up. He took the cell that Oleg handed him. Maybe an answer to his prayer? He hoped so. His source came from the Russian ambassador's residence in New York City. Yerik often did business with this mole. No one knew he worked for him and that's the way it would be kept.

"Helge, my old friend," he greeted as he walked down to the black limousine, "you called?"

"Yes. I have an address for you. It is where Sky Lambert is staying."

Yerik hesitated, focused. "You found her?"

"Yes, by a great deal of sifting and moving quietly," Helge said, talking in a low tone into the cheap burner phone. He gave him the address.

"What else do we know?" Yerik demanded, committing the address to memory. In their business, emails and phone calls must remain untraceable.

"Nothing, so far."

Nostrils flaring, Yerik said, "I will find out. Thank you. As usual, you can expect a sum of money to appear in your offshore account for your fine work."

Yerik felt like yelling triumphantly. Instead, he kept his poker face on and entered the car. Vadim shut the door and climbed in. Pyotr rode in front. Oleg, in back with him. On the way into Manhattan, Yerik made several phone calls. He would find out more about where Sky Lambert was hiding. A feeling of glee flowed through Yerik. At last, months of hard work, and a lot of money spent, had paid off. Now he knew where his son's wife-to-be was at. It was only a matter of time until he had her.

Lauren dropped Sky off at her home after finishing the mid-afternoon appetizer. Before she could get her Jeep Wrangler in gear, Alex Kazak appeared almost magically at the driver's side door. She had the window down, her arm resting on the frame. Instantly Lauren scowled at him. The man was sweating, somewhat out of breath. This afternoon, he was wearing an olive-green t-shirt across the massive expanse of his chest, black cargo pants, and black combat boots. He wore a harness around his waist that contained two quarts of water and probably some protein bars, she guessed. He'd been running hard. Most likely a daily discipline in his life, like it was in hers. Lauren ran five miles a day with a fifty-pound pack on her back to stay in shape for the demands of her job.

Alex gave her an apologetic smile, shoving wisps of short black hair off his brow. "I want to say," he murmured formally, "that I am very sorry I treated you like a piece of meat yesterday, Lauren. Will you forgive me?"

Lauren watched him struggle with the English words. The look in Kazak's hazel eyes was one of abject apology. He was sincere. She could feel it. And he appeared humble in her presence. Black ops men were good and they knew it. They were all type A's, super confident and competitive. "What do you want, Kazak?"

He blinked once, cocked his head, studying her. "Why… to make you feel okay about me. I did not mean to be rude to you the other day in the office." He shrugged, opening his large hands. "Am I saying this right? My English is very bad."

"Yeah, for sure," she said wryly. "You don't go around telling a woman that she's a piece of meat. Okay? That's slang no woman wants to be seen as or hear." Lauren saw his face fall, the desperation in his eyes. She almost felt sorry for him. Almost. "And you haven't told me why you're really doing this."

"But… I just did. I was not a gentleman. I did not treat you as the lady you are, and how you should be treated. The American way."

Rubbing her face, Lauren shook her head. "Kazak, bone up on English, will you? You're slaughtering it."

"I am at fault, Lauren. I am sincerely sorry," and Alex pressed his hand to his chest in a gesture of heartfelt apology.

Lauren studied his hands. Even though she knew Kazak was from a farm life in Ukraine, his hands reminded her of artist's hands, beautiful in their own masculine way.

"You're sorry? I doubt it, Kazak. All I felt and saw around you was lust yesterday. You wanted to screw me. And I'm NOT interested."

Wincing, he murmured, "That was true, I felt you were beautiful. What does screw mean? Is that a construction term?"

Surprised, Lauren stared at him. "Well," she muttered, "I'll give you an E for effort, Kazak. At least you're more honest than most American men will ever be." And then she added, "Men use the word screw to mean you take a woman to bed."

Alex gapped at her. "Oh....no....I would NEVER use such a word like that with ANY woman! In Ukraine, we honor our women, we admire them, we see them as equals. They would NEVER be treated like that. "Then," he pleaded, holding out his toward her, "can we start over? I promise never to look at you like that again or treat you without respect."

Her nostrils flared and Lauren felt her heart wrench. An odd reaction for her, for sure. But the earnest look in his puppy dog eyes got to her. Kazak reminded her of a big, slobbering St. Bernard dog; somewhat bumbling, shaggy, and inept, but nevertheless, lovable and huggable. Well, dogs were, but men were not. "Fine," she said flatly. "But you know what? Actions speak louder than words. Just remember that."

He frowned, his eyes moving upward as he considered the words. Trying to understand what she'd just said.

"Is this American slang again?"

Lauren smiled a little. "I suppose it is. Ask Cal. He'll know what it means." She gunned the engine, the Jeep taking off down the road with a rooster tail of rising dust behind it.

Alex wiped the sweat off his brow. His heart was pounding in his chest. He'd so desperately wanted to make peace with beautiful Lauren. Watching the red Jeep speed away like a banshee flying down the long, graveled drive, he smiled a little. Well, that didn't go too badly, did it? Rubbing his sweaty hands off on his cargo pants, Alex climbed the stairs to go to his guest room and take a shower. His heart lifted a little because just as Lauren, the vaunted sniper, could sense the subtleties, so could he. In Spetsnaz, he had been cross-trained as a back-up sniper. He possessed the same sniper sensing equipment she did. But the deeper truth was that he was a healer. He honed those sensory abilities to read his patients, to learn what they needed to save their lives. And if his senses were right, Alex had just gotten an inch inside those Kevlar-like shields she wore like a good friend around herself.

He met Cal in the hall on the way to his room and stopped him.

"What does 'actions speak louder than word's' mean? It is American slang?"

Cal nodded. "Yes. It means how you act on a daily basis shows a person more about you than any amount of words you speak." He saw Alex scowl. It wasn't computing. Cal tried again. "Okay, let's say you tell someone you're honest."

"Yes?"

"That person may wait, watch and listen to you over days, weeks or even for months at a time to see if you're really honest or not. The words you speak and the actions you take, they have to be the same, they can't be different."

Alex's dark brows flew upward. "Ah, I see! That would be like me saying I am a good guy. But I would have to prove I was one every day with everyone I met. Yes?"

"Sort of," Cal said with a grin. "What's this all about?"

Alex told him.

Cal rolled his eyes.

"Have you got a death wish, Alex?"

"No. Why?"

"You just don't ambush Lauren like that. You have to give her a helluva lot of room to maneuver. She'll cold cock you."

"What is a cold cock?" The vision he had in his head wasn't pretty.

"It's more slang. It means she could punch your lights out."

"But I do not have lights to punch out."

Letting out a long breath, Cal said, "Lights is another word for being conscious. If she cold cocks you, you will be unconscious after she hits you with her fist."

"Oh…," he mumbled. "But I was honest with her. I told her I would no longer treat her like a piece of meat."

"No…," Cal groaned, "you TOLD Lauren that?" and his eyes rounded with disbelief.

"Yes. Why?"

Cal drew in a deep breath. "Listen, you need to stay the hell away from her, okay? She's not like other women at all. You're damn lucky she didn't break your nose or put your lights out." He rubbed his face and then shook his head in disbelief.

"She did not seem as angry with me this time. Perhaps I amused her instead?" Alex had seen laughter in her eyes even though it hadn't translated to Lauren's sensual lips in the form of a smile.

Sky came wandering down the hall from the kitchen, hearing them talking.

"What's going on?"

Cal gave her a grim look and told her about Alex's apology to Lauren.

Sky brightened. She grinned up at Alex. "That was really sweet of you to apologize to her. That was a good idea."

"Sweet?" Cal muttered. "I'm surprised Lauren didn't get out of her Jeep and deck 'em."

Laughing, Sky said, "Give Lauren some credit, will you? I think she saw Alex was struggling to be sincere with her. Like I said before, she has a bullshit meter, and she can peg someone's intentions real fast." She tapped Cal's shoulder, seeing the amazement in his eyes. "Alex did the right thing. Lauren knows that. That's why she didn't let him have it. Consider it progress, Sinclair. Give Alex a gold star."

"Well," Cal grumped, "when he called her a piece of meat again, that must have gone over well."

Sky chuckled. "You guys. You're so entertaining to us women. You give us a good laugh." She looked up at Alex. "How was your run?"

"It went well," he said, grinning. "Beautiful country. Reminds me in some ways of the Carpathian Mountains in southwest Ukraine."

"Good," Sky murmured. "Grab your shower Alex, and then come join us out in the kitchen for a beer and some chips and avocado dip afterward?" She slid her hand beneath Cal's arm. "Come on, big guy, you can help me make spaghetti sauce for dinner tonight. That will wipe the shock off your face," and she laughed lightly, shaking her head. Men!

CHAPTER 4

June 3

"WE HAVE NEWS," Ivan Orlov told his boss, Yerik Alexandrov, bringing in a sheet of paper with him. The walnut-paneled office was located in mid-town Manhattan, a respectable place, upscale, providing them a convincing cover. To the casual visitor, it was a global import company with ties around the world, Yerik's legitimate business that fronted his drug-running trade that fueled the millions of dollars he made daily.

Yerik looked up from his large mahogany desk. "Yes?"

Orlov halted and gave the young male assistant a look that told him to leave and shut the door behind him. Although thin and short in comparison to Alexandrov, Orlov was respected as a geek or the bean counter for the organization. Few suspected the power he carried, except those in the very highest of circles of their Russian Mafia group that ruled New York City. He was their number two man. Orlov unbuttoned his four-thousand-dollar grey Italian suit coat, straightened his conservative dark blue silk tie, and sat down when Yerik pointed to a chair nearest his desk.

"Ah," Yerik said after quickly reading the paper, "this is good news. They've gathered intel on Sky Lambert and where she lives."

"Well," Orlov cautioned, holding up a thin hand, "it is news. Not necessarily what I'd consider GOOD news."

Scowling, he read the rest of the report. "The cabin she lives in is a security nightmare. And the team is suggesting we don't try and kidnap her at that location?"

Steepling his hands, Ivan said, "She's marrying an ex-SEAL by the name of Cal Sinclair on June sixteenth. I'm sure that name is familiar to you." He saw his boss make a face, his fingers tightening on the report.

"He was the bastard who rescued Sky from my son."

"Exactly."

"He's marrying her?"

Shrugging, Ivan murmured, "It appears so. I've had my people in Coronado and San Diego snooping around, dredging up information here and there.

According to their report, the two are going to get married on the island of Coronado, at the SEAL Team Three base. Of course, there's no way we can crash that party."

Alexandrov snorted and looked over at Ivan. "Not likely. What are our other options?"

Ivan ran through the details with his boss. "The house she is living in with Sinclair cannot be breached. My scouts ran into sensors half a mile away from the house. Short of parachuting into the cabin directly, Sinclair will be alerted by any attempts to access the property. In a week though, they are flying to San Diego to make preparations for their wedding. Our best option is to act while they're staying at a condo on the island."

"Is it a security nightmare, too?"

Shaking his head, Ivan said, "The condo building belongs to an ex-SEAL by the name of Joe Harrison. He's loaning Sinclair and his new bride the first-floor condo during the wedding, a gift from him and his wife. They will be attending the wedding. A number of employees from Shield, a security company out of Alexandria, Virginia, are also attending. Sinclair is an operations mission planner for Shield, but that was as far as we could go into their computer network. They've got firewalls bigger and meaner than the Pentagon has."

Sitting up in his chair, Yerik pondered the situation. "I know you well, Ivan. I'm sure you've had your planning team doing some creative planning on how to kidnap the woman?"

Smiling a little, Ivan sat back in his chair, folding his hands in his lap. "Having ex-Spetsnaz in our ranks is a tremendous tool, Yerik. We have two plans that we can initiate, depending upon the circumstances that present themselves at the time."

"What are you going to do about Sinclair?"

Shrugging, Ivan said, "It depends. What we're hoping for is that Sky Lambert will go off somewhere by herself. Or perhaps shopping with a girlfriend. We don't want to tangle with a former SEAL if we can help it. We can't leave a string of dead bodies behind us. It's going to require a very careful surgical strike and extraction."

"I agree," Yerik growled. "The only way we grow powerful is to remain in the shadows. Dead bodies will point to us sooner rather than later. This must be handled very, very carefully. I want Lambert delivered to me in good health and with no marks on her body. She was my son's future. Understood?"

"Quiet," he said, giving a sharp nod of his head. "We are going to have to wait for an opportunity to strike. We must catch her in that condo alone, or somewhere without her new husband around. We will render her unconscious with a drug, and we'll get her out of San Diego and to an offshore boat as soon as possible. From there, I assume you want her either in the villa in Guerro, Mexico or at La Paloma in Costa Rica?"

"Costa Rica. It is my hiding place from the US government. I don't believe we've been compromised at that villa yet. It hides very well in the Monteverde Cloud Forest in the northern part of that country. Satellites can't get through the surrounding triple canopy around the house and grounds. It parallels a very famous tourist resort near Arenal, the volcano, but there is enough jungle in between there to keep nosy tourists from discovering us."

"Good choice," Ivan congratulated. He tapped his fingers lightly together, watching his scowling boss. "What plans do you have for her? Is it going to take long? Do you want me to stay here in New York to handle things while you're away?"

Yerik leaned back in his chair, rocking in it gently, his eyes on an oil painting of his son in Russian military uniform, on the opposite wall. Vlad was receiving a medal for his bravery as a Spetsnaz officer. "I don't know yet, Ivan. It depends upon her willingness to cooperate or not."

"I'm sure you will have your way."

He slid his friend a look. "I've been working out the best way to manipulate her. I believe she will bend to my will." He smiled a little. "And I'm going to be there to watch it happen. Every minute of every day is going to be designed for her to leave her old life behind."

Ivan smiled. "Care to share? Now you have my curiosity piqued."

"No," Yerik murmured, rocking back and forth, his fingers tapping the ends of the chair arms, "I'm going to assess her once we capture her. I may change my mind. I may not."

"Well," Ivan said, rising and straightening his coat, "no one is more skilled than you when it comes to breaking a person. When you were in Spetsnaz, you were the best interrogation officer in the Russian Army. You had no equal."

"My son was almost my equal," Yerik whispered, pain in his voice. "He had such promise."

Coming over, Ivan patted his shoulder gently. "Perhaps, old friend, when we capture her, this will help you heal from your loss."

Nodding, Yerik muttered, "I will break her. And then, I will see what happens next..."

June 4

IT WAS THEIR last night at their home in Virginia before the wedding. Sky had made sure everything was ready for their trip to San Diego, California. Tomorrow morning, they would be taking a flight out and her dreams of their wedding would begin. But tonight, was special in so many ways. After Cal had come out of his shower and joined her in their bed on the second floor, she needed to ask him for one last favor.

"I want you…" Sky whispered raggedly against Cal's mouth as they lay naked upon their bed. "Now…," she whispered, huskily, holding his burning gaze. "Without a condom…"

Reality hit Cal. He blinked. And he saw the seriousness in Sky's eyes. His mind spun. In two weeks, they would be married. What was she saying? He knew she was near ovulation because she was sexually hungry at those times more than any other time. Ovulation meant if he took her, she could get pregnant. He propped himself up on his elbow, grazing her cheek. The look in Sky's eyes was fearless. Barely able to think he rasped, "Are you SURE?"

"I'm VERY sure, Cal. I want you. Inside me. Now. I'm ready."

Cal wasn't going to argue with her. It was nearly midnight, and he was wide awake. "Okay," he rasped.

"I'm ready, Cal."

"You know, you're ovulating?" He knew her body as well as his own. He was sensitized to her because he loved her.

"Yes."

He grinned a little. "You're such a fearless little hell cat. Do you know that?" and he rolled her over on her back. "How do you want me?"

"Just like this," Sky coaxed, opening her thighs to him. "I want to see your face when you come inside me, Cal. I want to experience us like never before… I want to remember every second of us coming together… mating…"

Her words triggered a powerful male sense of protection toward the woman he loved with all his life. "Okay, Sweetheart, this is for us, for the baby we're going to make tonight…" and he covered her, his knee pushing her thighs wider, "because I want to see you come, too. I want to see what our love can create between us… together…"

Sky closed her eyes, smiling, her hands moving gently across Cal's broad, thick shoulders. She felt her lower body flex as his flesh pressed thickly against her entrance. Without a condom it felt so different. So… wonderful. Raw. Flesh against flesh. Oh, yes, this was the way it should be, and she arched her hips, sliding her long, slender legs around his narrow hips, the need to couple with Cal so primal within her that it took her breath away.

The elemental pleasure of Cal sliding into her, deliberately teasing that knot, bringing her body to glowing life once again, made Sky moan. Now, she felt Cal in every possible way, the walls of herself stimulated even more, and it made Sky open her eyes and drown into his narrowed ones, his intense gaze riveted upon her as he thrust teasingly into her. He had such a hard face, weathered, toughened by so many years outdoors in dangerous, harsh conditions. And as Cal cupped her breast, Sky arched into his hand, her flesh tingling wildly as his calloused fingers triggered an avalanche of fiery sensations, tightening her below. Leaning down, he teased one nipple and then the other, tight points begging to be lavished by him. Sky felt herself dismantling, the heat imploding within her, and she arched, crying out Cal's name, her fingers digging deep into his biceps, feeling animal-like, raw pleasure singing through her as they mated.

Just as she orgasmed, her body ravenous, wanting more of him, Cal slid one hand beneath her hips, angling her just so, milking that orgasm of hers until she flushed, her cries turning into sweet mewls that made him love her even more. It was then that Cal thrust into her, feeling the raw grip of her surrounding him. Gritting his teeth, Cal held her gaze, her half-opened eyes dazed, gold shimmering in their depths. He took her deeper and deeper, so damned sensitized to Sky's body, every sensation amplified times ten.

Cal couldn't control himself like before, the sliding friction squeezing him, pulling him so tightly against her that he felt the climax erupt and explode through him. The fiery heat tore down his spine, tightening his balls until it was damn near painful, and then unleashing within her hungry, welcoming body. He drowned in Sky's loving gaze. A guttural growl tore out of him as he felt the throbbing release pouring into her and it was all he could do but freeze in place, the pleasure searing his brain, burning through his groin, hurtling him into a space he'd never been before. And through it all, Sky pushed her hips against his, bringing him to total collapse as he sank against her slender form afterward.

Cal couldn't think, only feel. He weakly framed Sky's face, kissing her, feeling drugged and satiated as never before. She was so hot and fluid, her sex scent drawn deeply into his flared nostrils. Sky was was his life, she tasted good, her skin warm velvet beneath his exploring fingers, her lips soft and hauntingly strong in a way only his woman could be beneath his searching mouth. Their breaths were sharp and gasping. Her breasts rose and fell against his chest. He'd never felt so strong, so powerful as a man, until now. Cal never, ever wanted to forget this moment torn out of time and place.

"Don't leave me," Sky panted softly, holding him with her woman's strength, glorying in him being deeply lodged within her. There was something incredibly beautiful, so ethereal about their union that she pressed her cheek against his, tears leaking out of her eyes. She WANTED his baby. Her heart was wide open, ready to be written on it by him for the rest of her life. Sky gloried in every breath he took against her, felt the caring strength of his arms, felt him adjust how much weight he was placing upon her. Cal had told her once that he was always situationally aware of her. Sky believed it. SEALs had a sixth sense that was evolved to a place few humans would ever achieve, and he always monitored her, felt, and sensed her. Because he loved her. She sobbed against Cal, her arms tight around his neck, holding him close, loving him passionately.

"Hey," Cal rumbled, easing away just enough to look into her glistening eyes. He lifted his hand, smoothing strands of hair away from her temple, drowning in their turquoise color, seeing unparalleled happiness in their depths. "Did I hurt you?"

Sniffing, Sky rolled her head back and forth. "N-no… just the beauty of us… feeling you inside me for the first time like this. It's wonderful, Cal… I'm crying because I'm happy," and she smiled brokenly, his face blurring before her eyes. Sky saw the tenderness burning in Cal's understanding gaze, in his smile, as he leaned down, brushing small kisses across her brow, her eyes and finally, across her mouth.

"This was," Cal growled, moving his tongue across her lower lip, feeling her respond, "the best sex I've ever had." And he gave her a look of awe. "I don't know what did it. Maybe without a condom? Maybe," and he shrugged a little, "because I just got you pregnant?"

"You feel so good inside of me, Cal. I can't explain it," and Sky touched his jaw, feeling the sandpapery quality of it beneath her fingertips. "It was wonderful for me too. It's so much better without a condom," and she smiled a little, wiping the tears from her eyes.

"Maybe because we really do love one another," Cal rasped, moving his hips slowly, feeling himself becoming thicker, growing within her. He saw Sky's eyes grow darker, telling him she liked what he was doing. Her body was so wet, the smell of her sex driving him to hardness once again.

"I like you in me like this. Don't leave."

"I'll roll us on our sides," Cal reassured her, kissing Sky once more and then guiding her beside him. He brought her leg over his so they could remain coupled, the sensations continued to be exquisite, satisfying, as never before. Sky sighed and nestled her brow against Cal's jaw, sliding her arm across his hard torso. "I love you," he growled, drawing Sky tight against him, letting her know it in every way possible. He slid his hand across her hips and embraced her tight against him. She moaned that soft sound, telling him she enjoyed him remaining deep within her, giving her renewed pleasure.

"Sometimes," Sky murmured, her voice wispy, "I think my love for you will make my heart explode and I'll die from the utter joy of it."

Cal closed his eyes, holding her so he could feel her heart against his. "I know. You can't put it into words what I feel for you, Sky." Threading his fingers through her silky hair, Cal watched the moonlight dance across her multi-colored strands. "You are my life. You know that, don't you?" and he pulled back just enough to engage her druzy looking eyes. The tenderness she shared with him told Cal everything. "You're mine," Cal growled. "Always and forever…"

June 5

SKY FOUND HERSELF surrounded by Cal's old SEAL team. Joe Harrison and his wife Abby had given them the first-floor condo on a three-story building he own on Coronado Island. They had flown in midday and had picked them up at Lindbergh International Airport hours earlier. They had left their two-year-old twins, Michael and Dawn, with Abby's mother, Poppy, back in West Virginia. They would be staying in the other ground-floor condo next door to them. Abby had thoughtfully brought a huge bouquet of flowers arranged on the coffee table, giving the spare, clean condo some bright color. The windows looked out over San Diego Bay to the south and Sky found herself staring at the smooth, marine-blue, sun-dappled water.

Cal's ex-SEAL friend Ben Gordon and his wife Leah had also arrived. They had a one-year-old baby girl, Samantha, who Ben's mother was caring for their child in their absence. They were staying at the posh historical and famous Del, the massive hotel on one end of the island. Jack Driscoll would arrive two days before the wedding with his crew from Shield Security. Hunter Gibson, still a SEAL, had gotten permission to come out of the Chocolate Mountains training area in Arizona to attend their wedding. Sky could see that Cal was happy being surrounded by his SEAL team buddies.

"Hey," Abby called, gesturing for Sky to come over to the pink granite island where she was pouring some wine, "let's sit here and let the guys gab." Abby wore a white pantsuit and a tasteful silver tee beneath it. She pushed her curly light brown hair away from her face and quickly tamed it into a ponytail.

Sky grinned and nodded. "Thanks, Abby," she said, holding up her glass of water and gently clinking it against Abby's wineglass. She liked Abby's freckled face. Cal had shared with her that Abby was part of a top-secret group of volunteer military women who had been assigned to black ops groups around the world a few years earlier. Abby had been assigned to Joe's SEAL team in Afghanistan. Over time, she had fallen in love with, and later married SEAL Joe Harrison. They were now the proud parents of twins who were two years old. She glanced toward the living room where the men were sitting and talking, beers in hand. The SEAL drink of choice.

"I'll bet you're plumb tuckered out from all the travel and the excitement?" Abby asked.

Sky nodded. "Just a little. But it's nice to see Cal's friends, too. He often talks about them, sometimes shares a story with me about an op. Now, I get to put faces to the names."

Abby sighed. "You'd think these guys were still SEALs. Look at 'em," and she laughed, pointing toward the group of men sitting, laughing, and telling stories amongst one another. They were like a pack of male alpha wolves, competing mercilessly with one another, a take-no-prisoners way of life for them.

"It's good that they are together," Sky murmured. "I don't think you ever take the SEAL out of a man. It's bred into their bones."

"That's for sure," Abby said. "Joe stays in regular touch with his team, too. It's a positive, healthy lifeline for all of them."

"And then they have us."

Abby laughed. "Well, if Cal hasn't been sold on marrying you yet, Joe will set him straight. He'll tell you it's the best thing that's ever happened to him."

"Oh," Sky said, moving her finger delicately up and down the glass, "I think Cal is more than ready to go there." So was she.

"Good."

Just then, the door opened. Sky gasped. It was Dylan McCoy! He was balancing at the entryway on crutches. All the SEALs stood and quickly came over, pounding him hello on the back, shaking his hand and opening the door so he could swing into the condo. Sky said, "I'll be right back. Dylan is giving me away at the altar…"

"Hey," Abby murmured, "I need to go call our children. I promised my Ma that I'd do it," and she looked at her watch.

"Oh," Sky said, "I understand. We'll see you later for dinner?"

Abby grinned and finished off her wine in a hurry. "Better believe it. When I come back, I'll join ya'll out on the patio."

The men parted as Abby left the condo, opening the door for her. Sky slipped between them so she could reach Dylan. She laughed and threw her arms around the former SEAL. "How are you?" she asked, kissing his shaven cheek. She saw him blush, his grin lopsided with embarrassment.

"Better, now that I'm here."

Sky stepped aside, ushering him in, gesturing him to an overstuffed chair. "Come on, sit down. Do you want a beer?"

Cal came to her side, slipping his arm around her waist. "We've got this handled," he told her, kissing her temple. Dylan excused himself and merged with his old SEAL team. Sky noticed he wore a serious external brace on his left thigh. McCoy had been shot in February when Vlad Alexandrov's men had attacked them at an Indian village in Peru. The bullet had shattered his femur.

If not for an Army Special Forces team nearby who had a vaunted 18 Delta combat medic among them, he would have died outright from blood loss. Because of the exemplary skills of Nate, the Delta medic, Dylan hadn't bled out and he kept his leg. Sky's smile dissolved as she went back to that day, the screams, the ear-splitting roar of gunfire, the smell of blood, watching Julie, Dylan's wife, dying as she threw herself like a shield between the Russians shooting at them to protect Dylan, who was already wounded and down. She felt Cal squeeze her shoulders and looked up.

"Okay?" he asked, searching her eyes.

"You're scary sometimes, Sinclair." She watched him give her a slow grin.

"No, just attuned to you, is all," Cal reassured her gently. And then he dug into her gaze, as if silently asking her what she was thinking about.

"Just… memories," she admitted softly. Forcing them away, Sky whispered, "I want to be with Dylan for a bit at some point. Can you guys go outside to the barbecue sun deck? Joe was firing up the barbecue out there. Maybe help him grill those steaks?"

Cal nodded. "Sure, we can do that." He dropped a quick kiss to her lips. "Remember? That's the past. We're here now. And I love you…"

Dylan McCoy barely touched his beer and Sky felt her heart squeeze in anguish for him. He'd lost his wife, Julie, four months ago and she knew how much he loved her. She sat down on the couch and waited until Abby and Joe had taken the platter of steaks outside to the deck where everyone else was gathered. The condo was quiet, and she tucked her legs beneath her, holding Dylan's sad gaze.

"How's physical therapy going for your leg?"

"Painful as hell." Dylan shrugged, "they said I'd almost lost the leg. And then they told me I'd never walk again."

Snorting, Sky said, "Good thing you're a SEAL. You don't listen to anybody but yourself. You guys are tougher than what the medical field realizes."

He lightly touched the contraption around his thigh that gave it the continued support it needed. "Mostly, I don't listen to them," and he smiled a little. "How are you doing, Sky? You look good. Happy."

Her heart wrung with grief and pain for Dylan. "I'm very happy," she admitted. "Happier than I've ever been." Sky opened her hand. "I never thought in my wildest imagination that I'd ever meet someone like Cal."

"I can see he really loves you. He always did. From the gitgo."

Nodding, Sky held his warm gaze. "Yeah," she laughed a little, "I was the last to know it. When Cal showed up in Peru, I was torn. I guess I fell in love with him at Camp Nichols, but I was running scared. When I was hit by a bullet while climbing into my Black Hawk, Cal saved me, and I sort of knew then."

"Knew what?" Dylan asked softly, taking a sip of his beer.

"That there was something very special, one-of-a-kind, between Cal and me. I was way too scared, though. I'd been running since I was sixteen, trying to hide from Vladimir Alexandrov, and I fled to Peru after I recovered from the bullet wound."

"See? I never knew any of this about you." Dylan smiled a little. "You're black ops, Sky. You say little, listen a lot."

Flushing, she sipped from her glass of water. "I learned from an early age on not to say much. Listen, watch, and you live. That was my unspoken motto growing up."

"You and Cal shared similar bad childhoods," Dylan murmured.

"Sort of." Sky didn't want to talk about the past. "So what are your plans, Dylan?"

He gave her a sudden grin. "To hobble down the aisle with you and not fall flat on my face and ruin your wedding."

Laughing, Sky shook her head. "We have a rehearsal in three days at the SEAL team HQ. I'm kind of excited. I've never seen the inside of a SEAL team building."

"It's a rare look at our inner space," Dylan agreed. "I understand Master Chief Butch Carpenter is going to be the master of ceremonies and make it happen inside the HQ."

Fondly, Sky nodded. "He was the Master Chief of Ben Gordon's team. I've yet to meet him, but Cal truly admires the man."

"We call him Butch for short," Dylan murmured, a wry smile on his face. "He's forty-four years old and got twenty years in with the SEALs. I think he'll die with his boots on and never leave the team. Someday, they'll drag his dead body out of there," and he chuckled fondly.

"Cal said Butch has red hair."

"Yeah, and he had a helluva temper to go with it when things went south. The man is a master dancer politically speaking, but then, most Master Chief's are. They run the SEAL teams top down."

"Cal said he's got ties clear up to the President's office. Do you think that's true?"

Dylan shrugged. "Butch Carpenter is a force of nature, Sky. If you want something done, the man is a magician. That's why Cal wanted him on this wedding ceremony. Butch will make sure it goes down right or else."

"This guy is like a legend in ST3," she murmured, shaking her head. "I can hardly wait to meet him."

"Tomorrow, Cal and all of us are going over at 0900 to HQ to sit down in one of the briefing rooms with him. You and Lauren are invited along, of course, because it's your wedding and she's your maid of honor."

Looking at her watch, she said, "Lauren's supposed to be here any time, now."

"Cal said she's hell on wheels. Is she?"

Grinning, Sky said, "I'll let you decide that, okay?"

"And what about the combat medic who saved you?"

"Oh, that's Alexei Kazak. We call him Alex. He's been hired by Shield as a security contractor. Even better, he's being given political asylum with his sister Kira, here in the U.S. They've been given a pathway to earn their green cards and eventually, become U.S. citizens. It's a happy ending for this guy, Dylan. Alex saved our lives."

"Spetsnaz operators are almost as good as SEALs," Dylan said. He looked up and saw a tall, red-haired woman in a black t-shirt, dark green cargo pants and black combat boots at the front door. "Hey, is that Lauren?"

With a shriek, Sky leaped up, quickly placed her glass on the table and hurried to open the front door.

"Lauren! You made it," and Sky gave her a quick hug of hello.

"Like I wouldn't make it," Lauren teased her. She walked through the door, saw Dylan and halted.

Sky quickly introduced them.

Dylan slowly stood up and picked up his crutches. "Tell you what. You ladies enjoy a nice quiet chat with one another. I'm going to go get a beer and join the guys outside."

"Yeah," Sky teased him unmercifully, "you can't stand missing a good joke, Dylan." She quickly got up and slid the door open so he could hobble through and be with his buddies.

Turning after she slid the door shut, Sky said, "They are a rowdy group." She returned to the living room where Lauren stood and asked, "Want to meet everyone else? Or get some wine first?"

Lauren tossed her long hair across her shoulder with a movement of her head. "Wine first." She looked toward the sliding glass doors leading out to the patio. "Oh, hell, leave them be. They're all sharing SEAL stories out there," and she followed Sky to the kitchen.

Laughing, Sky said, "Yeah, it's like old home week for these guys. How was your flight?"

"Okay," Lauren murmured, taking the glass and holding it still while Sky poured the white wine into it. "Slept most of the way. So, I'm refreshed. I met Abby Harrison on the way out. I like her a lot." She looked around the condo. "Nice digs."

"It's a very Japanese decor," Sky agreed, "very peaceful feeling to me."

There was a loud burst of laughter out on the sun deck.

"Well, almost peaceful," Lauren corrected wryly, wrinkling her nose. She followed Sky into the living room, and they sat down on opposite corners of the couch.

"Those guys need this," Sky said.

Lauren snorted. "Hell, they're black ops boys. It's all they know how to be. It will be your job to train them to be civil."

Sky grinned and sat down. "Don't you want to go out there and carouse with them? You were black ops, too?"

Giving the group a hard look, Lauren shook her head. "No thanks. I like having girl time with you. Much more intelligent, quiet conversations, thank you very much," and she toasted to Sky and took a sip of her wine.

"Hey, how are you getting along with Alex?" It had been a week since their fateful meeting at the office. Sky saw Lauren's face go blank. Uh oh… when she put her game face on, she knew it hadn't gone well.

"I'm just thanking my lucky stars he isn't coming out here for another three days," she drawled.

"That bad, huh?"

"He's on my training roster for upgrading his shooting skills. The type of weapons he's used to using, we don't carry. So he has to requalify and get real friendly really fast with our weapons."

"Is he that bad?"

"No," Lauren said. "Actually, and don't you DARE tell him this, he's a damned good shooter. He was a trained sniper in Spetsnaz, a back-up in case the main snipers were put out of commission. He trains easily, gets it first time around, and he'll hit ten out of ten bullseyes. Jack is very pleased with him."

"Then why aren't you happy?"

Squirming, Lauren griped, "He gives me moon eyes."

"Moon eyes?" Sky grinned.

Sitting up, Lauren took a huge gulp of wine and set her glass on the coffee table. "You know I work with training security dogs, right? And I also devote time to the Humane Society?"

"Yes." Sky could hardly wait to hear how moon eyes and dogs went together. She'd never heard the term.

"You know those big, sad-eyed looking dogs? Like St. Bernard's?"

"I've seen them, yes."

"Well," she huffed, "Kazak sometimes gives me one of those looks, you know? Moon eyes. Big sad, soulful looking eyes. I swear to God, the guy could make a flower bud and bloom by just looking at it," she groused.

Sky said, "Oh... I see now..."

Giving her a dirty look, Lauren growled, "You see WHAT?"

Covering her mouth with her fingers, Sky tried not to smile but Lauren caught her at it anyway.

"What is so funny, Sky? You're sitting there like you know something. Spill it?"

"Oh, nothing I can say is a fact," she parried, holding her friend's unhappy stare. "Why does it bother you?"

"It irritates the hell out of me!"

"Really?" Sky's brows rose and she couldn't help but smile. "Honestly? It does, Lauren?"

"Yeah." She glared at Sky. "So what?"

"It just seems that if you were immune to Alex, it wouldn't matter how he looked at you. You'd have NO reaction. Right?"

Lauren suddenly moved and flicked her hair across her shoulder. "You're reading too much into this, Sky. You're head over heels in love with Cal and you're starry eyed. You see love everywhere. Even when it's not there, you're misinterpreting it."

"Maybe," Sky allowed, seeing how twitchy Lauren had suddenly become. She couldn't sit still, had got up and started pacing the length of the room like a caged lioness.

"Well, how else is Alex doing at Shield?" Sky thought talking business instead of touchy-feely topics with Lauren might calm her down. She'd never seen her friend nervous like this before.

"Jack's been congratulating himself on hiring Kazak. He's a combat medic and apparently, a very good one. We're always needing medics, so he's filling a big hole we have in our company roster. Actually, we can use two more and I've talked to Jack about that. He's in agreement."

"But Alex is doing okay?"

Lauren's mouth tightened. "I have to teach him Krav Maga starting next week."

"But you've always taught classes on it to other team members."

Lauren halted and threw open her hands in frustration. "I just don't want—I don't LIKE to be near this guy, Sky. He makes me twitchy as hell. I'm NEVER nervous, but being around him, I feel like a Mexican jumping bean. It's spooky."

Sky decided to swallow her smile. "I see. And has he been respectful of you?"

"To a fault," Lauren said, shaking her head and going to the refrigerator and bringing back the bottle of white wine. She filled her glass. Sitting down, she griped, "You'll never believe what he did the other day."

"What?"

"The guy brought me a bouquet of red roses out to the shooting range! In front of six other team members. I about died of shame."

Sky compressed her lips, knowing what was happening between the two of them. But Lauren was absolutely oblivious. She was crawling out of her skin when Alex was too close to her, a sure sign that he was getting to her sexually. She knew Lauren had very little relationship experience to read the signs or the signals between them. "That was sweet of him."

"Sweet?" Lauren took a gulp of wine. "I call it damned embarrassing. I told him to take the flowers and get rid of them. They had no business out on a shooting range. Hell, he had to qualify. He shouldn't be thinking of flowers."

Sky remained silent, happy for Lauren. Alex was like Cal: once he saw something he wanted, he went after it. Alex was trying to be nice, to behave how he thought an American gentleman should toward the lady he wanted to court. But it was sailing over Lauren's head like a helium balloon. She didn't have a clue. "He meant well," Sky murmured.

"I can't hardly stand the fact he's coming out here for your wedding. I have to play nice because I don't want to ruin your wedding by getting into a snit with him."

"Thank you," Sky said, sincerely meaning it. Lauren, despite her outer toughness, was very sensitive. And she loved the idea of being Sky's maid of honor. Lauren hated the idea of wearing that gooey dress, as she referred to it, and she refused to wear heels or nail polish, but she had conceded to let a hairdresser style her red hair. Those were things Sky could live with. She liked her friend just the way she was independent, headstrong, and blunt. She was a perfect picture of a female version of Cal Sinclair.

CHAPTER 5

June 6

"CAL... THIS IS so beautiful!" Sky looked around, absorbing the beach. The pounding of the ocean waves, the seagulls sailing lazily overhead on the warm June afternoon, crying and floating above them as they walked along the beach, it all filled her with an overwhelming joy. Cal was carrying a ruck on his back that contained a blanket, picnic food, and water. He was wearing his black baseball cap with the SEAL insignia on it, a black t-shirt, and black shorts that showed off his powerful legs to perfection. Last night, she'd been exhausted by the day's ceaseless activities. This morning, Cal had slowly awakened her with kisses from her mouth to her feet, simply caring for her, not making love with her. Sky was sure he'd sensed the depth of her tiredness from all the excitement leading up to their wedding. Caring was part of loving, and his tenderness filled her heart and soul.

Cal turned, feeling the warmth of the sun. From behind his wraparound sunglasses, he looked over and grinned at Sky, who was struggling through the fine, sugary white sand. There was a rosy flush to her cheeks, and she looked winded from their mile-long trek across the public beach at La Jolla, a small, but very rich town north of San Diego. "We need to make our way around that," he said, pointing to the five-hundred-foot dark brown rocky cliff coming up. "That's the surprise I have waiting for you," he teased.

Huffing, Sky gave him a game smile. "I'll do it..." Cal must have seen her struggles and slowed his stride. He reached out, grabbing her hand. "Sorry," she said, breathing unevenly. "It's my stupid asthma acting up. No big deal. I'll be okay."

Cal halted and tucked Sky beneath his arm, pointing her in the direction of the marine-colored ocean, the waves at least six or seven feet high at low tide. "Let's rest a minute," he murmured, dropping a kiss on her mussed hair. In the sunlight, her blond strands gleamed like molten gold. Cal would never get tired of looking at Sky. She was utterly flushed from the mile-long walk along the beach. Sky, he knew, would never ask him to slow down. When they lived in Cusco, Peru, which sat nearly twelve thousand feet above sea level, she often labored to catch her breath when her asthma decided to intrude. Sky never complained, though he wished she would. What he had to do instead was monitor her and constantly keep his senses oriented to her.

"This is incredible," Sky whispered, looking around.

"Is this your first time to the San Diego area?"

"Yes." She flashed him a smile. "I hope it isn't our last?"

"I'm a SEAL and I took my training here," Cal told her wryly. "We'll always make time to come back here." He pointed out to the waves breaking against the golden sand. "That's Mother Ocean. We were taught she would always keep us safe. If shit happened on land, you go into the ocean and swim out as far as you could, and then get picked up by a sub, helicopter, or by a boat."

"The water's cold," Sky noted because she'd been walking barefoot, allowing the foamy bubbles to slosh around her feet and ankles.

"It is." Cal grinned. "Brings back a lot of memories of when I was in BUD/S at Coronado, hoping like hell to make it through that six-month school in order to become a SEAL."

"I was listening to Dylan, Ben, and you talking late last night about BUD/S." Sky shook her head. "That sounded like six months of continuous torture. Being forced to stand up to your chest in this cold water? Freezing to the point where your teeth were chattering? No thanks." She shook her head, giving Cal a look of admiration. "You guys are REALLY tough."

"And you aren't?" Cal gave her a serious look, noticing her breathing was calming down and evening out once more. Her face wasn't as flushed, indicating she wasn't struggling any longer to inhale a deep breath.

"I could never make it through BUD/S!"

"There's all kinds of challenges in life, Sweetheart," he told her, becoming solemn as he held her close to him. "And you have strength. A kind that can't be made by going through something like BUD/S. Your childhood was a make-or-break kind of strength for you. You handled it for sixteen years, I only had to handle training for six months. And you have the heart." Cal placed a kiss on her brow, "There's a core of resilience in your soul, enough to overcome anything thrown at you." He smiled down at her. "You're a survivor, Sky. Not all people are, but you are."

Sky pushed her toe into the damp sand. "Well," she muttered, "I'll agree with you that I'm strong. But Cal, you guys have an incredible physical and mental strength I just don't see much of anywhere else in this world of ours."

He pulled her along with him, keeping her on the damp sand where it was easier for her to walk. Checking his stride even more, Cal wanted to make the last part of the journey to his secret beach would not become such a battle for her. "SEAL training sorts out those who have mental toughness and heart and who don't," Cal told her. The breeze was warm and danced around them as they approached smooth stones covered with slippery green moss. Cal halted. "You're mentally tough, too, Sky or you wouldn't be here today, with me." He leaned down and brushed a kiss across her smiling mouth, tasting the salt that was in the fresh air surrounding them.

Sky sighed, squeezing his large hand, feeling the monitored strength of Cal's fingers around hers. "Well, today we don't have to be anything but happy." She looked at the expanse of tidal pools in among the smoothed rocks they had yet to traverse. On the other side of the cliff that rose to their left, she glimpsed a small beach hidden behind it.

"I think after yesterday," Cal told her, releasing her from beneath his arm but holding her hand, "you need to rest. Maybe," and he flashed her a slight smile, "more downtime with me."

Groaning, Sky said, "Thank you. After last night and then meeting with Master Chief Butch Carpenter at the ST3 HQ this morning, I felt like my mind was turning into rubber."

Laughing, Cal led her across the drying rocks, holding her hand and helping her to remain balanced. With the tide out, the mossy plants growing on the long, smooth boulders were dry enough so as not to be as slippery as they could become during high tide. "Butch likes you," he said.

Laughter bubbled up Sky's throat as she slid on her sandals to negotiate the rocks and tide pools nestled throughout there. "Butch is a piece of work. I mean, really, Cal, is that guy for real?"

"Oh yeah, he's for real. Every pound of him."

"He's a powerful person. I never saw you guys become so quiet, respectful, or attentive as when he walked into the condo yesterday afternoon to have a barbecue with all of us."

"No question he is our SEAL god," Cal said drily. "Master Chiefs rule the SEAL universe and beyond. He kept our asses out of trouble in Afghanistan. Butch is one of the best in the business when it comes to planning an op. Our SEAL team was lucky to have him."

Sky halted at a small tide pool; wonder mirrored on her face as she saw all kinds of small, colorful creatures beneath the clear, mirrored surface. "He scared the hell out of me when we visited your team HQ this morning."

Cal laughed. "Yeah, he comes across as a hard ass, but nobody cares more than Butch. He liked you, Sky. Really."

She squatted down by the pool, resting one hand on the spongy surface across the rock, the other at the edge of the pool for balance. "I couldn't tell if he saw me as a bug to squash or what." She pointed to the pool. "Cal? What is that? It looks so beautiful."

Cal knelt beside her. "That's an anemone that has opened. See the long white and pink arms slowly waving around?"

"Yes," and she was mesmerized by the graceful movement of the translucent tentacles, which were so many she couldn't count all of them.

"It's trying to lure a fish into coming over," Cal explained. He pointed to a tiny silver and black fish swimming around in the pool. "If that fish gets into the arms of the anemone, he'll grab the fish, draw it down inside itself, into its mouth, and eat it."

"So beautiful but deadly," Sky said, giving him a quick look. "I'll bet because you've swam so much in the oceans of the world, you know the creatures that live in it like the back of your hand?"

"Sort of," Cal hedged. He picked up a rounded shell sitting on the bottom of the pool and placed it in the palm of his hand. "Watch this…"

Sky saw a creature suddenly pop out from beneath the huge shell. "Oh…"

"This is a hermit crab. They're a soft-bodied crustacean and they go scuttling around in the tidal area searching for a shell home. When they find a shell that an occupant is no longer living in, they make it their home. When it outgrows the shell, they'll abandon the old one and go in search of a larger shell to accommodate their new size." Cal put the hermit crab back down in the tidal pool. "Another way to survive." He saw the wonder on Sky's face. She'd been born in Trenton, New Jersey, and to his knowledge, had never been taken to the Jersey shore to appreciate what nature had in store for those lucky enough to walk the sands along the Atlantic Ocean.

Sky stood up and pulled her small digital camera out of the pocket of her shorts. She had never taken a liking to capturing photos on her cell phone. "I'm going to take some pictures." She grinned. "Then, once we get home, I'll try my hand with pastel chalks and capture all of this. It's so colorful!"

Cal watched her turn into a curious child in that moment. Every day, he glimpsed another facet of Sky. She was excited now, and he was grateful she trusted him enough to be herself around him after so much had happened to her. The breeze lifted strands of her hair. The awe in her expression was priceless to Cal. He liked watching Sky make discoveries, liked being able to share what he knew about the ocean with her.

Sky loved to swim. One of the surprises Cal had for her was to teach her to scuba dive during their honeymoon. He'd already rented a dive boat and he was going to take her out to the famous kelp beds off La Jolla. There, Cal would swim with her, showing her the underwater beauty, he was sure would amaze her even more. He'd find them lobster for a meal that he'd make for her that evening. His heart opened fiercely with the love he held for her. Sky didn't know it, but another wedding gift he'd bought her was a Canon underwater camera so she could photograph while they scuba dived. He knew she'd be thrilled.

"Your drawings are getting better with each one that you create," Cal told her, watching as she stood and moved around the pool to get some other shots.

"Oh, I'm such an amateur," she protested. "But I do love to draw. It relaxes me."

He stood and backed away so she could easily maneuver around the pool and take more close-up photographs. "Where did the love of art show up in your life?"

"Marielle Zimmerman, my foster mother, was an art teacher. She taught the middle grades, and one day she came home with her student's art project. I was so taken by their work." Sky slid the camera back into her pocket, pushed strands off her brow and looked up at Cal. "I didn't know I liked art, but Marielle began to tutor me." She sighed. "She was so good to me, Cal. I'm just so sorry Vlad murdered my foster parents. To this day, I think about and miss them so much." She touched her heart and frowned, her voice growing wispy. "Jack introduced me to flying the helicopter. I think he sensed I needed to get into the air, away from everything. When he took me up in the helicopter he flew for the Trenton police department, I felt truly free for the first time in my life."

Cal saw the grief and loss of her foster parents in her eyes. He reached out, caressing her cheek. "That time spent with them showed you love and hope, Sky. They gave you gifts money can't buy. It was the most important time in your life." And Cal knew it on levels he couldn't explain. Those two stellar human beings had opened their home and their hearts to Sky. Unfortunately, the Zimmermans had also taken Vlad Alexandrov into their home. He had been their foster son since he was nine years old.

Yerik Alexandrov, Vlad's father, was in a fight to take over the Russian Mafia in New York City back then. He'd wanted to protect his only son from being killed during the take-over. He'd gotten Vlad into the state foster program with lies and fraud. Vlad had landed on Jack and Marielle's doorstep, and they'd taken in the young boy with open arms, without question, giving him only their love. They never realized that the boy who appeared so sweet and innocent looking on the outside was bad seed, a sadistic, brutal killer. Cal often wondered at the shock Jack and Marielle must have experienced when Vlad, at age seventeen, pulled a gun and shot them. It was a tragedy for them and for Sky, who had witnessed their murders.

"I like your art," Cal murmured, pulling Sky into his arms, wanting her to stop thinking about the past, about another loss in her life. Cal gave her a teasing look. "Want to see my secret beach? A place where I would bring my wet suit, my tanks, and wade into the ocean and then swim out there when I was a SEAL," and he pointed out toward the ocean where the kelp beds sat.

Sky nodded, leaning against his strong body. Cal's flesh was sun warm, slightly damp with sweat, feeling so steady and calm to her. "I don't see kelp beds," she said, shading her eyes, looking out at the restless ocean.

"No, you can't see them from here," he said. "They're about half a mile out."

"And you'd swim from here to there?" Sky's eyes widened with shock over the distance.

Chuckling, Cal kissed her cheek. "Sweetheart, during BUD/S, we'd don wetsuits and tanks and swim five miles underwater. A half a mile swim is a warmup. It's nothing."

"Amazing," Sky said, reaching up, placing her lips against his mouth. She wasn't disappointed, feeling Cal's arms slide around her, pinning her against himself. Slipping her arms around his neck, Sky reached up on her toes, taking his mouth, making a happy sound in her throat as he returned it. Everything was perfect to Sky. The heat of the sun, the playful breeze, the constant call of seagulls wheeling above the beach, all conspired to make her feel euphoric. Cal had a way of getting her distracted from her past, or even worrying about last-minute details about their wedding. His mouth cherished hers and she felt his fingers caress the nape of her neck. He treated her with such tenderness, such adoration, that Sky felt like a goddess, not the mere, flawed human being that she really was. Cal made her feel alive, made her feel hope, something she'd lost a long time ago. Most of all, as he deepened their kiss, Cal fed her incredible happiness.

Reluctantly, Cal eased from her wet mouth, feeling his lower body awakening. It wasn't going to be tough to see he had an erection thanks to her. And when Sky sinuously pressed her belly against him, he saw the wanton look come to her eyes. Groaning, he released her and took her hand in his. "Come on, let's get to that secret beach…"

Sky's eyes widened as they made their way across the rocky tidal pool area and rounded the massive cliff rising above them. There was a small, crescent-shaped golden beach bracketed by cliffs on three sides, making it, indeed, a secret of sorts, she thought. There was no one here, unlike the public beach at La Jolla. Cal chose a nice, gently sloped area of gleaming golden sand and shrugged out of the ruck. He pulled the dark blue blanket out and spread it across the undisturbed sand. Next came the food and their water. Sky kicked off her sandals and sat down on the blanket, arms around her drawn up knees.

Here, she realized, the cliffs became like silent guardians to either end of this hidden jewel. A rocky embrace of sorts. "Do people not know this is here?" she wondered as Cal sat down cross-legged on the blanket, facing her.

"Locals know about it. The tourists don't." He grinned a little as he poured some water into a plastic cup and handed it to her. "And locals don't talk about it. It's their secret."

"It's beautiful here, Cal," and Sky sipped the cold water, not realizing how thirsty she'd become after their mile long trek. Looking up on the cliffs dotted with thousands of blooming, colorful ice plants and surrounded by a wooden fence along the boundary, Sky imagined that it looked like Nature's afghan, the bright colors making it look dazzling. Sky gave him a teasing look. "Is this where the SEALs brought their girlfriends? It's VERY private."

Cal had the good grace to look guilty. "Yeah, it's one of our hideaways. There are others, closer to Coronado, but I always liked this one because the chances of some tourist coming upon you and interrupting you were minimal."

Shaking her head, Sky muttered, "You guys... all you have is sex on your mind."

"Guilty," Cal said smugly, pulling out the sandwiches he'd made earlier. Handing one to her, he added, "This was a serious beach for us SEALs, though."

She opened her sandwich and saw he'd assembled turkey, cheese, and lettuce on the bread slices. "Oh?"

"Yeah. If a SEAL was in love, he brought his lady here." Cal waved his hand in a gesture around the cove. "This is a place where you asked her to marry you," and he gave her a heated look.

"Ohhh," Sky murmured between bites, "I see..."

"Joe brought Abby here when they were living together. He loved her and they were getting pressured by her military commitments she had to fulfill for the top-secret program she'd volunteered for. Abby had to deploy in a week, and Joe was desperate to cement their relationship. He brought Abby here and professed his love, his dreams for both of them."

"That's so romantic," Sky sighed. "And you can see how much they love one another. It's written all over them."

"Like it is us?" Cal baited, hearing the wistfulness in her voice, her eyes getting that dreamy, faraway look. Sky, despite everything, was an idealist and a dyed-in-the-wool romantic. And he loved her for those qualities. He watched her flush and avoid his look.

"Well, yes... I just love how Joe looks at her. And there's such warmth in Abby's eyes when she looks up at him. They're so deeply in love with one another."

"Even after two years of marriage."

She snorted. "What's wrong with that?"

"Nothing," Cal murmured, grinning. "You're so easy to get a rise out of, Ms. Lambert."

Shaking her head, Sky muttered, "And you're SUCH an unmerciful devil, Sinclair."

"I'm not a mean teaser, though," Cal gently pointed out, finishing off the sandwich. He rubbed his hands down the sides of his shorts.

"No, you're not." Her brows fell. "Vlad was a mean tease."

"No you don't," Cal growled, not wanting her to drag up the past. He pulled Sky between his opened thighs, brought her back up against the front of him, and gently held her. "Look at the way the waves break out there," he said, pointing toward them. "Feel the sun on your skin. The way the breeze touches you. Look forward, Sky. The past is behind you where it needs to remain. Today is all that counts."

She leaned her head against his shoulder, brow against his jaw. "You're right... sorry... I didn't mean to spoil it."

Cal took her half-eaten sandwich and set it aside. "Listen," he growled, hauling Sky closer to him, kissing her temple, "you've come a long way, Sweetheart. Every time a bad thought enters your mind, replace it with a happy one."

Sky opened her eyes, drowning in his burning golden gaze. "Until recently, I had no happy things to replace it with." She watched his chiseled mouth curve faintly.

"Well then," Cal said gruffly, "I guess I'm going to have to give you another happy memory." He reached to the left and pulled his ruck over to him. He dug in an outside pocket until he found what he was looking for. "Open your hand."

Stymied, Sky did as he asked. Cal placed a small, dark green velvet jewelry case into her palm.

"What's this?" Sky asked, sitting up in his arms, touching it delicately.

"Open it and find out." Cal watched her closely, seeing sudden excitement in her eyes. Sky was so utterly readable. She had no way to hide how she really felt. Unlike him, who could put on a game face and no one on Earth would ever know what he was really thinking or feeling. Cal was grateful Sky entrusted herself to him, allowed him the privilege of seeing her. He watched as her slender fingers delicately touched the gift.

"What did you do?" Sky accused, smiling up at him.

"Something good," he gloated. "Are you going to open it?"

With a breathy laugh, Sky carefully pried opened the gold clasp. As she raised the lid, a gasp escaped her. "Cal!" She stared at him, thunderstruck, and then gazed at the two blue diamond earrings glinting in the sunlight. "Oh, you didn't! These are the exact same color of diamonds on my engagement ring," and she held up her left hand where they rested.

Cal felt warmth flow through his chest as Sky pressed her fingers against her opened mouth, just staring at them, her eyes huge. "My gift to you for our coming wedding," he said thickly, emotions welling up in him because he saw tears come to her eyes. Taking the jewelry box, Cal eased one of the blue diamonds from the velvet and placed it in her hand. "Here, try one on? See if it fits?"

"Oh, Cal, they're so beautiful! They match the color of the ring perfectly." She shook her head, stunned. "Did you go back down to Cusco, to that jeweler, and buy these from him?" He'd bought the wedding ring with three carats of blue diamonds that had cost him forty thousand dollars in Peru before they returned home to Virginia.

He grinned. "No. I went to a jeweler on Coronado. He found them for me. Want to try them on? Maybe wear them for your wedding day? You know? That wearing some new? Something old? Something borrowed? Something blue?"

Fingers trembling, Sky stared at the earring in palm. "How many carats, Cal? These are not small diamonds."

"Two carats each," he said, and pointed to her engagement ring. "The main stone is two carats. I wanted them to match." He saw how shaken she'd become. Sky had been poor all her life. When he'd bought the expensive wedding set in Cusco for her, she could barely accept it because it had cost so much money. Cal had finally set her down once they had arrived home, and step-by-step, shown Sky his financial worth and structure. She hadn't realized he was worth over five million dollars from playing the stock market since he was eighteen years old. Still, Cal knew that huge outlays of money still shook Sky. She wasn't used to spending such amounts. And he could see she was going to ask him how much. "Twenty thousand," he said, cutting her off at the pass. Sky's eyes went huge with surprise.

"Oh... Cal..." and she stared down at the earring like they might bite her. The sunlight was lancing through the facets. She swore they were the same color as her eyes. It was a perfect match.

"Listen," Cal said gruffly, "consider them a life-long investment, all right?" He pinned her with a look, trying to get Sky to realize his financial world and reality. "These diamond earrings will look beautiful on you when you walk down the aisle to me. They are insured, Sky. Even if they were lost or stolen, the insurance company would pay for them. And in another way, this is an investment that over time, will only increase in value."

Sniffing, Sky wiped her eyes self-consciously. "You were telling me about how an investment accrues interest over time," she said, her voice wobbly with emotion.

"Right," Cal murmured, proud of her, proud that Sky remembered his careful explanation of how he made his money. He was a keen investor but not a risk taker. Over time, his portfolio had grown even during the worst of Wall Street times and increased exponentially during robust times on the stock market. "So," Cal murmured, kissing her cheek, "will you wear these for me? It's my heart's investment in YOU, Sky. Because I love you and," he smiled a little, "because women like matched sets of jewelry if they're going to wear jewelry?" He saw her laugh a little and nod. His heart mushroomed with so much love for her that he sat there embraced in an invisible tsunami of happiness. Sky liked the earrings, there was no question.

"Now," Sky whispered, "I'll be afraid I'll lose one... or one will drop off from my ear lobe..."

"No way," Cal muttered. He turned it over, showing her the delicate clasp on gold post. "Once on, they aren't falling off, okay? I made sure of that because I know you. You're SUCH a worry wart," he teased her gently, watching her lift her lashes, those amazing turquoise eyes of hers stealing his breath away.

With trembling fingers, Sky carefully placed the earrings on her lobes. She touched them often, making sure they stayed put. "They're so beautiful."

He gazed at her, a grin on his mouth. "Gorgeous from where I'm sitting. I don't have a mirror. I guess you'll have to wait until we go back across that tidal pool area. You can lean down over one of them and see your reflection in it. Then you'll know how beautiful you look wearing them. You'll see what I see. Or, if you'd like? Give me your camera and I'll take some pictures."

"Let's do both! I love you so much," Sky quavered, sliding her arms around his shoulders. "You're spoiling me rotten, Cal. You really are."

Cal brushed her lips, tasting the tears in the corners of her luscious mouth. "I'm going to continue to spoil you. I've got a whole lifetime planned of surprising you, making you happy, watching you smile, and hearing you laugh. I promise you, I'm going to make up for those lost first sixteen years of your life."

CHAPTER 6

June 14

"LORDY," ABBY HARRISON murmured, "that's one beautiful wedding gown, Sky."

Sky brought out her wedding dress from the guest bedroom at the condo. Two days from now she would be changing here with the help of Abby and Lauren.

"It's a stunner," Lauren agreed from the kitchen, pouring two glasses of chardonnay and a glass of ice-cold water for Sky. Sometimes, as much as Sky liked wine, it didn't set well with her. Given all the stress and excitement of the coming wedding, Lauren figured her stomach was probably on the fritz. Hers probably would be too, but she wasn't ever going to get married, so she didn't have to worry about that.

Abby watched as Sky gently laid the dress down on the granite island so she could closely inspect it. "Oh, I like the blue and pink beading across the top," she said, lightly running her fingers over the plastic encasing the satin dress. "The blue beads will emphasize the color of your gorgeous eyes."

"Lauren helped me pick it out," Sky admitted. Lauren brought over the drinks to the women and walked back to get her glass.

Abby smiled over at the redhead who wore her standard costume of black t-shirt, green cargo pants and black combat boots. "You have really good taste, Lauren."

Lauren smiled and wrinkled her nose. "Abby, I'm NOT a fashionista as you can tell. Sky is giving me all the credit and it's really hers to take."

Sky shrugged. "Well, Abby, to tell you the truth, I never really had much schooling in feminine things. I didn't feel confident in choosing something myself and Lauren's a sniper. She's got a good eye, so I dragged her along for her valuable second opinion."

Grinning, Lauren said, "Yeah, kicking and screaming. Let's see... How long has it been since I wore a dress?" She struck a thoughtful pose, her finger on her dimpled chin. "The last dress I wore was for my high school graduation."

"And you've never looked back," Sky said, returning her grin. "Hold that thought. I want to put my dress away."

Abby sat down on the stool. "The boys are gonna be gone all day on their scuba diving adventure out in the kelp beds. You don't have to worry about Cal unexpectedly showing up and seeing it."

"I know," Sky said. "I hope they'll have a good time."

"You'd better hope they find enough abalone steaks for all of us tonight for dinner or he'll be showing up with McDonalds!" Lauren said, sitting down at the island.

They all laughed.

Sky said, "I've never eaten an abalone steak."

"Me neither," Abby admitted. "But Joe told me last night they taste good. He said the SEALs would often go out, rent a dive boat, and anchor it off the kelp beds near La Jolla to dive for abalone and lobster. I guess they grilled a lot of those things back at their HQ on Coronado."

Lauren shook her head. "Things is the correct word. They're a certifiable bunch. Forget mermaids. We have Aquamen."

Sky put the dress away, closed the door and joined her friends at the island. She sat at one end of it, appreciating female companionship. "Cal said I'd love them."

"Do you like oysters?" Lauren asked.

"Ugh, I HATE oysters because they're so slimy... Oh no, don't tell me abalone tastes like them?" and Sky gave them a stricken look.

"It's a shellfish," Lauren reminded them. She raised a brow. "Just in case the three of us don't cotton to abalone, I bought some nice New York steaks yesterday. They're in the fridge. We can force the boys to put them on the grill and we'll eat beef instead."

Abby smiled. "You truly are a sniper, Lauren. Always thinking ahead of the curve."

Lauren nodded and sipped her wine. "I understand you were a sniper, too?"

"Oh, no," Abby said quickly. "I was assigned to Joe's SEAL team in Afghanistan, and he was a sniper."

"But," Sky interjected, "Cal said you shot like a sniper."

Abby wrinkled her nose. "My Pa, Floyd, was a Marine Corps sniper. He began teaching me to shoot when I was a young'un. When I got to Joe's team, they were short a sniper. I told them I could shoot pretty well."

"Bet that went over well," Lauren deadpanned.

"Yeah, like throwin' a red-hot horseshoe in a bucket of cold water," Abby agreed, chuckling.

Sky gave Abby an admiring look. "What happened?"

"Well, one of the SEALs who really disliked me being there was a sniper, too. His name was Hammer and he challenged me to a shooting contest with a Win-Mag .300, their sniper rifle of choice for certain distances. My Pa shot a civilian version of that rifle, so I knew it pretty well. Joe saw his team ganging up on me, so he came over and volunteered to be my spotter and coach for that shootin' match."

Sky hung on every word. "And? What happened? Did you win?"

"Well," Abby said, giving her a bashful look, "I held my own. I outshot the guy and technically, I won the match. He was pretty pissed off. Half the team was with him. But the other half, including Master Chief Butch, the officers, and Joe, were on my side and congratulated me."

Lauren rolled her eyes. "Men are SUCH weenies. Women are well known to be better shooters and snipers than any man will ever be. Our brain is wired for details and that's what being a sniper is all about that. During World War Two, Russian women were snipers and helped save their country. All their men were fighting the Nazi's, and the women picked up the rifles and went to work. What they did? It's legendary to this day. So don't tell me women can't be snipers and outshoot any man."

Crowing, Abby said, "That's right."

"Did Joe's team ever get over that loss to you?"

"Sure they did." Abby smiled. "They were short a sniper. As long as I could shoot straight and hit targets, they didn't care if I grew horns."

The women laughed.

"It's still like that out there," Lauren griped. "Our country may have thrown open the doors to women going into combat, but there's a helluva lot of push back by the military, and the black ops community in particular, to not allow us women through their doors. But the horse is out of the barn. SEALs are already opening their doors to women candidates."

"But," Sky said, "you busted down the door before that, Lauren. You became a Marine Force Recon sniper."

"Only because I was twice as good as any man carrying a set of balls," Lauren said grimly. "Twice as good. I outshot all of them. Repeatedly. Consistently." She pulled out a hog's tooth on a leather string around her neck. "When I passed Marine Corps sniper school with a 950 out of a possible 1000, I'd done better than any man who passed through that brutal school. But they refused to give me the hog's tooth. Every male sniper who passed the test got one." She scowled and tucked it down inside her black t-shirt. "It took me a year of haggling, getting a lawyer, and then suing the Marine Corps to force them to acknowledge that I passed with the highest score ever and that they owed me that hog's tooth as proof of it."

"Wow," Abby murmured, "you really took them head on."

"It's the only way they understand force vs. force. Anyway, it's the story of my life," Lauren said tightly. "I eventually was put on the roll call as passing the school course and given my rightfully earned hog's tooth. It's SUCH a boy's club, even to this day. It will be interesting to see how the sniper school evolves now that it's open doors to women. My bet is that they'll have more women snipers graduating than men, in the long run."

"Is that why you left the Marine Corps?" Abby wondered.

"Yes, after six years I walked away. I figured the hassle, the continual sniping behind my back about me being a woman, hurting a lot of male feelings, and just generally expending a lot of energy defending myself and trying to get good on ops, took an emotional toll on me. I was fighting an outside enemy and I was also fighting Marines who were supposed to have my back. I had enemies in two camps."

"And then you found Shield Security?" Sky asked.

"Actually, Jack Driscoll went looking to hire me. He knew my sniper scores and didn't care if I was a woman or not." Lauren's voice tempered a bit. "He'd heard how good I was, how many kills I had. The day after I left the Corps, he called me up and offered me a job and a mind-blowing salary, as well as a leadership position in his company."

"Jack's a fair guy," Sky said to Abby. "He was in SEALs for seven years before he left. He started Shield with the intent of getting the best of the operators, no matter what service branch they came from."

Abby looked over at Lauren. "Are you the only woman in it?"

"Oh, no," Lauren murmured, her shoulders relaxing. "About half of the operators there are women. Jack has a hundred employees, and his company is growing so fast, they're building on to the original office complex. His services are wanted around the world, and he's got a very good name for himself."

"Impressive," Abby said, nodding. "I like a man like that."

"Don't we all?" Lauren said.

"Joe strikes me as that type of man," Sky said.

"Oh, he is, believe me. We'd never have gotten along if he hadn't treated me like an equal." Abby grinned a little and opened her hands. "I come from Hill people in West Virginia. Most folks consider us ignorant because we live in the mountains, raise our own food, and live in tight knit groups."

Raising her brow, Sky said, "You don't strike me like that at all."

"No," Lauren said with an evil grin, "one look into how Abby canvases an area, she doesn't miss a thing. It's a sniper's way of operating in the world. Details count. She learned that from her Pa in the hills of West Virginia, I imagine."

Abby flushed. "Well, I admit I do still operate more or less like a sniper, paying attention to details, but I'm not as paranoid about it anymore."

Sky laughed. "Cal told me once being a sniper and paranoid went hand-in-hand with one another."

"Paranoia keeps you alive," Lauren added archly, finishing off her wine. She slid off the stool. "Second round ladies?"

Sky shook her head. It was barely eleven a.m. "No, I'm going to nurse my water for a while, Lauren, thanks."

"Me too," Abby chimed in. "Well," she said, "how do you think our guys are doin' out there in their dive boat?"

"Hopefully having fun," Sky said. It was Cal's bachelor party. He'd rather do something like diving than drinking himself into a drunk. "Cal loves the water."

"Those guys are water dogs, no question," Lauren agreed.

"How do you think Alex will do? Does he know how to swim at all?" Sky wondered. She watched Lauren's mouth twitch. Alex had arrived at Coronado almost a week ago. He'd been keeping his distance from Lauren so far. Earlier this morning, he went out to eat with the guys at a local SEAL restaurant and then on to the dive boat.

"Probably drowned."

Abby hooted. "You can't mean that, Lauren."

"Don't try me."

Sky shook her head. "Alex is from Ukraine, and he joined the Russian Army. I don't know enough about Spetsnaz to understand how they train their operators."

Lauren shrugged. "They're almost as good as any SEAL."

"Then," Abby murmured, "he's got to know how to swim."

Sky saw Lauren make a prudish face. There was no question in her mind that Alex got under her skin, and she didn't know what to do about it. She hid a smile and said nothing.

It was late afternoon when all the ex-SEALs in the dive boat shed their gear, their wetsuits, twin oxygen tanks, and harnesses, and headed back into San Diego harbor. Cal sat with Alex in the back, both of them slugging down a well-earned cold beer. Joe, Jack Driscoll, and a few other guys from Shield were at the bow of the boat, drinking beer as well.

Alex pushed his damp black hair off his brow and gave Cal a grin. "Lots of abalone steaks for tonight, eh?"

Cal nodded and gestured toward the huge ice chest where the abalone had been quickly separated from their rainbow shells and chilled. "The girls are going to be happy. Though Abby wasn't sure about eating one."

"Oh? Joe's wife?"

"Yeah," Cal said, "she's West Virginia Hill people, and they don't eat a whole lot of shellfish or ocean-going vittles. Frogs and fresh-water fish are okay, though."

Alex grinned. "And what about Sky?"

Groaning, Cal muttered, "The jury is out on that one. She hates oysters, so I don't know how she's going to react to eating abalone."

Alex wore a pair of faded Bermuda-style blue swim trunks that hung nearly to his knees. Like Cal, he was naked from the waist up, eagerly absorbing the hot sun's rays. "And Lauren?"

"Ask her yourself."

"What? And get killed at twenty yards with her drop-dead stare?"

"That bad, huh?" Cal took pity on him when he let his game face drop for a moment. "Look, you shouldn't have shown up with a bouquet of roses on the shooting range where she was the instructor."

"But you said red roses and a box of chocolates always fixed it with an American woman."

Cal grimaced. "There's a time and place for that, Alex. Not in your work-place and certainly not on a shooting range where you had to qualify that morning."

"These American rules to get a woman to notice you are very, very strange," he muttered, his black brows dropping.

"Yeah," Cal commiserated, "it's a long, tough ordeal, believe me."

"Did you have to chase Sky like that?"

Cal chuckled. "Hell yes. She ran the moment she could get away from me. I didn't even get a chance to give her roses or a box of chocolates."

Straightening and throwing his broad, thick shoulders back, Alex growled, "But you caught her, without them?"

Cal remained patient. He felt sorry for Alex, who was obviously so damned in lust with Lauren that he couldn't think straight. "I didn't catch Sky. I did go to her, but I left the door open as to whether she was going to let me stay in her life or not. She made that decision."

"Then, she was a smart woman to let you stay," Alex said, gesturing as the boat gently rocked in the waves. "Look at her now. She is very happy with you. Everyone can see that." He snorted. "I would like to see that look on Lauren's face when she looks at me."

Grimacing, Cal tried to put things gently to Alex. "Look, you need to chill out. Give her room. Don't keep pressing her, Alex. All she's going to do is round on you." Cal scowled. "And I saw Lauren in a bar fight once. You

DON'T want to goad or crowd her. She will respond."

"Really? She was in a bar fight?"

"Yeah, a long time ago."

"And you were there?"

Squirming, Cal said, "It was in a canteen at a black ops camp in Afghanistan. We'd hooked up with Marine Force Recons and Lauren was one of their snipers. The op was successful, so when we all flew back in a Chinook to Bagram Air Base, we went to one of the bars and got stinking drunk. An Army doggie type saw Lauren knocking back whiskey with us and started getting nasty with her. One of the Marines tried to tell the guy to shut the fuck up, but he was drunker than hell. When he called Lauren a bitch, she came over and took a swing, broke his nose, and sent him flying six feet from the table he was sitting at."

"Impressive," Alex said, his voice admiring.

"Hell, it got us into a brawl," Cal growled. "The SEALs cleaned it up and the Army dudes went slinking out out of the bar with their tails tucked between their legs." He grinned a little. "Lauren made a good account of herself. We made her an honorary SEAL, which she accepted."

"No one should call her such a name," Alex said, frowning. "If I had been there, I would have stood up and defended her honor."

Groaning, Cal gripped the man's shoulder. "Look, this isn't the 1800's in Ukraine. Okay? Lauren is fully capable of handling herself in all situations."

Alex grabbed a towel, wiping his damp face and pulling it around his thick neck. "I will always see every woman as needing a man to protect her."

"Oh, nooooooo," Cal muttered, "NEVER say that around Lauren. Please... you really don't want her reaction to that kind of male, neanderthal statement."

Frustration lined his expression and Alex looked out at the dark blue ocean for a moment. "Then," he said darkly, as he stared over at Cal, "how do I tell her I like her?"

"You don't," Cal growled. "Just give her time. And space."

"Could I not compliment her on her hair. It is a beautiful red color."

"No."

"Then, her eyes. They are like emeralds."

"No."

"I could compliment her on how well she walks."

"Oh, shit, no. You don't understand the line between sexual harassment and dealing with a woman coworker in your workplace, Alex."

Shaking his head, Alex sighed. "You Americans have so many rules. It is confusing even to me. In Ukraine, things are simple: if you like a woman, you sing her love songs, you take walks with her, you listen to what she thinks is important…"

"Don't work that way over here, partner," Cal muttered. "Just take my advice: pretend Lauren doesn't exist. If she likes you, she'll eventually come around to you."

"That's impossible," Alex said heavily. "How can I ignore such combined beauty with brains?"

Ivan brought the latest information to Yerik. It was near quitting time, and his assistant had already left for the day. He handed his boss a thumb drive. "Put this in your laptop," he suggested, moving to the other side of the desk to stand next to him.

"News?" Yerik asked hopefully, shoving the thumb drive into his PC.

"See what you think," Ivan said.

Yerik eagerly waited for the file to load and opened it up. He saw many digital photos taken by the Russian men on the ground in Coronado. His face lit up. "So, these are good. Your team caught them alone on a beach with one another?"

Pleased, Ivan nodded. "Yes."

Yerik studied the photo intently. "This is good. Clearly, she is in love with Sinclair."

"Clearly," Ivan smiled a little. "The next photos are of the three women in the condo. We're trying to identify the redhead. The other woman next to Sky is Abby Harrison. Her husband is an ex-SEAL. You'll see him in a minute."

Yerik scowled. "That redhead looks military."

"We think she is. We're trying to find out who she is."

Yerik studied several photos of a dive boat coming into dock at the San Diego yacht club basin in the late afternoon.

Ivan leaned over, pressing his finger on one particular closeup. "Now, what I find very interesting about this is the man next to Sinclair?"

"Yes?"

"That is Alexei Kazak, a Ukrainian. He was with your son's team down in Peru. Ex-Spetsnaz and a combat medic. He had been shot in the leg after Sinclair found and rescued Sky Lambert from that village. Later, when the Army Special Forces team arrived, they attacked Vlad and his team who refused to give up. The analyst THINKS that maybe one of those Special Forces soldiers killed Vlad, but there is no concrete proof of it. We never found out where Kazak went after the Americans took him into custody. His Ukrainian medic partner, Nikita Morozov, disappeared also and we cannot locate him. Now? Kazak finally shows up in the U.S."

Scowling, Yerik studied the young Ukrainian soldier. "This smells, Ivan."

"Indeed. I think so."

Turning in his chair, he gave Ivan a black look. "Did he turn traitor on my son? Did he tell these Army Special Forces men where my son was at? Or did he kill Vlad himself?"

Shrugging, Ivan said gently, "I do not know, my friend. But I believe once we kidnap the woman, she will know. You will break her. She will talk."

His fingers curved into a fist and Yerik's eyes turned angry as he studied the photo. "Get Kazak's file. I want to know where the bastard's family is at in Ukraine. Run this down now, Ivan."

"I already have," Ivan responded quietly. He tapped another file and a document opened on screen. "Kazak has a sister named Kira. I sent your men in Moscow to Ukraine, to hunt her down. Their parents and their close relatives are dead. So are their uncles and aunts. Both sets of grandparents are dead. They all died during a Chechen rebel attack on their family farm years earlier. The only reason Kazak and his sister lived was that they were elsewhere when the attack happened…"

Rubbing his narrow chin, Yerik studied the document. "But they didn't find this Kira? She just disappeared, too?"

"Yes." Ivan placed his hand on Yerik's tense shoulder. "I have men looking deeper into Russian military records on Kazak. We're not done with this, we've just begun our search. Kira Kazak is nowhere to be found. We have NO idea where she is at."

"But Kazak is with Sinclair!" Yerik yelled, slamming his fist on the desk. Breathing hard, he glared up at Ivan. "This makes NO sense unless Kazak was working WITH Sinclair! Why else would a drug running ex-Spetsnaz soldier be with an American ex-SEAL? You tell me, Ivan."

Wringing his hands, Ivan murmured, "It does not look good. I agree with you." Sweat popped out on his brow as Yerik's breathing became uneven, his eyes black with rage as he stared across the room at his son's picture.

"Sky Lambert is the key," Yerik ground out, his nostrils flaring. "She will know. She is the easiest of all of them to capture."

A little relief fled through Ivan. "That is true. I would not want to tangle with Kazak under these current circumstances. He is a traitor as far as everyone is concerned. I don't believe he's on our side any longer."

"Sinclair would know who killed Vlad."

"More than likely, yes. But he's as dangerous, if not more so, than Kazak. Remember, Yerik, we want this extraction done as quietly as possible. Our motto is raise no ripples on the surface of our lake. We leave no footprints for this government to follow us."

"Yes, yes, I know." Yerik drummed his fingers impatiently on his desk, staring at his son. Vlad was incredibly proud and virile. He could see his mother in his face. He was glad Darya's influence was there because Vlad had drawn women like bees to honey. They all had wanted his attention, wanted to marry him. Yerik's heart twisted with grief. But his son had fallen helplessly in love with Sky. He'd become smitten with her from the moment she'd been taken into the Zimmerman household. And he never stopped loving her, wanting her as his wife, wanting her to be the mother of his many children. He'd turned the world upside down trying to find her.

"Our team is following them at a safe distance," Ivan soothed him. "They know the players, now. We know their hangouts. All we need is one break, just one, and we can extract her."

Nodding, Yerik muttered, "The sooner, the better. I want to know if that bastard Kazak is a turn coat. If he is…"

"Yerik, my friend, focus on the woman. She is the key. She will have all the answers you seek."

Wiping his brow, Yerik growled, "This makes it imperative to break her quickly so she will give me the truth on who killed my son." He turned slowly in his chair, glaring up at Ivan. "And if it turns out to be that bastard Kazak did it, I will have him caught and his skin stripped off his body an inch at a time. He will die a death even the Devil fears."

CHAPTER 7

June 14

S KY SAT WITH Abby and Lauren when the men came trooping back with a huge ice chest carried between them. It was five p.m. and the quiet of the condo suddenly amped up with booming male voices, laughter, and joking. It reminded Sky of warriors returning from a successful hunt.

Lauren was in one corner of the couch with her wineglass, Sky was tucked into the other corner of the couch, and Abby sat in a chair across from them. They all smiled at one another as the men came in like an assault wave. They were in swimsuits, naked from the waist up, and barefoot. Sky smiled when Cal entered first, opening the door wide for Alex and Joe, who were proudly carrying their booty in the ice chest. Every man had a cocky grin on his face.

"Obviously they were successful," Lauren drawled, eyeing the triumphant grins on their collective faces. She avoided the hello smile Alex gave her.

Sky lifted her hand in greeting to Cal as he walked toward the kitchen.

"Hey," Cal told them, "we got plenty of abalone for everyone."

Sky saw the pride in his eyes. He looked gorgeous to her, his chest broad, shoulders thrown back with such natural pride, that wicked grin tugging at his mouth. "That's good to hear. We won't starve now," Sky teased. Her heart swelled with love as he winked at her and took off for the kitchen.

Once the former SEALs were in the condo, Lauren unwound from her position on the couch and shut the door behind them. She saw them put the ice chest on the counter next to the sinks. Turning, she said, "I think those New York steaks are going to look really good to us…"

Abby grinned, her feet stretched out on the wooden coffee table. "I'll try the abalone," she said. "But if I don't like it, I'm heading straight for your steaks, Lauren."

"Hey," Alex called, coming over and standing near the couch. "I caught these rock sea bass in case you ladies do not like abalone steaks."

Sky saw he had three huge fish laying in some freezer paper between his hands. "What are those, Alex?" She saw the Ukrainian give her a boyish smile, excitement in his eyes.

He crouched down in front of her and canted the paper with the fish on them. "Well," he told Sky, astutely making an effort not to connect with Lauren's gaze, "I was worried that some of you may not have eaten abalone before. I asked Cal if he minded if I went spear fishing in the kelp beds for some fish in case any of you preferred these instead."

Abby sat up and said, "Ohhhh, that's so sweet of you, Alex. Thank you," and she beamed at him. "I've never had abalone and I was tellin' the girls here that I wasn't sure I'd want to eat them."

Nodding, Alex said, "Yes, I thought about that."

Sky scooted over and pulled the paper back enough to look at the large fish. They were ugly looking. Each had been speared. "I didn't know you could swim, much less spear fish," she said, smiling at him. She saw Alex blush, his cheeks growing ruddy.

"Well," he said, clearing his throat, "when you are Spetsnaz, you are trained to do everything. Learning to spearfish is a way to eat instead of starving." He shrugged his thick shoulders. "These are rock sea bass. They taste very good, Sky."

"I love fish," Sky murmured. "These are huge, Alex!" She moved aside to show Lauren and Abby the catch.

Abby craned her neck, checking out the fish. "Alex, do you know what they taste like?"

"Yes," he said. "Have you ever eaten halibut?"

Abby nodded. "Yes."

"They are a very firm flesh," he told her, hooking one of the fish in its gill and holding it up for her closer inspection. "Very firm, flaky and it tastes very good. I know you would enjoy it."

Abby smiled. "Well, I think that was awfully nice of you to think about us girls. Did any of the other guys think about fish for us in case we didn't like abalone?"

Alex carefully placed the fish down with the rest. "Well," he murmured, "perhaps they would have. I just came up with the idea first, was all." He brightened. "Cal had brought along a spear, so I think if I had not asked to use it, one of the other men might have."

Sky patted Alex's shoulder. "You're being much too humble," she said. Sky turned and looked at the women. "Are you two up for grilled sea bass to-night?"

Alex dared to sneak a quick look in Lauren's direction. He was surprised that he didn't see anger or disgust in her eyes as he had every other time, he talked to her. Instead, he saw thoughtfulness in her expression. Seeing her nod toward him made him feel good, but he quickly averted his look to Abby, who was eagerly nodding her head.

"If you do not mind?" he said to Sky and Abby, carefully avoiding looking directly at Lauren, "I have a very nice Ukrainian recipe for grilled sea bass. Would you trust me to make your dinner for you tonight?"

"I'd love it," Sky murmured. "Abby? Lauren?"

"Go to town," Abby told Alex enthusiastically. "I'll put my life in your hands."

Alex smiled a little, his nervousness showing as he shifted in his crouched position between them. Lauren said nothing. He started to feel hurt when she spoke up.

"I'll take that check ride with you, Kazak. Go for it. If you kill me, I'll come back and hunt down your sorry ass."

Abby and Sky burst out laughing, knowing Lauren was teasing him. The look on Alex's face, however, made it clear he took her seriously.

"I would never hurt you, Lauren," he said in an an emotional but somber tone.

Lauren said, "It's my black humor, Kazak."

Alex frowned. "What is black humor?"

Groaning, Lauren said with a slight grin, "I was teasing you. Go ask Cal for a definition of what black humor means. Okay?"

Alex looked a little relieved. "Yes. Thank you." As he slowly rose to his feet, carefully holding the sea bass in his arms, he felt his chest expand with sudden, inexplicable happiness. Lauren's voice had been almost friendly. Not condescending as it always had been before. Maybe Cal was right: ignore her. Let Lauren come to him. Giving Lauren a wide smile, he said "I will take care of you ladies tonight. I promise, you will like the way I grill these sea bass for all of you," and he turned, walking cockily back to the kitchen.

Sky turned to Abby. "Wasn't that kind of Alex? He's so thoughtful."

Abby nodded. "He's a really sweet."

Lauren shrugged and sipped her wine. "Before you heap him with praise, why don't you wait and see how the sea bass turns out tonight. Proof's in the pudding."

Abby giggled. "Spoken like a true sniper. Taste it first THEN make up your mind."

A grin edged Lauren's lips as she lifted her head and watched Alex with the other SEALs crowded around the kitchen sink. There was raucous kidding and teasing going on between men and it appeared the SEALs had easily embraced and included the Ukrainian. "Let's see," she murmured with a grin, turning her attention to the women, "if he can deliver the goods. Talk is cheap. It's the action that counts."

"Well," Sky sighed, laying her head on Cal's chest, "it's been a wonderful day." She moved her fingers across his damp flesh. Her body still rippled with the multiple orgasms he'd given her earlier. Loving Cal without a condom was, in her mind, incredible. Her body seemed so much more sensitized to him, and she relaxed across Cal, contentment washing through her.

He slid his hand across Sky's long back, caressing the firm warmth of her flesh that felt like velvet beneath his exploring fingertips. Cal smiled and closed his eyes as she nestled her head in the hollow of his shoulder. Moonlight slipped silently through the gauzy drapes from windows on the west side of their large bedroom. "It was. Sex was good too," and Cal grinned, lifting his head to see her response. He heard that soft sound he loved so much in Sky's throat as she looked up, smiling into his half-opened eyes.

"Sex? It's making love, Sinclair. Anyone can have sex. What we have transcends that by a mile. It's about loving one another."

"Okay," he murmured apologetically, feeling the strength in her small shoulder, "you're right."

She laughed softly and caressed his jaw. "You guys are NEVER going to change."

"But you love us anyway?"

"Well," she murmured, feeling sated and drowsy, "I love YOU, that's for sure."

"Did you girls have fun today while we were out on the dive boat?"

"Yes, we had a lot of fun."

"Damn good dinner tonight, too," Cal said, pride in his tone. "You three girls seemed to really like the way Alex fixed that sea bass he caught for all of you."

"It was delicious," Sky agreed. She absorbed Cal's touch, his calloused fingers sliding in a grazing motion slowly up and down her spine. No one would ever guess how gentle a man he really was except for her. She was privileged to share this side with him. If she had known this when she'd first met him, she would never have run away from Cal.

"And, were my eyes deceiving me?"

"About what?"

"Lauren? She wasn't her grumpy old self tonight at the dinner table with Alex present."

"I know. I thought that was an amazing turn-around from her snarky looks she always gave Alex before." Sky lifted her head. "What did you say to Alex?"

Laughing a little, Cal shook his head. "I told him to ignore her. Make as little eye contact as possible."

Sky laughed with him. "Well, it must have worked. Alex was sitting as far away from Lauren as he could get."

"Yeah, with us," Cal murmured, sliding his fingers through her silky hair. "I wasn't sure Lauren would eat the sea bass because Alex had made it."

"Me either, to tell you the truth."

"Well, who knows?" Cal said, "maybe there's a truce of sorts developing between them?"

"That would be nice. I was worried Lauren's attitude would spill over into our wedding day."

"Naw," Cal murmured, lifting his head and pressing a kiss to her hair, "she's a professional. She knows how to set her emotions aside and get a mission accomplished. Don't worry about that. She'll be fine."

"You're right," Sky admitted, stroking his jaw and outlining his strong, thick neck and shoulder. "But I think Alex's thoughtfulness has given Lauren a different perspective of him."

"Yeah? I gotta admit, none of us guys thought about going spear fishing. We all thought you three ladies would like abalone steaks. Alex wasn't so sure, so I told him to go hunting. See if he could come up with some fish as a second choice."

"I like his thoughtfulness," Sky murmured. "It was a lovely surprise."

"It was," Cal admitted ruefully, "Alex showed us SEALs up tonight, for sure. The three of you ladies had nothing but praise for the fish and for him. I think it did his ego a lot of good."

Laughing softly, Sky shook her head. "It wasn't a test, Sinclair. It just shows us a side to Alex that no one knew was there until now. I think he'll be a really good team member to whomever he's sent out with on missions, don't you?"

"Absolutely," he said, inhaling the almond fragrance of her shampoo she'd used earlier on her hair. "But remember? He's a combat medic. He's got that nurturing, caring side to him or he wouldn't be in the business of patching up people."

Sky sat up, facing Cal, placing her arm across his narrow waist, smiling down at him. "I guess I should have expected that from Alex. He was the one who cared me for those hellish days while I went through the malaria cycles. Him and Nik Morozov, the other medic. Alex had him running all over the village trying to find a woman who had made chicken soup. Nik found some and brought it back to Alex. I remember how delicious it tasted. I was so thirsty and starved for anything salty tasting."

Raising a brow, Cal appreciated the way the moonlight caressed her slender body, the light curving provocatively around her small breasts. It made him want Sky again. "Nik's disappeared into the jungles of Peru from what Alex said. He doesn't like being separated from his best friend. I guess they were close as brothers. He's worried about him."

"That's so sad. I remember Nik helped Alex wrap me in as many blankets as they could find to keep me warm." Sky smiled fondly. "You're right. Alex has good traits an operator should have. It means he's going to be there for his teammates. I think Jack saw those qualities in him, too."

"I'm sure that entered into his evaluation regarding hiring Alex."

"Alex deserves good thing to happen to him and his sister, Kira. She's here in San Diego. I know Alex took a day earlier this week to go see her."

"I'd talked to him when he came back, and he seemed happy. He said Kira was blooming here by the ocean, that he felt it was really helping her to come out of some of her depression."

"Wonderful," Sky said. "He worries a lot about her."

"She's the only family he has left. And they've always been close to one another. I'm hoping the salt air, the ocean, and the sun will help Kira."

"Alex is a healer by nature. He's a natural born medic. I know he is a trained black ops guy, and a stand-by sniper also, but his real love is serving and helping those who need help."

He nodded. "I think Jack is looking at him to perhaps, after a few years of doing missions, create a department that would solely be medics that could help us out in the field. They save lives."

"Well," she whispered, kissing him softly, "you have certainly helped save my life, too."

"Hey, what are you girls doing tomorrow? The day before the wedding?"

"Ummm, Lauren's staying at the condo to make sure the florist and all the other details are taken care of..."

"And you and Abby? What do you have planned?"

She pushed her fingers through her tangled hair. "If it's okay with you, I'd love to take Abby out to our hidden cove? I told her about it this afternoon and she remembers it. We thought we'd go out there together and just enjoy the quiet, undisturbed beauty of the day. It's a special place for Abby, too. We'll take a picnic lunch, and I want to take more photos of the tidal pools for possible future art projects."

Cal slowly sat up, leaning against the headboard. The moonlight caressed Sky's body, making her look like a Greek goddess sculpture he'd seen at the Louvre Museum in Paris. She was extraordinarily beautiful. Caressing her hip, he murmured, "Why not? You'll be alone, no prying tourist eyes. Have fun."

"We'll be back about four p.m.," Sky promised. "We want to avoid rush hour traffic coming back down I-5 to Coronado. And we have the big dinner at The Del for everyone at seven p.m. tomorrow night. If we get home at 1600, that's plenty of time to get cleaned up and put on my new dress."

"Sounds good. I'm going to be out with the guys tomorrow. We'll be working over at HQ putting the final touches on the hall where we'll be getting married. I think Lauren will be having the flowers delivered, the runner laid down, and all that detailed stuff."

"I can hardly wait to see it," Sky breathed, excited. "But," she murmured playfully, giving him a wicked look as she eased her leg across his body, "Abby and I are going to have the most fun tomorrow. All of you are going to be in work mode."

Cal groaned as she settled against his erection. His hands automatically fell around her hips. "Woman, you know how to get my attention."

Smiling softly, Sky slowly slid against him, watching his eyes glitter with hunger. "I want you, Cal…"

He met her smile with a feral look. "You're such a tease, Ms. Lambert, soon to be Mrs. Sky Sinclair…"

June 15

"DID YOU GET the pictures you wanted?" Abby asked, leaning over Sky's shoulder and peering at the digital photos she'd taken earlier. They sat on Cal's dark blue blanket in their secret cove.

"I think so," she said, and Sky held up one picture in particular to Abby. "Look at this one. The colors are phenomenal!" The breeze sifted by them. They had spent an hour on the rocks at low tide photographing nearly every tidal pool nestled between the damp, rounded rocks.

"Ohhh," Abby whispered, "I like that one!" She sat down cross legged, facing the ocean. "Will you draw that one in pastel chalk?"

Sky smiled, her legs tucked beneath her. The sun felt delicious upon her skin. They wore white tees and dark colored shorts, their feet bare as they sat on the blanket. "I think so. I just love drawing, Abby. I'm not very good at it, but I love putting colors together, smearing them with my finger and watching it make a third color. Sort of magical."

Abby chuckled and opened the picnic basket she'd carried with them. "Cal said you were very good. I don't think you should shortchange yourself."

Sky pushed strands of hair off her brow. She frowned. "Abby?"

"Yes?"

Pointing out toward the ocean, she said, "Look at that…"

Abby lifted her chin. There was a small sea plane coming in for a landing not far from where the waves were forming. "Wow, a sea plane."

Sky took several photos of the white and dark gray striped plane landing. They could barely hear the engine as it shut down and the pontoons drifted expertly onto the smooth ocean's surface. Today, without much wind, Sky noticed the ocean was almost like glass, the waves very small compared to when she was here with Cal the other day. "Cal said there was a lot of sea plane traffic in the area, mostly civilian."

They both looked north when they heard a helicopter engine. Sky squinted as she took off her sunglasses to see what kind of helicopter it was. "Oh, it's the Coast Guard Search and Rescue helicopter coming by," she murmured, taking more photos as the orange and white helicopter buzzed past them on its way south. "Cal said they're constantly patrolling the area beaches. Sometimes swimmers get in trouble, and he said there aren't life guards at every beach, so the Coast Guard patrols to help out."

"Well," Abby said, retrieving roast beef sandwiches from the picnic basket, "we don't have to worry about being rescued today. That water's too cold for me to even put a toe into it!"

Laughing, Sky watched the sea plane. It was a good quarter mile away and the noontime sunlight made it tough to see many details. She saw people begin to emerge. She thought she saw a raft inflate and get put into the water next to the pontoon. Several people, probably men judging from their size, got into it. She took more pictures. "I wonder what they're doing out there. Hunting for lobster or abalone in the kelp beds?"

Abby handed her the sandwich and looked. "I don't know. Looks like a raft. Are they fishing, I wonder?" She laughed and looked over at Sky. "Can you fish off a sea plane's pontoons?"

Shrugging, Sky said, "I really don't know. This is the first time I've ever been out here." She set the camera aside and began to eat her sandwich, her gaze on the raft as it floated closer and closer.

"Maybe they're scuba divers?" Abby wondered, opening a sack of potato chips and setting them between them.

"Could be," Sky murmured, fascinated. "Cal said there's lots of people at the kelp beds area. Scuba divers, snorkelers, and abalone divers who swim down to the sea floor, find them, and shoot back up to the surface."

"Looks like they're coming ashore," Abby said.

"What a fun thing!" Sky said. She laid down her half-eaten sandwich and picked up her camera. The three men in the raft were dressed in black wet suits with weight belts around their waists. As the raft bobbled and rode in on the foamy waves to the edge of the beach, she took more photos. "Maybe some SEALs?" she whispered excitedly. "Wow! They look like SEALs, don't they?"

Abby laughed. "You've got me. Joe said they were always practicing missions along this stretch of water. You're right, they're in wetsuits just like SEALs." She grinned. "Take lots of photos. I'll bet Cal and Joe, when we show them to them tonight, will know who these guys are," and she chuckled. "It's a small, tight fraternity, and everyone knows everyone else."

Sky saw the three men pull the raft up beyond the water line where it would not be washed back into the surf. Something wasn't right. All of them had their gazes on her and Abby. As they turned toward her, she gasped.

"Oh, my God!" Sky whispered, stricken. "I recognize one of them!" Her heart took off at a furious beat. "Abby! Get up! Run! Run!" and Sky leaped to her feet, dropping her camera on the blanket.

"What?" Abby said, confused. She looked at the three men quickly walking toward them, their wetsuits gleaming in the sunlight.

Sky grabbed her by the hand. "They're Russians!" she cried, jerking her to her feet. "That one! He was with Vlad's drug running team! Come on!" and she cried and yanked Abby forward.

Sky pushed Abby ahead of her, digging her toes into the warm, deep sand. Terror shot through her. Abby was confused, but ran, sprinting at her side. They hadn't gotten more than fifty feet when Sky felt the sting of something biting into her calf.

Abby cried out in front of her, tripping and falling. She grabbed at her lower right leg as she slammed into the sand.

Sky turned, open-mouthed, as she saw a dart of some kind stuck in Abby's leg. And then, she stumbled. Her vision began to gray. Staggering, Sky tried to stop herself from falling sideways. Tumbling into the sand, landing on her back, she felt her body not obeying her commands to run, to escape. More terror sizzled through her as she saw the man she recognized from Vlad's team. Triumphantly grinning down at her.

And that was the last thing Sky remembered.

CHAPTER 8

June 15

SKY FELT LIKE she was floating. There was vibration all around her. Frowning, she tried to lift her hand, but it wouldn't obey her. Male voices, clipped and in a foreign language, caught her woozy attention. What had happened? Her mind wouldn't work. She felt like limp spaghetti, her body unresponsive to her needs. Her mouth was dry, feeling as if cotton were stuffed inside it. She tried to speak, but all she heard was a moan coming out of her. There was a sudden movement around her. Plane... she was in a plane. Her mind wouldn't focus. The jostling continued, sharp up and down movements. The engine sound changed, deepened. Where was she? What had happened to her?

She felt as if she were lying on something soft. The male voices were close and guttural. Her nostrils flared, and she smelled sour male sweat. Fear started zigzagging through her. This wasn't right! She wasn't supposed to be here! Some primal instinct was slowly coming back online. Her mind wouldn't coherently function, but now, Sky felt threat. Fear tunneled through her as never before. Men were talking in a language she couldn't understand.

And then, Sky felt the jab of a needle entering her upper left arm. The bite of it made her moan. She felt a man's thick, strong fingers gripping her arm, holding it still, almost hurting her. This wasn't Cal's hand. She could tell the difference. WHY was she here? What was going on? And as the needle slid out of her arm, the hand released her. Within moments, darkness descended upon Sky once again and she slid back into oblivion.

ABBY GROANED. SHE was lying face down in the sand, grains in her mouth and nostrils. Dizziness assailed her. She felt weak, almost like a puppet filled with sawdust. She heard the cry of gulls floating in the sky, and the sound of waves crashing upon the beach. The tang of the salt air entered her nostrils. She felt incredibly weak. Her mind spun. What was she doing on the sand like this? She was sprawled out on her belly, arms flung above her head. What the hell was going on?

It took nearly fifteen minutes before Abby was able to push herself weakly up into a sitting position. Her sunglasses had been knocked off, and she squinted, slowly lifting her hand to shade her eyes. The sun had shifted dramatically. Frowning, Abby forced herself to look at the watch on her left wrist. The dials and numbers blurred. Making a frustrated sound, Abby forced her wandering mind to focus. It was four p.m.

Frowning, she tried to wiped and spat the sand out of her nose and mouth. Something was wrong. Terribly wrong. Every simple movement took a huge amount of effort. Turning her head, Abby saw the blanket further down on the beach. Where was Sky? Making a rough sound, Abby felt like she was going to vomit. She barely got rolled to her side, on her hands and knees, before she did. The retching was violent, and everything came up. Eyes watering, nose running, Abby weakly wiped her mouth and nose with the back of her hand.

Sky?

And then, her mind gave her back the memories. Eyes widening, Abby sat up, hands on her thighs, looking around the empty beach. Where was Sky? The raft? The seaplane? And those big men in black diving suits? Abby felt a new terror work through her. Her cell phone had been in the picnic basket on the blanket. With a grunt, Abby shoved to her feet. She wobbled. Her knees collapsed out from beneath her. She struggled again to stand up, wavering badly, arms out to try and not fall again. She had to call Joe and Cal. They had to know something terrible had just happened.

Abby felt adrenaline burning through her, giving her the strength, she needed to make it to the blanket. Sand had been kicked up on it, but to her relief, she saw the basket was still there. Falling to her knees, Abby opened it up with shaking hands. There! The cell phone! Making a relieved sound, Abby saw the numbers blur. Frustrated, she blinked several times. She had to call Joe! Now! Finally, she punched in his cell phone number. Dizziness assailed her. Abby was on her knees, and she leaned downward, phone pressed to her ear, trying to remain conscious. *Please, please, answer your phone, Joe. Please... oh Lordy... answer it...*

"Abby?"

Joe's deep voice was like balm washing through her. She sobbed. "Joe, something's happened to Sky and me. Th-there was a seaplane that landed nearby. Three men in a raft..." and she sobbed. "They came ashore. Sky told me to run, that there was a Russian she recognized." Tears started down her drawn cheeks. "Joe, she's GONE! Sky's gone! Th-they shot us with darts of some kind. I-I just woke up. I was drugged and she's not here..."

"Are you at the cove?" Joe demanded, his voice deadly calm.

Abby nodded. "Y-yes, the secret cove."

"Are you alright?"

"I-I think so. Th-they must have drugged us. I-I can't walk much. I made it here, to the blanket. God, Sky isn't here!" and her voice broke.

"Okay, Baby, listen to me."

"Y-yes..."

"Is there anyone else around you right now?"

Abby slowly sat up, the effort huge. She twisted her head looking from one end of the crescent beach to the other. "N-no. Alone... I... I'm alone..."

"And the raft?"

"Gone. No seaplane, either." She could hear Joe giving sharp orders to someone in the background, his hand over his cell phone.

"That's good. You're safe then?"

"Y-yes, I think so," and she slowly turned, looking out toward the ocean. "Th-they're all gone. Nothing out on the ocean, Joe."

"Good."

Abby could hear the relief in his tightened voice. "W-what should I do?"

"Stay right where you are. We're coming to get you right now."

"W-what if they come back?"

"Cal doesn't think they will. They wanted Sky. You have my cell number. Stay put, we're coming to get you. Alex's coming along because he's a combat corpsman. He's bringing his medical ruck with him, and he'll take care of you after we arrive. All right?"

Wiping her tears away with a shaking hand, Abby whispered, "O-okay. I'm so drugged up, Joe. I-I need to lay down on this blanket. I-I feel like I'm gonna faint..."

CAL'S EYES WERE slits as he worked with Alex to give Abby, who had fallen into a drugged stupor, a shot that would revive her. Joe was at her side, his face showing the terror he felt.

"Okay," Alex said, gently placing Abby on her back and placing a rolled-up towel beneath her neck so she could breathe easier, "she should come around very quickly." He gave Joe a worried look. "She's drugged, but her pulse is strong, and her blood pressure is becoming normalized. She is going to be fine, Joe."

Joe nodded, swallowing hard, his gaze never leaving his wife's pale, freckled face. "Good, good," he rasped, holding her hand tightly in his own.

Cal stood up, looking around. He couldn't afford to cry. But a huge fist of terror and tears were ramming up through his chest, heading for his tightening throat. Walking around, he followed the tracks of the three men from the beach. The tide was starting to come in, but he could see imprints of where a raft had been dragged up on the beach. Taking photos with his camera, he looked out at sea, finding it empty. Swallowing several times against a forming lump, he continued to follow the trail in the sand. Moving quickly beyond the blanket, he saw where both women had fallen in the sand. He discovered a small dart partially hidden in the sand and picked it up. His brows fell as he examined it. Turning, he took it back to the men.

"Tell me about this, Alex," and Cal handed him the small dart.

Scowling, Alex studied it. "It's Russian. It's a Spetsnaz drug we would use to render someone quickly unconscious." His mouth thinned. "This is a big dose."

"What's that mean?" Cal growled, barely able to hold himself together. He knew in his gut that Vlad Alexandrov's father had kidnapped Sky. Worse, he knew he would take his revenge out on her. And Sky wouldn't live long. His heart thrashed violently in his chest and tears burned in his eyes. He looked away, choking them down deep inside himself. He wouldn't be any good to Sky, unable to find and rescue her, if he let his emotions howl through him. It was a distraction that would slow down their rescue efforts.

Alex examined the dark wound on Abby's leg. There was a dribble of dried blood below where the dart had entered her calf. "It means that whoever has her, wants to make sure she remains sedated for a long trip." He looked at his watch. "When did the ladies come here to the cove, Cal?"

"Noon," he growled, restless, wanting to do something… anything…

"And it's four-forty-five now," Alex said, thinking aloud. "That's a long time to be unconscious."

"What the hell does it mean?" Cal demanded tightly.

Shrugging, Alex looked over at the ocean, frowning. "They took Sky, drugged her heavily. That means a long distance must be flown. Probably to Mexico or beyond."

"It's Alexandrov," Cal snarled. "Vlad's father, Yerik Alexandrov, has done this. I fuckin' well know it even if I can't prove it."

Joe moved his hand gently up and down his wife's arm. He looked up at Cal. "Abby said Sky recognized one of the Russians."

"Yeah," Cal rasped, taking off his black baseball cap and pushing his fingers angrily through his hair. "Vlad had a group of ex-Spetsnaz soldiers on his drug-running team. One of them escaped. It must have been him."

"I was one of them," Alex told Joe, apology and sadness in his tone.

"Who do you think it was, Alex?"

Shrugging, he said, "I don't know. Maybe, when Abby becomes conscious, she can give us a description? The only one that escaped the Quechua village was Lev Zuyev, and I'm sure he held Nik, the other Ukrainian medic, as a prisoner."

"Shit!" Cal snarled, pacing back and forth.

Abby moaned. Her lashes fluttered open.

"Baby?" Joe whispered, touching her brow, "it's all right. It's Joe. You're going to be okay. Look at me?"

Abby sighed deeply and slowly turned toward her husband's low, emotional voice. She whispered, "You came…"

"Always," Joe promised her, his voice shaken with emotions he couldn't contain. "Can you sit up?"

Nodding slowly, Abby saw Alex and Cal standing nearby. "Y-yes… help me up?" and she offered Joe her hand.

Alex knelt and slid his arm around Abby's shoulders, levering her into a sitting position, keeping his arm around her because she wasn't fully coherent yet. Joe placed his body against her right shoulder and then took over holding her.

Cal came around and knelt at Abby's bare feet. "Abby? Can you tell us what happened?"

Joe held up his hand. "Give her a minute?" He pointed to a bottle of water in the basket. Alex quickly picked it up, unscrewed the cap and handed it to Joe.

"Baby, are your thirsty?" and he held the bottle up for her to see it.

"Ugh… yes… I'm dying of thirst…," and she weakly reached for it.

"I'll give it to you," Joe murmured, positioning her beneath his arm to give her head a place to rest. He gently pressed the bottle to her lips. Abby drank sloppily, water leaking from the corners of her mouth. In a minute, she'd drunk the entire pint of water.

Alex took the bottle. "That is good. She needs to be hydrated." He hunted in the basket, finding another bottle and opening it. "Let her have as much as she'll drink. It will aid in washing the drug out of her system much faster."

Nodding, Joe took the bottle. This time, Abby wrapped her hand around it. He could feel her strength returning. Her blue eyes were more clear, less cloudy. She gulped down another half bottle of water before sinking wearily against him.

"Cal," she whispered, her voice hoarse, "Sky saw a seaplane land," and she pointed out toward the ocean. "We saw a raft inflate by the pontoon. We thought… God, we thought it might be SEALs coming ashore because they had wet suits on and wore belts around their waists." She rubbed her face, trying to focus because Cal's face was hard, and she could see the anxiety buried deep in his slitted gaze. His fists were clenched at his sides, and she felt his desperation. She wanted to cry for him, for Sky.

"Sky recognized one guy. She screamed at me to get up and run. I was shocked and confused at first. I didn't know what to think," and she gulped, giving Cal an apologetic look. "I-I slowed us down. Maybe, if I'd reacted faster—"

"Don't go there," Joe warned her, giving her a gentle squeeze.

Cal nodded, his voice gruff. "You'd never outrun them, Abby, so don't be hard on yourself. What happened next?"

Rubbing her face, Abby thought, her mind shorting out. For a moment, there was clarity, and then, she lost her focus and her memory. "I—uh—we ran. Sky pushed me ahead of her and we took off. I remember something painful hitting me here," and she looked down at her leg that showed where the dart had struck her. "I screamed, and then I saw Sky get hit in the leg with the same thing. All of a sudden, I just crumpled, Cal. I couldn't control my body. I remember slamming into the sand and then I blacked out."

Alex nodded grimly. He wrapped the blood pressure cuff around Abby's other arm, taking another reading. "That's how the drug works," he told them. He smiled a little over at Abby. "You are normal. You are going to be fine," and he slipped the cuff off her upper arm.

Miserably, Abby looked at Joe and the up at Cal. He was standing so tensely, as if he might suddenly crack and explode into a million pieces. And then, she gasped. "Oh GOD!" and she suddenly pulled out of Joe's arm, lurching toward the edge of the blanket.

"What?" Joe asked, alarmed.

"The camera!" Abby cried, pushing her hands along the folded edge of the blanket. On her hands and knees, she frantically searched. "Sky had taken photos of the seaplane, the raft and the guys coming ashore... wait! Oh, thank GOD, it's here," and she jerked the camera from beneath the fold.

Cal took it, immediately flicking it on, staring hard at the digital screen. Alex came over, looking over his shoulder.

Joe pulled his wife back into his arms, holding her because she was crying softly, her hands pressed to her face.

"Sonofabitch," Cal breathed, holding one photo up of the three men advancing upon Sky and Abby. He held it steady so Alex could look at it. "Recognize any of those bastards?"

Alex's face went hard. "Yes." He pointed to the bald man in the center. "That's Pyotr. The bald one." Swearing, Alex shook his head. "You are right, Cal. This is Yerik Alexandrov's work. Pyotr is his main soldier who does his dirty work," and he gave him an apologetic look. "I am so sorry, my friend..."

"Don't be fuckin' sorry," Cal snarled, quickly flicking through the photos, looking for more information. "Tell me where they're taking Sky." He saw the seaplane, enlarged it, making the numbers readable on the fuselage. Holding it up, he asked, "Do you recognize this plane?"

Alex frowned and studied it. "Alexandrov has a fleet of sea planes on both coasts of the U.S. as well as in the Gulf of Mexico. It is how he transfers cocaine and fentanyl from Central and South America to North American shores," he told him grimly. "I was never part of those operations. The plane does not look familiar to me, but that means nothing."

Joe called, "Let's get Butch on this. Run those numbers on its fuselage. Maybe it will turn up the owner."

Cal looked over the camera at the former SEAL. "More than likely, the numbers are painted on and changed all the time to confuse American officials."

Nodding, Joe grimly agreed. "Make a call to Butch? We're going to need him on this if we're going to find her in time."

Cal's heart squeezed violently in his chest. He nodded, mouth thinned. Alex left his side and knelt by Abby. He gently picked up her wrist, fingers against her pulse.

"You are doing fine," Alex soothed, patting her shoulder awkwardly. He looked over at Joe, who still had worry in his eyes. "She is going to be all right," he reassured the ex-SEAL. "Just keep her drinking water when she wants, and when we get her back to the condo, she will want to lay down and sleep."

"Sleep sounds good," Abby agreed wearily, reaching out, sliding her fingers into Alex's hand. "Thanks… we owe you…"

Alex shrugged, gently squeezed her fingers and then rose to his full height. "I am nearby at the Del. If you or Joe need me tonight, even if it's midnight or early morning, you call me and I will come with my ruck. I am a very good medic. I know how to treat drug reactions."

Joe gave the Ukrainian a silent look of thanks. Alex nodded and turned away, placing the medical items back into this ruck laying on the blanket.

"Ready to be carried?" Joe asked his wife with a slight smile.

"Oh, I can walk," Abby protested weakly.

"We need to get back to Coronado as soon as we can," Cal told her.

"You're right," Abby whispered. "Okay, carry me, Joe?"

"In a heartbeat, Baby," and he slowly released her and slipped his arms around her, easily bringing her into his arms as he stood.

Cal's cell phone rang. He answered it. Butch was on the other end. As Alex gathered up the blanket and picnic basket, Cal listened intently to the Master Chief. When he hung up, they were ready to roll. As Cal broke into a trot, heading toward the tidal pool area, he said, "Butch said he'll get those photos as soon as we get back to him. He's already making calls to his contacts at all the intelligence agencies in North, Central, and South America."

Alex trotted easily at his side with his eighty-pound ruck he carried on his back. "What does that mean?"

"Butch is going to be calling in favors from every U.S. government bureau we've got NSA, CIA, FBI, ATF, DEA, SOCOM, everyone. He's going to find something out about Alexandrov, where he lives, where the bastard hides, and he'll find out where Sky's been taken. And then, he'll spread out to Central and South American contacts in governments who work with us." *Sooner rather than later*, Cal prayed, because Sky's life hung in the balance. He tried to stop his mind from going to the dark places he knew about. Being in black ops, Cal knew the terrible torture techniques utilized. He wanted to cry as he jogged. He didn't feel the heat of the sun, hear the cries of the gulls floating overhead, or smell the tang of salt in the air. His heart felt as if it had been shredded, torn and bleeding, making a cavity in his chest that ached so much it felt like he was in the middle of a heart attack.

Alex gripped his shoulder for a moment. "My friend," he said as he jogged by Cal's side, "Sky is a brave, resourceful woman. You must have faith that she will survive this. She was in the military. She was in black ops. You MUST have faith that she will do whatever she needs to do to escape," and he gave Cal a hard look, his face tight, his voice fierce with passion.

Cal nodded. When Alex released his shoulder, he felt his chest tighten. He needed to scream out his fury, his terror. Somewhere... anywhere... But Alex was right. He couldn't forget that Sky had gone through SERE, Survival, Evasion, Resistance and Escape training. She knew torture methods. She knew what to expect when captured, and that often made the difference. Above all, Sky was mentally tough. And that's what Cal had to rely on, her internal strength that she had been forced to develop since early childhood. In a sick kind of way, the horrors of her childhood that had cultivated that inner strength in her could possibly save her life now. Wiping his eyes with a swipe of his hand, he felt the fist of grief jam into his throat. He was grateful that Alex remained at his side.

The Ukrainian medic would become an important part in the planning that would start the moment they walked into ST3 HQ at Coronado. Alex knew Russian mafia techniques. He knew how the men worked under Alexandrov's direction. Any information he could give them might yield out where they were taking Sky.

"Alex?"

"Yes?" he asked, looking at Cal.

"Why did Alexandrov kidnap Sky? Why would't he just put a bullet in her head?" Cal gave him a look that told the Ukrainian to tell him the truth, no matter whether he wanted to hear it or not. They approached the tidal pools and slowed to a walk, carefully making their way across the rocks.

Alex became grim. He hesitated.

"Dammit," Cal snarled, "tell me what you know!"

"Alexandrov likes to slowly, psychologically torture someone he hates," he admitted, his voice low, hesitant. "I had heard this from his son, Vlad, that he has special places he takes such a prisoner. Usually, it is someone that has deeply wronged him."

"Yeah," Cal growled, "Russians are big on revenge."

Alex shrugged and gave Cal a pained look. "I have never been to these places. Only heard stories…," and he wiped his mouth, his brow furrowed.

"What stories?"

"That Yerik Alexandrov enjoys slow killing of the person. He will spend weeks, maybe a month or longer, watching them slowly die. He enjoys watching the process, I guess," and Alex shook his head. "He is a sick bastard, Cal. He was considered one of the best Spetsnaz interrogation officers in the Russian Army. His son used to enjoy slowly pulling wings off flies. I am sure his father does the same kind of torture to his enemies, psychologically rather than Vlad's way of doing it."

"Yerik is exactly like his sick fuck of a son," Cal growled. They finished crossing the tidal pool area and were now on a nearly mile-long public beach that was scattered with colorful umbrellas, adults and children playing in the shallows. The scene looked idyllic to Cal. As they broke into a trot along the wet, damp sand, their strides long and cadenced, Cal saw smiling faces, mother's closely watching their children who shrieked with glee in the sand or near the water's edge. Everyone was relaxed, sunbathing, enjoying the beauty of the day.

"What kind of torture?" Cal demanded. He saw Alex give him an agonizing look. "Okay, we'll discuss that later," he muttered. Because he really didn't want to know. His mind was churning wildly over all the possibilities. Sky had to know, sooner or later, who had kidnapped her. She had been around Vlad. She knew the son's predatory, hunter-like stalking of her. The old man would be far worse than his son. Vlad was a chip off the old block.

But now… his mind waffled with denial. Cal's mouth thinned. But he couldn't afford to be in denial about anything. Already, he was forming an extraction team in his mind. He'd want Alex along for obvious reasons, plus he was a damned good combat medic, and they wouldn't know what kind of shape Sky would be in when they found her. He'd want Lauren along because her sniper skills were better than anyone else at Shield. Jack would want to come along. They worked well together, plus he had all his assets and would work directly with Butch, who would remain as the central hub of intel here in Coronado. There was no question in Cal's mind that the Master Chief would bring the full weight and help of the SEAL community to them on this mission to locate Sky. It was going to be a top-secret civilian-military black op. And he was grateful to Butch because this Master Chief was a god among military gods. If anyone could shake loose assets to help them find Sky, it was him.

As he jogged past the women, the children, the dogs barking at them, watching the surfers out further in the ocean catching waves, Cal felt a little more steady. The fact they would have this kind of military help was going to make the difference in this mission. He hoped they were not too late. He hung on the medic's information that Alexandrov would keep a victim alive weeks or months at a time. That gave him hope. But it was hanging by one, thin thread that could sever at any moment...

CHAPTER 9

June 15

ABBY ONCE AGAIN repeated, clearly this time, what had happened when Sky had been kidnapped. The assembled team in the briefing room of ST3 was composed of nothing but grim-faced people as they took notes, listened, and asked questions, their game faces on. It was nearly six p.m. when Abby finished.

Butch sighed and gave her a kind look. "You've got to be tired, Abby." He looked over at Joe. "Take her home?"

"I'm not leaving her alone in that condo," Joe said. "The Russian mafia may still be hanging around the area."

"It's okay," Abby protested, standing, giving them all a weary smile. "Master Chief? If you have a hidey hole somewhere around here that I can just go lay down in? I'll be fine until ya'll break up this mission planning meeting. Joe can take me home at that time." She gave her husband a fond look and he nodded.

Butch said, "Good time for a break, people. Let's get more coffee and I'll show Abby where she can crash. Let's take a fifteen-minute break and then we'll regroup."

The chairs scraped back on the tile floor, and everyone rose. Not much was said. Cal rubbed his face and turned, following Butch and Abby out of the small, windowless room. These rooms were security safe, lead lined walls to prevent anyone from spying or snooping with any type of electronic equipment while they conducted a top-secret meeting.

Lauren was the last to leave. She saw how haggard Cal was, felt deeply for him. He loved Sky with his life. Abby looked exhausted. Anger stirred in her as she closed her notebook and stood up. She tucked it in the thigh pocket of her cargo pants. Outside in the passageway, she saw Alex head outdoors, head hanging, shoulders slumped. He looked the worst of everyone, and she suspected she knew why. Following him out, she saw the area was cordoned off with cyclone fences and concertina wire strung across the tops of them to prevent access. The sandy yard spilled out all the way down to the ocean. Alex was slowly walking toward the empty beach, beaten. It was very unlike him. He usually had the confident walk of an operator. *Not now. Not this time.*

Lauren hesitated and remained on the concrete steps, hand on the metal pipe railing, feeling the warmth of it beneath her fingers. The sun was close to setting, the Pacific Ocean glassy smooth. Inhaling deeply, she drew the tangy salt air into her lungs. Her mind spun with questions that only Alex could answer. Shoring herself up emotionally, she watched him sit on the golden sand, draw up his legs, and rest his head across his folded arms. Something broke within her. He looked like a lost child needing care. From this distance, with her hawklike eyesight, she saw Alex's partially revealed face. His eyes were closed. He was vulnerable. Her instincts were finely honed, her senses acute as few people would ever experience. The sense around Alex was one of grief-stricken loss and abandonment. Lauren knew he doted on Sky. He treated her like his little sister. And she knew he was completely emotionally invested in trying to find her, no matter the danger to himself.

Tapping her fingers on the metal railing, she decided to push the river and walked down the steps and into the sand toward him. The breeze was soft against her face. Earlier, she had pulled her long, thick hair into a ponytail that moved gracefully between her shoulder blades. She didn't want to feel anything for this operator, but she did. As she drew closer, she saw his cheek glistening. He was crying.

Halting, Lauren scowled, watching his massive shoulders shake. Her hearing was extraordinary, and she could hear soft, deep sobs wracking out of his opened mouth. Closing her eyes, Lauren felt tears burning in hers. *No.* She couldn't go there. If she released her emotions, she'd be no good at all to Cal and the assembled team. Lauren turned and walked toward the building, took the steps, and walked back inside. She couldn't handle anyone crying right now. Shock rolled through her because she'd never seen a man cry before. The sounds coming out of Alex had been terrible, clawing at her heart, tearing into her in ways she had no defense against. The last tears she'd shed were one of utter relief when the state sent a social worker to take her out of that hellhole of a family who had abused her.

"All right," Butch growled, looking at everyone around the table, "we've got our first break." He tossed a piece of paper toward Cal. "We can thank a Coast Guard contact of mine for these. It's a URL from the CG database on drug runners and drug dealers. Every time the CG finds a boat or a plane carrying drugs, they photograph it, take down the serial number, and keep it in their main database. Cal, when we get done with the initial planning, I think you'll want to spend some time trolling through that database for that sea plane Sky snapped a picture of?"

"I'm on it," Cal said, pulling the paper toward him.

"I'll help you," Lauren volunteered.

"Good," Butch muttered. He clasped his thick hands in front of him, dressed in desert cammos, his face hard. "Driscoll? You got a plan?"

Jack nodded. "It's forming. Until we get solid intel, there's not much we can do but choose a team and get ready to mount up."

"Who are you going to have on your team?" Butch demanded, pulling a pen out of his pocket.

Jack said, "Cal, Lauren, Alex and me. I want the team small and mobile. Alex knows Russian tactics and the language. He knows the way Alexandrov and his soldiers behave." He pointed toward Lauren who sat across from Cal. "No matter where we go or where Alexandrov is taking Sky, we may need a sniper. Cal's a breacher. No one was better than he is in that business."

"I'd go even if you didn't invite me along, Driscoll," Cal growled, giving him a drilling glance.

Jack managed a slight grin. "Yeah, I know, but I need your talents, too. There's every possibility we're going to have to breach and enter a building of some type to reach your lady."

Cal grunted, taking down notes as well. "Why do we need you?"

Driscoll snorted. "Because I'm damn good at radio, electronics, and know how to use a Raven."

"So do I," Cal said. As SEALs, the Raven drone was indispensable tool. It was as a large as the bird it was named after, flew silently above the enemy, and gave them lap top real time video on what it was seeing below where it flew.

"My strength is communications," Jack told Butch. "You know that better than most. I can call in an airstrike if that's what it takes. I'm the only one with with forward air controller training and experience."

Butch nodded. "It's a good, small team with strengths, and no weaknesses. You also need a medic and Kazak can fulfill that role as well. He also can translate Russian to the three of you, if necessary. I think you have everything you need."

"Satellite?" Cal demanded. "Can you get the use of one?"

"I can once we find out where the hell they've taken her."

Jack sat up. "What about comms traffic? Can you get your hands on a satellite that's listening to all cell phone, land line, and handheld radio traffic communications?"

"It's already done," Butch told them. "Got a high up in the Air Force who runs that north-south satellite. I've got him positioning it from La Jolla all the way down to Central and South America on the Pacific side."

"Have they got the names of the players?" Cal demanded.

"Some," Butch said, "but I need all of them." He looked directly at Alex who was sitting at the other end of the table. "Kazak, you want to start peeling off names of the leaders you know about. Any soldier's names. Anyone else you can think of."

He nodded. "Of course. Do you have a Russian translator who is working with this satellite?"

"I'm getting her. My Air Force connection knows the bastards will be speaking in Russian to one another. I'm going to give you an email address for this woman who is supposed to arrive at Vandenberg Air Force Base shortly. She's been tasked to stay on this electronic surveillance until we can locate Sky."

"That is good to hear. I will write all the names down. Give them to you?"

"No, you're going to type them into a computer."

Alex's faced folded. "I am not so good at typing, Master Chief." He held up his large, square hands. "Big, awkward fingers."

"I'll do it," Lauren volunteered, looking over at Master Chief. "I type nearly two-hundred words a minute. We'll get it done in no time."

"Wow," Jack murmured. "You never told me you were that fast."

Lauren wrinkled her nose. "I'm a sniper, not a damned office pogue, Driscoll."

There were titters around the room, and it broke some of the tension.

"Guess she put you in your place," Cal told Driscoll drily.

"I cannot even imagine hands flying that fast over a keyboard," Alex admitted, giving her a look of astonishment.

"You have to strap in or you'll fly out of your seat, Kazak," Lauren deadpanned.

There was more laughter at Alex's expense, but the Ukrainian gave everyone a goofy grin and a good-natured shrug.

"Okay, let's focus," Butch muttered.

Everyone instantly became serious.

"Alex, where are Alexandrov's safe houses? Places he goes to torture unfortunate victims? Or places he visits on vacation?"

"I do not know all of them, Master Chief. I heard Vlad say his father liked his villa in the state of Guerro, Mexico. He has a villa in Oahu, in the Hawaiian Islands. I know he lives in New York City, in a penthouse in Manhattan."

Butch wrote them down. "Where else?"

"I do not know. I wish I did."

"Did Vladimir ever speak of where his father preferred to visit? A favorite place? Even if you don't know if he has a safe house there?" Butch pushed.

Rubbing his wrinkled brow, Alex thought. He closed his eyes, rerunning conversations between Vlad and the men. Opening his eyes, he said, "Yerik Alexandrov likes jungle areas. That is why he has a home in the Hawaiian Islands."

Lauren said, "The state of Guerro is a well-known drug runners paradise. It's mountainous, and I know drug lords have villas there. Why not Alexandrov?"

"I'll have my resources check it out," Butch promised.

Cal growled, "If he likes jungles… where is the closest jungle around here?"

"Central America," Jack spoke up.

"Alex, does he have a villa in that area?" Cal pressed.

Giving them a frustrated look, Alex said, "Not that I have heard."

"What's Alexandrov's favorite hobby?" Butch demanded.

"I heard he prefers aquariums and falconry," Alex replied, giving the Master Chief a confused look.

"Fresh or salt water?" Butch shot back.

"Er… I think salt water. I remember Vlad telling us one time his father had one of the largest wall aquariums in the world. That he collected poisonous saltwater fish like the lionfish and the puffer. He said he collected jellyfish and sharks as well."

Cal grimaced, saying nothing.

"Does the elder Alexandrov scuba dive?"

"No, but I heard Vlad say his father was an avid snorkeler."

"Okay, those are leads," Butch said with finality. "What about this falconry angle?"

Alex frowned. "Only that it is a hobby. He prefers raptors. Vlad had no interest in the birds, so he rarely spoke about them to us."

Cal didn't ever question how Butch's mind worked. This was like finding puzzle pieces and then trying later to put them together, so they revealed a larger, more cohesive picture. He gave Alex a look. "What else does the elder Alexandrov like?"

"He likes quiet," Alex said. "Nature." Snapping his fingers, he sat up. "Wait… I remember something Vladimir said one time. His father loved the mountains. He said when his father retired, he was going to the cloud forest. But I do not know where that would be."

"Good work," Butch murmured, pleased, scribbling down the intel.

"And Vlad said his father preferred Japanese ways of living."

"Maybe Asia?" Cal wondered. "Lots of jungles and lots of clouds there?"

"Possible," Butch murmured.

"What we need," Driscoll said, "is a satellite that saw that seaplane land

and take off. Are you checking to see if there was a satellite in the area at the time of the kidnapping?"

"I'm already on it," Butch said coolly, giving Driscoll a one-eyebrow raised look. He looked at his watch. "I'm hoping to get an email or phone call shortly from another Air Force contact. They're checking the video feed as I speak."

No sooner had Butch spoke, when his land line phone, which sat in front of him, sounded off. Because of the lead lining in the room, only land line electronics were utilized.

Cal held his breath as Butch talked on the phone. Everyone sat quiet. Waiting. God, if they had had a satellite passing over at that time, it would be so damned helpful. He watched Butch's face carefully. But he was a SEAL, unlikely to give anything away. Butch ended the call. Opening his laptop, he growled, "Let's watch this satellite feed they're sending me..." and after he hit a few keystrokes, the large screen at one end of the room suddenly lit up with grainy black and white video.

Cal's stomach knotted. The satellite had caught the entire kidnapping on its overhead cameras in space. His heart started hammering in his chest, he felt adrenaline leaking into his bloodstream. Joe sat at his elbow, and he felt him tense up as they all watched the kidnapping. Just as the satellite moved out of range, the seaplane took off and headed south. The screen went blank. Cal wiped his mouth, trying to settle his emotions down, stuff them in his kill box, trying to not feel anything.

"That plane was heading south," Butch said quietly. He hit a number on his phone.

Cal heard the Master Chief speaking to someone. Could his source get another satellite fly over? Maybe pick up the path of the seaplane? Pinpoint its location? Maybe where it landed? Cal slowly drew his hand into a fist, feeling an incredible need to do something besides just sitting here. Cal he knew without proper surveillance, good, actionable intel, they were spinning their wheels. He had to be patient. But that was the last thing in the world he wanted to be right now. Closing his eyes, pinching the bridge of his nose, Cal tried not to think of Sky. Tried not to worry about how she was. Or worse, about what was happening to her.

June 16

A STABBING PAIN brought Sky awake. She groaned as someone lifted her eyelid, flashing a bright light directly into her eye. Reflexively, she tried to lift her hand, but found it incredibly weak. The light stabbed into her other eye.

"She's coming around," a man with a thick accent said.

Sky felt so thirsty, her mouth dry, her lips feeling cracked.

A hand gripped her shoulder, giving it a solid shake.

"Wake up!"

The male voice rolled through her head like thunder, and she winced, the sound magnified so that it actually caused her to flinch. His fingers dug deep into her upper left arm.

"Don't bruise her!"

Instantly, the man's fingers left her arm.

"Stupid dolt! He told you not to mar her skin! He'll have you punished for that!"

"Go fuck yourself, Vadim."

Sky felt movement around her. She was lying on what felt like a bed. She was warm. It took every effort to raise her lids. She saw early morning sunlight cascading through an open window. Her mind was like a wobbling top but sounds and smells got her attention. Birds were singing. Harmonious melodies she didn't recognize. Drawing in a slow, deep breath, she could smell the humidity, the heaviness of it along with a fragrance of a flower that was unknown to her.

"Remove the IV."

Sky winced as someone with shaking hands removed the needle that had been inserted into the vein of her right arm. She closed her eyes, feeling so exhausted, her lids too heavy to keep open.

"Kesera, remain with her. Let me know when she's fully conscious."

"Si, si, Señor Vadim."

Sky heard rustling of feet across a floor, men talking in Spanish or Russian, and then... silence. She felt a woman's hand gently move across her brow.

"You are safe now, Señorita Sky. Just rest. Do not listen to those big, ugly dolts."

Sky relaxed beneath the woman's Spanish accent. She felt a cool cloth being applied to her brow, cheeks, and neck. Right now, she felt sweaty, the blanket too hot, and she wanted to pull it off her. As if realizing it, the woman removed it.

"It is the drug, Señorita. You will sweat a great deal now. The stupid dolts, they gave you too much. But do not worry. Kesera will take care of you from now on."

Sky felt a pat of the woman's hand on her shoulder. *Drugs?* Her mind refused to work. She felt the coolness surrounding her and it felt good. When Kesera placed a wet, cool cloth against her lips, Sky eagerly began to try and suck the moisture from it.

"Ahhh, you are getting stronger. That is good."

Sky was so grateful as the woman repeatedly gave her a wet cloth dripping with water close to her parted, cracked lips. The liquid flowed into her mouth, making her groan with gratitude for the woman's kindness. The water infused her with a bit more strength and Sky forced open her eyes. The older woman looking down at her, smiling, was in her forties. Her black hair was in two thick braids over what looked like a nurse's white uniform. She even wore a white cap in her hair. Frowning, she whispered, "W-where…?"

"You are here, with me, Señorita. I will take care of you from now on."

Frowning, Sky watched the room slowly congeal before her eyes. The plaster on the walls was a pale, soothing blue. She saw thick velvet blue drapes opened across an open window to her left, sunlight splotchy. The birds singing sounded like beautiful music, and it served to put her at ease. There were a lot of shadows around the windows. Sky thought she saw lots of green foliage and trunks of trees nearby.

"Would you drink some chicken soup if I brought you some?" Kesera asked, leaning over, smiling at her.

Sky barely nodded. She was starving to death. Her stomach growled. She heard Kesera titter. The nurse went to a dresser at the end of the bed where she lay and picked up a phone mounted to the wall. She spoke quickly in Spanish and then returned to her.

"You look so much better. You need many fluids to help chase the drug out of you." She walked over to Sky. "Come, I will bring the bed up so you can sit up a little…"

The whirring sound beneath the bed began and in no time, Sky was sitting up at a comfortable angle. The bed folded gently beneath her knees, taking the strain off her back. She felt minimally better. Kesera puttered around like a bird landing here and there. She poured some pink juice into a small glass.

"Here, guava juice. Very high in potassium, Señorita. Drink?"

When Kesera pressed the glass to her lower lip, nothing had ever tasted as good as that juice. Sky gulped it down, wanting more.

"More? Yes?"

"Y-yes, please?" Her voice was hoarse. Sky slowly looked down at herself. There was a dressing over the inside of her right arm. Her lower left calf ached intermittently. She felt too weak to move much. Every joint in her body ached and Sky wondered why. She tried to remember, but her brain was stuck in neutral.

The soup arrived, and another woman, short and heavy, wearing a white apron around her gray dress, gave the tray to Kesera. She kept her eyes down, not looking at Sky, and quickly left the room. The soup smelled good. Sky watched Kesera placed the soup on a tray with wheels, bringing it over to the bed.

"Our chef, who is the best in our country, cooks for the Don. And now, you get to taste his wonderful soup." She lifted the spoon, blew on it to cool it and then pressed it onto Sky's lower lip so she could sip it.

"That tastes… so good…," Sky whispered. She tried lifting her hand. Every attempt, she felt it getting a little stronger. Sky knew the food would help, and she eagerly consumed the noodles, carrots, celery, and chicken in the thick, delicious broth. By the time she was done, she felt her strength begin to return.

"Where am I?" she asked the nurse again, her voice stronger.

"Ah, Señorita, I am not able to say," Kesera said, giving her a sad look. "You will know soon, I promise. The Don is flying here. He will arrive tomorrow morning. He will tell you everything. I am only to care for you. Si?"

Sky slowly lifted her hand and rubbed her aching brow. Now, she had a splitting headache. Due to the drug? How did she get drugged? Why was she here? Nothing made sense, but she had no access to her memory, either.

Her lids grew heavy.

"Ah, you need to sleep a little, Señorita. I will put the bed down." She patted Sky's shoulder. "Just rest, rest…"

Sky nodded and felt the bed move her back into a prone position. She sighed, feeling better but feeling utterly spent. It bothered her she couldn't remember anything. The birds were singing melodically. It soothed her frayed emotional state. Who was the Don? Kesera's face took on a fearful look when she spoke his name, as if she were afraid of this man. Or was Don the man's name? Her mind tumbled in free fall and Sky couldn't hold her focus. The songs of the birds lulled her into a deep, healing sleep.

CHAPTER 10

June 17

S KY SNAPPED AWAKE, breathing in rasps, sweaty, her heart pounding. It was dark. She dizzily sat up in the bed, looking around. Faint moonlight filtered in through the black wrought iron bars across the window. Terror seized her as she remembered the seaplane landing and men in a raft paddling toward them.

"Oh, God…" she whispered, pressing her hands against her eyes. Wild with fear, Sky realized she'd been kidnapped. The Russian's face glared back at her in her mind, and she forced open her eyes, breathing raggedly. She had to escape! She had to get out of here!

Sky pushed her legs across the bed, the sheet and blanket tangling between them. Dizziness assailed her. Gripping the edge of the mattress with both her hands, she gulped, trying to steady herself. *Kidnapped. Captured.* The words thundered through her head in time with the frantic beat of her heart. She squinted, her eyes adjusting to the murky darkness of the quiet room. Scanning it, she found one door that was closed. There was another room, the door partially open, a tiny light dimly shining in it. Sky looked around the large room, realizing she was in a bedroom. But who's? Where was she?

She slid herself off the bed. Her knees buckled as her ankles caught in the sheet. With a cry, she slammed to the wooden floor. The wood was cool against her sweaty cheek and she lay there, stunned. Pushing her hands against the polished surface, she tried to get up, but couldn't. Her legs were entangled in the bedding, and weakness still gripped her. Tears squeezed from her tightly shut eyes.

Cal! Oh, God… Cal!

Sky's mind roiled and tilted. Her emotions were amplified, ripping through her, making her shaky and unable to think coherently. There was a brushing sound against one of the windows. She slowly sat up, trying to pull her legs free of the binding sheet. Looking toward the sound, Sky realized it was a large leaf slapping against the window because of the wind. Gulping, her eyes adjusting, she saw two large wooden dressers, an antique armoire, and the door that opened to another room. Was there a way out of this place? An escape? Where the hell was she?

Swallowing painfully, Sky forced herself to sit up more. She was shaking, and she could feel remnants the drug still lingering in her bloodstream. Fear tore through her as she realized how alone she really was. The menacing glare of the Russian's black eyes drilled into her when she closed her eyes. Brushing her leg, Sky remembered feeling pain. Rubbing the area that was now tender, she examined herself, trying to take stock, trying to calm down and think.

Sweat was dripping off her, the blue gown she wore clinging to her body. She saw a bandage on the inside of her right arm, touching it with trembling fingers. *Thirsty.* She was dying of thirst. Spotting a pitcher of water on a silver tray on top of one of the dressers, Sky pushed carefully into a crouch, testing her strength. This time, as she stood up more slowly, the dizziness didn't fell her. Arms raised out from the sides of her body in order to balance herself, she walked unsurely toward the dresser. The outside of the glass pitcher was beaded, ice cubes melting inside it.

Taking the pitcher in both hands, Sky crouched and set it down on the floor. She didn't have the coordination to pour the water out of it standing up. She slowly stood up once again, picking up the nearby glass. Sitting on the floor cross legged, it took both her hands to hold the pitcher and tip the spout downward. Water sloshed all around. Not caring, Sky gripped the glass, drinking the contents in several gulps. Closing her eyes, she felt like a camel who had been out on the desert for too long. For the next ten minutes, she filled and drank until there was no more water left in the pitcher.

Almost miraculously, her head cleared. Her thoughts began to string together. Sky pushed to her feet. She saw she was wearing a blue hospital gown with nothing beneath it. Grimacing, she stumbled her way toward the partially opened door. Inside the large, tiled room was a shower, a toilet, and washstand. Her legs were quivering almost uncontrollably now. The smell of fear, sweat, and the drug stench clung to her body. She sat down on a nearby vanity chair, staring longingly at the shower. Torn between getting clean and testing the door on the other side of the room to see if it was open, Sky tried to find out what time it was. There was no clock in the bathroom.

Heaving to her feet, she felt steadier. Every minute, she was getting stronger, more clear-headed. Her mind sprang to Cal, and she felt her heart wrench. She loved him so much. What must he be going through right now knowing she had been kidnapped? Step by step, Sky made it to the thick, wooden door. Sliding her hand around the black iron knob, she quietly twisted it, praying it was open.

The door was locked. Sky tried tugging on it, but she was in no shape to do anything physical, much less tear a door of this immense size open. Instinctively, she knew Vlad's father was behind her kidnapping. Since Vlad had died, she'd felt a kernel of terror gnawing deep in her soul, like grit an oyster would have rubbing against its raw vulnerable innards. She'd never brought it up to Cal because they were both stressed out from nearly dying in Peru. All Sky had wanted was the peace of his home and his love to help heal her.

Why hadn't she told Cal about her deepest fear? That Vlad's father, Yerik Alexandrov, would come after her? That he would somehow blame her for Vlad's death? Wiping her mouth, Sky turned and grimly walked to the dressers. There was just enough moonlight to look into each drawer. They were filled with women's clothing, some casual, others, elegant, worth a great deal of money and all designer fashions. Sky rummaged through several drawers, tearing clothes out, trying to find something to wear that would fit her. She finally found a blue tee and a pair of wheat colored linen slacks. There were no shoes to be found. That wasn't good if she could manage to escape.

She walked to the two windows. Each had black wrought iron bars across them. Sky opened the first window. A gust of humid wind, heavy with the scent of rain upon it, burst strongly into the stuffy room. Sky saw lightning somewhere in the far distance. The full moon was being hidden by the coming storm. Peering out, she could see what she thought was jungle surrounding the house, with tropical looking plants growing next to the villa's wall.

Sliding her fingers around the bars, Sky tried to move them. They didn't budge. And she couldn't slide between the bars because they were set too closely together. Another form of panic began to gnaw at her. Quietly closing the window, Sky walked into the bathroom. There were plush pink terrycloth towels all neatly stacked on the cream-colored tile counter. She desperately needed a shower in order to get the drug smell and sweat off her skin.

As Sky washed with a pink hard-milled soap that smelled like roses, she cleaned herself up, discovering a bottle of shampoo on a tray sitting on the tile wall of the shower. Within twenty minutes, her hair was washed, and she was clean. Her mind was starting to work. Finding a brush and comb, Sky got her hair into some semblance of order. There were no bras or panties to be found in any of the drawers. She slipped into the tee and the slacks, wishing desperately for a pair of shoes.

How could she escape? How many people were here? Where was Alexandrov? Sky shivered as she slowly sat down on the bed, looking around the room for anything she could use as a weapon. What time was it? Lightning flashed outside and she winced, her eyes sensitive to the sudden, bright light.

Chewing on her lower lip, Sky stared at the only entrance/exit point in the room. Was there a guard outside it? Armed? What was going to happen to her?

Why had she been kidnapped? Was it really Alexandrov or her wild imagination? Sky didn't know for sure. Thunder shook the villa, the sound like cannons being fired from nearby. The wide tropical leaves slapped against the one window, the wind gusting.

Sky was scared. And alone. Cal would try and find her; she knew that with every cell in her body. But how would he locate her? She didn't even know where she was! Laying down on the bed, drawing her knees up against her chest, she felt suddenly chilled. Reality rolled over Sky, crushing her, destroying her hope, and she began to softly cry, the hot tears rolling down her cheeks. Pressing her face into the pillow, she rocked herself, needing help, needing some sense of safety, but there was none. What was going to happen tomorrow morning? Would she die? Would they rape her? Torture her? She wasn't even sure who had kidnapped her. But something told her it was Alexandrov. And she knew the Russians were cruel and sadistic. Living with Vlad had taught her that.

Sky cried herself to sleep, arms tight around her body, knees drawn upward into a fetal position. She could die tomorrow. All she could do as she cried was picture Cal, his hard face, feel his rock-solid confidence, that feral look in his eyes when he had his game face on. Somehow, just visualizing him gave her a sense of safety. She clung to that tiny piece of solace. Sky knew Cal would turn heaven and hell over to find her. She knew he would.

Cal halted at the closet where Sky's wedding gown hung. It was two a.m. in the morning, and he was exhausted in every possible way. Lauren had driven him back to the condo and dropped him off. He ached for Sky. Walking through the condo, the deathly silence only reminding him that she was somewhere unknown, probably feeling the same way he did. Lonely. Torn in half. Not whole anymore. She was his life. His mouth twisted as he stood at the door. He remembered Sky telling him not to look at her wedding gown before they got married; that it was bad luck. His hand moved to the handle. He was superstitious more than he'd ever admit, and he allowed his fingers to drop away from the handle.

Turning, he walked out of the room and closed the door. Looking around, Cal knew he was in shock. Two nights ago, this condo had rung with laughter, joking, and good times. Now... He ran his hand across the granite island, remembering their breakfast together in the morning, what they talked about, the way Sky looked shortly after taking her shower, how clean she smelled, the scent of almonds in her blond hair. He had to get a hold of himself, but it was impossible. At 0800 tomorrow morning, Butch had ordered the team back to the briefing room. By then, more intel would be available, he hoped. Lauren had worked with him until one thirty a.m. and finally pushed him out of the briefing room. They left everything there, the laptops, the notebooks, and pens, not to mention a pile of empty paper coffee cups.

Cal halted at the bathroom door, hands on the door jamb, staring numbly into it. Sky and he had made love in the shower the morning before their wedding day. It had been nothing short of mind blowing. Her cries had echoed sweetly around in the huge, steamy glass enclosure. She had clung to him, her face buried against his neck and shoulder, sobbing as he brought her to orgasms so many times that they'd both lost count. And then, when he came into her sweet, wet body, he nearly lost his footing, the power of the ejaculation tearing through him with raw, scalding pleasure. She brought out the best in him in every way, even when having sex. Cal corrected himself: when making love to Sky. She had been right, as he recalled their conversation with bittersweetness. Their last together, just before she got on top of him and rode him into more mindless pleasure, she'd said it wasn't just sex they shared. It was love. He loved her more than life. Cal didn't give a shit about living if he couldn't have Sky in his life.

He pushed away from the door jamb, cursing richly. Turning, he walked into the bedroom. The bed was still unmade. Standing at the foot of it, he could still see the small indent in the sheet where Sky had slept. This was so damned painful. He rubbed his chest, his heart hurting so much that he was beyond tears, beyond screaming out his terror and frustration. Cal walked to the bed and sat down on his side of it. He saw Sky's silky golden nightgown nearby. Picking it up, Cal pressed the silk to his face, inhaling deeply, smelling her scent on the material. Desperately, he wanted to hold her. He knew Sky was still alive, and she had to be so damned frightened. He wanted to enfold her into his arms, against his body, protect her as she deserved. How had this happened? HOW?

Cal pulled the material away from his face and held her gown between his large hands, staring down at it. Some of the material caught on the rough callouses across his fingers. Sky was like the silk, so smooth, soft, and beautiful. Cal hung his head, feeling the hot prick of tears at the back of his eyes. He crushed the silk between his hands, drawing it against his chest, over his heart. He felt an earthquake-like spasm roll up through his chest. A terrible, raw sound tore out of his mouth. He couldn't stop it, it overtook him like the mindless, crazed animal he felt running wild inside of him.

Sky...

Cal swore he could feel her, that invisible connection they had with one another. He could sense her moods every time. And now, he felt such fear deep within him, he knew it was her fear that he was somehow experiencing. The only fear Cal had was of losing Sky. He swore, as the tears flowed unchecked down his cheeks, he would find her. He wouldn't stop looking until he died. He'd hunted for her for two years trying to locate her, and he'd finally persevered and did the impossible: he'd discovered Sky in Cusco, Peru. And against the odds, he'd been able to track her down in that remote Indian village Vlad had carried her away to and rescued her. He would do it again.

Lifting his head, Cal stared at the top of their dresser. The blue diamond earrings he'd gifted her with were sitting there. She'd been so excited about them, so eager to wear them with her ring on their wedding day. His fingers plunged into the silk nightgown, and he shook with grief and terror. Tears dropped upon the fabric, soaking into it. This was his only physical connection with Sky. She'd worn this last night until he'd taken it off her. His mind violently rejected it would be the last time he'd ever touch Sky, love her.

"Señorita Sky?"

Sky jerked awake, sitting up. She blinked, her heart thundering. A petite woman, Caucasian, with long blond hair and wearing what she thought was a designer dress of bright red, stood by her bed. She was very young, she realized, maybe eighteen. Her face was artfully made up, her full lips painted a glossy red. She was beautiful. Sky gulped, looking down to see the dress barely covered half her thighs. She was wearing bright red designer shoes to go with the dress. Looking up into her soft blue eyes heavily made up with mascara and highlighted with charcoal above her eyes, Sky could smell the faint scent of spicy perfume around her. The woman looked like a fashion model who had walked out of the pages of Vogue Magazine. Sky quickly looked at the only door leading out of the bedroom. It was closed.

"I'm Catarina," the young woman said, offering her a smile. "How are you feeling this morning?"

Gulping, Sky realized she was still in the clothes she'd taken from the dressers the night before.

"Are you hungry? I have a lovely breakfast ready for you. If you'd like it, I'll have them bring it to you?"

Wiping her face, Sky felt groggy. "I'm thirsty," she croaked. But she knew she had to eat to keep up her strength. "Who are you? And where am I?"

Catarina smiled and walked over to the wall phone. "I'm Don Alejandro Tobar's favorite," she murmured proudly. She picked up the receiver, speaking to someone in a foreign language.

Sky sat there, trying to reorient. Sunlight slanted by the opened window and into the dark green jungle nearby. There were still raindrops clinging to the glass. There had been a thunderstorm sometime last night. She remembered falling into an exhausted sleep while hearing the sounds rolling across the house. Vaguely listening, the woman was speaking in what could only be

Russian. Living with Vlad for a year and hearing him using Russian often when he talked to himself, her sluggish brain finally recognized the language.

Sky looked toward the door. It opened. Kesera entered with a smile of hello. The Latino woman in her early forties, overweight and wearing her white cap, white dress with a green apron today, bringing in a tray filled with food. She nodded to Sky and placed the food on the rolling tray table and eased it over toward her. Thanking her, Sky saw plates of fresh fruit, croissants, jam in small jars, a carafe of coffee, cream, and sugar. Her stomach growled. She picked up the tall glass of guava juice, drinking it down in thirsty gulps.

The door closed.

Catarina floated by, the epitome of feminine grace. "That was Kesera, she is a nurse and will be your maid. I'll be back shortly, Señorita Sky. I will return with your clothes…"

Frowning, Sky saw two guards, men in cammo's with military rifles, standing outside the door as Catarina opened it and walked out. Where the hell was she? This morning, Sky felt more like her old self. The drug given her had made her feel like an emotional wet rag and she had felt out of control. This morning, Sky felt more solid, even confident. Food was fuel. If she was going to escape, she had to eat. Her appetite was non-existent, but Sky forced herself to eat all three croissants, spreading the unknown pink jam that was sweet and flavorful on the warm, fragrant bread. She drank the other glass of orange juice and then drank three cups of coffee, finally feeling sated, no longer violently thirsty.

Sky had barely wiped her mouth with the white linen napkin provided when the door opened again. It was beautiful Catarina, and this time, she had clothes folded neatly over her left arm and a pair of sensible brown leather shoes in her right hand. The door was shut by the men with the weapons.

Sky frowned, wondering about the timing of the girl's entrance. Looking around for a camera, she found them discreetly hidden up in each corner of the room. Fear worked through her. They were recording her every move. Shutting her eyes for a moment, Sky wondered if there was a video in the bathroom where she'd showered and then walked naked out into the surrounding area to dry off and dress. She felt violated.

"Don Tobar is arriving shortly," Catarina said in her sweet voice. She laid the clothes next to Sky. "He always likes us to dress beautifully when he graces us with his presence. I hope you don't mind. I saw your beautiful blue eyes and so I chose a pale lavender blouse with dark blue linen slacks and a thin leather belt." She held the belt up in her long, graceful hand, her nails matching the color of her lipstick. "Isn't the buckle gorgeous? Look, it is eighteen carat gold set with tiny turquoise gemstones set in it. The gemstones perfectly match your eyes. I think Don Tobar will be very pleased with the clothes I've chosen for you."

"Where am I?" Sky demanded, her fingers digging into the mattress where she sat, her legs hanging over the bed. She saw Catarina's long, oval face grow flushed. She seemed artless to Sky. Innocent, maybe. But incredibly gorgeous.

"Don Tobar will tell you," she said in a wispy voice, her smile growing. "He is a man of many surprises. Our job," and she gracefully gestured around the room, "is to make him happy. He's a very stressed businessman, and when he comes to La Paloma Villa, we are here to please him, make him relax and forget his business world."

"Your job?" Sky said, frowning.

"We are here to please him."

Scowling, Sky stared at the woman. "How old are you?"

"I just turned eighteen last week," Catarina said with a giggle.

"And how long have you been here a La Paloma?"

"Three years." Catarina tossed her head, her long, silky blond hair covering her small shoulders. "I am Don Tobar's favorite."

"Favorite what?" Sky asked, staring at the clothes she'd carefully laid out for her.

"Why," Catarina said, "to please him, of course."

"How many of you are there here?"

Catarina moved to a chair and sat down, crossing her long, slender legs. "There is Arina and Elga. We live here."

"And," Sky rubbed her brow, feeling the fear begin to move and grow within her, "how often does this Don Tobar come and visit you here?"

She gave an elegant shrug. "Perhaps once or twice a year. It just depends upon his very busy schedule."

"Where am I, Catarina?" Sky drilled a look into the girl's widening eyes, her tone a low growl.

Fluttering her hands, she said, "I am advised to allow Don Tobar to answer all your questions. I will not go against any order he gives me."

Flattening her hands against the mattress, Sky bowed he head, thinking. Who the hell was Don Tobar? She looked up.

"Are you Russian?"

"Oh, yes."

"Where do you come from, Catarina?"

Shrugging, she said sadly, "I was orphaned at birth. I do not know who my mother or father was."

"Then… you have parents who adopted you?"

"No," she said, her voice taking on a sad note. "I was placed in an all-girl orphanage. I grew up there outside of St. Petersburg." She rallied and opened her hands. "Elga and Arina were there, too. They were my best friends." Catarina smiled. "They taught us how to walk, how to dress, how to put on make-up, and how to please a man. Don Tobar bought us, and we're very happy here at La Paloma." She sighed and looked around the room. "He is very, very rich. And we want for nothing. We live in unimagined luxury."

Sky closed her eyes, unable to hold Catarina's enthusiastic gaze. They were sex slaves? She'd heard of girl orphans who were gathered up in Asia, living together in a communal area, trained to please a man, then sold to the highest bidder. And yet, as Sky opened her eyes and gazed at Catarina, she realized she was utterly innocent of who and what she was. They had trained her from birth, brainwashed her in subtle, daily ways, orienting her young mind to always please a man, her lord, her slave master. "And you were bought by Don Tobar when you were how old?"

"I was thirteen."

Wincing internally, Sky felt rage tunneling though her. She knew Vlad had been a sadistic, sexual monster. She had lived through him stalking her, always talking about sex to her, telling her he loved her, that he wanted to make love to her to produce his strong sons. It had scared and sickened her. Like father like son? Was Don Tobar another name for Yerik Alexandrov? Sky would bet her life on it.

"Tell me, Catarina, what does Don Tobar look like?"

She brightened. "Oh, he is a very, very tall man, very broad shoulders. He has blond hair and green eyes and is so handsome."

Her gut tightened. She'd seen a photo of Yerik Alexandrov when Vlad had shown it to her the day he'd trapped her in her bedroom. He'd locked the door, the proceeded to tell her that he really had a father. He'd been very proud of that fact he had one. Even her foster parents, Jack and Marielle, had believed he was an orphan. Vlad had strutted over to her, pulled out the photo, and pushed it into her face, saying this was his REAL father, Yerik Alexandrov. Vlad bragged openly that his father was now king of the Russian Mafia in New York City. He'd just been invited back to his side, to fly over to Russia and join the military. Sky had stood there like a deer frozen in headlights as he'd continued to extol his REAL father, how proud he was to be his son, that they had fooled everyone.

Sky swallowed, her throat tightening with tension. "Catarina? Does Don Tobar have a scar on his left cheek, just below his eye?" Because in the photo of Vlad's father, the scar had been prominent. Vlad had bragged he'd gotten it when he was a young officer in the Spetsnaz, in a fight with an Afghan when Russia had invaded that country.

"Why," Catarina said, amazed, "he does! How did you know this?"

CHAPTER 11

June 17

S KY SAT VERY still, feeling iciness flow through her veins. Catarina looked surprised. Fear mixed with hatred within Sky as she realized it really was Yerik Alexandrov, Vlad's sadistic, murdering father, who had kidnapped her. She licked her lips, her mind whirling with what could happen to her next. Old, familiar dread flowed through her, dark memories of Vlad stalking her, catching her off guard, whispering sickeningly sexual things into her ear, scaring her to death. She sensed Yerik would be even worse. What was she going to do? What did he have in store for her? Sky knew without a doubt he was going to take his revenge for Vlad's death out on her. No question.

Catarina rose gracefully. "Come, it is time for you to dress, Señorita Sky. Have you taken a lovely, fragrant camellia bath?"

"I took a shower last night," Sky said, "I don't want another one."

"Oh… I see. Well," and Catarina gestured gracefully to the clothing she'd laid out next to Sky, "Don Tobar expects his women to look their best. Please, I will help you dress. Put make-up upon you. I will comb and brush your hair so you look presentable to him."

Gritting her teeth, Sky bit back a rich curse. Catarina was clueless. She was brainwashed. A beautiful doll whose only purpose in life was to be a sexual object for that sick bastard. Thirteen years old? Catarina had been taken sexually at such a young age? It turned Sky's stomach. Her fingers dug into the mattress as she struggled to hold her anger within herself. "Look," she told the girl, "I'm wearing what I have on. I could care less what Don Tobar wants. And I don't do make-up. My hair is fine as is."

Sky saw the girl blanch, her face literally, go white. She saw fear in Catarina's pale blue eyes.

"But-but… if you do not wear these clothes, Don Tobar will be angry with me," and Catarina pressed her manicured hand against the low-cut dress that exposed her full breasts.

"What do you mean?" Sky demanded, hearing the sudden terror in Catarina's girl-like voice.

"H-he will beat me! You have no idea what Don Tobar is capable of! I-I don't want to be beaten by him again. Please, please, you MUST wear those clothes," and her voice broke, and she pressed her hands against her opened mouth.

"He beats you?"

Squeezing her eyes shut, Catarina lowered her voice. She whispered, "Come to the bathroom with me? Pretend you want to shower?" Her eyes were huge and pleading.

Nodding, Sky said, "Fine, I'm taking a shower," and she walked into the room. Catarina scooped up the clothing and quickly followed her into the room, shutting the door.

She turned, keeping her voice low, she whispered. "There are no cameras or microphones in this room." She gripped Sky by the arm. "You cannot cross Don Tobar! If you do not do exactly as he orders, he will beat you." She gulped. "Once, I did not want to him to take me. He got very angry with me. He called in two of his guards and ordered them to rape me as punishment." She shook her head, tears coming to her eyes. "You MUST not cross him, Sky! You must not! He will hurt you! Badly." She placed the clothing on the counter, her voice cracked. "Another girl, one of my sisters, Olga, fought him. He had her raped by every soldier here at the villa while he watched. She died the next day."

Sky felt nausea rise in her throat. She stared disbelievingly at Catarina, who was shaking, tears huge in her wide blue eyes. There was no way she wanted Catarina hurt. "Okay, okay," Sky whispered, reaching out, touching the girl's shoulder, "I'll wear the clothes. You can put make-up on me, fix my hair. I don't want you punished."

"Oh... thank YOU, Sky! Thank you!" and Catarina sobbed, throwing her long, slender arms around Sky's shoulders. "You are so good to me! Thank you. We cannot disobey Don Tobar. Not EVER! We must stay a team to protect all of us from his rage."

Sky stepped out of the girl's embrace. "I'll take a shower. You go back out there and wait for me?" She looked at the clothes. "Where's a bra? Panties?"

Sniffing, Catarina said, "Don Tobar wants us naked beneath the clothes we wear. He likes us that way."

Sky grimaced. "Okay. Just go wait for me. Those cameras in the other room? Are they working?"

"Oh," Catarina said, looking at how the tears had marred her make-up in the mirror, "Yes. Two soldiers watch those videos in every room of the villa twenty-four hours a day. Everything is recorded and saved. There are many cameras in the Don's bedroom. He likes to film us when he has sex with us. It pleases him."

Shooting the bastard in the head would please her about now, but Sky kept those thoughts to herself. "Where will you be taking me to see him?"

Catarina pulled several tissues from a nearby box, blotting her cheeks. "To his den. The tea will be served to you two. He wants to see you alone."

"And the soldiers? Where will they be?"

"Out of sight, but not far away. He is always protected, Sky. Never assume that they aren't close enough to kill you." She turned, gripping Sky's shoulders. "They said you were very special to Don Tobar. He's ordered that no one bruise or touch you in a painful way. He wanted you perfect."

"Perfect for what?" Sky asked, her stomach tightening, fear arcing through her.

"I-I don't know." Sniffing, Catarina said, "Later, when he is finished with you, you will be sent to our wing of the villa. There is a bedroom apartment prepared for you."

Scowling, Sky tried to shake the fear stalking her. "What will he do to me?"

Helplessly, Catarina whispered, "I do not know. I'm sorry. I wish I knew. You are being kind to me. You are protecting me, and I wish... oh, I wish I could tell you more..."

"It's all right," Sky soothed. "Get out of here. They may suspect something's going on if you don't leave soon."

"Yes, yes," Catarina whispered. She hurried to the door. "I-I will fix my make-up out there and wait for you. Do not be long?"

Sky hated how she looked as she studied herself in the bedroom mirror. She hated make-up, her skin stretching beneath it. She wore a mauve lipstick to go with the terribly revealing lavender silk blouse that hung open halfway down her chest, revealing the swell of her breasts. Worse, her nipples, being rubbed by the soft material, were standing out, and it made her feel like a piece of meat on parade. The linen slacks were tight across her ass, making her feel vulnerable, under inspection.

"You look beautiful!" Catarina praised enthusiastically, finishing placing lavender nail polish on her short nails. "I know the Don will be pleased."

Sky shook her hands, drying the nail polish, hating wearing it. This wasn't her. She saw how upset and sensitive Catarina was, feeling sorry for the girl. And that's what she was, a girl. Innocent. Not mature. Trapped in a box with no way out. "Thank you for your help."

There was a sharp knock on the door.

Catarina jumped.

Sky cringed. It was a man knocking on the heavy mahogany door. Her heart skittered with fear.

"It's time," Catarina whispered, gesturing for her to stand. "Hurry. We cannot arrive late, or Don Tobar will be angry. He will take it out on me."

Sky stood, pushing her damp palms against her revealing linen slacks. Thankfully, she was given a low-heeled pair of leather shoes; something she could walk in unlike those five-inch spike heels Catarina wore. The girl wobbled on them, and Sky was sure she would one day break her ankle wearing those torture devices. If men had to wear them, they'd ban them forever in a millisecond.

"Let's go," Sky murmured, following Catarina to the door. It was going to be her opportunity to see where she was at, to case the villa, memorize the rooms, the hallways, and especially, exits for escape.

The door opened. Sky saw the bald Russian, his bulk filling the narrow, dimly lit hallway. She decided to refer to him as 'Baldy.' The polished flagstone floor gleamed dully as light from a window at the other end of the hall revealed enough for her to see where they were going. He grinned, showing half his front teeth that were missing. He took his large hand and rubbed his crotch suggestively. Sky avoided the hungry look in Baldy's small, glittering eyes, feeling bile rise in the back of her throat. She was sure he was hoping she'd defy Don Tobar and she'd end up being raped by him and his other Russian goons.

The villa was huge. She caught sight of a placid river, about fifty feet wide and about thirty feet away from one side of the villa. It was airy and light around them as Catarina led her out into an open, plaza-like area. The windows were all thrown open, the breeze warm and humid. Sky knew they were in a jungle, no question. She saw other servants, all women, dressed in prim and proper black dresses, white aprons, and plain black leather shoes. They were all older women. They looked Latino to her, with black hair and brown eyes. They barely looked up, their heads bowed as Catarina swayed by like the goddess-in-charge that she was. Sky heard Baldy's thunking combat boots behind her, cringing inwardly because he was closer than she ever wanted him to be.

The room was open, filled with expensive black leather couches and chairs, large rectangular golden-framed coffee tables, and sculptured art of naked women in each of the corners. The flagstone floors were neat, clean, and highly polished, reflecting the light. Sky spotted some sunlight lancing through what looked like a triple canopy of jungle trees. Wherever this villa sat, it was well hidden from a strategic point of view. Sky was going to utilize her military background on everything she observed. They passed a grand looking kitchen where three men in white uniforms and chef's hats worked. The scent of bread baking mingled with the aroma of cinnamon and cloves, being carried throughout the area. Catarina turned to the left, down what appeared to be another wing of the villa.

The light was low and there were at least six doors, three on each side, suggesting these were bedrooms, or perhaps apartments. Catarina hadn't said a word, just the sound of her heels clicking smartly against the flagstones filled the corridor. Maybe rooms for his soldiers? Or visitors that Alexandrov brought with him? At the end of the hall, there were two other passages. Sky looked down one hall and saw two doors, one on each side of it. Catarina chose the left hallway, giving her a quick glance. Sky saw the anxiety in her eyes. Her heart rate picked up. She tasted fear, knowing she would see Vlad's father in person for the first and maybe the last time in her life. Sky wanted to run, but two armed Russian soldiers with rifles stood at the entrance to another room. Everywhere she looked, there were big, hulking Russian guards. There was no escape.

Catarina swayed into a huge room, the den, with a floor-to-ceiling flag-stone fireplace. The windows all had wrought iron bars across them, but were open, allowing the heavy, humid warmth to flow through the high-ceilinged room. Catarina led her over to a black leather wingback chair. "Please," she murmured, "sit here."

Sky swept the place with her gaze, seeing no one else but them in the room. Her throat was dry, and she felt like running, but there was nowhere to hide. She slowly sat down.

Immediately, a maid appeared and silently placed a fragile China cup filled with amber tea on a nearby round desk sitting next to her arm. Next came cream, sugar and a fresh, hot cinnamon roll, as well. The anxious maid wouldn't meet Sky's eyes, instead she bowed and scuttled away.

Catarina turned and looked down at her. "Don Tobar will arrive shortly. Please, enjoy the Earl Gray tea and the cinnamon roll."

Sky watched the woman leave. And so did Baldy. She looked around, sitting up in the chair, trying to see everything she could, to memorize it and tuck it away.

"You are more beautiful in person than any photo my son Vlad ever sent me of you."

Sky's head snapped straight ahead. A little gasp escaped her. Yerik Alexandrov stood on the other side of the coffee table, dressed in a white peasant shirt, loose white linen slacks, and a pair of brown sandals. Her gaze lifted to his. Sky felt dread move through her.

Unconsciously, she gripped the arms of the chair, feeling his intense inspection of her, his flat green eyes, the same color as Vlad's. Yerik had the same face and strong chin, giving his eyes more emphasis, close set together. Sky felt the air whoosh out of her lungs because he was practically a carbon copy of Vlad. His skin was darkly tanned, his blond hair military short. What threw her was Yerik's mouth. It was a full one with an almost pouty lower lip, and there was a faint smile hovering around it. She felt as if she were staring at a slightly older version of Vlad, and it nearly paralyzed Sky. Yerik's voice was low, cultured, and he spoke precise English without a Russian accent attached to it. Compared to Vlad, who had always reminded her of an animal on the prowl, his father was cosmopolitan, at ease with himself. Sky swallowed hard, holding his look.

"Please," he said, gesturing toward the tea and food, "be at ease, Sky. "I think you know who I am? Vlad's father? Yerik?"

Sky barely nodded, her hands knotted in her lap. There were so many emotions veering through her that she knew she had to keep her face expressionless and her voice flat so as not to give away her real feelings. Alexandrov had snake's eyes: flat, unblinking, and intense. She could feel herself starting to crumble inwardly as he stood there, relaxed, hands at his side. "I know who you are," Sky whispered.

Nodding, Yerik smiled a little. "Let us have some mid-morning tea and get to know one another?"

She saw a maid scuttle like a crab toward where he sat down in a wingback chair opposite of hers. Glad the coffee table was between them, Sky forced herself to relax. Her heart was pounding so hard, she could hear it in her ears. The maid carefully delivered the same cup of tea and two cinnamon rolls. Yerik nodded and thanked her. The maid never made eye contact with him, relief on her face as she quickly and silently left the den.

"You know," Yerik said conversationally, taking the plate with the rolls and tearing one of them apart, placing a piece in his mouth, "you are missing the most delicious cinnamon rolls in the world. Please, take just a taste? For me?"

She saw his eyes crinkle, a smile flexing at the corners of this mouth. It did not reach his eyes. Sky knew better than put up a fight, protest, or do anything other than what was asked. Catarina gave her a head's up on that. Right now, Sky had to be subservient. It didn't come easy, but her life was on the line, making it a helluva lot easier. She picked disinterestedly at the roll, the fragrance sweet and spicy. It tasted like warm wood in her mouth because she was too frightened to focus on anything other than surviving this meeting without being raped.

"Very good," Yerik praised, nodding deferentially in her direction. He wiped his manicured fingers off with a white linen cloth he'd spread across his lap. "Vlad told me, in an email, that you loved cinnamon rolls."

Shock rolled though Sky. She stared at him, her lips parting momentarily.

"He did?" The words burst out of her before she could stop them. Yerik had hooked her, caught her off guard.

Picking up his cup of steaming tea, Yerik smiled slightly and nodded. "Indeed, my son did. You used to make them with your foster mother, Marielle. I believe she taught you how to bake? Vlad said he always looked forward to when you got enthused about making fresh bread and cinnamon rolls for the family." His voice faltered. "Vlad loved eating them, too."

Her heart wrenched in her chest. Sky lowered her gaze, feeling tears prick her eyes. Valiantly, she fought them back, but her voice came out husky and unsteady. "I loved my foster parents with my life. They were always good to me. And to Vlad." She wanted to snarl, *but your bastard son murdered them in cold blood right in front of my eyes.* Sky bit down on her lower lip, fighting to keep the words choked back. She watched Yerik eat both rolls delicately, but with appreciation of a gourmand. He slowly licked his fingers, and it sent revulsion through her. Sky couldn't eat any more, picking up the tea in both hands because she was afraid, she'd spill it otherwise.

"What you didn't know, dear, sweet Sky, is that my son was sending me many photos and daily texts about you. When you arrived at the Zimmerman household as a lost waif, he fell madly in love with you upon first meeting you." Yerik sipped his tea, watching her face closely. He saw surprise flare in her unearthly blue eyes.

Sky went icy inwardly. Vlad professed his undying love to her, but she wasn't going to let Yerik know that. "N-no... I had no idea. I mean..." and Sky shrugged and placed the teacup on the table.

"Why tears?" Yerik probed softly, cocking his head.

Yerik sounded genuinely as if he CARED. Sky knew he didn't. It was all a game with Alexandrov, just as it had been with his evil, plotting, manipulating son. She never forgot that Yerik was Spetsnaz from age eighteen and spent ten years as an interrogation officer for his black ops group. There was a group of them that were psychological experts, able to bend and mold their prisoners to squeeze what they wanted out of them. Yerik was one of the best of them. Blinking, forcing the rest of her tears away, she whispered, "Vlad was always taking cell phone photos of all of us. I didn't know he was sending them to you."

"Quite right," he agreed. "And text messages, sometimes long emails from my son as well." He smiled a little. "The emails were always about you. How beautiful you were. How graceful. He loved your blond hair and went on and on about it in several emails." Yerik sipped his tea. "And Vlad was right: your hair is an arresting, natural color. In fact," and Yerik set his tea aside and snapped his fingers.

A man dressed like a butler arrived silently with a small silver tray balanced on his white gloved hand. The man was bald, older, and darkly tanned. He bowed to Yerik and extended the tray in front of him. She watched as he took a stack of documents off the tray. The butler made an about face, whispered by her, and left the den.

Yerik leaned forward, putting some of the papers on the table and choosing one. "Here, I want you to see these, Sky." He stood and walked to the coffee table, leaned across it, and offered the photo to her.

Sky stood and took it, being careful not to touch his fingers. She sat down and turned the photo over. Frowning, she saw a very beautiful blond-haired woman with blue eyes smiling back at her. She looked up, frowning. Yerik had sat down, legs crossed, elbow on the chair, his chin resting against his fist, watching her. "Who is this?"

"My beloved wife, Darya. Vlad's mother."

Sky stared at the woman. She saw a bit of Vlad's face in hers, but little else. What intrigued her the most was Darya's long, shoulder-length blond hair had streaks of wheat, caramel, and gold in it. Just like hers. Sky had rarely seen this natural coloration in blond hair unless it was dyed in. "She's beautiful," Sky admitted, sitting the photo on the table between them. Her heart plunged because she saw tears glimmering in Yerik's eyes. His face had softened, and she couldn't believe it. Was that a performance for her, or genuine, emotional grief in his expression? She didn't know.

Suddenly, Sky felt caught in something that was far beyond her. In SERE, they had tortured her with mind games. An enemy soldier would come in, her captor, and he would smile, offer her food, water, and be nice to her. If she didn't give him the information he wanted, he left. Then, another man would come in, who was the exact opposite, cruel and harsh toward her. Could Alexandrov so easily create crocodile tears to manipulate her? Sky sat there, unsure, suddenly off balance by the man's display of tears and grief in front of her.

"She died shortly after giving Vlad life," Yerik murmured, pulling a linen handkerchief from his pocket, blotting his eyes. He gave her a watery smile. "I must apologize. Family is everything to me. I lost my best friend, my lover, my life, when Darya died in my arms after birthing my beloved son."

Sky closed her eyes, trying to stop herself from feeling sorry for the man. She had expected him to rage at her. Perhaps slap her. Rape her. Call her names or even torture her. But not this.

She heard the rustling of paper and opened her eyes. Yerik stood and handed her another photo. She reluctantly took it.

"This is Vlad when he was three hours old. My wet nurse from Russia, bless her heart, cared for him the first seven years of his life when we lived in New York City."

The photo showed a squalling, red-faced Vlad, angry at the world. The wet nurse looked very sad. Swallowing hard, Sky set the photo down. "Why are you telling me this?"

Yerik drank more of his tea. "Because Vlad loved you."

Shock struck her. "You can't be serious!" The words came out harshly. Sky cringed, watched Yerik's eyes narrow upon her for a moment. And then, that furious look disappeared, replaced with a mild, reproachful look instead.

"You did not know?"

Sky hesitated. Vlad, when he'd cornered her at seventeen in his bedroom, professed his love of her, wanting to marry her, to have her carry his children. He'd been telling her that for a year and Sky blew him off. His cruelty and actions always spoke louder, and not of love. "Not at all," Sky lied, her hands damp and sweaty in her lap. The urge to run roared through her. She wanted to scream. This was mental and emotional torture of the worst kind. She'd never expected Alexandrov to be nice. Not to her.

"I see," he murmured, rustling through the papers. Yerik pulled one paper out of the stack and handed it to her. "You will see the date on Vlad's email to me. This was about two weeks after you arrived at the Zimmerman home. Please, read it?"

Sky unwillingly looked down at the paper.

"Read it out loud?"

She gritted her teeth, trying to control her emotions. "Papa, I have met the woman who floods my heart with such joy—" and Sky looked away, compressing her lips. She couldn't go on, terrible, raw emotions ripping through her.

Yerik stood, walked around the coffee table, gently took the paper from her hand, and read the rest of it. "…with such joy that the sun truly rises and sets upon her glorious hair that she wears like a crown of gold. I go to sleep each night, wishing she would give me just one smile, one look of yearning, the next day. I dream of her at night. Smiling at me. Laughing with me. Running in the park next door to where I live. Papa, is it possible to feel so much in love that I can barely breathe when I see her? When Jack or Marielle call her by name, I feel like my heart is going to break open, there is just so much love for her within me that goes untouched, unknown to her."

Sky gripped the arms of the chair, choking back the shock. She felt more than heard Yerik leave her side. He sat down, a pensive look in his eyes as he watched her struggling with her emotions. This time, she wasn't lying. "I-I didn't know…"

"I believe you," Yerik said softly, carefully folding up the precious email.

"Vlad once said he saw exactly how you felt because you could not hide your feelings from your face."

Grimacing, Sky raised her chin and stared at Yerik. "I've heard that from everyone." She saw him give her a kind smile and nodded as he slowly set the email on the table next to his chair, treating it as if it were the most sacred item he had in his life. "Vlad was right. But then, my son was a great observer of the human condition, just like me. He had his mother's face. She worked for the KGB and had been an undercover agent for Mother Russia. I met her by luck in St. Petersburg at an Army conference. When I saw her hair, I was smitten. But then," Yerik added wryly, fondly recalling those times, "so was every other able-bodied male officer in that room, too. Darya was a stunning, very powerful young woman. And I knew," he murmured, picking up her photo once more and fondly studying it, "that I was hopelessly, suddenly in love with her. I knew I wanted her. And I would move heaven, hell, and anything else in between to catch her attention, woo her, and make her mine."

Sky saw the parallels. Vlad had tried to get her to like him. At first, he'd bent over backwards to please her and smile at her. There wasn't anything he wouldn't do for her, whether she asked him to do it or not. Vlad had his father's genes for hunting down the victim he sought. "How long did it take until you caught her?"

Laughing pleasantly, Yerik murmured, "Two years. Two years of seeing her every chance I could, bringing her flowers, singing her old Russian love ballads, because I could play the balalaika with the best of them. I took her on long walks, asked her about herself, what she liked, what she loved. What made her cry? What made her laugh? What were her favorite colors? What was important to her? What touched her heart?" Yerik waved his hand and gave a slight shrug. "She was a crafty one, highly intelligent, not given to fools, always blunt and to the point. Darya, bless her, never let me get away with a thing. She was a strong woman, but she also had an equally soft, tender side to her as well. I fell in love with all aspects of Darya. She was interesting. She provoked me into thinking in broader terms and and exploring deeper realms. She was relentless and never gave me an inch of breathing space when I would try and become arrogant with her because I was a man." Yerik grinned and looked up at the high ceiling of mahogany timbers that trussed across it. "Darya was a woman who knew her own mind and she knew mine, as well."

Sky nodded, thinking that Vlad had two very highly intelligent, sharply observant parents. Vlad certainly was the same way, and he'd just as relentlessly pursued her as Yerik had Darya. He never stopped hunting her, wanting her. "I'm sorry she died so young," Sky said, meaning it.

"Ah, I approve of your humanity, Sky. It becomes you." Yerik's smile faded. "You see, every feeling you have is written across that very beautiful, fragile face of yours. I know you are disgusted by me. I know you hate me. And you fear me. I see the rage in your eyes as well." He sat up, elbows on his thighs, studying her with a kind look on his face. "But I hope, as I show you my family, acquaint you with my dead son's correspondence, and how he truly loved you, that you will begin to mellow a little toward me."

Sky felt her heart thud with more terror. She sank inwardly because she had always known she couldn't hide how she felt. That put her at a disadvantage here. "I don't know that it could ever happen," she rasped, holding his expectant stare. Why did Yerik have to be so likable? There was no hint of threat, violence, or danger around him as there had been around Vlad. Was his father really what she saw? Or was this nothing more than a deep mind game, a manipulation far more dangerous to her than any other she'd ever encountered?

"You don't trust me," Yerik said, his voice pained. "I cannot fault you on that. After all, I sent my best Russian soldiers to drug and kidnap you. For that traumatic event, I truly apologize." He opened his hands. "In my eyes, you were Vlad's princess, someday, to become queen of all that you see here, Sky. My son had even gone so far as to come for a visit the last month before your high school graduation and begged me to help him find a suitable set of wedding rings for you."

Sky's mouth dropped opened. "Oh, no..."

Nodding, Yerik whispered, "He truly loved you, Sky. He had my genes. Once he met the woman he loved, he would never give her up. He would somehow convince her to love him, marry him." He rose. "You look very stressed, and it is not my intent to make you feel badly. I want you to know you have complete freedom around La Paloma, my villa in the clouds of the Monte Verde." He gestured around. "There will always be a guard with you, should you go outside. But I do invite you to go outdoors. The air here is delicious. The beauty of the Costa Rican jungle is like none other in the world." He shrugged. "Who knows? Perhaps you will deign to ask me to walk with you sometime in the future? To discuss life? I do want to hear what makes you laugh. What makes you cry. My son wanted to hear those thoughts from you, but he's no longer with us. But I am." Yerik touched his heart with his hand. "You would give his father great solace if you could one day find in your heart to take such walks with me."

Her stomach rolled. Sky felt like vomiting. It had come out of nowhere. Standing, she clasped her belly. "Please, I need a bathroom. NOW!"

CHAPTER 12

June 24

LAUREN WIPED HER watering eyes, the text blurring on her laptop. She sat in the briefing room that had been converted into a war room to locate Sky. The clock on the wall read 0200, two a.m. A week had passed, and they'd found no clue to Sky's whereabouts. Lauren felt horrible, her mind imagining snatches of what she must be going through.

"Knock, knock?"

Lauren lifted her head, looking toward the opened door. She saw Alex hesitantly come in, two cups of coffee in his hands. She was too tired to raise her defenses. "What are you still doing here? I thought you'd left already."

Alex shrugged and pushed the door shut with the heel of his combat boot. "I just got done looking at a thousand photos over in another department with Master Chief Butch." He smiled tiredly and held up the cups. "Would you like some?"

Rubbing her face, she muttered, "Yeah. Thanks…"

Alex leaned across the table and placed it near her laptop. "Do you mind if I remain for a minute? Or would you like to be left alone?" He was fairly sure Lauren would send him away. For a week, they had rarely seen one another. Everyone was focused on their individual tasks. He saw Lauren lift her head, her beautiful emerald eyes red rimmed. She was exhausted. Everyone was putting in twenty-hour days. They were sleeping in chairs, head resting on their arms across a table was the norm, only going to the condo to shower and grab clean clothes.

"Have a seat. Thanks for the coffee," Lauren murmured, picking up the cup and carefully sipping from it.

Heartened, Alex sat down, placing his large hands around the cup. "I… uh… I am worried about Cal. You know I moved in with him at the condo a few days ago? That Joe told him to let me stay with him?"

"Yes." Lauren rubbed her smarting eyes. "I'm worried about him, too." Joe and Abby had flown home yesterday. They couldn't leave their children with Abby's mom any longer and had to resume their parental duties in West

Virginia. Lauren now shared their condo with Jack Driscoll, next door to where Cal and Alex stayed. Ben and Leah Gordon had reluctantly left as well, their one-year-old child needed them home in Kentucky.

Giving her a furtive look, Alex said, "I do not know that I could hold up like Cal is holding up. If my woman... I mean... If I had one..., was kidnapped and I knew she was in harm's way, I would go berserk."

"Your Ukrainian blood," Lauren suggested wryly, giving him a blunt look. She saw Alex flush. The man, despite being so tall and massive, had a teenage boy's reactions sometimes. Maybe that was upbringing. Lauren wasn't sure. She saw his strong, full mouth pucker into a boyish pout.

"Could be," he agreed.

"What are you worried about regarding Cal?"

Sitting back in the chair, Alex felt grateful just to be talking calmly with Lauren. She wasn't being defensive with him. Perhaps it was because of the sleep deprivation, it sure as hell tore the veneer off people in a hurry, and what you saw in that state was the real person. The shadows beneath her glorious eyes told him she was catching only two or three hours of sleep a night. Lauren was tired, no question, her eyes clouded, stress lines around her luscious mouth, a perpetual V between her slender eyebrows as she poured through thousands of photos trying to identify possible sites for Alexandrov's hidden villa in the clouds.

"Cal does not sleep. Oh, he goes into his bedroom, but I am a light sleeper. I hear him get up, walk the hall, pacing. Always pacing." Alex scowled and sipped some of the coffee. "Do you know how to help him?" and he gave her a searching look.

Shrugging, Lauren said, "Are you asking from a woman's perspective or are you asking what men do when they're caught in a vise?"

"I know," Alex admitted quietly, "we are very bad at talking, are we not?"

"Worse about admitting your feelings. And yes, men in general are terrible communicators. Add to the fact we're black ops, and being closed mouth is just part and parcel how a man or woman operates in that environment. Worse than a clam."

"Yes." Alex gave a huge sigh, feeling defeated and helpless. "What would you do if you were in my footsteps?"

"In your shoes," Lauren corrected, a self-deprecating grin tugged at one corner of her mouth. Alex was having a terrible time with American slang. He slaughtered it, and sometimes, it was funny as hell, but Lauren tried not to embarrass the man. He had worked just as hard, just as many hours as any of them to find Sky. And if it hadn't been for his memory and knowledge of Alexandrov, they wouldn't even be this far along in their search.

"Oh… okay," and Alex gave Lauren gave an apologetic look. "What would you do if you were in my shoes?"

Sometimes Lauren had a tough time believing Kazak was Spetsnaz. Those Russian black ops warriors were tough. There was a soft, almost tender side to Kazak, that she couldn't ignore. Lauren slowly found herself warming up to him because he was laid back and easy to get along with in the team. "Cal needs to talk, pure and simple. He needs to bawl his eyes out. Somebody needs to just hold him and let him cry." She saw Alex grow uncomfortable. "You guys really suck at emotions and showing anyone a little human care. Do you know that?"

Alex sighed. "I can listen. But if he starts to cry…," and Alex gave her a desperate look and admitted hesitantly, "it makes me very uncomfortable to hold him. I feel helpless. I do not know what to say or do."

Snorting, Lauren shoved the chair back and stood up. She stretched and began to walk, getting circulation back into her body after sitting far too long. "You know, God gave men tear ducts. Now, that isn't lost on you, Kazak, because you're a combat medic. You know anatomy." She turned, hooking her hands over her hips, giving him a bruising stare. "Tear ducts mean you can CRY, big guy. And Cal needs to cry. He's got to let it out, because anyone with a set of eyes can see it's eating him alive from the inside out." She remembered when he'd cried out on the beach shortly after Sky was kidnapped.

Alex nodded. "You women are much wiser and far stronger than any man will ever be."

Brows flying up, Lauren stood there, shocked by his quiet admittance. Alex wasn't smiling now. He was utterly honest, his eyes reflecting the truth. "God, save me. A man has actually admitted the fact. You're damned right we're stronger. We know how to work with our emotions, not sit our asses with them and pretend we don't have any." She jabbed a finger toward him. "No one can force Cal to cry. You just can't walk up to him and tell him he needs to cry and get it off his chest."

Alex nodded. "Yes, you are right." He rubbed his wrinkled brow. "But how can I talk with him, Lauren? What should I say to help him speak of what he carries?"

Lauren groaned, closed her eyes, and shook her head. The silence deepened in the room. Finally, she raised her head, her eyes narrowed on Kazak. "About the only way any of you operators are EVER going to cry is to get stone drunk out of your minds. Drink him under the table. Then, maybe he'll talk. Or if you get lucky, cry."

"No… I do not want to do that. Alcohol… well… it is a crutch."

"Obviously, you aren't Russian." Lauren walked back to her chair and sat down. "Those guys drink vodka like it's water and not alcohol."

"Which is why so many Russians have died of alcohol poisoning."

"Or pickled their livers and died early," Lauren added, sipping more coffee. She didn't want to be moved by his gesture to help Cal. The guy was
without guile. He truly cared for Cal and his predicament. And whether Lauren
wanted to admit it or not, she was touched by Alex coming to her for counsel.
Only her close circle of teammates trusted her to that depth. And Kazak was a
shadow in her life.

Alex cocked his head, studying her grim face. "If I try to trigger him to
talk, then I just sit and listen?"

"Yes, without comment. Unless he asks your opinion, then give it." She
saw the worry in the medic's large, intelligent hazel eyes. "You would act like a
witness. Just sit and listen. That's what Cal needs."

Alex compressed his lips, his brow furrowing deeply. "I have a sister, Lauren. Kira is two years younger than me." He sat up and opened the pocket on
his cammies and produced a photo of her, handing it to Lauren. "I love my
sister with my life. When she was a young nurse in the Russian Army, her unit
was attacked by Chechen terrorists. They killed all the men who were already
injured there at the medical forward operating base. Then they killed the
doctors. They gathered up all the nurses and they were all gang raped repeatedly. Many of them died of internal hemorrhage." His voice fell and emotions
clearly showed in his thickened tone. "Kira was never the same after that. I was
not there. I felt guilty because I was supposed to protect my sister, and I could
not. She became a shadow of herself. When I finally got emergency leave to fly
home, to be at her side at the St. Petersburg hospital, I was nothing but a mess
of emotions. When I sat with her, tried to find out what happened, she was like
a wooden doll. She refused to speak of it."

He gave Lauren a sad look. "I am not very good at getting anyone to talk.
Not even my sweet, loving sister." Alex rubbed his face and rasped, "It was me
who cried. I cried for her, for all the pain she experienced, the terror she felt
being violated like that. I cried for myself because our parents were gone. We
had very little family left, just far distant cousins. Kira had no one. I visited her
every day for five days. Every day I asked her so many questions. She just laid
there in bed, her eyes blank, as if her soul had been murdered. And perhaps it
has been."

"God," Lauren whispered, shaken. "I didn't know this, Alex…" Lauren
managed, her voice strangled. She reached out, briefly touching his hand that
had curled into a fist on the table as he'd spoken about Kira. "I'm so sorry…"
Lauren choked, her throat tightening with unexpected emotions. She saw him
raise his head when she'd grazed his thick, hard knuckles. There was something

in his darkened eyes that she couldn't decipher, but whatever it was, it was warm and good, flowing around her like an invisible embrace. She had to be tired and wasn't reading Alex accurately. She must be exhausted so much that she was beginning to hallucinate, which is what sleep deprivation spiraled into.

"That is why I asked you for advice about Cal. I am not good at this. Now you know why. I am terrible at it. But I lay in bed listening to Cal pace. I swear by all that is holy," and Alex pressed his hand to his broad chest, "I can FEEL how he is feeling."

Lauren grunted, pulling her hand back, her fingers tingling where she'd connected with Kazak's fist. "I understand now," she murmured. "But you're being too hard on yourself. There's horrible shock after being raped, Alex. Surely you know that because you're a combat medic? Or do they just teach you how to fix men and not women out on the battlefield?"

"No… it is male oriented," he admitted. "But I took other courses regarding women, pregnancy, and childbirth, because I was out in the field. Often, women in remote villages needed help of that kind. I wanted to be able to render them aid." He smiled a little. "I have delivered six babies to date. They all lived."

Lauren felt her heart open. It was the strangest, most uncomfortable feeling she'd ever had. "You'd be good with babies," she muttered. "You've got an obvious tender side."

"Is that a compliment?"

Lauren gave him a flat stare. "Well it wasn't an insult, Kazak." She watched him blush and avoid her gaze for a moment. *Unbelievable.* The guy wore his heart on his sleeve. Who knew? Kazak wasn't like the Spetsnaz she'd met. Lauren wrote it off to the fact he was a medic and therefore, passionate about saving lives, helping to aid those who suffered. He had a more sensitive conscience, was all.

"Look, just ask Cal how he's doing. Ask if there's anything you can do for him. All right? That should get the ball rolling." Lauren sighed. "I'm so damned tired, I'm going to keel over."

"Me too." Alex rose. "May I will drive you home?"

Usually, Lauren hitched a ride with anyone else but Alex. Tonight, she felt differently. Jack, her roommate, had already left, and she had no way to get home. Probably because she was so rummy she couldn't add two and two together, her usual defensiveness wasn't in place. "Yeah, fine. Let's get the hell out of here…"

June 25

CAL SAT OUT on the picnic table on the sun deck, looking at the cold, glimmering stars overhead. It was 0300, the middle of the night. He'd tried to sleep, tossed and turned. He imagined Sky being tortured by Yerik Alexandrov. It tore him up. He couldn't stop the terrible scenes he imagined that kept running through his sleep deprived brain. Cal allowed himself to be soothed by the gentle lap of ocean slapping against the huge rocks that surrounded Coronado Island, guardians that stopped it from being eaten away by the Pacific Ocean. He sat in his pajama bottoms, perched on the tabletop, his feet resting on the bench below. He leaned his elbows onto his thighs, hands clasped between his opened legs. His heart felt like ground up, raw meat. It never stopped hurting. In the last week, Cal had made grief his best friend. The frustration ate at him until all he wanted to do was scream and go ballistic.

His team, Lauren, Jack, and Alex were working like dogs twenty hours a day, nonstop. Master Chief Butch had thrown several SEALs down on sick leave onto the project as well, doing grunt work for them, going through thousands of pieces of intel. He heard the rear door open and quietly closed. Sensing it was Alex, he turned. There was enough light from the kitchen night light to see the medic's tall, muscular figure. Alex wore a pair of loose shorts, naked from the waist up. He looked exhausted.

"Why don't you go back to bed," Cal growled in way of greeting as he Cal and sat on the picnic table with him.

"Could not sleep," Alex said thickly, rubbing his face tiredly.

Snorting Cal said, "Yeah. Fuckin' disease at this point for me."

Alex wiped his watering eyes. "Want to talk about it?"

Rubbing his hands down his thighs, Cal muttered, "I'm just frustrated, Alex. Frustrated we haven't found a damn trace of that seaplane. Or where the hell it went."

"It did not help that the satellite passing over Central America had already flown over that area minutes earlier. It left a hole we could not fill in." Alex glanced at Cal's hard profile. He could see the anxiety, the worry, in his narrowed eyes, the way his mouth was taut and thinned. Even his clasped hands were tight. He reached out, patting Cal's taut shoulder. "We will find Sky. I know we will." Removing his hand, he anchored his elbows on his thighs as well. The Pacific Ocean felt calming to Alex. He liked the lapping of the water against the rocks that were no more than a hundred feet away from where the condo had been built.

"We need a break," Cal uttered. "Something… anything…"

"I know," Alex rasped. "I have been working with this Lieutenant Anderson on the comms satellite that picks up cell phone, radio, and land line traffic. Yesterday, I asked Butch to get the satellite parked over Central America. Anderson knows Russian. She is the one that's been picking up more Russian traffic in that region of late. We both felt if we could get the satellites in synchronous orbit so they remained over that area, we would have a better chance of finding something."

"I didn't know you'd have any Russian being spoken in Central America. Maybe South America," Cal uttered.

Alex snorted. "Russian mafia is spreading out like a cancer through all Central and South America. The mafia is now on both coasts of the U.S. They want to take those markets away from the Latin drug lords." Alex rubbed his hands slowly together as he watched the lights glimmer along the curve of the San Diego Bay. Ordinarily, he would be mesmerized by watching the beautiful colored lights dancing off the glassy surface of the ocean, but tonight, Alex wanted to try and reach Cal, to help him. He kept Lauren's advice about letting Cal speak and answer only when appropriate in the front of his mind. "In fact," he added, "the West Coast leader of the Russian Mafia has more or less claimed Central America as his territory."

Cal cocked his head, looking at Alex's profile. "And Alexandrov has claimed Peru?"

"Oh, no. Yerik Alexandrov wanted all of South America," Alex said wryly. "His son Vlad often bragged that other teams just like ours were infiltrating Brazil, Columbia, and Belize. No, Alexandrov is like Genghis Khan of Mongolia: he wants to dominate the whole world of drug trade on that continent."

Snorting, Cal muttered, "You think these two kingpins will end up fighting one another someday after they eradicate the Latin drug lords?"

"I do not know."

"Well," Cal said bleakly, "look at it another way: the Latin drug lords we've been trying to kill, or capture have a new, stronger enemy: Russians who want to wipe them off the face of the earth. Shows you the savageness in this battle."

"Yes," Alex murmured, "and they are far more lethal, far more ready to put a gun to their heads and kill them. Russians do not want to capture the drug lords. They want to scour the earth of them."

"No need to tell me how nasty Russians can be," Cal said.

"We will find Sky. You need to hold onto that," Alex urged him quietly. He saw the corner of Cal's mouth flex, as if he'd just poked an open wound in him and poured salt in into it. "Hold your faith, my friend. I know Sky looks fragile, but her spirit is strong."

"I can't close my eyes at night, Alex. All I see is Alexandrov torturing her. The bastard is sadistic. Just like his son. Sometimes... sometimes I wish I didn't know what I know about the torture methods Russians use on their enemies."

"I saw Vlad toy with people who he wanted to manipulate or wanted something from," Alex offered quietly. "There was a Quechua chief in a particular village in Peru. He was very powerful, well known and beloved by the people in the region. Vlad wanted his cooperation. He knew if we went in guns blazing and killing the chief, we would not get the cooperation of the villagers who were carrying sacks of cocaine down trails through the jungle. Usually, Vlad would grab a daughter of a chief, tear her clothes off in front of the father and his village, and rape her. That was his usual tactic." Alex's mouth turned downward. "But with this one chief, he was very different. He spent a month manipulating him, becoming a friend, bringing gifts to him and food to his family. He played it smart, Cal. There was never any violence, which surprised me, because Vlad took a scorched earth policy with most of the Indian villages."

"Why did he change tactics?"

"Because it served his purpose. The chief eventually granted him permission to use those jungle trails. Vlad brought in medicine to help his people, and of course, I and Nik were the ones who were administering it. We were able to vaccinate all the children, and I helped deliver two babies in the village."

"So, you're saying Alexandrov didn't kill or rape anyone?"

"That is what I am saying. And," Alex turned and looked Cal in the eyes, "Vlad loved Sky. I know you do not want to hear that, but the man was insanely in love with her. That is all he ever talked about at night when we made camp. He carried several photos of her. He would often show us her photo, tell us stories of how he lived with her while growing up."

Cal muttered, sitting up, "I wasn't aware…"

Alex shrugged. "I did not think it was important to tell you this, at first. I did not want to hurt you or her. I know Sky never loved him, she feared him, and she was right to do so."

"What are you saying?" Cal demanded, turning fully toward him. "What does this mean?"

Shrugging, Alex said, "I really do not know. But I can conjecture. Vlad loved Sky. He said his father knew all about his plans to ask her to marry him when they graduated from high school. Vlad even bought a set of wedding rings and was going to ask her to be his wife. And he wanted to get her pregnant right away, to give him big, strong sons. That was his dream. He talked to our team about it endlessly."

Blinking, Cal felt a surge of terror along with hope. "His father knew all about this?"

"Of course. The Zimmerman family had no idea what kind of monster and master manipulator they had under their roof. Vlad was was in constant touch with his father in New York City by email and cell phone, and often Vlad sent photos he'd taken of Sky to his father."

Cal felt his stomach twist. He felt sick. He slowly got off the picnic table, the concrete cold beneath his bare feet as he considered the new information. "So the elder Alexandrov knew his son was in love with Sky?"

"Yes," Alex admitted. "And I did not think this was important enough to tell you before. But now, I do." He watched Cal thinking about the information, his hands tense on his hips as he stared out at the black water, unseen by the moonless night.

"And the bastard just kidnapped her."

"Yes."

"Why? Do you think it's because Alexandrov believed Sky killed Vlad?"

"Doubtful. I am sure Yerik has secret, undetected ties into the U.S. government. I heard Vlad once brag that his father had moles inside the State Department, inside NSA and the CIA. He can find out who really killed his son. I am sure Yerik knows by now it was not Sky."

Cal began to pace. "Then why the hell did he kidnap Sky? This doesn't make any sense to me, Alex."

Alex gave him a sympathetic look. "A very old Russian way of seeing the world, Cal. Family," he rasped softly.

"What?" Cal halted, confused. "What the hell are you saying?"

"Alexandrov had seen his son, who was madly in love with Sky, buy wedding rings for her. I am sure there were many emails and phone calls between father and son about her, about how happy he was to be in love with Sky. Yerik helped Vlad pick out those rings. He was already planning to have a huge wedding for his son in New York City. From the elder's point of view, Cal, Sky was already his daughter-in-law."

"Only," Cal snarled, feeling rage flow through him, "Vlad made several fatal mistakes. He cornered Sky in her bedroom. He damned near raped her, Alex. And when she pushed him away and started screaming for help, her foster father, Jack Zimmerman, broke down that door to see what was wrong. Vlad shot him point blank. And then, Marielle, his wife, ran in. Vlad murdered her on the spot. Sky saw it all. She escaped out a window after hitting Vlad with a bronze statue, nearly knocking him out. That's how she got away and ran to a neighboring house and called 911."

Heaving a sigh, Alex said, "He never told us about that part of it at all. All we heard was how deeply in love he was with her. His dreams of her and a having a large family."

"That explains why he never stopped hunting for her then," Cal growled. It made so much more sense to him now. What a sick, obsessed sonofabitch

Vladimir Alexandrov really was. Sky must have felt tortured by knowing he was stalking her no matter where she tried to hide in the world. He turned, looking over his shoulder at Alex, who looked agitated. "So, when Sky went missing, I wonder if the father ever knew what Vlad had done to her? That he'd murdered two people. Tried to rape Sky? I wonder what he told his father?"

"I do not know." He shrugged. "Remember? Vlad was a like his father. He could have condoned such acts. None of us know…"

Cal said, "I do know that when Vlad escaped the police, he fled back to New York City. His father gave him new a new identity, a new passport, and sent him to Russia to become trained as an officer in the Russian army. Yerik had many powerful ties with Spetsnaz, because he was once in the Psy Ops branch as an officer himself. He wanted his son to follow in his footsteps, and he did. It kept Vlad safe and secure, the trail on him and the murders of the Zimmerman's growing cold, and eventually being dropped by the Trenton police department."

"None of us knew this," Alex said, apology in his tone.

"Okay," Cal muttered wearily, "how does this affect Sky's status right now? Is Yerik torturing her if he saw her as a prospective daughter-in-law?"

"That is what I have been thinking a great deal about," Alex said hesitantly. He opened his hands. "Russians value family above all other things. They will kill for family. They will protect family with their own life if they need too. They are fierce about family, caring for and protecting them."

Cal gave him a scowl. "Are you saying that Alexandrov kidnapped Sky because he STILL sees her as his daughter-in-law? Even though Vlad and her never married?"

"I cannot be sure, but that is my present thinking," Alex admitted. "And if that is so, he is not going to torture her. He would, instead, be nice to her. Try to convince her that he is her father-in-law, that he is there to take care of her. She is like family property to him. I'm sure he knows Sky did not kill Vlad. If that had happened, then yes, I would think he would torture and kill her. But knowing what I heard Vlad say constantly, I do not think in my heart that Yerik Alexandrov is going to harm Sky."

"What's he going to do with her, then?" Cal demanded angrily.

"Alexandrov the father," Alex said, "he collects things. He collects fish for his aquarium. He is a falconer, and he collects raptors from around the world and flies them. I believe," and Alex gave him a sympathetic look, "that he has now collected Sky, made her a part of his family, whether she knows it or not. What he has in store for her, I cannot guess. But I earnestly believe, Cal, he is NOT torturing her."

"Not physically," Cal rasped, pacing, his head down, his mind in turmoil, relief trickling through him. "Sky is being brainwashed by the bastard, then. She's being lulled into being a prisoner somewhere, being cared for, fed, and hidden. It's Stockholm Syndrome." He halted and stared at Alex. "Do you think she realizes this?"

"I do not know. I think she fears Yerik even more than Vlad. After all, his bad seed of a son was gotten directly from the father's rotten genes. Yerik is far more of a mind torturer than his son could ever have possibly been. He's smoother, more elegant, and quieter about the kind of mind games he will employ on Sky. I worry she will not realize it. I worry, like all those who are captured for a long period of time, she will develop feelings of trust or affection towards her captor."

Cal cursed, staring out at the black water. "Fuck."

"At least, Sky is not being physically tortured."

Running his fingers through his hair, Cal shook his head. "That would be a huge relief to me. She's being tortured in other ways, though. Far more lethal to her sanity in the long term."

"I am afraid so. In time, if we cannot find her soon enough, Sky may come to see Yerik as her benefactor. She may see him as a kind father figure she never had. He will give her family, Cal. Something Sky never had and always yearned for."

"Sonofabitch!" Cal felt terror clawing up through his chest. He glared over at Alex. "Is there anything else you're not telling me? Us?"

"No. That is it. I honestly did not feel this was important until now. The fact that Alexandrov has gone to ground, that we can find NO evidence of him, forces me to come to this conclusion and to tell you this, Cal. I believe Alexandrov has Sky somewhere in Central America. We have sources telling us he has not been at his New York penthouse for over a week. Yerik is with her. And the longer he stays away from New York City, that tells me he is working to brainwash Sky into believing she is his family, that he has her best interests at heart. He will impress upon her that Vlad, who loved her with his life, would have wanted her to be a part of the family, even though she never formally married him. In Yerik's eyes, Vlad and Sky were already married. The ceremony was just a formality. In other words, he sees her as blood. Family blood."

Cal stared disbelievingly at Alex as he digested the man's impassioned words. "That is sick. Absolutely sick..."

"Vlad was insane," Alex said, shaking his head. "The father, worse."

"So, now it's not a race to save her physical life? It's a battle for her heart, her mind?" *Her soul.* Cal reeled internally, his emotions raging. Would Sky realize what was happening? That she was a prisoner in a gilded cage? Would she still try to escape? Find a way out? A way to contact him?

"Listen to me," Alex said heavily, getting up, walking over to Cal and placing his hands on his slumped shoulders. "What this REALLY comes down to is if Sky's love for you outweighs anything Alexandrov can do to convince her otherwise. She must love you more, to see through the manipulation he is pulling on her. If Sky loves you more, she WILL try to escape. She will reject Alexandrov's games, although Sky must be very careful and not show her true feelings." He gave Cal a gentle shake and released him. "Now, you must go to bed. Put the torture scenes away. We must refocus and reorient ourselves to a new way of seeing her abduction tomorrow morning."

CHAPTER 13

July 1

"COME, SKY, I have something that will cheer you up." Yerik smiled and held out his hand to her after they had eaten lunch together on the outdoor patio. The pergola overhead was covered with thick vines that grew colorful orange trumpet flowers, their fragrance enveloping the noontime area.

Sky set her linen napkin aside and stood, repelled by him offering his hand. She didn't want to touch him. "I'm very tired," she protested. Two weeks had passed, and she realized that he was not going to physically torture her. At least, not yet. Still, Sky did not trust the Russian at all. Yerik had been nothing but kind, thoughtful and seemed truly invested in her welfare and state of mind. When she told him irritably that she hated wearing the clothes he insisted she wear, he asked what she'd like to wear instead. And she pushed further and demanded to be able to wear a bra and panties. He'd eagerly seen to her request. Her heart ached for Cal. She lay in a beautifully appointed apartment, reminiscent of the condo she'd stayed at in Coronado, with Japanese-like decor. In fact, the entire massive villa, with the exception of the Russian sex slaves he kept, was all in the same spare, tasteful design.

"Please?" he pleaded. "I promise you, this is worth seeing."

Grimacing, Sky rose. The servant pulled her chair back so she could stand. She wanted for nothing. The best of food. Constant servants to do her bidding. If she wanted a glass of guava juice, all she had to do was asked for it. Yerik discovered her passion for board games. Every evening, after dinner, they would play Monopoly or Scrabble. She found him to be warm, engaging, and even an enjoyable companion. He'd even made her laugh last night. A first. The look on his face was one of humble pleading. His green eyes danced with mirth, and she had come to realize when Yerik had that expression, he had a surprise of some kind in store for her.

"I promise," he said, "you will be awed. You will love what I show you."

Sky refused to touch Yerik. She shied away from any kind of close contact with him. He seemed to realize her discomfort and dropped his hand. Yerik gave a sharp order in Russian to a man she'd not seen here at the villa before.

He snapped to attention and did an about face and quickly left the pergola. "You have a surprise for me, don't you?"

He grinned. "Vlad had said you were extraordinarily observant of people, and he was absolutely right." Yerik gestured for her to come around the table. "Come, walk with me? I'm going to show you a new path to a place you have not been before. I think you will be magically transported by what you see." He waited patiently for her to walk around the table. Yerik thought the Levi's she wore, the tennis shoes, and the dark green tee made her look less beautiful. But Sky was more at ease wearing loose, comfortable American clothes that were not sexy or revealing. Above all, Yerik wanted her to be relaxed. Happy even, although she rarely smiled. He could see Sky was grieving for the man she was going to marry. And every day, he schemed to find ways to get her mind and heart off that man and centered on him, on the fact that she was HIS family, whether she accepted it yet or not.

The flagstone path was three feet wide, and Sky had begun walking it at least once a day with Yerik because she hated being indoors so much. He'd been good for his word: she had the freedom to range in or outside the massive villa hidden beneath a triple canopy of jungle trees. He'd let her know she was in Costa Rica. If she asked a question, he'd usually answer it. And Sky kept a mind map in her head of the villa's layout. Yerik had not told her where she was in Costa Rica, but she knew from her many walks outside the villa, casing the place, understanding her prison, that it was in a mountainous area. Computers were nowhere to be found. She'd have quickly figured out where she was with Google GPS.

The sun was hidden by soft, gossamer clouds at noon. Sky had come to realize the jungle breathed in and out, just like a human being. Each morning the clouds floated above the tops of the trees, silent, twisting, graceful and beautiful to watch. By noon, the low hanging clouds were burned off by the intense equatorial sunlight. The sky would turn a pale blue and then, around four p.m., almost like clockwork, thunderstorms would pop up and roll noisily over the area. As they walked, she noticed that Yerik always shortened his stride for her sake. He was a tall, broad-shouldered man who reminded her so much of Vlad. Sometimes, when Yerik caught her off guard, she would see Vlad's intense face staring at her, not his. It always frightened Sky.

"Today, I'll show you another passion of mine," Yerik said, excitement in his deep voice.

The path paralleled the deep, quiet green river on the eastern side of the villa. Sky had found it calming to sit by the water. The path winded downward on a gentle slope. On either side of the carefully maintained and swept path, jungle rose over a hundred feet tall. Sky realized it was a jungle she could run through. It had lots of trees, but very few bushes beneath them because the sunlight couldn't penetrate to the jungle floor. It made it possible for her to escape. But she had to know where she was at, where there might be a highway or road, to find civilization. To get help. To get home to Cal and into his arms. To be held, loved, and cared for once more. Sky yearned for him, crying herself to sleep nearly every night, missing him so much.

At night, she ached with loneliness, thinking of Cal holding her, remembering the times they'd made love, the intimacy so strong and beautiful between them. Sky knew Cal was going crazy trying to locate her. She knew Jack Driscoll's team would be deeply involved in trying to find her. Alex could help them in ways no one else could because he had run with Vlad's team in Peru. She took a deep breath, trying to stay ahead in the fucking mind game that Yerik played with her. Never once did she fall for his kind look or his tearful, emotional moments when he spoke about his dead son. None of it touched her. She wouldn't allow it. But she was doing her damnedest not to let him see that. If he thought she was a helpless victim incapable of escaping, she would let him think that, and eventually he'd let down his guard. Already, only one soldier remained in sight when she walked outdoors. There used to be two guards. When she did escape, it would catch them all by surprise. And Sky swore she would escape, she would or die trying. It sickened her to be with Yerik daily. It was like rubbing salt in the open wound of her torn, bleeding heart. Yerik had spawned Vlad. He had been bad seed, evil and sadistic. Sky never forgot for a moment that that bad seed had come directly from Yerik.

"Ah, here we are," he announced proudly as they walked around a long, gentle curve in the path that revealed a large, oval meadow.

Sky looked and saw huge wire cages that stood ten feet tall and probably twenty feet wide. There were birds in each of them. Frowning, she counted fifteen such cages. They were all arranged neatly beneath a huge tin roof that protected them from the rain. "What are these?" she wondered. Gazing around, Sky had never realized this meadow existed. It was just another piece of the puzzle of trying to find out where she was at, what escape routes were available.

"My dear daughter-in-law," Yerik said grandly, "welcome to my world of falconry."

Frowning, Sky winced inwardly. For the last week, he'd been calling her that, as if it were a beloved term of endearment, he was bestowing upon her. She hated every time he said it. Her lips thinned, but Sky didn't want to upset Yerik. She'd seen him slap a servant who had not brought his coffee soon enough to him. She'd seen bruises on beautiful Catarina's arms two mornings ago. Sky knew Yerik slept with one of his three sex slaves every night, without fail. Her heart wrung with agony over their plight. Guiltily, she was relieved that Yerik had not made any type of sexual advance toward her. At least not yet. And she hoped with all her heart and soul that he never touched her, because she'd fight back. She'd never allow Yerik to rape her. Sky would die first. But he didn't know that, and she wasn't going to broadcast it, either.

Every room had four cameras in it. She knew that in some hidden room, guards monitored the video feeds of the complex on over forty television screens. And Sky was sure some Russian soldier was watching her sleep at night. It was disconcerting, invasive, triggering all of Sky's paranoia. Vlad had tried to get into her bedroom at least once a month when she was at the Zimmerman household. She never slept well knowing he was stalking her, always keeping her door locked. Sky was afraid to tell her foster parents about it, for fear of being blamed because Vlad had lived with them much longer than she had. Sky had thought they would believe whatever lie he told them. Then, she would be kicked out of the house, out of their lives. And Sky couldn't bear that, because for the first time in her life, she was being loved, as if she was their child.

She followed Yerik down the path. There were two men waiting for them with heavy leather gauntlets on their left arms. The taller man, a thin Latino, stepped forward, producing two more gloves and gave them to Yerik.

"My dear," Yerik murmured, "this is known as a gauntlet. It is a specially designed glove to go on like this," and he pulled his onto his left arm. The leather was supple, yet thick. He wiggled his fingers and pulled the cuff of the glove halfway up his forearm. "Now, you must put yours on."

Sky gritted her teeth as he picked up her hand. His fingers were long and smooth. Every morning before breakfast, Yerik has his hands manicured, clear nail polish brushed on his fingernails, his feet massaged by one of his female servants. She wanted to jerk her hand out of his, but forced herself not to react as he gently pulled the gauntlet over her hand and settled it expertly around her lower forearm.

"There!" Yerik murmured, pleased as he stood back and observed how well the glove fit her. "Now, you look like a falconer." He gazed over at the thin Latino. "Juan, bring me Casca."

"Si, Don Tobar," and he quickly turned, running to a second set of cages behind the first row.

"Now," Yerik said in a conspiratorial tone as he waited for the raptor to be brought to him, "you watch what I do, Sky. And then, once I have taught you, we will transfer the White Hawk, a personal favorite of mine, to your glove. She's a beautiful raptor found only in Central and South America. Her favorite haunts are woodlands such as these."

"Okay," she said, seeing the man return with a white hawk with black banding on its wings and a black bar across its white tail. It's beak and legs were yellow.

As the hawk cried out, it sounded like a bleating goat to Sky. The raptor opened its wings that appeared to be about four and half feet in length, which made Sky gasp. It was a big raptor.

"Do not be afraid," Yerik said with a smile. "This is Casca. She is a three-year-old female White Hawk. Females are larger than males. Her wingspan is nearly five feet. She is impressive, is she not?"

Sky nodded. The hawk's eyes were brown, sharp and missing nothing. Her long, yellow claws were dug deeply into the falconer's glove, and she saw why they were padded in order to protect a person's arm. "She's huge."

"She is a Buteo hawk, Daughter. If you have ever seen a Red Tail hawk? They are near the same size to one another. She weighs around 2.7 pounds and she prefers reptiles, is a lethal snake killer, and will indulge upon small mammals, also. If she could not find any other food, she would dine relentlessly on insects found in the woodlands where she ranges." Yerik grinned. "I like to fly her against snakes. She is phenomenally skilled at killing them. It is quite a spectacle in and of itself. Reminds me of the gladiatorial fights in Rome's famous arena." He held out his glove and the falconer placed his nearby. The White Hawk hopped over to Yerik's glove.

Sky saw the hawk had soft leather jesses around her stout, strong looking yellow legs. Yerik casually wrapped the jesses around two fingers of his glove and proudly turned, smiling toward her.

"Now, my dear, I will transfer Casca to your glove. It's important that you give her an unmoving perch so she can relax and not have to be flapping around, trying to always get her balance. Rest your elbow against your hip. It will steady your forearm and will not tire you out as quickly. Once I make the transfer, just quietly and slowly reach up for her jesses and unwind them from around my fingers. That way, if she begins to flap or try to fly away during the transfer, I still have a hold of her jesses and she cannot escape."

Sky felt sorry for the beautiful, huge hawk. She too was a captive of Yerik's. The transfer went without incident. After wrapping the jesses around three of her fingers, Yerik nodded, pride in his eyes.

"This was one thing I could never share with Vlad. I had him put into foster care at a very young age to protect his life against my enemy factions who would have loved to have kidnapped and killed him." Yerik sighed. "By giving up my son, though it was to keep him hidden from other Russians who were fighting me for supremacy in our mafia, I gave up much." His eyes twinkled. "But at least I get to share this passion of mine with you, daughter. Vlad would be happy that you are here, learning how to work with hawks and falcons."

Her stomach turned, but Sky only nodded. She hated that he called her daughter or daughter-in-law. The man was insane. Did Yerik think she was falling for that manipulation? That she was a part of his evil, sadistic family? Sky smiled slightly. She'd ruthlessly observed Yerik, and it was something she was good at because she'd developed the ability early on as a child. It kept her from getting abused by her drugged-out father. Later, it kept her safe from Vlad's repeated, constant attempts to touch her, try to kiss her or catch her in a closet where she couldn't escape from him. "I didn't know Vlad had an interest in falconry."

"No, you wouldn't. He loved you, but there were many secrets he carried. I would send him photos and videos to his cell phone when I would fly a hawk or falcon from one of my mews. He got to enjoy it secondarily." Yerik's voice dropped and he smiled softly at her. "You have NO idea how much this day means to me, Sky. To see you standing there…," and he turned away, quickly wiping his eyes.

She wanted to vomit. Sky tried so hard to not allow her reaction to show. When Yerik turned around to look at her once more, he shrugged.

"I can see you are touched by this, also, Sky."

"I am," she forced out, trying to sound properly emotional. "I hope Vlad is watching us. Seeing this day unfold, I'm sure he's happy about it." Sky saw Yerik's face grow grief-stricken. More tears glimmered in his eyes, threatening to fall.

"You have no idea what your words, spoken from your heart, mean to me," and Yerik started to reach out, but stopped himself. Allowing his hand to fall to his side, he rallied. "Come, I want you to fly Casca. I will walk to the other end of the flight oval. Juan will stay with you, teach you how to launch her and how to stand to allow her to fly back to your gauntlet."

Her stomach rolled with nausea. Sky was relieved when Yerik turned and walked quickly to the other end of the quarter mile oval carved out of the jungle that surrounded them. She vaguely touched her belly, feeling the nausea finally subside, blaming it on her careening nerves tearing through her. She hated Alexandrov. And worse, he'd almost reached out to touch her in his moment of emotional weakness. She NEVER wanted him to touch her! Not EVER!

WHEN SKY ARRIVED at the villa an hour later, she saw a petite woman with black hair piled up on her head waiting for them in the den. She wore a white lab coat over a conservative blue pant suit. She didn't recognize her, but Yerik seemed pleased to see her as he walked into the den.

"Ah, Dr. Allegra Zapato! Welcome, welcome. Thank you for taking the time from your busy practice to come for a visit. Come, I want to introduce you to a very dear friend of mine, Sky Lambert. Sky, this is Dr. Zapato."

Sky moved forward and shook the doctor's hand. The woman was in her mid-forties, attractive, with light brown eyes. She was petite and shorter than Sky. Allegra's hands were long and thin. "Hello, Dr. Zapato."

"Now," Yerik said, smiling at them, "she is a very, very famous doctor from San Jose, where she has a huge practice. I've persuaded Allegra to allow me to fly her by helicopter up to the villa to come and give you a physical, my dear."

Blinking, Sky frowned. "Why?" She looked at the doctor, who seemed tense. Her golden face was neutral, however, her full lips somewhat compressed.

"My dear child," Yerik murmured, "you've been throwing up and you are saying you are tired nearly every afternoon. I am concerned for you, of course. I have brought you the best woman physician in Central America to take a few blood tests, a urine sample, and perform a quick physical exam to ensure you are all right." He gave her a pleading look. "Sky, I have just found you. Your health is important to me for many reasons. Please? Will you go with the doctor? I am told this won't take long. And you will make me very, very happy."

Sky frowned. She was vomiting because her nerves were raw and on edge. She was exhausted by midday because she couldn't sleep at night knowing a man was watching her on a video. But she couldn't say any of that. "Well... all right." Maybe, just maybe, the doctor would give her information she could use.

"Oh," Yerik said, sliding his hand around Allegra's elbow, "I must be forthcoming and tell you, doctor, that the examination room has cameras and audio. In all fairness to you, I always have such sessions taped. It stops assumptions and I can view the video at my leisure. That way, we are on the same page. Yes?"

Sky saw the doctor frown slightly.

"Of course, Don Tobar. I don't normally allow such a thing, but if you insist..."

Yerik led her toward the stairs where the butler stood. "You must understand, Doctor, that Sky is very, very important to me. We had spoken earlier of what I wanted done for her. You do remember our conversation?"

"Yes, of course I do," Allegra said, pulling her elbow away from his hand and taking the stairs in her sensible white sandals. "I will do as you directed."

"Wonderful," Yerik murmured. He smiled as Sky took the steps, following the butler and doctor.

Sky dressed in a pink, knee length gown in the bathroom next to the examination room. She hadn't known until right now that this medical room had existed. It seemed to her as if this place was a small city that had exactly what it needed to exist without outside help. Even the electricity was created by massive generators, quiet and far away from the main house. In the exam room, there was another woman, Galena Vidales, an RN, who was there to assist Allegra. Sky thought it strange, and she was wary. Were these two women working for Alexandrov? The placed was bugged and cameras were rolling. She couldn't just speak openly and directly question either of them. Nurse Vidales gestured for her to come sit on the end of the massive examination table. Sky did so. She had peed in the bottle while changing, and handed it to the nurse, who thanked her. Several vials of blood were drawn from her.

The women were efficient but said little. She felt the tension in the room. No one liked being videotaped. Allegra gave her a slight smile as she listened to her heart, to her lungs, and pronounced her healthy and normal.

"Please lie down," the doctor instructed. She pulled out metal stirrups from the end of the examination table.

Sky knew what they were going to do. "No."

The doctor looked harried. "A pelvic exam in a natural part of this because you are a woman. I must make ensure you do not have cervical cancer."

Sky hated anyone touching her down there. Memories of Vlad's attack on her, roughly shoving his fingers up into her, tearing at her, making her bleed, made her cringe. She hesitated.

Allegra patted her gowned thigh. "Sky, I will be very gentle. This will take no time at all. I will just examine your uterus, check for fibroids or any other possible abnormalities. How long has it been since you had such an exam?"

Sky liked Allegra. She trusted her because she was a woman. "Well," she stumbled, "not for a long time. I hate for a man to touch me…" The last time was when she'd endured a physical examination shortly after entering the Army.

Allegra nodded, giving her a softened look. "Well, then, let us just ease into this? The nurse handed her a form to fill out on a clipboard. "First, let's just discuss your menstrual cycle. The time of the month it comes. It's regularity? Any problems during menses? Clots? Excessive bleeding? Perhaps as I ask these questions, you will begin to relax a bit, eh?"

Nodding, Sky said, "I'll try. I'm sorry. I'm just… well… sensitive about it, is all."

"And Don Tobar was worried about your vomiting. You have thrown up seven times since you have arrived here. He's concerned about that. Can you tell me if you have ever had ulcers?"

Sky shook her head. "No. No ulcers. When I get upset, really upset, I throw up. I've done that ever since I can remember." She threw up a lot as a child.

"Ah, you are one of those unfortunate people who has a very sensitive vagal nerve response. When you get upset, do you first feel it in your stomach? Do you feel nausea?"

Sky rolled her eyes. "Exactly like that. I hate it, but I can't control or stop it."

Patting her arm, Allegra murmured, "You poor child. Of course, you can't control it. Our vagal nerve connects to our stomach. If a person experiences any type of trauma, sheer terror, or a life-or-death situation, it is normal to throw up after it has happened. It is a human response to a dire threat."

Sky chewed on her lower lip. The last two weeks had been a special hell on her. She felt as if she were teetering on the edge of an abyss where, if she fell into it, she knew she'd die. And she didn't want to die. If anything, her strong sense of survival had kicked in and she wanted to get home to Cal. To love him. To care for him as much as he cared for her. She shrugged. "Stress will do it," she quietly agreed.

"So, no gastrointestinal issues?"

"No... none."

"Good, then this is nothing to worry about." Allegra smiled a little sadly. "You are simply a very sensitive person, is all."

"Lucky me," Sky griped, giving her a grin, feeling the doctor's sincere warmth and concern about her.

"Well, let's move on, shall we?" Allegra said sympathetically. "Can you tell me about your period?"

Sky hated even talking about herself. She knew it was all going to be taped. She wouldn't put it past Yerik to be in the video room, watching and listening intently right now. It made her skin crawl. She felt invaded. Again, as when Vlad had pinned her down on the bed, ripping her panties off her, plunging his fingers deep into her as she screamed, she had no control over the situation. That sense of helplessness snaked through her.

"I... well... six, maybe seven weeks ago, I think."

"Do you skip periods?"

"When I'm under stress? Yes."

Allegra wrote quickly. She looked up. "And you have been under stress the last two or three weeks, yes? You mentioned earlier you were?"

Sky deadpanned her expression. She'd like to tell Allegra she'd recently been drugged, kidnapped, and was now a prisoner of a sadistic monster who was listening to every word she said. That wouldn't go over well on the video feed, however. "Yes, under tremendous stress," she murmured, hoping Allegra wouldn't push the issue and ask why she was so stressed out.

"Does this happen often? With stress, you skip a menstrual cycle?"

"All the time," Sky answered, emotion in her voice. She'd been in the military. During helicopter training with the Black Hawk, she'd gone five months without a period.

"That's very normal for a young woman of your age," Allegra murmured, giving her a gentle look of understanding.

Sky wanted to suddenly cry. Allegra was so maternal and nurturing. She was genuine, unlike Yerik who hid the monster he was beneath that thin veneer of civility he showed to the outer world. She fought back the tears, hungrily absorbing each kind touch that Allegra would bestow upon her as she finished off the long list of questions.

"Well done," Allegra murmured, handing the nurse the clipboard. "Now," and she looked Sky in the eyes, "I would like you to lay down. My nurse is going to put a sheet across your waist and legs. As I gently move each of your heels into the stirrups, she will ENSURE you are completely covered. You will not be exposed in any way to any camera. I will not allow that to happen. Do you understand that Sky?"

There was a fierce protectiveness in Allegra's voice. "Thank you," Sky whispered unsteadily, afraid and vulnerable. Never wanting any man to see her helpless, laying on her back, exposed to their depraved eyes again, Sky felt Allegra pat her arm. The doctor was protecting her, and Sky had never felt so grateful as she did right now. It only took a few minutes, and the doctor had been good for her word, she was exceedingly gentle, and Sky eventually relaxed as she fully examined her. When it was over, the nurse ensured that Sky was protected from prying eyes as she sat up and smoothed the gown down across her legs.

"We're done!" Allegra announced lightly, pulling off her examination gloves, dropping them into a nearby wastebasket.

Sky thought she detected some worry in the doctor's eyes. There was some kind of unreadable look in the woman's gaze, but Sky was not a mind reader. "I'm really okay?"

"Of course," Allegra murmured, offering her hand to help Sky step off the examination table.

"You looked... well... concerned?" Sky probed.

"Oh, it is nothing, nothing." Allegra forced a smile and said, "I'm fairly sure you are a tad anemic. I'm going to order nurse to give you a B-12 shot right now. And some packets of vitamins and minerals. The lab tests will, of course, bear this out."

"Is that why I'm tired?"

"It certainly can contribute," Allegra said cheerily, removing her lab coat. "Well, I must be flown back to the capitol. I have a long and busy day of patients waiting for my attention upon my return."

"Wait," Sky said, "what about my tests? Can you tell me what you find?" She saw Allegra's open face become guarded. It was a dramatic change. The doctor put the stethoscope she had hanging around her neck into her leather medial bag sitting on a chair.

"I'm sure Don Tobar will be more than happy to pass on any comments I may have about your tests to you, Sky." She looked up, smiled, and said, "I would suggest you continue to take naps when you want. I would also order more walks in fresh air for you. You are pale and you need some sunlight to make Vitamin D for your body."

Sky nodded, feeling better. "Okay. Thanks so much, Dr. Zapato. I really appreciate your making this trip to see me."

"It's not a problem. I will visit you in a few weeks and then we can discuss any questions you may have personally with me. The lab reports will be sent to Don Tobar in approximately one week. I'm sure he'll be first to tell you if I've seen anything important in the results. But I doubt there will be any issues."

Sky watched them leave the room. Her skin prickled as she felt eyes on her. She hated those damned cameras. Moving quickly to the bathroom, she decided to shower, to wash herself clean and hopefully feel better than she did presently.

CHAPTER 14

July 8

CAL'S HEART LEAPED as he spotted Lauren hurrying into the war room. She placed a piece of paper down in front of him. She was grinning like a feral wolf. Alex was on her heels, his expression hopeful. Driscoll looked up from his laptop from the other table.

"What's this?" Cal demanded, picking up the paper that showed latitude and longitude coordinates plus a message in Russian.

Alex grinned hugely. "It is possibly the break we were looking for! But the credit goes to Lauren. She was taking all the comms coming out of Central America. She was running computer simulations on GPS signals." Alex looked up at Lauren with no small amount of pride and said, "You tell him."

"There's been a lot of cell traffic from a specific spot in Northern Costa Rica. It's been with San Jose, the capitol of that country. Always in Russian. Always encrypted." She smiled over at Alex, who was practically glowing with excitement. "Alex ran it through encryption." Lauren leaned over, placing her fingertip on the paper Cal laid down between his hands. "Whoever is making calls is using the code name White Hawk. And guess what, Cal? Where we're getting this signal? It's in the Monteverde Cloud Forest. Remember? Alex had said Alexandrov wanted to retire to a cloud forest, but couldn't say where?"

Alex clapped his hands, startling everyone. They were now into their third week without a break, all bone tired, living on coffee and donuts. "Remember me telling you about Alexandrov's passion for falconry?"

Cal rubbed his watering eyes. "Yeah? So what?"

Alex was almost bursting. "Alexandrov collects raptors. When I saw that call sign after I unencrypted it, I recalled Vlad telling me his father had a special interest in a hawk in South America. It's called a White Hawk. That could be a connection."

Cal let out a long, slow breath, staring at the jumble of words and numbers. He glanced sharply up at Alex. "White Hawk? It's a bird? It lives in Costa Rica?"

"Yes," Lauren said triumphantly. She pulled out her laptop, opening the lid and turning it around so Cal could see it. "I Googled the hawk. Look: it lives in woodlands like they have in the Monte Verde Forest."

"And," Alex said excitedly, leaning over and pointing at the map where the hawk was found, "the cell phone calls are emanating from this one spot in the woodlands. In fact, it is near the Arenal volcano. Very close to it."

"And," Lauren added, growing excited, "the hawk is said to be very common in that specific area."

Frowning, Cal rapidly read up on the hawk and the type of area it liked to hunt in. He picked up the paper, studying it. "Okay, who are the calls going to in San Jose? To a specific number? Or to a bunch of individual numbers?"

Lauren sat down and quickly pulled up the map showing the cell phone calls from the satellite over Costa Rica. She turned it so Cal could study it. "We don't know yet. That's our next step. But if you look at the lines, you can see this past twenty-four hours, wherever that is originating from in the Monte Verde Cloud Forest, it's been intense traffic. Far more than normal."

Alex sat down on Cal's right and opened his laptop. "But we cannot get too excited yet." He turned the screen around, showing a map of the area surrounding Arenal. It was ringed with about fifty resorts, hotels, inns, and bed and breakfast. "Now, I've been in Costa Rica a number of times. Maybe five years ago." Alex tapped the laptop. "Arenal used to be one of the most active volcanos in the world."

"I didn't know that," Cal muttered, his brows drawing down.

"Arenal is Spanish for sandy," Lauren told him, going to the same webpage, and then throwing it up on the overhead screen so everyone could view it. She pointed toward it. "The volcano is moving in a southeasterly direction, which is why you don't see any resorts or villages in that direction."

"Which means," Cal growled, "a shitload of cell phone traffic by the tourists visiting them?"

"Yep."

"Lauren said," Alex offered, struggling with the slang, "that there is a haystack with needle in it and we must locate the needle."

"Needle in a haystack," Driscoll corrected him, grinning over at the medic. "You make my day, Kazak. Thank you for slaughtering our slang," and he chuckled.

Everyone laughed, including Alex. He was red faced and looked humble.

"Stop picking on Alex," Lauren ordered them sharply, the only one who was not laughing. "He's doing his best."

Alex blinked, seeing the fierceness in Lauren's narrowed green eyes as she took on her team in his defense. That was new. He felt good. But when Lauren snapped a look over at him, her eyes were green ice. So much for a feel-good moment, he thought. "Okay," he mumbled apologetically, pointing to the map, "we are searching for a needle in a haystack."

"But who would use a call sign from one of those resorts?" Jack demanded.

"We don't have a clue," Lauren muttered. "At least, not yet."

"We must pare it down and look closely," Alex said. "I am going back to our office and find all the names and numbers of the resorts. Lauren and I will begin a cross-comparison."

"Do any of these resorts have falconry offered to the tourists?" Jack asked.

"Unknown," Lauren said.

"I'll check that out," Cal muttered, writing it down on a notebook placed next to his laptop.

"Because, if they do, maybe there's a head falconer whose nickname is White Hawk and we're off on a wild goose chase," Jack said with a rueful shake of his head.

Alex frowned. "A what? A goose that is wild? What does that mean?"

Groaning, Lauren said, "I'll explain it to you later, Alex. Not now, okay?"

He nodded, apologetic. "Yes, of course. Thank you."

"We need to verify if this one cell number, whoever it is, is calling ONE individual several times in San Jose or not," Cal said. "For all we know, it could be tourists calling from resorts, calling home to the capitol, talking to their family or friends who live there."

"Mmmm," Lauren said, warning in her husky tone, "I'd be careful going there. Alex and I have been looking at comms in Central America for damn near three and a half weeks. We know the normal flow call patterns. This," and she jabbed her finger down at the document in Cal's hand, "is different. It's sticking out like a sore thumb." And then she groaned, rolling her eyes. She held up her hand toward Alex, who had a blank look on his face because he understood only half of what was said. "I'll clue you in on that slang later, too," Lauren promised.

Alex smiled a thank you and gave her a nod, gratefulness in his expression. Why the hell did he have to be so damned nice all the time? Lauren swung her attention to the rest of her team. "You have to rely on us to tell you what's the normal and what isn't. Cal, this burst of cell phone traffic is abnormal and deserves a much closer look."

"Okay," Cal said, "then let's get at it. At least it MIGHT be a clue."

Ryan muttered, "I hope so. We're way past due for a fucking break."

Alex gave Lauren her laptop. He handed to her as she walked up to him. He was finding she'd allow him to do small things for her. Perhaps accept a cup of coffee. Or he would become what she called a 'gopher' and run errands for her when she needed something done here at HQ to help in the search for Sky. When she took her laptop, their hands touched briefly. He felt an electric shock in his fingers. A secret thrill went through him as Lauren took it and turned away, muttering a thank you over her shoulder in his direction.

Cal rose and stretched, the afternoon sun beckoning to him. Being closed up in a lead lined room for hours on end, he craved the salty fresh air of the Pacific and the sun beating down on him. But not now. They'd just possibly gotten a lead they needed so desperately. "I'm taking a head break," he told them, following Lauren out of the room and into the passageway. Alex moved by them, hurrying with long, ground-eating strides and diving into the room where he was working with Lauren.

"Hey, is he growing on you?" Cal teased as he walked at Lauren's shoulder.

"Like mold."

He chuckled and shook his head. "Alex's not a bad dude, Lauren." He saw her mouth twitch, refusing to be baited. "Well, at least now," Cal drawled, "when we get boots on the ground, I don't have to worry about you shooting him in the balls so you don't have to work with him out on this op."

"Cal!" Lauren jerked to a stop, glaring up at him. "That's not fair!"

He knew she was tired. They were all exhausted. His grin increased. "Oh," he murmured, "you had murder in your eyes ever since you met Alex. Now I see it's thawing a little, that's all," and Cal turned and went into the restroom, hearing her curse him richly out from the passageway. He laughed for the first time since Sky had been kidnapped.

July 9

"CAL?"

Cal had fallen asleep on the couch at the condo, too tired to even make it to the bathroom to get a shower after leaving SEAL HQ after midnight. Alex had a worried look on his face as he came out of the second bedroom. "Yeah? What?" He sat up, rubbing his burning eyes. The medic was holding some papers in his hands.

"I was digging in a lower drawer for some clothes space, and I found these in my bedroom." His voice thickened. "I think... I think they are from Sky?" He motioned awkwardly to the lavender bow tied around them. "Have you seen these?"

Cal reached out, drowsily taking the packet. "No," he mumbled, barely awake.

"Maybe," Alex said, "it was a wedding gift for you? Something personal? I did not look at them."

Cal grimly looked at the thick batch of papers. It was Sky's art paper she used to create pastels drawings on. "I don't know. I didn't know about them if it is."

Alex gave him a sorrowful look. "I am going to hit the shower and then go to bed. Good night."

Alone in the quiet condo, Cal saw the satin bow tied around the thick sheaves of art paper. His heart started to pound, and he felt suddenly wide awake, sleep torn from him. Carefully, Cal untied the satin ribbon and set it aside. He placed the papers on his lap. Some were square, others rectangular. Some were photo-sized to fit into an album or perhaps a picture frame. He touched the first thick, white paper, almost afraid to turn it over to see what was there. This was the paper Sky used to draw and paint on. Cal knew she'd brought out her pastel chalk and drawing paper with her. He didn't remember her drawing, but he had been gone a lot of the time, too. Each of them had different responsibilities before their wedding.

Fear moved through Cal. He had to turn the drawing over. When he did, he felt his soul rip open. Sky had always drawn landscapes. And animals. Cal had never seen her draw a human. He stared in disbelief down at her artwork. It was a portrait of him. Cal's throat tightened. He'd once shown her an old photo album of pictures from when he and his SEAL team had been stationed in Afghanistan. She'd chosen one of him, kneeling, the butt of his M4 planted on his thigh. Her talent was far more than he realized, because, literally, it damn near looked like color photo of him in haji gear, his Afghan clothing. He wore his thick beard, his hair long, and an Afghan rolled cap on his head. She'd captured his intense stare, a fierce look toward the man who had taken the photo.

Cal's heart began a slow pound as he realized Sky had written something in black ink at the bottom. *To the man who will always be a hero in my eyes and heart. Thank you for your service. I love you so much. Sky.* The words blurred. Cal cursed softly, blinking rapidly, wiping the tears out of his eyes.

His hand trembled as he picked up a five by seven-inch paper and turned it over. He had never seen Sky draw in ink, but she had this time. Cal marveled at her raw talent. It was a portrait of him in his SEAL work uniform, a close-up, and he was smiling, looking out of the picture directly at the person holding it. Beneath it, Sky had written: *Your smile makes me smile. I had such darkness in my soul until you walked into my life. I was so lost until you found me. I love you. Sky.*

Cal took in a ragged breath, his chest feeling squeezed, a fist gripping his heart. He carefully placed it right side up on the larger one he'd already looked at. The next one was the same size. Turning it over, it was an ink sketch of his hand, fingers splayed outward as if reaching for something. The detail in the drawing were stunning, even down to the many small white scars across the back of his hand. It almost looked alive. His gaze dropped to the the bottom of it. *When you touch me, I feel your love. Your touch is so gentle, so tender with me. I never knew a man could be like that with a woman, but you are. Never stop touching me. Ever. Love, Sky.*

Sky must have created these over time and brought them with her from their home in Virginia. They were like Hallmark cards, only better. Made by her. Personal. Intimate. Loving. Cal looked up, staring hard at the door, visualizing Sky walking through it, with her beach towel draped over her arm, her hair tangled, her incredible blue eyes shining with such life. What was he going to do if he never found her? Cal swallowed hard.

He felt anxious, turning over the next sketch. It was as large as the first one. Sky had drawn the meadow below their bedroom. It took his breath away because the composition looked almost alive. The elk herd crossing it was perfectly drawn. A corner of Cal's mouth drew slightly upward. Sky had captured the alpenglow, that pale, gossamer pink that occurred just at dawn or dusk. He knew she had struggled through God only knew how many attempts trying to get it just right. Well, she had. He wanted to read what she had written at the bottom. It was as if he were hearing her voice whispering near his ear. Cal swore he could feel Sky so close to him, her slender arms draped around his shoulders, her breasts pressed against his back, her head nestled on his shoulder, eyes closed. *Promise me always that we can live in the house you built? I feel so safe there. I feel as if you built a beautiful womb just for me to thrive in, to know happiness, to feel so alive because you are there with me. I'll love you until I take my last breath. Sky.*

Wincing, Cal turned it over. He felt as if some invisible claw was tearing his chest apart. He missed Sky so damn much. Every day that passed, he felt more pain. More agony, not less. There was one last sketch left. He wasn't sure he could emotionally handle it or not. Cal wanted to cry. He wanted to hold Sky so damned badly, give her the safety he knew he'd always given her before. She'd lived a life without any security at all. The misery and anger of not finding a trail to follow, to find her, rammed up through him. Cal's hand shook as he reached for the last sketch.

He groaned as he turned it over and pressed his hand against his eyes, the tears squeezing out of them, leaking through his fingers. He pushed the sketch away. He felt ripped wide open. Staggering to his feet, Cal caught himself, pushing toward the front door and jerking it open. It was 0200. The night sky was clear, dark, and moonless. The stars glimmered but blurred as Cal walked steadily toward the rocks and the lapping of the water. He couldn't stop the sobs that were tearing out of him. Pressing his hand against his constricted chest, he made it to the rocks. Cal sat down, facing the bay, trying to find some kind of solace juxtapose his anguish, some kind of peace. But there was none. The terrible animal-like sounds surrounded him. His shoulders shook and he leaned forward, elbows planted into his tense thighs, his face buried in his hands.

Cal didn't know how long he cried. His throat ached. His chest hurt. He could never recall feeling this hopeless, this terrified or grief stricken. Not even when he was a boy of seven, after his father cut his back open with a belt buckle, he had been beaten with. Cal had run out of the house, escaping to a shed, hiding, trembling with abject fear. He'd lain there all night, huddled into a tight ball, crying softly, hurting so much, unable to understand why his drunk father would hurt him like this. Those feelings were still sharp and clear within Cal, but paled compared to the loss of Sky, the woman he loved with his soul. It jagged through him like a raw, bleeding wound that would not close and would never be healed.

Slowly, Cal straightened, wiping his wet face, then shoving his damp palms against his cargo pants to dry them off. Slowly, the world around him gently returned. The lapping of the water was so damn comforting to him. He was a SEAL. Water was his mother. She would always protect him, guard him, save his life if it came to that. Cal felt as if he were emotionally hemorrhaging. He understood now, as never before, how Sky saw him. Symbolically, he was her water, her security, her safety. And now... she had no one to hold her. No one to give her that sense of protection he knew she so desperately needed. He felt so damn powerless. As a SEAL, they were men of action. That's what they were very good at. Sitting around? No. Not their style. Not his. Cal couldn't sit for longer than fifteen minutes at any time. He got up, stretched, and walked around. The restlessness in him gnawed like a wild animal's fangs sinking deep into his chest, tearing at his muscles, clawing and snapping his ribs apart. The pain was excruciating. His love for Sky was so deep, he couldn't feel where it began or ended.

Cal sat there, recalling one very serious talk with Sky a few mornings after their return from Peru. They were both still in shock from the series of events, battle weary and feeling emotionally gutted. As they sat in the living room, Sky curled up against him, her head on his shoulder, coffee resting on her slender thigh, she'd whispered to him, "Hell is the absence of love."

God, she was so right. So damn right. He rubbed his chest, trying to will away his grief and loss. Cal hadn't realized it, but his life had been hell until he'd met Sky. She had brought her love into his dark life. He hadn't even known he lived in Hell until now. Until she had been ripped away from him.

Cal watched the lights dancing and twinkling across the San Diego Bay. The crescent shape reminded him of the curve of Sky's arms holding him after they made sweet, hot, hungry love with one another. Her arms were not heavily muscled like his. But they were firm and strong in other ways. And when her long, slender fingers lightly grazed his cheek, caressing him, Cal knew love for the first time in his life. Sky didn't realize that with every grazing touch she gave him, she fed him, as though he was a starving pauper, dying until she sent light deep into his dark soul, chasing the blackness away, making him feel love. Feel hope…

Somehow, he had onto hold hope. Scrubbing his face ruthlessly, Cal knew in his heart that Sky was strong. Much stronger emotionally than he would ever be. Right now, he felt like fragile glass that was going to shatter into a million pieces, never to be put back together again. Sky had a woman's strength, soft, quiet, soothing, and calming, that tamed the savage beast that always prowled within him. She had tamed him.

Cal had never seen himself as married. Or hell, even being in love, whatever the hell THAT word meant. He knew sex well. But love? No. Sky had entered his life and triggered his hope, had opened his heart. At the time, he hadn't even known what the hell was going on, except that he NEEDED her like oxygen in order to live. Meeting her changed his life forever. Instead of just existing, he'd discovered what it was like to be alive. No longer did he simply exist. Sky made him want to live. She made him laugh, and the striking sketch of him smiling had totaled Cal emotionally. Because before Sky, he never smiled. Never laughed. Life was one rough son-of-a-bitch, day in and day out. That was all.

He'd been in total survival mode since he could remember. Yeah, he shared black humor with his SEAL team. And when he was home between deployments, he would always go visit his sister Tracey and her husband on the farm in Oregon. She always wanted him over to their house to eat dinner. To be a family that they'd never been. Cal cared deeply for Tracey. She'd been raped, nearly died of the beating, but she'd survived. And Cal was there every step of the way through her grueling recovery. Tracey had fought a fight Cal never thought anyone could survive. But she had. And today, as he fondly looked across the bay toward glittering San Diego in the distance, his sister was happily married, the terror of her past put to rest by the devoted love of her husband. John loved Tracey fiercely.

Cal had always stood back, watching them together, unable to be a part of it. Because he didn't know love. He'd never loved. Afraid of that kind of deep, magical, scary connection, he'd avoided it at all costs. Cal was happy for Tracey because she had a rough childhood too and deserved someone like John. Best of all, Cal thought, watching the lights dance on the water, John worshipped his sister. There was a gentleness he had toward her that Cal had never seen in a man before. He wondered what was wrong with him. Being a SEAL, the word gentle or tender simply did not exist in their world. But Sky had brought those qualities out in him. He had not known he was capable of such emotions. And she had taught him tenderness in four short months.

Wiping his jaw, feeling the stubble, Cal slowly rose. He pushed his hands deep into his pockets and slowly walked back into the condo. Now, he was ready to look at her last sketch and read what she had written below it.

Quietly shutting the door, Cal sat down on the couch. He took a deep, ragged breath and picked up the sketch, turning it over once again. It was a black-haired baby, newly born, with blue eye, smiling from the pink swaddling around her. She was looking directly at him. Cal looked at Sky's handwriting. He saw splotches where the ink had spread from the clean lines as it was written. Barely touching the script, Cal knew Sky had cried while she wrote these words. *I wish in my heart of hearts, that one day, we will create a beautiful baby girl just like this one. Love allows us to grow, to hope, to dream. I dream of at least two, maybe three beautiful, strong, courageous children with you, Cal. Love forever, Sky.*

CHAPTER 15

July 10

D R. ALLEGRA ZAPATA studied the lab results on Sky Lambert in her office in San Jose, Costa Rica. Her thin black brows drew downward as she considered everything. The woman was roughly eight weeks pregnant. She'd known Sky was pregnant when she'd examined her at La Paloma. However, Allegra didn't trust the fact that the room was heavily monitored with cameras. Sky seemed not to realize she was pregnant. Something didn't feel right to Allegra, and she wasn't going to tell anyone just yet, not even Sky. Riffling through the lab reports, they all clearly confirmed that Sky was pregnant.

What was going on at that villa? Don Tobar did not seem Latino at all. He was a foreigner, but she wasn't sure where the man had come from. Allegra was very well off economically because she was one of the best fertility experts in Central and South America, and she recognized the expensive Italian shoes the man wore. They cost him thousands of dollars. Further, the goons he had working with him looked like soldiers, even though they wore casual civilian clothes. There was an air of unspoken tension at the villa, the servants all had wary looks on their faces.

Rubbing her brow, she sat watching the late afternoon sun moving quietly through her large office window on the fifth floor of the skyscraper in downtown San Jose, capitol of the country. Allegra shook her head. Sky Lambert was clearly North American by her speech patterns. Who knew where Don Tobar came from? The servants were all Costa Rican from what she could observe.

Her phone rang.

"Yes, Maria?" She was the receptionist outside her office who took all incoming calls.

"Dr. Zapata, there is a call from a Don Tobar? He said it is urgent…"

Speak of the Devil… Allegra sighed. The man had called her at least three times a day since she'd examined Sky Lambert. She looked at her watch. It was 4:45 p.m. In another fifteen minutes she would leave to go home to her family. Her husband, Jaime, was planning on taking her and their two young daughters to a picnic, a special outing for them. "Put him through, Maria."

"Dr. Zapata?"

Why did her skin crawl? "Don Tobar?"

"Yes, Dr. Zapata. I'm inquiring about the results on Sky Lambert? I've called you repeatedly and your office assistant is a very unnecessary guard dog to reach you."

"I haven't yet received them. Tomorrow," Allegra lied.

"I'm not a person accustomed to waiting, Doctor. You've tried my patience tremendously. I paid you well and I expect results quickly."

"With all due respect, Don Tobar, I'm a very, very busy fertility specialist and I have many demands on my time. I promise, I'll get to the lab reports tomorrow."

"Very well."

Allegra heard the growl in the man's voice. Why did it feel like a warning? She placed the phone down in the cradle, concerned. Things just didn't feel right about this case at all.

Cal was going through hundreds of photos from the satellite fly overs across Central America when Lauren and Alex entered the room. Looking up, he saw Lauren's face was radiant, like a hunter who had located her prey. He sat back, expectant.

"What did you find?"

Lauren grinned and sat down at this left elbow. Alex sat opposite her. She slid some paper in front of him. "First, every call made from that area of Monte Verde Cloud Forest in northern Costa Rica, near the Arenal volcano, went to ONE phone number." Triumphantly, she tapped the paper, the phone number on it. "They all went to a Dr. Allegra Zapata, an M.D. in San Jose."

"What about the caller?" Cal demanded.

Alex roused himself. "All throw away phones. We cannot track any of them. There have been a total of sixteen calls in last two weeks to this doctor. Perhaps it is White Hawk? There was one encrypted phone call from that same GPS coordinate, and it wasn't a throw-away cell phone. I am thinking it is from the same person."

Cal rubbed his brow. "Who is this doctor?" he demanded. "Have you done any background checks on her?"

"She's a fertility expert," Lauren provided. She pulled more papers out and pushed them in front of Cal. "She's clean. Dr. Zapata is a specialist in fertility. One of the head honchos in Central and South America."

"Any law enforcement ties to her? Does she have ties to Russian mafia? Al-Qaeda? ISIS?"

Lauren shook her head. "She's forty-five years old, a mother of two young daughters, is happily married to a rich businessman, Jaime Zapata. Allegra is considered one of the top ten world experts on infertility treatment."

"This doesn't make sense," Cal growled.

"No," Alex said, "but I think we need to move a step closer to this woman." He risked a look over at Lauren and then focused on Cal's scowling face. "I suggest Lauren and I fly down to San Jose and check her out. We should have photos of Sky and Yerik Alexandrov that we can show her. If she positively identifies one or the other, then this is a genuine lead." He saw Lauren's brows drop, very unhappy with his suggestion. Holding up his hand, Alex argued passionately, "This COULD be our break, Cal. If we go down there and pose as a husband and wife with an infertility problem, we will be able to get in to see her. Once Dr. Zapata is in her office, we can show her the photos. We can verify if she has seen Sky."

Cal rubbed his chin, giving Lauren a glance. She was glaring at the medic. "We have clues. Nothing solid."

"This fertility expert," Lauren said, her voice tight, "could have patients up in that region of northern Costa Rica. Maybe a patient in crisis? That would account for the phone calls, perhaps?"

Alex gave her a studied look. "My hunch tells me there is something to this." He opened his hands. "If I walked in there alone to Dr. Zapata's office, it would look suspicious, Lauren. You are the only woman on the team, and we would have to go there undercover. We will have to pose as man and wife, so it would not tip the doctor off. What we are really after is for her to verify she's seen Sky or Alexandrov. That is all."

Lips quirking, Lauren barely nodded. "That's a three-day round trip," she told Cal. "Can you really afford to have us gone that long? There's so much intel to plough through here."

"Hey," Jack muttered. He was at another table with his laptop, his voice suddenly turning excited. "Holy shit, look at this! Get over here, now!"

All three of them walked over and huddled around Jack and his laptop.

Jack jabbed a finger down at a satellite photo. "This satellite is doing a fly over above the Monte Verde Cloud Forest in northern Costa Rica. Look at this," and he traced an oval area cut out of the surrounding canopy jungle. Down below was a man flying a white bird.

Cal's eyes narrowed. The man's back was toward the satellite photo, making it impossible to identify him. A white raptor was lifting off his gloved hand. There was another man, standing back and to the side of him. "Can you enlarge the photo on that bird?"

Jack hit a key stroke several times and the bird came up in detail.

Lauren gasped, gripping Jack's shoulder. "My God," she whispered, leaning down, looking closely, "that's a White Hawk!"

"But we cannot see who the man is," Alex said, frowning.

"Jack, get me the GPS coordinates on this meadow?" Lauren said, quickly straightening. "Send them to my computer? I want to compare this place with where the burner phone calls were originating from."

Cal tried to remain calm. "Do it," he ordered them.

Alex stepped back so that Lauren could extricate herself from the group. She quickly walked out of the room, heading for the other office. "That is a White Hawk." He saw the hope suddenly flare in Cal's eyes. "Whoever is flying that raptor is a falconer."

"None of those tourist resorts at Arenal had a falconer or hawks. We called every one of them," Jack pointed out.

"You're right," Cal murmured. He looked up and saw Lauren returning, triumph on her face. "What did you find out?"

"Bingo!" Lauren crowed, laptop under her arm. "The meadow GPS coordinates are within three hundred yards of where all those burner phone calls were made from." She came around and opened up her laptop to show them.

"So?" Jack wondered out loud, "this isn't a resort? Or is it?"

"No," Lauren said, her voice a rasp, excitement underlying her husky tone as she brought up the diagram showing the location of the cell phone calls and the meadow. "Not a resort. I don't know what it is yet. We're going to have to do some more investigation on it."

"I'll get on it," Alex volunteered.

Cal sat there, feeling restless, hoping against hope that they had really found some intel that would lead them to Sky. This was the first piece of possible evidence.

An hour later, Lauren and Alex returned. She sat down with her laptop and a satellite map from Google. Turning it toward Cal, she said, "This is a villa owned by someone. Don't know who, yet, but look: you can see the villa beneath the trees and then the oval meadow north of it."

"A single residence," Alex told Cal.

Jack Driscoll walked over, craning a look across Cal's shoulder and studying the Google map. "I can barely see the villa. That damned triple canopy is pretty much hiding it from everyone. Any chance of getting infrared readout in the villa?"

"Yes," Lauren said. "But the canopy cover prevents us from detailed identification. A cow could be a human, or vice-versa, unfortunately."

Cal sat back. "Okay, but this is such a long shot. We have a fertility doctor in San Jose and the calls originating from this villa. We have a White Hawk." Cal looked over at Alex. "The ONLY thread connecting these disparate pieces of intel is the White Hawk."

Alex gave Cal a pleading look. "My hunch tells me this is where Alexandrov has a hidden villa. It is in a cloud forest. He is a falconer. He favors the White Hawk. We have just seen a photo of a man with a White Hawk. Those are more than just pieces of intel. They are like pearls stringing together to create a necklace."

Lauren looked up. "You're a romantic, Kazak."

He grinned shyly. "No. I just see things in visual symbols sometimes, is all." The look on Lauren's face made him feel good. Her usual icy green gaze had thawed, as though she realized there was more to him than just being an operator. THAT made him feel even better.

Cal's mouth thinned. He gave Lauren an intent look. "You and I are going to catch the fastest flight down to San Jose and drop in on this doctor." He looked at Alex and Jack. "You two stay here, keep getting sat photos and comms on that villa while we're gone. Do some tracing on the owner. Also, reach out to the CIA agent down there in San Jose. I want that spook to give us and any logistics and assets he's got or knows about in case we do find Sky there."

Lauren nodded. "You and I will pose as husband and wife?"

Cal stood up. "Yeah." He gave Alex an apologetic look. "Sorry, but I'm going instead of you. If Sky's down there, I want to know and I want to be on the ground."

Alex swallowed his disappointment. It would have been good to be alone with Lauren, and hopefully, to get to know her a bit better. "It is a good plan," he agreed with Cal. He thought Lauren looked utterly relieved that Cal was going instead of him. It hurt, but Alex was a team player, and this was about finding Sky, not his personal issues with Lauren.

Lauren typed in some info. She grinned. "Guess what? There's an American Airlines flight to San Jose, Costa Rica in eight hours out of Lindbergh International Airport in San Diego. We make a stop in Miami, Florida, change planes, and leave an hour and a half later for the capitol."

"Book us," Cal ordered, standing up. Hope flowed strongly through him. He desperately wanted something to turn up, to prove Sky was at the villa. It was such a long shot. But it's all they had right now. He loved her, he ached to hear her voice, see her smile, and watch those blue eyes of hers sparkle. Rubbing his chest, he muttered, "Get us first class tickets."

"I've got fake passports and ID's already," Jack said. "You'll have the cover you need. I'll get busy acquiring them," and he turned, going back to his laptop. His company worked with the U.S. government, and they produced passports and other documents for his undercover operators.

Alex said, "You'll need a car from the San Jose airport, I'll get it rented."

Jack looked up from his computer. "Okay, girls and boys, here's Cal and Lauren's new identification: They're going in as Jim and Emma Anderson. I'll have their driver license intel over to your laptop in a minute, Alex, because you'll need to give that info to the online car rental agency. I'll also send you four credit cards in Jim and Emma Anderson's names."

Nodding, Alex said, "Excellent." He grinned and rubbed his hands together. "I have a good feeling about this. I believe this doctor will be able to identify one of them."

Cal hoped like hell it was Sky. But what the HELL was a fertility specialist doing in the mix? It made NO sense to him at all, but he kept his thoughts to himself.

July 11

ALLEGRA WAS SHOCKED when Don Tobar walked into her office at nine a.m. the next morning. Her assistant was running after him, upset, trying to stop him. "It's all right, Maria. Please let my next patient know I will be a few minutes late while I speak to Don Tobar?"

"Yes, Doctor. I'm sorry," Maria said, her voice tight, her glare scathing at the intruder who pushed by her.

Yerik ignored the upset assistant, his gaze trained on the doctor who sat behind her massive mahogany desk. He sat down and waited until the door closed. "I'm not happy with you, Dr. Zapata."

Allegra pushed a file aside, her heart beating harder in her chest beneath her white lab coat. There was a dangerous feeling around this man. "And I could say the same of you. You cannot just walk in here, unannounced, without an appointment. I have twelve patients I must see today."

Alexandrov crossed his legs. He'd flown in earlier in his helicopter. Wearing an expensive gray Armani suit, a white silk shirt with platinum cufflinks, and a Golden Ellipse Platinum watch by Patek Philippe. His tie was a tasteful dark blue silk to match the watch's face. "Now, good doctor, I will make this brief. Have you read Sky's lab report yet?"

"No," Allegra lied, frowning. Her skin crawled again. The man's eyes were a forest green, slitted upon her. She felt hunted. "I told you I would read them today. I just got in the office," and she placed her hand on Sky's file that had all the results.

"Quite right, doctor." Yerik waved his manicured hand. "I'll get straight to the point. I want my semen, which you will collect at the appropriate time, inserted into Sky, and I want you to get her pregnant."

Opening the file, Allegra didn't show her surprise. Instead, she said, "Don

Tobar, you need to know she is ALREADY pregnant."

Yerik's eyes narrowed. "What are you talking about?"

"Sky's blood and urine tests confirm she's about one and a half month's pregnant." Allegra looked up at him. "I assumed you knew this?"

Yerik froze, stunned by the information. His mouth thinned. "Then you will abort it. I want her pregnant by ME."

"But...," she said, opening her hands, "I ASSUMED she was pregnant by you. That you already had some kind of relationship?"

Waving his hand dismissively, Yerik said, "Sky has decided to throw her lot in life with me. She knows I want a child from her."

Blinking, Allegra stared at him. "When my nurse took Sky's information, she made no mention of being pregnant."

Shrugging, Yerik murmured, "Maybe she did not know? That is very early in a pregnancy, doctor."

"Yes, I suppose that is possible," Allegra admitted. "May I enquire as to your relationship with her?"

"No, you may not. I'm a very wealthy man and I don't like headlines about me or my private life. So, when can you do this?"

Hesitating, Allegra's mind spun. She sensed he was lying. "Don Tobar, to do this, I need to talk to Sky much more thoroughly than that examine I gave her a week ago. In our country, abortion is allowed ONLY if the woman's life is in danger, or the fetus is in danger or has not developed properly."

"I want her to carry my son," Yerik growled. "She's young, healthy, and I'm sure, very capable of doing just that. How soon after the abortion can she be ready to be impregnated with my semen?"

"Have you tried this method before? Has she suffered a miscarriage previously? Sky obviously has no issue in getting pregnant. There are all kinds of hormonal tests I must do first. Generally, after an abortion, it takes a woman's body about one to three months to return to normal, to ovulate, so that her egg can be fertilized and she becomes pregnant once again."

Yerik said, "I want this done as quickly as possible." He saw the doctor frown, confusion in her eyes. "I want you to impregnate her with my semen." Yerik saw the doctor become upset, her brows drawing down, a slight tremble in her fingers as she brought over a pad and pen to make notes. He sensed she was not trusting or believing him.

"This is highly irregular, Don Tobar. Normally, the woman comes in and requests an abortion, not the man in her life. Are you married? Living together? There are many things I must know before I can do this. Because the woman must sign a great deal of legal and medical paperwork beforehand—"

Yerik gave her a cold smile. "Doctor, you will do as I request," he told her quietly. "Because if you do not show up within the next five days to do this, I will ensure your two beautiful little daughters are kidnapped." Yerik glared at her. "You will never see them again. Do I make myself clear?"

Allegra gasped, coming halfway out of her chair, and then quickly sitting down. "Who are YOU to threaten ME?" she demanded in a low, furious tone.

Yerik smiled a little and rose. He looked at his watch. "As I promised, doctor, I will not take up much of your time. I expect you at La Paloma villa in five days. I want Sky to carry my son. And if you need a little persuasion, I advise you to pick up your phone, call your house maid, and asked if she can find Belicia, your daughter."

Terror thrummed through Allegra as she pulled out her cell phone from the pocket of her lab coat. When she connected with the maid and asked where Belicia was, the girl could not be found. Allegra signed off, telling the maid she would call her back in a moment. Her throat ached with tears as she stared at Don Tobar, who was smiling confidently at her.

"What have you done with my daughter?" she cried.

"Belicia is fine," Yerik said smoothly. "She will be returned to you within the hour. The maid will find her outside, playing on her swing set in the back yard once again."

Touching her throat, Allegra whispered, "WHO are you?"

"Someone you do not cross, Doctor. Now? May I expect you in five days at my villa? To see Sky's fetus is aborted?"

"Y-yes, of course…"

"I am going to tell Sky that you discovered some minor problem in her uterus, and that she needs a small medical procedure to correct it. You will NOT tell her that she's pregnant." He drilled a hard look into the doctor's widening eyes. "You will NOT tell her a thing. If you do, you'll never see your daughters again. Do you understand?"

"Y-yes, I understand," Allegra whispered brokenly.

Yerik strolled into his villa, still smiling inwardly. He saw Sky sitting out on the patio in the mid-morning sun, reading a newspaper in Spanish. She was good at learning languages, he'd discovered. Joining her on the patio, sitting in the shade beneath the umbrella, a servant brought him coffee.

"And how are you this fine, beautiful morning?" Yerik inquired, sipping his fragrant coffee. Sky wore a bright red tee, her body-hugging jeans, and tennis shoes. The sun glinted off her blond hair, making it look almost like a halo about her head. Yes, he would have her carry his son. And what a fine, strapping son he would be. Of course, Sky had no idea what was coming. He wondered if she knew she was pregnant. It did not appear as if she knew anything. He contemplated the joy of getting her pregnant, carrying HIS son, a replacement for Vlad. And she would not know she was pregnant until months afterward. By then, Yerik would have her under twenty-four-hour-a-day guard to ensure she didn't try to kill herself or abort his son. Because he knew she would.

Sky folded up the paper and set it across her lap. The morning sun was warming, burning off the fingers of clouds that always twisted and moved like a maze through the trees surrounding the villa. "I'm fine." She saw Yerik was in a particularly buoyant mood. She rarely saw him in a business suit. "I heard the helicopter take off earlier this morning."

"Yes, I had some urgent business in San Jose to attend to. I dropped in and talked to Dr. Allegra Zapata, as well." He tried to look properly concerned. "She said there was a minor issue. Have you been feeling any discomfort or different the last few months?" Yerik watched her face carefully.

Frowning, Sky said, "No. What problem?"

Shrugging, he said, "It's nothing, my dear. Dr. Zapata will be coming up five days from now to perform a simple surgical procedure. Wipe the worry off you face. It's nothing to be at all concerned about. All right?"

"Okay," Sky said, feeling tentative.

"Dr. Zapata will tell you everything when she sees you. She'll go over all your lab tests. Apparently, many young women have this condition and it's easy to remove and fix."

Sky felt trapped. She could feel Alexandrov maneuvering her. Why? She knew better than to confront him. Instead, she played along and said, "I've never seen you in a business suit before." Sky was always on guard around Alexandrov, even though there seemed to be a truce of sorts between them. She had realized that, at least for now, he wasn't going to torture her. Rather, she felt like a kept pet, something he wanted around and enjoyed playing with.

"Sometimes, when I must, I dress for the part," he murmured, giving her a slight smile. "What are your plans for today?"

Shrugging, Sky said, "I'd like to walk down to the meadow. I love walking there, seeing the raptors in their mews." Actually, it was to continue memorizing escape routes she'd chosen. She had been quietly collecting food and depositing it in the falconer's office near the mews. If she was going to escape, she had to have food. Water was plentiful. In fact, the other day, one of the men who cared for the raptors had shown her a thick, woody vine that, when cut open, yielded fresh, drinkable water. And these vines were everywhere in the surrounding jungle. That was good news for her.

"By all means. Would you like to fly one?"

Sky shook her head. "No. I just need to walk. Get my exercise."

Yerik nodded. He trusted Sky only so far. She had been a black ops U.S.

Army officer and had taken SERE training. His gut told him she was casing the property, looking for ways to escape. He never allowed her to go anywhere without a guard. The two falconers were tasked with watching her when she was in the meadow. "There is an Olympic-size pool. Why not start swimming every morning? Before breakfast?" He knew Sky was getting bored. He would not allow her near any television or computer. She had the newspaper, that was all. But he could see she was looking for something to keep her busy and occupied. Once she was pregnant with his son, he would keep her more than entertained.

"I thought about that. But I don't have a bathing suit." Sky dreaded wearing one. The guards always gave her looks that made her feel threatened. If Alexandrov wasn't present, she feared they might rape her. It was nothing overt, but the feeling was there, and it was enough to scare Sky. She was grateful Alexandrov had never made a move to touch her. He seemed respectful. Circumspect. More than willing to please her if he could.

"That can be remedied," Yerik assured her. He made a gesture and a servant waiting near the entrance to the villa who quickly walked toward them with a tray. "Here, I brought you a little something from the capital." He smiled at her.

Sky sat up as the servant placed the silver tray near her elbow. On it was a box. It said Giacomin Chocolates on it. The white box had a purple ribbon around it. "What is this?"

"For you. A sweet for a sweet." Yerik lazily gestured toward the small box. "A dozen of the finest chocolates, all handmade, in this country. I don't know a woman who doesn't love chocolates. I thought you might find these something to smile about." Because Sky rarely smiled at all, Yerik found himself wanting to see her smile. To be happy. He watched her pick delicately at the bow, graceful and feminine. The look on her face was also sweet. He felt his heart swell because finally, she was honestly reacting to the unexpected gift with genuine pleasure. But it was all part of getting her to trust him. Maybe, over time, to even like him. Yerik wanted her to bear him many sons. It would be Sky's way of paying him back because she was the reason Vladimir was dead. It was her karma to give back what he had lost. He knew things between them would turn hellish after Sky discovered herself pregnant. The months leading up to the birth would be stressful on her and him. He hoped to continue to forge small steps of trust with Sky. He wanted her to deliver him a fine, strapping son. An heir to his empire. Once again, he would have a large Russian family surrounding him. The prospect made him giddy.

"This is so nice," Sky whispered, opening the box. The chocolates looked delicious. "Did you get these this morning?"

"Yes, while in San Jose on business, I went to the shop that carries them." Yerik saw her lift the box and inhale the scent of the chocolate within it. Just the way Sky closed her eyes, a haunting slip of a smile across her lips, told him much. He'd broken men swift and hard. And he'd broken men slowly by killing them with kindness. The concept of Stockholm Syndrome wasn't lost on him at all, and he was waging a war to get Sky's trust. To get her to realize that he was her sun, and she was a planet that orbited him. And to forget the man who had impregnated her. He felt cold rage moving through him. Even he had blind idealism regarding Sky. How had he overlooked this fact she was pregnant by another man? She was slated to marry Cal Sinclair, the former SEAL, after all.

Sky looked over, forcing herself to sound compliant. "Thank you. This is a very thoughtful gift." She wondered why Yerik had done it.

"Well," Yerik said grandly, "if you continue to relax, to enjoy this place and acclimate, I was thinking of buying you an iPad so you could download ebooks. I know you like to read."

An iPad! Sky kept her face very still. Would it have email capability? Internet access? How far did Alexandrov really trust her? "I would love to have books to read," she said, her voice full of emotion. This time, she was being completely honest with him.

Nodding, Yerik murmured, "Well, as always, it depends upon you, Sky. I'm a very kind and generous man, as you know. If you continue to be compliant, to treat this villa as your new home, you will never want for anything. I have taken excellent care of you, and I will continue to do so. More than anything," he delved into her widening eyes, "I want you HAPPY."

A lump stuck in Sky's throat. What would make her happy was to find her way back to Cal. To be in his arms. To have a life with him. Not this oily monster who pretended to be nice when she knew damned well he could order her killed with a snap of his fingers. The need to escape overwhelmed Sky. Somehow, she had to get out of here. She didn't want any surgical procedure. She felt as if she were being maneuvered into something she didn't want to do.

CHAPTER 16

July 12

AT NOON THE next day, Allegra went to her office to find a moment's respite to think about Don Tobar's threat to her and her family. She was in complete emotional turmoil over the man's unexpected threat. Something was terribly wrong with the situation regarding Sky. What if she didn't want the abortion? Did the woman even know she was pregnant? Allegra didn't think so. She had just set down at her desk when Maria knocked at the door and entered.

"I'm so sorry, Doctor," she said, standing unsurely in the entrance to her office. "There are a man and woman out here who say it is urgent that they speak to you. A Jim and Emma Anderson?" She gave Allegra a pleading look. "They are insistent that it is important, that you must see them immediately."

"What?" Allegra muttered. She frowned. "Oh, send them in." Maria looked relieved and opened the door fully, gesturing for the couple to come into her office.

Allegra saw a tall, well-dressed couple enter. The woman was a stunning redhead dressed in a cream-colored pantsuit and emerald silk blouse that matched the color of her wide, gorgeous eyes. The man was casual, in a loose white short-sleeved cotton shirt, Levi's and sneakers. Alarms went off in Allegra and she didn't know why. She stood up and offered her hand as they approached her desk.

"I'm Dr. Allegra Zapata."

Cal took the doctor's thin, long hand. "Jim Anderson. This is my wife, Emma." He released her hand and added, "We're very grateful you would see us on such short notice."

"Nice to meet you, Emma. Please, both of you, sit down," and Allegra gestured gracefully to the two chairs in front of her desk.

"Thank you, doctor," Lauren said, giving her a slight smile while shaking her hand. She sat down next to Cal.

As Allegra took a seat, she saw the man's hard face, his light gold-brown eyes were completely unreadable. He pulled two photos out his wallet. He got up and slid them in front of her.

"Have you seen either of these two people, Doctor?" Cal stood, watching the doctor's face. Allegra frowned and pulled the small color photos closer.

"Oh," she whispered, "yes, I know both of them. This is Sky Lambert and that is Don Tobar." Confused, she looked up into the man's expressionless face. Allegra realized something else was going on here. This was not a couple with a fertility issue.

"Where is she?" Cal demanded, his heart taking off in hard, wild beats.

"Why," Allegra stumbled, unsure, "she is at La Paloma. She lives with Don Tobar up near the volcano, Arenal. Excuse me, but who ARE you?" and she gave them a confused look. For a moment, Allegra saw the man's face thaw, saw something in his eyes she couldn't interpret.

Cal pointed to the male in the photo. "You called this man Don Tobar?"

"...Yes. Why?"

"Because his real name is Yerik Alexandrov. He's the leader of the Russian mafia in New York City," Cal told her. He saw Allegra's face fall and the immediate terror in her eyes as she sat back, wrapping her arms around herself.

"How do you know this? Who ARE you?"

Cal tried to remain calm. Sky was here! She was with Alexandrov! She was so close... so close... "That woman, Sky Lambert, Dr. Zapata, is my fiancee. She was kidnapped off a beach in San Diego three and a half weeks ago." His voice turned to a growl. "Sky and I were to get married the next day. We've been trying to find her. We picked up some suspicious communications that led us to you and decided to come see you."

Gasping, Allegra sat forward, shocked. "YOU were going to marry Sky?"

"Yes. Why?" Cal demanded, watching the doctor pull over a file.

"Because she's nearly two months pregnant, Mr. Anderson. With, I'm assuming, your baby?"

Stunned, Cal blinked. He wasn't prepared for this. "Sky's pregnant?"

Allegra gave him a frown. "I examined her a week ago. She's pregnant. All the tests confirmed it." She saw the man flinch, saw raw grief in his eyes for a split second. And then the emotion was gone, replaced by that same hard, expressionless mask. She tapped the file with urgency. "You must know that Don Tobar wants me to abort her fetus four days from now. He wants her impregnated with his sperm. He wants Sky to carry HIS baby."

Lauren gasped, sitting up in the chair, hands gripping the arms. "What the hell are you talking about? That's SICK!"

Allegra heard the woman's husky voice turn to outrage. She looked at them and placed her hands protectively over Sky's file. "I'm telling you nothing more until you tell me who you really are. This is privileged medical information."

Cal moved and gave Lauren a warning look and then turned to the doctor. "As I told you, I am Sky's fiancé. We work for a U.S. security contractor based out of Washington D.C. that is coordinating Sky's rescue. We are here to find her and rescue her from her kidnappers, Dr. Zapata. We've been working nearly a month to locate Sky." He tried to keep his voice calm and firm, but damn, his heart was twisting in his chest. A part of him soared with the joy that Sky was pregnant. Pushing back on the gnawing ache growing in his chest, Cal focused on the upset doctor. "We need to know more about where this Don Tobar has her held."

"*Dios,*" Allegra whispered, rubbing her brow. She looked up at the man. "Then, you must know what happened yesterday morning," and she told them everything about Don Tobar's unexpectedly coming to her office and threatening her.

Cal sat down, listening. The sonofabitch now knew Sky was pregnant. With HIS child. And Alexandrov was going to force Zapata to abort his baby. He could barely sit still to listen to her entire story. When Allegra told them about Tobar kidnapping her oldest daughter, Belicia, to prove he could do it, Cal became grim. By the time the doctor finished, she had tears in her eyes she was dabbing away with a tissue.

"I-I'm terrified," Allegra whispered to them. "My daughters... *Dios...* they are MY life! And if I don't do what Don Tobar wants, he will take them away from me." Her voice cracked. "Forever!" Allegra gave them a desperate look. "Can YOU stop this from happening? Are you WORKING with the Costa Rican *policia?*"

Cal sat down, his mind moving at the speed of light. "We can help you, Doctor. We have connections with the police in your country." He saw her face fall with relief. "This Don Tobar is a wanted man by U.S. authorities. He's kidnapped my fiancee. And we're tasked with getting her back, safely, to U.S. soil."

"T-then, what can I do to help you?" Allegra asked tearfully. "I've NEV-ER had anything like this happen to me before."

Cal held on to his emotions. Rage churned through him. So did revenge. He wanted to kill Alexandrov himself. "Did Sky know she was pregnant?"

"No, I don't think so," Allegra sniffed, blotting her cheeks. "My nurse took her complete medical history. She had many bouts of not having her periods for months in her life because of the stress due to the type of flying she did. And she vomits when she is threatened."

"She was an Army helicopter pilot," Cal provided. "And Sky had told me she wouldn't have a period for months at a time because of the constant stress and danger." Never mind she was a black ops pilot, but Cal wasn't going there. The less the doctor knew, the better.

"Yes, she said stress stopped her period. When you're less than two months along, many women have no idea they are yet."

Cal grimaced. "All right, Doctor, here's what I suggest: cancel the rest of your appointments for today. We have a lot of work to do, and you need to tell us exactly where this La Paloma villa is situated."

"DON TOBAR!"

Yerik jerked his head up. He was in the den, reading a newspaper. His lead soldier, Oleg, came running in. His blue eyes were wide with shock. "What is it?" he demanded irritably.

"Sky Lambert has escaped!"

"What?" Alexandrov roared, leaping to his feet.

"The sensor alarms down by the falcon meadow just went off!"

Cursing in Russian, Alexandrov ran toward his soldier. "You know what to do! Send out a team! You head it up!" He grabbed the thickly muscled soldier by his arm. "Do NOT harm her! Be gentle with her! Find her, bring her back here! Take her to the basement interrogation room."

"Yes, sir," Oleg murmured, spinning around and running down the hall, talking into the radio unit he had clipped on the shoulder of his dark green cammo shirt.

Yerik breathed hard, cursing again. He hurried out to the patio and then ran down the path to the falconry area. Down there, he saw five soldiers amassing with rifles in hand and pistols on their hip. The two men who took care of the falconry area and fed his raptors, were gesturing excitedly toward the jungle behind the mews.

He cursed as he ran to where the group was huddled. He glared at the falconers, but said nothing, listening to what they had to say. One of them saw Sky in a dark green tee, carrying a small black canvas bag over her shoulder, and saw her slip into the jungle. It was he who had called in the initial alarm. Yerik had sensors out for half a mile in all directions around his estate. They would warn him of any incoming intruders. Or, in this case, the sensors would alert and pinpoint exactly where Sky was located. He was angry at her. What the hell! Yerik had badly miscalculated. She seemed compliant. She seemed to accept that she was his prisoner. Despite the fragility of her appearance, she had escaped! Angry at himself because he'd downplayed her military background, her ability to escape, he wanted to wrap his fingers around her slender throat and choke her until she passed out. The little bitch!

Oleg quickly got his five men fanning out into the jungle. Yerik knew he could do no good here. He headed over to his security control room, where he would watch the situation with the two soldiers manning the monitors. The sensors would report her activity, one after another. It was like an invisible string of breadcrumbs that would lead his men directly to where Sky was located. The jungle was fairly easy to traverse, and the alarm had gone out almost as soon as his man saw her run away. Turning, Yerik smiled grimly. Once they caught her, he would have his way with Sky. She'd disobeyed him. She'd flaunted her ability to escape. Now, she was going to pay the price.

Sky tripped and fell. Her go bag that contained her food and other items went flying out of her hand. She landed hard on her belly. She'd tripped over a partially hidden root beneath wet leaves on the floor of the jungle. Breathing hard, her heart pounding, Sky scrambled upward, fueled by adrenaline. Had anyone seen her escape? Had the man who fed the raptors seen her slip into the edge of the jungle? Sweat stood out on her face as she leaned down, grabbing her go bag. Everywhere around her were trees of varying sizes and heights. The floor of the jungle was littered with leaves that had fallen, exposing some roots, and hiding others.

She had to get out of here! All she wanted, all she needed, was Cal. Her sense of direction was nil, surrounded in all directions by the hilly jungle. Pulling out her compass, Sky pushed forward after pocketing it. She desperately needed to intersect a dirt road... anything... to escape. The land sloped downward, and she jogged forward, trying to keep her balance. To run hard would defeat her purpose. Sky knew from SERE training that the smartest way to travel was a constant jog. Her legs stretched, long and cadenced, as she moved down the hill. Up ahead, she could see another swell, topped with trees. In the distance, she could hear howler monkeys, their screeching muted by the surrounding jungle.

Just as she reached the area between the two hills, Sky skidded to a halt. She recognized Oleg standing off to her left. As she turned to the right to run, she saw Pyotr and Vadim. These were Yerik's best soldiers. And they stood there, panting hard and grinning triumphantly at her. Sky realized with a sinking feeling, terror filling her, that she'd been caught.

Yerik waited patiently in his office. He drummed his fingers on his desk. Oleg opened the door. His face was beaded with sweat, his uniform darkened with splotches of perspiration.

"We've put her in the interrogation room."

"Her condition?"

"We flex cuffed her once we located her, and she came back without a fight. She's tired."

"Did you give her water?"

"Yes, as you instructed."

Yerik smiled a little. "Excellent. Well done, Oleg. Dismissed."

Oleg nodded and left the door open.

Holding on to his rage, Yerik made his way down to the basement. There was a padded interrogation room wired with cameras and audio recording. Next door was the torture room. Next to it, a deprivation room that Yerik felt was an even better torture, because it took a person down mentally and emotionally, as well as physically. Two soldiers stood at the entrance to the interrogation room. They stepped aside and opened the door. Yerik strode in. Sky sat at the small, rectangular table, a pitcher of water and two paper cups on it. He saw wariness come to her eyes as he entered and quietly shut the door.

"You disappoint me," Yerik said softly, coming around and sitting on the opposite side of the dilapidated table. He picked up the pitcher and poured himself some water. Sky's face was scratched, but not badly. She was dirty. He saw debris and mud plastered across the front of her green tee. Saw the palpable beat of her heart beneath against her slender throat. Her hair was tangled, bits of leaves and soil in it. She must have fallen at least once. Sipping the water, his eyes never leaving hers, he knew the value of silence. Torture was all about timing. And he was a Master of It. Yerik saw her hands gripping her cup, saw her knuckles going white as she stared back at him. Yes, she was terrified. Sky wasn't as stupid as he'd thought. She knew he was angry. The look in her eyes told him she was waiting for him to physically strike her.

He smiled shortly as he set the glass down. "What? Nothing to say, Sky?"

Sky stared at Yerik's hooded eyes, felt his leashed rage toward her. "I want to go home," she said in a firm voice. "I was going to marry Cal. You took me away from him. I don't want to be here."

"Ah, I see." He sat back, relaxed, watching her. Yerik's respect for her backbone of steel increased. "And here I thought you were happy with me here at La Paloma. You seemed resigned to stay. Why, you even seemed happy at times."

"How would you feel if you'd been torn away from someone you loved?"

"Oh," Yerik murmured, "it has happened twice in my life. First, my beautiful Darya dies giving birth to my son. And then," his voice dropped, and he allowed some of his rage to be revealed to her, "Vlad falls in love with you and all you do is run away from him. He spent years trying to find you. And when he did, you got him murdered."

Sky compressed her lips. She felt her heart beating like a wild bird trapped in her chest. "I NEVER loved Vlad! It was always one sided!"

"Hmmm, well my son loved you. He was obsessed with you."

Sky felt panic and forced it down. She was in a padded room. She saw the cameras in all four corners of it. There was a reflective mirror behind Alexandrov, and she had no doubt there were soldiers watching her from behind it, even though she couldn't see them. "Vlad got himself killed." Her nostrils flared. "He kidnapped me in Peru! Against my will!"

"The last satellite phone call I received from my son was that you had malaria and two of his men, combat medics, were caring for you." Yerik stared at her. "My son cared for you even then, Sky. He didn't shoot you in the head. He gave you medical help."

"Yeah," Sky ground out, "when I came out of the malaria cycle, he was going to RAPE ME! So much for love!"

Scowling, Yerik growled, "Rape you? He LOVED you!"

Her nostrils flared, and Sky leaned forward, her voice hard, her eyes locked with Alexandrov's surprised gaze. "Rape! Your son was going to rape me! That sure as hell isn't love!" She slammed her fist down on the table. "Vlad tried to rape me when I was seventeen! He cornered me in my bedroom and threw me on the bed against my will." Her breathing became uneven, her voice cracking. "You have this sick idea that Vlad was a good person. Well, he wasn't! In Peru, he would deliberately rape a chief's daughter in front of him and his village, then force them to work with him and carry cocaine. Your son was a sick, sadistic bastard!" Tears splattered down Sky's taut face. "When I managed to push Vlad off me on that bed, he went and got a pistol. He was going to force me at gunpoint to lay on that bed and give him what he wanted. Only, my foster father, Jack Zimmerman, heard my screams and came running into my bedroom." She sobbed and forced out, "Vlad shot him! He murdered him! And when my foster mother came because she heard Vlad's gun go off, he killed her too!"

Yerik scowled. "If you would have surrendered, it would have turned out different. You should have submitted. Not fought."

Sky angrily wiped tears from her taut face, breathing hard. "He murdered the two people I loved most in the world! And these people had taken care of him since age nine! Vlad enjoyed killing. He enjoyed torture! And he routinely raped the women down in Peru. Him and his gang of men. No woman was safe from them."

Shrugging, Yerik growled, "That does not matter."

Sky sat back, wrapping her arms around her breasts, feeling naked even though she was clothed. "Let me go, Yerik. Let me go home. I will NEVER stay here. I will keep trying to escape. I will NEVER be compliant, as you put it, with you ever again!" Sky watched in terror as his face grew savage, saw his lips lift in a snarl. She knew Alexandrov would torture her, even kill her, but she no longer cared. Sky had hoped for rescue. She had prayed Cal would find her. But a month had gone by, and she felt her hope crumble day after day. There was no rescue coming. Sky knew that Alexandrov had probably gone to ground, leaving no trail that Cal could possibly follow. She could feel Cal wanting to find her, but after a month, her hope had died. The Russian knew how to hide from the world. Instead, she had tried to escape on her own.

"Do you know," Yerik said softly, giving her a bit of a smug smile, "that you're pregnant? That man you were going to marry. It must be his brat you carry."

Shocked, Sky sat up, her arms falling to her side. "What the hell are you talking about?" Instinctively, her hand pressed protectively against her abdomen. She saw Yerik smile fully, enjoying himself.

"When Dr. Zapata came here? I found out yesterday morning that you are pregnant."

"No...," and Sky sat back, her mind spinning. Her heart and mind fled back to that beautiful lovemaking when she'd felt it was so special. One-of-a-kind. Her hand tightened against her belly. Of late, her jeans wouldn't fit around her waist anymore. She had thought she was just gaining weight. Reflecting, Sky realized lately her emotions had been like violent up and down drafts. She'd cried so easily the last four weeks, and that was completely unlike her. She thought it was because she'd been kidnapped and held prisoner here. Worse, she had begun to vomit every few days, unlike her unless... unless she was pregnant...

"Yes." Yerik smiled more. "You did not know?"

Frowning, Sky muttered defiantly, "No."

"Well, it doesn't matter."

She stared at him. "What do you mean?"

Shrugging lazily, Yerik picked up his glass and sipped from it. "In a few days, Dr. Zapata is coming here. She is going to abort your brat. You'll have the surgery and be done with it."

Sky gasped. She shoved away from the table, the chair falling to the floor as she jerked upright. "NO!" and she backed away, her hands over her belly. "You wouldn't do that! It's MY BABY! I refuse any surgery!"

Torture was so enjoyable. Yerik let her sweat. Let her feel the full terror of her situation. "You will have nothing to say about it, my dear. You are mine. I OWN YOU." He gestured lazily in her direction. "And once you're rid of that brat you're carrying, then Dr. Zapata is going to monitor you. She wants your uterus to be receptive and ready."

Sky backed against the padded wall, staring at him. "What are you raving about? Receptive for what?" She saw Yerik's thick lips twist.

"She is going to impregnate you with my sperm, Sky. And you will become pregnant. This time, with MY son. You see? You took Vlad from me. And I must have a son to give my empire to someday. So, I've chosen you to carry my son. Just karma. Don't you think?"

The words shattered through Sky. She gasped, her eyes rounding as she heard Alexandrov's plan for her. "NO!" she screamed. "I will NOT carry your bastard!"

Yerik was up on his feet, swiftly covering the distance. He grabbed Sky, his fingers wrapping around her throat. He slammed her against the padded wall. The door swung open, and two soldiers stepped in. They grabbed her arms, holding her firmly against the wall. Sky sputtered, her face turning red. She tried to kick out. Yerik easily avoided her flailing feet. Smiling, he held her throat just tight enough to shut off some, but not all of her air. "Now," he snarled into her waxen face, her eyes filled with terror, with the realization she was his in every possible way, "you are going to be the mother to all MY children. You are going to understand what it means that I own you." Yerik suddenly released her. The soldiers let go of her as well. Sky collapsed to the floor, hand against her throat, gagging for breath.

Yerik stepped back. "Take her to the deprivation cell. Make sure she has food and water." He smiled down at Sky as she sank weakly to her hands and knees, sobbing rawly. "You know," he drawled, leaning down, sliding his fingers through her hair and jerking her head up so he could look into her eyes, "deprivation is a swift, brutal way to break a person's spirit. You need to be broken, and I promise, I will break you..." He pushed Sky down hard, hearing her cry out as she slammed to the floor.

"Take her there now!" and Yerik spun on his heel, leaving the room.

Sky shut her eyes, feeling the soldiers slide their hands beneath her armpits, hauling her upright. Faint, black dots still dancing in front of her eyes, she couldn't fight, her feet not working properly. They dragged her out of the room. They took her two doors down and put her into a dark room that had no lighting. The light spilling in from the hallway revealed the rough shapes of a table and a chair, the entire room padded like the other one. In the corner was a toilet. There was an old mattress, stained with blood and other fluids, in the other corner. They jerked her over to the mattress and let her collapse upon it. In moments, they were gone, the door shut with a finality that made her panic. It was pitch black. There was no light, anywhere.

Oh, Cal...

CHAPTER 17

July 12

S KY SAT ON the mattress, back against the padded wall, arms wrapped around her drawn up knees. Tears trickled down her cheeks and she tried not to sob. Her throat burned and ached where Alexandrov had grabbed and choked her. She'd been so shocked by his sudden violence that she'd completely forgotten how to fight back. But what good would it have done anyway? Sky knew she was being watched all the time and it made her feel desperate, like a caged wild animal with no place to hide. Her heart swung back to the baby she carried. Cal's baby.

As she settled down, the adrenaline crashing through her finally dissipating, Sky slid her arms around her belly, rocking a little, feeling her way through the fact she was pregnant. The signs had been there all along. Why hadn't she recognized them? Swallowing painfully, she noticed the throbbing in her throat was gradually subsiding. The past month she'd been vomiting but hadn't thought anything of it. At first, Sky thought it was flu. Or that some food odors repelled her, making her suddenly nauseous. Her stomach would roil, and so many times here at the villa, Sky thought her reaction was triggered by the stress of being kidnapped by Alexandrov.

It had been over an hour since they had thrown her in this dark room. Sky slowly got up, dying of thirst. The room was stuffy and the humidity heavy. Feeling as if she were starving for a breath of fresh air, Sky kept her hands out in front of her, knowing that in the center of the room was a table. There was a pitcher of water on it and a paper cup. Finding it, she sat down and poured the water with shaking hands. She was pregnant. Would the stress of all this harm her baby? Would she miscarry? Above all, Sky did not want to lose Cal's baby. She sat there, fear and grief roiling through her. Hanging her head, her hands wrapped around the glass, she shook.

The thought of Dr. Zapata coming to abort her baby made her nauseous again. Her stomach revolted. Sky vomited violently. She kept retching, arms against her stomach as she leaned over, head between her legs. Her mouth burned with acid. Tears squeezed out of her eyes. She floundered with her hand, finding the glass of water. She took a drink, swishing it around. Where was the toilet? She couldn't see it, everything suffocatingly black. She was afraid to get up, feeling that if she did, she'd collapse. Spitting the water out on the ground, she cleaned out her mouth. The horrible stench of the vomit made her stomach roil again.

The darkness, the airless room closed in on Sky. She tried to remember SERE, tried to remember what to do to combat the despair tunneling through her. She finished the water and then pushed the chair back from the table. Getting up, holding on to the chair, Sky moved in slow, unsure steps, trying to locate the mattress. Once she found it, she collapsed upon it, laying on her side in a fetal position, her arms around her stomach, trying to protect her unborn child. She knew Yerik would force her to have the abortion. More than likely, Dr. Zapata would be forced to do it because the bastard would threaten her life and family if she didn't. Oh, God, what was she going to do?

July 14

YERIK SMILED AS he watched Sky laying on the mattress in a fetal position. She'd been in the deprivation room for two days. Once a day, ample amounts of food were delivered and plenty of fresh water was always available for her on the table. He'd watched Sky begin to lose ground with herself. It had been enjoyable watching her slowly surrender to the inevitable. He had infrared cameras installed in the room and he could see her every expression. She'd been vomiting two to three times every day, much to his delight. He was sure the stench of the vomit was making her even more miserable. *Good.* He wanted to break her. That way, she would become compliant. Sky had no way to bathe, no way to clean herself. Deprivation did wonders to a person when everything was taken away from them. It was an easy form of torture, and given Sky's hormonal state, knowing he was going to rip that brat out of her uterus shortly, she had to be going through a very special hell. All of it, Yerik knew, would begin to dismantle Sky's desire to escape, to fight back.

In a few more days, Dr. Zapata was driving to his villa with her assistant, and she would abort the fetus Sky carried. He'd ordered the doctor to do whatever necessary to force Sky to have the abortion. The doctor had assured him she would give Sky a shot to make her go unconscious and then perform a D&C. He was going to be in that room, watching the doctor do it. He didn't trust Zapata at all. He smiled a little. That thrilled Yerik. There was nothing like ultimate control over another human being, and he was going to take extra pleasure in watching it all unfold.

"I'm going down to see her. Get the guard to open the door. And turn on the lights as the door opens. I want to surprise the bitch."

The guard nodded, giving a quick call to the two men who stood outside the deprivation room.

The door was opened for Yerik. The stench of vomit assailed his sensitive nostrils. The lights suddenly flashed on. He heard Sky give a sudden cry, her hands reflexively moving up to her eyes, turning away from the light where she lay on the mattress. Yerik smiled to himself as he jerked the chair away from the table and sat it a few feet opposite of the mattress. Sky's face was pale, her lips drawn back in a grimace as she slowly sat up, hands protective against her eyes.

"Do you have any idea of how long you have been in here?" Yerik asked her in a gentle tone.

Sky shook her head. Her heart pounded with fear. The light blinded her. She could see nothing. But Alexandrov had entered, and she could feel him nearby. Fresh air tunneled into the room and Sky desperately dragged in huge draughts of it.

Yerik spread his thighs open, placed his elbows on them, hands clasped between them. "Time is a funny thing," he went on in a quiet tone. "You lose track of it with only the darkness. Just being alone with yourself and your thoughts. It's amazing how the mind will turn and spiral downward when there is no light. We humans are dependent upon it." Yerik watched Sky lift her head, squinting, her brow furrowed, hands guarding her eyes. The light was very low, as a matter of fact, but he knew from experience that for eyes going without light for that long, it would be exceedingly painful when they were suddenly exposed to it. He smiled a little, watching tears running freely down her drawn cheeks. Sky had eaten little. She'd vomited at least twice a day like clockwork. It had to be due to the pregnancy. That, or the extreme stress. Yerik knew one of the vagal nerve responses to stress was vomiting. *Perfect.* He had her exactly where he wanted her.

"Tell me, Sky? Would you like to get out of this room?"

"Yes," she rasped, her voice hoarse from disuse.

"Well, there's always a price to pay for your freedom, eh? You were a bad girl. You tried to run away from me. And you see what you get? Time in the deprivation room. It's not pleasant, is it?"

Sky shook her head, her eyes watering nonstop as the light stabbed into them. The pain was excruciating. She could do little other than try to shade her barely opened eyes, the tears streaming down her face. She felt so out of control.

"Well then," Yerik went on in a pleasant tone, "I need to you ask me nicely to leave this room. If you ask, I shall grant your wish." Compliance started with the prisoner being forced to ask something of his or her captor. It was the first step in controlling the prisoner. He saw her lips thin, saw her lick the lower one, her head bowed against her knees she hugged against her body. Yerik smiled as he saw her tremble.

"But," he murmured, his voice reasonable, "if you don't ask me, then I'm afraid I shall leave here quite soon and you can remain in here another three days. It is your decision."

"I-I want out of here."

Her voice had been low, emotionally off key. Yerik's spirit soared with joy. "You must learn to be respectful. 'I want out of here, please.'"

Sky whispered brokenly, "I want out of here, please…"

"Very good," Yerik praised, slapping his hands against his thighs. "Now, you must tell me what you want, Sky. You must always be honest and truthful with me from now on. Tell me what you desire." He watched her cower, her brow pressed to her knees, hands against her eyes. She was fighting him. It was to be expected. To be broken down and forced to do or say things under duress was tough on someone like her.

Yerik had changed his frame of mind on how he saw Sky Lambert. He'd allowed his own plans for her to gloss over the fact she had been a trained military officer. She was not stupid. As a matter of fact, she was damned intelligent. When he'd gone over her behavior the last four weeks when she was a prisoner here at the villa, Yerik realized he'd been played by her. Sky had pretended to be compliant when she was not. She had been very good at fooling even him, and few could do that. Ever. But now, he was going to get even. He had to break her before she was fertilized with his sperm. That meant he had a month to do it, because he wanted Sky in an even emotional space when she carried his son. There would be no more torture after she became impregnated. He had a month.

"Sky," he reminded her gently, "you must speak up quickly. I take your silence as a no. And my people learn quite speedily around here that they must answer me or do my bidding without hesitation. So, this one time only, I will be patient with you. But from now on," and his voice became a grate where he allowed his anger to be unveiled, "if you dare disobey me, I will have you thrown back into this room. Do we understand one another?"

"Y-yes, we understand one another."

Her voice was halting. Yerik heard no anger in it. Just… resignation. That was a promising start. "Very good. Now, tell me what you want?"

Sky lifted her head, squinting, trying to hold his gaze. He was dressed in a pale blue peasant's shirt, white linen slacks, and sandals. "I want to keep my baby. Do NOT take it. Please?" She watched him wreath in a smile.

"Very good. You are learning, Sky. Unfortunately, I cannot grant you your request. But I can reward you for speaking your honest and truthful thoughts. Would you like a shower? To wash your hair? A clean set of clothes?"

"Y-yes. Please..." and she sobbed, pressing her hands against her eyes, tears running down her cheeks.

Yerik felt as if he'd made a breakthrough with Sky. "That, my dear, I can easily grant you. I will have you taken to Catarina's suite. She will take proper care of you."

"T-thank you..."

"No. 'Thank you, Don Tobar.'"

"Thank you, Don Tobar."

Pleased, he stood, wanting badly to get out of this hellhole of a room. "Very good. You will join me for dinner, my dear." He stepped out and the guard shut the door.

"Get her out," Yerik told his guards. "Have Catarina take her to her bathroom suite and get her cleaned up. Tell her to dress Sky in a loose fitting dark blue caftan gown," and he grinned. "Then, bring her to the pergola and she will join me for dinner tonight.

"Yes, Don Tobar," the guard said.

Sky luxuriated beneath the warm spray of water from the shower. She'd washed her hair, soaped off the stench from her skin. Catarina had given her a thick pink towel and she'd dried herself off afterward. As she looked down at her belly, Sky thought she saw a slight bump, more than normal. That was her baby. *Cal's baby.* Her heart cringed in abject grief as she thought about her baby being aborted. Somehow, she had to convince Yerik to not do this to her.

"Here you go," Catarina said airily, opening the bathroom door. She presented Sky with a bra, panties, sandals, and a dark blue silk caftan. "Don Tobar expects you for dinner in about thirty minutes. I must prepare you, so hurry, come out here and sit down in front of my make-up mirror."

Emotionally, Sky felt numb. She recognized it from the time she'd escaped Vlad by going out a bedroom window, getting the police, and then coming back to the house, seeing her foster parent's dead bodies. She'd felt gutted. Out of control as if the world were controlling her instead. She was a puppet of circumstances. Despite feeling robotic, Sky caressed her belly where her baby lay protected. Swallowing hard, she followed Catarina out to the vanity.

When she sat down, she saw five bruise marks, bright purple, around her neck. Catarina said nothing. Staring at her face, Sky saw how lifeless her eyes looked. They had finally adjusted to light, and she was no longer leaking tears. The pain had gone away. Staring at her throat, Sky realized the violence in Alexandrov was barely beneath the surface. She tried to think as Catarina fussed with her hair and quickly put on make-up. Sky hated the make-up. It symbolized a mask to her, something she couldn't tolerate.

"Don Tobar wants you looking beautiful," Catarina cooed. "You have such great bones in your face. You're truly gorgeous Sky. I think he'll be very pleased when you sit with him at dinner."

Sky said nothing. If she fought the make-up, she knew there would be instant repercussions. She did NOT want to go back into that squalid, hateful, smelly room.

"Do you know? He chose the caftan for you. He requested a certain perfume for your skin as well."

"I hate perfume."

"Not anymore, you don't," Catarina laughed. And then she became very somber. "Sky, you must not make him angry. What he has done to you this one time is nothing compared to what he can do." She placed her hand on Sky's shoulder. "Please, just do as he requests. If you do, things will go better for you. I promise."

Sky nodded and said nothing. Catarina had to know she had been thrown into the deprivation room. Clearing her throat, she whispered, "Has he done that to you, too? Put you in that room for days without any light?" She looked up at the pretty Russian girl. Catarina grimaced.

"No. If I do not, please him, he throws me to some of his favorite guards. They have their way with me. They're allowed to do anything they want. They are animals compared to Don Tobar. I hate it. I hate when... well... when I do not, please him exactly as he wants."

Sky gave her a sympathetic look. Is that what was in store for her? How was he going to impregnate her? Rape her? Just as Vlad had tried to do? Her mind whirled and Sky felt a violent rush of emotions. She would NEVER let a man rape her. Vlad had nearly done so. He'd been a wild animal, the look in his eyes insane as he'd held her down, ripped off her panties... Sky closed her eyes, feeling lost. Feeling abandoned.

"Listen," Catarina said quietly as she leaned over to put eye shadow over her eyes, "Don Tobar enjoys watching me being raped by his soldiers."

Sky thought of Vlad enjoying capturing a fly and slowly pulling off it wings. The voyeur in him, she supposed. "I'm so sorry for you, Catarina. I really am..."

"It doesn't happen often," she breathed softly. "I feel badly when I do not please him. I try my best. I live to make him smile. To have him pet me afterward and tell me I pleasured him."

Sky's stomach churned. Would he rape her? It sounded like it. Her whole world collapsed in on her. Alexandrov was extracting his revenge on her, she realized dully. He was going to take her baby's life. He would rape her, get her pregnant, and then she would be forced to carry his baby inside her body. The thought was so repugnant that Sky would rather kill herself than allow that to happen. A horrible, snaking finality flowed through her. There was no help coming for her. Cal couldn't find her. Soon, she would have her baby aborted against her will by Dr. Zapata. And then, sometime in the future, Alexandrov would rape her and impregnate her. Hopelessness filtered through her. It was not a life she could live.

Sky saw the pleasure in Alexandrov's face as the guard escorted her to the pergola beneath the stars above. A white linen tablecloth laid across the table, place settings of white plates with gold rims sitting upon it. He was dressed in a dark blue silk shirt the same color as her caftan, black linen slacks, and sandals. She could tell he'd coordinated their clothing. It sickened her. The guard pulled out the chair and she sat down opposite him.

"You look beautiful, Sky," Yerik said, opening his white linen napkin. A servant came and placed a colorful small appetizer in front of him and then her. "Does it not feel wonderful to breath in clean, fresh air? To wear clean clothes? To smell the fragrance of your washed hair?"

Sky sat and hung her head, unable to look at him. Her stomach churned, her hands knotted in her lap beneath the tablecloth.

Yerik could tell Sky was completely stressed out. Ordinarily, he'd punish her for not answering him right away, but she was beaten. His heart lifted with joy. The days in the deprivation suite had done more than he had hoped. "Come, come, my chef has prepared a delicacy of lobster with a divine sauce. You must eat to keep up your strength my dear."

Sky forced her to look across the table at him. "I'm not hungry."

Nodding, Yerik savored the lobster. "Of course. I understand. There is much going on in your life presently. Soon, Dr. Zapata will abort the brat you carry." He saw her wince, tears come to her huge blue eyes. He smiled. "I never told you this, but you remind me so much of my beloved Darya, my wife. She too, as you know, had blond hair. I showed you her photo." He finished the appetizer and the servant quickly remove the plate. Another servant came and poured white wine in his wineglass. "I am hoping that when you are impregnated with my semen, you will have a blond-haired son for me nine months later." He smiled at her, lifting the glass to his lips. "A replacement for Vlad. A beautiful, blond-haired baby son. You will make me a very happy man, Sky. And I will see to it that you want for nothing. You will be treated as the queen you are."

Sky glared at him. "You're going to rape me time and time again? Until you get that son you want?"

Surprised, Yerik grinned and set down his glass. "Ah, I see. You are worried I will take you physically? That you become my nightly bed partner? Raping you against your will?" He held up his hands, laughing softly. "My dear Sky, I'm a civilized man. I have no need to upset you like that. No, Dr. Zapata will routinely come up here once every few weeks and see how your hormones are behaving. She will then know when you ovulate. At that time, I will donate my sperm and it will be placed into you without me ever laying a hand on you." He saw her eyes widen. Saw sudden relief in her expression. So, Sky was worried about being raped. Well, that was a useful piece of information. If she misbehaved during pregnancy and carrying his child, he could threaten her with rape to bring her back into line. The threat would make her behave and continue to gently carry his son in her young, healthy body.

"Then," Sky whispered unsteadily, "you won't touch me?"

"No, my dear." He sighed. "You are going to be the mother to all my children that I had dreamed of having with Darya. You will give them to me, instead. And you will be queen of all you see. You will have the best of medical care, designer clothing, gourmet food, and jewels that the world will envy. One day, you will realize how much you have, and I hope you will one day look upon me with some fondness. You are going to be the mother to many, many children to complete my dreams of having a large family. Russians like big families. Did you know that?"

Sky avoided the look in Alexandrov's eyes. He was a madman. Insane. And if he thought for one second that she was going to willingly carry his son, he was mistaken. Again, she thought of escape. Not physically leaving this villa but ending her own life. Sky's heart shrank with grief because she was going to not only lose Cal's baby, but he would never see her again. Would Cal ever know what had happened to her? Sadly, Sky doubted it.

"You know," Yerik said conversationally as the servants brought over their small salad as the next course, "you cannot escape this villa. I have sensors placed all around this area, Sky. The reason my soldiers caught you so quickly is because the sensors are monitored from the security control room here," and he pointed toward the villa. "We have cameras placed around, as well. When you walk near a motion sensor, it goes off. My men then switch on a camera in that area, and voila! There you are." Yerik stopped smiling and looked at her. "There is no escape from here, Sky. I think you know that now, don't you?"

"Yes," she whispered, "I know that now." There was some relief he would not touch her. Would not rape her to get her pregnant. Her heart shrunk with sadness as she thought of her baby beneath her hand pressed against her belly. *Cal... my God...* He would never know. Never know... Sky loved him so much, she felt as if she would implode from those beautiful feelings. He had given her so much in four months. The four most wonderful, happy months in her unhappy life. And now, it was at an end. A terrible, nightmarish end…

"Come, come," Yerik pleaded, "eat a bit of your salad, Sky. I cannot have you losing weight. You must maintain in order to be healthy and vibrant. That way, you will become pregnant more quickly."

CHAPTER 18

July 14

"**H**ERE'S THE BLUEPRINT for La Paloma," Cal told his team. Jack Driscoll and Alex had flown into Costa Rica earlier that evening. They were in a back room at the U.S. embassy in San Jose. Transferring the blueprint from his laptop to a white screen hung on one wall, Cal directed a red laser pointer at the floorplan. "According to Dr. Zapata, she was taken to several areas of this villa. What we're interested in is the security control room. It sits on the main floor of the villa. She caught a glimpse of the room because the door was open when she was taken to examine Sky. There were two security guards in it manning banks of monitors and camera feed."

"This is the heart and brains of security for the entire place," Lauren added. "La Paloma is entirely reliant on gas fed generators to produce electricity for the villa."

Cal nodded to her. "We're ASSUMING there's motion sensors and infrared cameras installed around the villa. Dr. Zapata didn't see anything, but she's a civilian and wouldn't know what to look for."

"How far out are the sensors?" Alex asked. "Does anyone know?"

Jack Driscoll grimaced. "Alexandrov is a control freak and security is his way of staying alive and ahead of those who want to kill him. I'd say a half mile radius around that villa, minimum. Probably more. We should go in expecting that kind of coverage."

Cal agreed. "Dr. Zapata was led past the security area and down this hall." He put his laser on a room that he'd labeled Examination Room. "After Sky was examined by her, Dr. Zapata saw her leave down this hall. She went into a room and I'm assuming it's her bedroom or apartment, here."

Alex studied it. "Sky is two doors down from the examination room?"

"Yes," Cal said, "and about fifty feet away from the security room."

Jack grinned a little. "Doesn't get any better than that. She'll be easy to extract after we take out the security room personnel."

"Assuming she's in there," Alex countered.

Cal nodded somberly. When running a mission, nothing ever went right.

They were always adapting to the unknown. "Correct." Cal didn't want to go there. If he allowed his emotions out of his kill box, he wouldn't be able to focus. And without focus, this mission was DOA, dead on arrival. He had his team, three people he trusted with his life. He wasn't going to let them down.

Lauren said, "There was a LOT of activity in that meadow several days ago. And we did confirm that Alexandrov was there."

"Yes," Cal said, "and we saw a helluva lot of his soldiers. They were geared up and going into that jungle and hunting someone."

"Could be an animal tripped a sensor," Jack said, leaning back in his chair at the long, rectangular table. "That's a routine event."

"Probably happened," Cal agreed.

"And if it was," Jack said, "then they were in serious response mode."

"Which means we can expect maximum resistance if they find us on the property or in the villa," Cal told them. It would turn into an ugly, close-quarters firefight. That's not what they wanted. Their goal was to extract Sky, ideally done with secrecy and silence. No one would know she was gone until the next morning.

"Because of the satellite fly over on that day," Lauren said, "we counted ten white and presumed Russian soldiers. Dr. Zapata saw two men manning the security room. That makes twelve."

"Alexandrov is not going to have light security," Cal said. "From the photos, we saw Russian weapons on these men."

"They are all ex-Spetsnaz," Alex warned them. "I recognize the way they move, the type of weapons they carry, and the gear they wear."

Cal nodded to the medic. "We're going up against first line defense operators. This isn't going to be easy."

"Your mission plan has you guys entering that river upstream a mile north of the villa," Lauren said.

Cal switched to the Power Point presentation and threw it up on the screen. "Here," he said. "We'll be dropped three miles upriver from the villa by a Night Stalker helicopter that has been given permission to come into Costa Rican territory by their government. We'll fast rope down to the bank of that river. We'll trot two miles. The three of us will then enter the river here, a mile from the villa. From hydrology reports, this river is slow moving, low current, and varies from three to twenty feet deep. We're going in with our gear, wearing rubber boots, keeping our combat boots in our waterproof rucks to keep them dry. We'll shadow the bank, remaining in the water. Reedbeds grow along both banks, running four to six feet in height. They will give us plenty of cover. We'll make our way towards the target and egress here." Cal threw up the blueprint of the villa. "We'll switch out our rubber boots for our combat boots and make our way into the villa at this infil point."

"Does anyone know if Alexandrov owns watch dogs?" Alex asked.

"So far," Lauren said, "the satellite flyovers have not detected a dog." She grimaced. "I hope like hell he doesn't have any, because they can raise alarm and wake up everyone at that villa. Not good for us."

"It's something we're going to have to deal with if it occurs," Cal said. "Also, we don't know if he has warning apparatuses between the villa and that river. There's ten-foot-tall cyclone fencing with concertina wire along the top of it at the ends of the villa. My bigger question is: are they going to have motion sensors WITHIN that area?"

Jack said, "Doubtful because of the heavy fence and concertina. It's probably one of the few areas that does not have motion sensors." He shrugged. "You'll find out pretty quickly when you egress from the river. If an alarm goes off? You'll know they are in place. If nothing happens, it gives your team the opportunity to get to the sliding glass doors and enter the villa without being detected."

"Infrared satellite has given us spotty intel," Lauren said. "There are so many trees right around the villa that it's not getting a clear picture of infrared body heat signatures inside each room." She added, "In all of the photos that we do have, there have been no animals detected, just blurred human shapes."

Cal kept the villa blueprint up on the screen. "There are two wings to this place. Down the south wing, there are three rooms. Human body heat detected in all three. They APPEAR to be female, but we can't confirm. Down the north wing, this is where we believe Sky is kept."

"I wonder if the door is locked from the outside?" Jack asked.

"There's been no guard standing outside it according to the infrared sat photos," Cal said. "We need to assume it's locked from the outside."

"Yeah," Lauren growled, "can't have Sky running around freely in that villa, can we?"

"There's wrought iron bars on all room windows," Cal noted. "There's no escape that way. Once I find her, she'll have to come down the hall, past the disabled security room, and egress out this door to the main parking area."

"And of course," Lauren said, "you will have called me on the radio, and I'll drive up that asphalt road and pick all of you up."

"Right," Cal said. "You're our driver. You'll have an SUV and will hide on the side of that road one mile away from the villa. We're going to assume Alexandrov has sensors out one mile in every direction."

"What if Sky is not ambulatory?" Jack demanded.

Cal's mouth quirked. "I'll carry her out. Whatever it takes."

Lauren looked across the table at Alex. "You have your combat medical pack ready to go? Sky may need immediate medical aid."

Alex nodded. "I am ready for anything."

"After we exfil with Sky," Cal continued, "we're driving thirty miles south, out of the mountain jungle area. A Night Stalker Army Black Hawk helicopter will meet us at this pre-arrange GPS point. We'll hand over the SUV to another driver, a local CIA agent, who will be coming off that bird. He'll drive the SUV back to San Jose, switch out the license plates, wipe it down, get rid of any prints, and hand it back to the rental car company."

"And then," Lauren said, "we get on board and fly out to meet the U.S. carrier off Costa Rica's coast, who just happens to be taking part in some war games in that area." She grinned. "Great timing, isn't it?"

Cal nodded. "Yeah, luck broke in our favor." *Finally.*

"I hope those Night Stalkers know how to land on the deck of a Navy carrier," Alex said.

"These are the best black ops helo pilots in the world," Cal assured him. "They're trained to land and take off on damn near anything. They'll take us safely to the carrier, no problem. From there, we get Sky to the Navy medical unit to be examined and taken care of. They can handle surgery if necessary." Cal hoped like hell it wouldn't be necessary, but he had no idea what shape Sky was in. Or that she was even alive.

"What about Alexandrov?" Alex growled. "Are we going to take him out?"

Cal saw the medic's face grow closed, and he saw the banked rage in Alex's eyes. "No. Our objective is to find Sky and extricate her."

"What if," Lauren said, "everything goes to hell in a handbag?"

Alex scowled and looked at her. "What is a handbag? Is that American slang for a woman's purse?"

Lauren groaned. "I'll explain later."

"Is it like a bag with grenades in it?" Alex pressed, struggling to understand. He was in a mission meeting. He needed to grasp everything now, not later.

Jack snickered. "Alex, it's like a woman's purse. I think women carry everything in it, and hell, maybe even hand grenades. Who knows? Nothing would surprise me as to what they're carrying in it."

"Oh, get a life, Driscoll," Lauren muttered, giving him a dark look. She saw Alex's brows go down. She felt sorry for him. "Alex, it's slang for Murphy's Law. Do you know that one?"

"No," he muttered. "More slang?"

Cal grinned. "Murphy's Law is a SEAL maxim, Alex. It means if anything can go wrong, it WILL go wrong."

"Oh... that... yes, we call that contingency planning. But you call it going to hell in a handbag, instead?"

Lauren groaned.

Driscoll howled.

Alex gave them a boyish grin. "Then I am right?"

Cal kept his face neutral. He understood the hapless medic was playing catch up. "It's Murphy's Law in disguise, Alex. If you can't remember Murphy, then yes, it's contingency planning because no mission goes according to plan." He saw the combat medic brighten, having grasped the concepts.

Jack wiped his eyes. He gave Alex a look of respect. "You've got it, Alex."

The medic nodded. "Good. You know, when I get a chance, I do write down all these slangs. I memorize them and remember they are a code for another definition. It is like," and he lifted his eyes to the ceiling, in thought for a moment, "like a stenographer writes in shorthand when a boss dictates a letter to her? Yes?"

"Yes," Lauren said. She admired Alex's tenacity. And his desire to understand American slang. "But we have a fall back. We have military lingo. Some of the concepts you know because you were an operator with that drug gang in Peru. You just know it by another name."

"Yes, I am catching up," and Alex gave her a warm smile.

Lauren didn't want to be affected by the sudden warmth radiating off Alex. He was so simple and straight forward for a man, it always caught her off guard. She was used to dealing with men who had layers of complexity. Being a farm boy in Ukraine, maybe Alex's simple way of living was preferable. She found herself appreciating his honesty. What you saw was what you got with Alex. There were no hidden agendas. He was easy to read, unlike the other operators she knew.

"Okay," Lauren said to Cal, "if we screw the pooch on this mission, all bets are off?"

Cal nodded and saw Alex's brow furrow. "Screw the pooch," he told the medic, "means the mission is completely compromised and we have to fall back on Plan B, C, or D. The rally point is our last chance to egress, to get out of dodge."

"I was having visions of this slang," Alex said, his face turning red. "It is quite sexually suggestive. But what does it have to do with mission compromise?"

Driscoll nearly rolled out of his chair, howling with laughter once again. Lauren couldn't help herself, her lips quirking into a smile. Even Cal's mouth pulled into an unwilling sour grin.

"It has nothing to do with sex," Cal told him, trying to remain respectful. "It's a mission gone sideways. It's corrupted or broken due to unknown issues suddenly arising and we have to be flexible, create a new extraction plan in the moment, in order to get Sky out of there alive."

Scratching his head, Alex wrote down the slang in a notebook he had in front of him. "You have very, very strange sayings," was all he muttered, refusing to look at Lauren, embarrassed by his own visualization of the words. "Mission compromise. Backup plan. Rally point. Yes?"

"Correct. We call it a rally point," Cal said. He took a deep breath. Inwardly, he thanked the medic for being here. It broke up the deadly tension in the room. Everyone here wanted Sky rescued, assuming she was still there, or alive. Cal knew they would give their lives to make it happen. He'd give his own. It was serious business, but black humor often rose at such times, a natural bleeding off of stress. Laughter was the best medicine. Even in cases like this, and these operators were no stranger to it.

"Do we know where these soldiers sleep?" Lauren asked.

"There's a two-story barracks fifty feet away on the southwest side of the villa. I'm betting the ex-Spetsnaz bunk in there. When they're not on duty, they're at that building."

"There can be guards IN the villa at night, too," Cal warned them. "We have already seen there are sentries twenty-four hours a day outside the villa. Thanks to the satellite flyovers, we know their schedule. We'll time entering the villa so we aren't going to be compromised."

"Which would mean," Lauren said, talking more to herself than anyone else, "that Alexandrov doesn't have motion sensors right around the villa. It's an open space. We can slip from river to inside the villa without being seen."

"Correct," Cal said. "And if this is true, that's a big plus for our side." He looked over at Alex. "Would Alexandrov have guards inside the villa at night?"

"Doubtful," Alex said, gesturing toward the blueprint on the screen. "Because he has three sentries outside. Why would he also have them inside? I think Alexandrov, like his dead son, wants his home free of everything. It's a place where he owns the territory."

"My thoughts are the same," Jack interjected.

"What about servants?" Lauren demanded. "Dr. Zapata said she saw a number of servants running around performing various tasks."

"There's another building here," Cal said, using the laser pointer. "It is due west of the villa, about half the size of the soldier's barracks. I'm guessing that the servants live there when they're not on duty over at the villa."

"The real question," Alex said, "is how many people are up and awake and walking around at 0300 in the morning within the villa?"

"That's the sixty-four-thousand-dollar question," Cal agreed.

Lauren saw Alex write down the slang. "It means," she told the operator, "that is the most important question."

"Thank you," Alex murmured, flashing her a grateful look.

Lauren nodded, feeling her heart tug. The man was a simple farmer at heart. She tried to resurrect her walls against Alex. Being around him was wearing her down. Ordinarily, she could keep anyone at arm's length. Since Jack and Alex had arrived, they'd all worked closely together, assembling the intel, moving like a well-oiled team. The more she was around him, the harder it was becoming to not let the big teddy bear get to her. She nodded, holding back the scowl she usually gave to warn him off.

Jack sat up, scribbling some info in his notebook. "If necessary, we will flex cuff servants if we find them within the villa, duct tape their mouths, wrists, and ankles so they can't raise the alarm or run off. If it's a guard, we'll use our pistols, which will have a silencer on them to muffle any sounds. We shoot to kill, not wound."

Everyone agreed.

Jack looked at Alex. "You're the lynch pin in all of this. Your mission is to get to the security room, kill the guards, and disable the villa's power. Everything in that room is probably written in Russian, and you're the only one who reads and speaks the language. Are you clear on your objective?"

Alex nodded. "Absolutely. After I get in, I disable guards and quickly read the set up, then I am to hit the kill switches on all the generators. That leaves them without electricity. We will all be wearing night vision goggles and we will be able to see through the darkness." He held up his large hand, spreading his fingers. "By denying the surrounding area of electricity, it means their sensors and cameras will not work, either. It will disable any device in or outside of the villa. I then radio you and Cal. Both of you will go down the hall and try to locate Sky. Once you have her in hand, you will call Lauren, who will start driving toward the villa. I will then leave the control room and meet you. I will provide back up. And we will exfil to the parking area."

Cal nodded. Everything hinged on Alex. They'd be up a creek if he didn't read and speak Russian. None of them knew that language. "We need to do a weapon's check after this mission briefing. All pistols and rifles will have silencers on them." He knew Alex would use Russian weapons because he was comfortable with the operation of them. And on an op, knowing one's weapon, if it jammed, could mean the difference between living and dying. Alex was training on U.S. weapons out at the firing range, but his muscle memory was in the use of the weapons he'd used for nearly a decade as a Spetsnaz operator.

"Any other questions?" Cal demanded. He saw his team shake their heads almost in unison. "Okay," he growled, "let's get to the armory."

July 14

CAL WISHED TO hell he had a mental telepathy link with Sky. To tell her they were coming. His gut instinct told him she was alive and, in that villa—somewhere. He sat on the edge of his bed, dressed in his black wetsuit, his balaclava nearby. They'd be donning Kevlar helmets with a rail system on top for their NVG's, night vision goggles. His mind moved over all the details. People got killed or wounded if they didn't pay attention to the details. An operator's existence hinged on them. He'd cleaned his SIG Sauer pistol, screwed the silencer on it. His M4 was cleaned and ready to go. It was a compact rifle, easy to carry, a multi-use weapon and hell on accuracy. And Cal knew how to unjam it and stay in the fight if it occurred.

His watch read 2300, eleven p.m. In fifteen minutes, they would be driven to the main airport, to a hangar that was out of the way. There, two Night Stalker pilots would be flying them by Army Black Hawk up to the area in the cloud forest. They would fast rope down because it was all jungle and no place to land.

He was restless, pacing, his mind focused on the mission. Occasionally, Cal would feel his chest heave, as if a ton of emotions wanted to escape from it and be given voice. His heart ached. He tried not to think about Sky, but it was impossible. Was she alright? Injured? Sick? Dead? No one knew. He hated not knowing. They were going into a hornet's nest where so much could go wrong in the blink of an eye. *So much…*

Would he ever see Sky again? Would he ever hold her in his arms? Kiss her? Feel her snuggle up against him at night in bed? Hear her laughter? Watch her incredible blue eyes go luminous with love for him alone? And she was carrying his baby. Their child. Rubbing his face wearily, Cal felt like he was literally carrying the weight of the world around on his shoulders. This op couldn't get started fast enough for him. And it was the most important op of his life.

July 15

THE BLACK HAWK hovered at one hundred and twenty feet, just above the triple canopy, as the team fast roped down into the shadowy jungle. The wheels on the Black Hawk were brushing the tops of the tallest trees. Wind slapped and hit Cal as he quickly slithered down the rope, his boots hitting the ground. Around him, his team silently dropped nearby. After giving the radio signal to the pilot above them, the ropes were released from the deck of the bird by the air crew chief, dropping around them on the ground. The helicopter rose swiftly, heading north, away from them and the villa. Quickly, they hid the ropes and got ready to trot two miles. The river was only a feet away, and

Cal had his NVG's down across his eyes as he studied the slow moving, black surfaced river. The good news was that there was plenty of bank vegetation, high enough for them to hide behind once they entered the water. Luck was always a big part of any mission. So far, it was on their side, as they all gathered and tightened the straps of their rucks. Jack led the way, followed by Cal and Alex. Lauren had left hours earlier and driven the SUV three hours up into the Monte Verde cloud forest. She was parked one mile up the road from the villa, lights off, hidden. Waiting and in constant radio contact with them.

They moved out at a swift, silent clip. If Cal had any doubts about Alex being in top shape, they were now put to rest. He wasn't a SEAL like the rest of them, but he easily kept the pace. A mile from the villa, they halted, hiding behind nearby brush, and pulled off their combat boots and stuffed them into their rucks. They replaced them with the rubber booties that completed their wet suit.

The M4 was in a sling across Cal's chest, ready if he needed it. He slipped quietly from the bank and into the warm, murky water. His feet found the bottom. It was muddy as hell, and he sank in up to his ankles. Holding on to some long, thin, sturdy reeds growing over the bank, Cal relayed the intel. It would slow them down. Their luck had just turned sideways.

Every sense he owned was online now as Cal walked through the river. They had to make sure they were far enough away from the grass along the bank so as to not make any noise. Above them, the sky was cloudy. The air was humid and heavy with coming rain. In the distance, Cal heard thunder rumbling. It looked like the thunder cell was quickly heading from the north, moving south, right over them. Cal liked a thunderstorm or high winds. Both helped keep his team hidden, making it harder for the enemy sentries to see or hear them coming. Lightning jagged above them. Cal cursed to himself, halting. The lightning destroyed his vision for several moments. He waited for his sight to return, pulling down the NVG's once more.

There would be no radio comms, no talking. Everything came down to hand signals or radio clicks. As Cal saw the villa emerge out of the night, he spotted a guard moving outside the cyclone fenced area, a rifle over his shoulder. He was alert and looking around. The wind picked up in a gust as the thunderstorm came marching down upon the villa. He watched the sentry pull his baseball cap a little tighter down on his head. He too, wore NVG's. Cal timed the guard. They stood quietly in the reeds, unmoving, while he timed the next circuit. *Five minutes.* They had five minutes to get out of the river. Looking up, Cal spotted a huge thicket near the bank. He made a signal that the team was to go there.

Slipping over the bank, not making a sound, Cal crouched and ran along the bank, diving into the brush that was at least ten feet high and twenty feet long, paralleling the river. He quickly shrugged out of his ruck, opened it quietly, and pulled out his combat boots. In moments, Alex and Jack joined him, doing the same. They worked with swift efficiency. Kneeling, they watched the next guard round the end of the villa. They had another five minutes. Cal made a signal. Alex shot out like a silent shadow, heading for the nearest door. Was the door rigged? Locked? Did it have a security alarm on it? No one knew. Cal held his breath.

Alex approached the glass door. He reached out his black glove-clad hand and twisted the knob. *Locked!* Swiftly, he took out his lock picks and went to work. In a minute, he heard the tumblers click. Shoving the tools back into his pocket, he twisted the knob. The door opened. Instantly, he moved in and shut it. No alarm sounded. After clearing the room, which appeared to be a den of some sort, Alex hid behind heavy floor to ceiling drapes. A sentry walked by the hallway. As soon as he disappeared, Alex opened the patio door again. He watched Cal and Jack sprint across the yard. In seconds, they were in. Alex quietly shut the door.

Pulling out their pistols, NVG's down, they prepared to move. They all had memorized the layout. Alex went first, his MP-445 Varyag .40 caliber Spetsnaz pistol up and ready to fire should he encounter anyone down the hall. He moved swiftly despite his height and bulk, the flagstone floor shining reflectively as lightning zagged across the villa. At the juncture of the two halls, Alex spotted the security room. Looking both ways, there was no human activity. He moved to the door, testing it. *Locked.* Pulling out his tools, he went to work, hoping whoever was inside wouldn't hear him jimmie the lock with the continual crash of thunder rolling around the villa.

Cal halted with Driscoll at his back, turned the other way, keeping watch for anyone coming up behind them. His heart was thudding slowly. His breathing was calm. The years of training and combat as a SEAL lowered his blood pressure and reduced his heart rate. He watched with anxiety, however, as Alex picked the lock on the security door.

Suddenly, the door flew open.

They'd been compromised!

CHAPTER 19

SKY JERKED AWAKE. There was a commotion out in the hall! Drowsy, she pushed off the bed, her feet hitting the cool wooden floor. She tried turning on the lamp on the bed stand. Nothing happened. Was the electricity out? Pulling on her blue silk robe, she tied it, hurrying to the door. There was more noise. Her heart sped up. It sounded like a pistol with a silencer being fired! Was Alexandrov under attack by his enemies? Sky hesitated, hand hovering over the doorknob.

Suddenly, the door was flung open. It was dark, but she was able to see Yerik standing in the doorway, glaring at her. He had a pistol in his hand. He shoved her backward and slammed the door shut. Breathing hard, he grabbed Sky.

"You bitch!" he snarled, gripping her by the upper arm, hauling her in front of him. Looking around wildly, Yerik held the pistol toward the door. "Your friends are here!" he rasped, dragging her back from the door, keeping her in front of him as a shield.

Gasping, Sky cried out as he yanked her hard against him, his arm going around her neck, almost crushing her airway and partially cutting off her carotid artery.

Lightning flared, eerily lighting up the room.

"W-what?" Sky rasped, trying to pull his arm away from her throat.

"Bitch! There are operators in the villa! I don't know how they got in! Stand still," and Yerik pressed the gun to her temple. "You're my ticket out of here."

Panic surged through Sky. Operators? Cal? SEALs? Her mind spun. Another bolt of lightning flashed, and thunder rolled, the whole villa shaking beneath the power of the booming sounds. The door suddenly swung open. She gasped. A man in black, rifle up, wearing NVG's, stood in the doorway. His rifle was pointed at her. Choking, feeling Yerik's arm tightening against her throat, Sky sagged against him, desperately clawing at his arm to release her so she could breathe.

"Back out," Yerik shouted at the operator. "Or I'll kill her!"

Sky gasped and struggled, but Yerik was much taller, much stronger. Her eyes were wide, her mouth contorted. The man in the black suit with the rifle didn't move. She recognized his form even though she couldn't see his face because of the balaclava NVG's hiding his face. It was Cal! Whimpering, Sky struggled more, feeling faint, her blood supply nearly shut off by Yerik's arm across the artery in her neck. She knew operators were the best at shooting in hostage situations. And that Yerik, although he held her as a shield, was still a target.

"Back off!" Alexandrov roared. He jammed the pistol against Sky's temple. She cried out in pain.

Cal watched carefully. Rage surged through him as Sky whimpered. He was waiting for a shot at Alexandrov's head. Yerik had come running down the hall until he saw them coming, then he dived into Sky's room. "Let her go and you live, Alexandrov," Cal snarled in a low voice.

Stunned, Sky stopped struggling. Cal's voice was quiet and deadly sounding. Emotions erupted through her, and she wanted to cry out his name, but she was barely able to breath. And then, she remembered something Cal had told her. He'd been training her in rescue techniques back at their cabin. And now, she was going to use one. She prayed it would work, prayed that Yerik wouldn't shoot her.

Sky suddenly dropped toward the floor. Even though Alexandrov had her neck in a choke hold, it jerked him forward and off balance. With Yerik distracted, Cal took the shot. Once to the head.

The Russian was jerked off his feet, flying backward.

Sky collapsed on the floor, coughing violently, holding her hand against her throat.

Cal moved forward, his eyes never leaving Alexandrov, who crumpled in a heap on the floor behind her.

"Stay down," he ordered her harshly.

Moving swiftly, Cal heard other commotion out in the hall behind him. Alex had run into trouble. He'd killed the two sentries in the control room and swiftly shut off the electric grid. One of the guards had gotten off a shot with a pistol before going down, and the roar of it had careened through the villa, awakening everyone, including Alexandrov, who had come running out with a weapon in hand.

Cal leaned down, seeing the Russian's head was blown half off, the spray of blood glittering against the wall and window as lightning lit up the area once again. It temporarily blinded him. Cursing, he pushed the NVG's up, blinking several times, trying to regain his sight so he could be assured the Russian was dead.

Turning, he moved over to Sky, who was gasping, her head hanging down, her hand against her throat.

"Sky," he rasped, kneeling, his hand on her shoulder to steady her. "Are you alright?"

The thunder caromed through the villa again, and Sky felt his hand, so steady and firm, on her shoulder. "Y-yes... Cal... you came," and she sobbed, sitting up, twisting a look up at him. All she could see were his slitted, black looking eyes. Tears jammed into her eyes. "I-I'm pregnant, Cal, I—"

"I know you are, sweetheart," he rasped. "We need to get you out of here. Now. Can you walk?"

Sky shakily nodded. Cal gently wrapped his arm about her waist, hauling her easily to her bare feet. Protectively, she placed her hand against her belly, hearing more gunfire ensue outside in the hall. She heard Cal speak quietly into the mic near his mouth as he pushed her behind him, facing the door, rifle lowered toward it.

"Do you have shoes?" Cal demanded.

"Y-yes, by the bed..."

Cal moved her toward it, always keeping his body between her and the opened door.

"Clear!" Driscoll said, his voice low key.

"Clear!" Alex called.

"Hurry," Cal urged her, the hallway safe for passage.

Hands shaking, Sky sat down on the bed, pulling on her sandals. Cal was here! She was being freed! Alexandrov was dead. She stood, but felt her knees become mushy. Automatically, she reached out for Cal's thick bicep, to keep herself steady.

"Follow me," he rasped, pulling down his NVG's. "Hold on to my belt, Sky. ALWAYS stay behind me. All right?"

"Okay," she whispered, her voice hoarse. Sliding her fingers around the narrow belt circling his waist, Sky's heart rate rocketed. Cal slipped to the door, snapping right and then left with his rifle. She waited, terror filling her. Would they get out of this alive? Cal moved swiftly, pulling her along, nearly lifting her off her feet. Sky gritted her teeth, trying to keep up with him as he progressed silently, like a shadow, down the hall. It was so dark; she couldn't see anything. His belt was her lifeline.

It was suddenly quiet. Sky sensed movement behind her. She gasped as she twisted a look in that direction.

"It's me, Alex," the voice said near her ear, his hand coming to rest reassuringly on her shoulder. "I'm protecting your back."

Relief slammed through Sky as she hurried to keep up with Cal. Alex was here! Who else was here? Where was Lauren? Her mind spun and gyrated. They moved as a shadowy unit down the hall, heading for the outer door down at the end of the corridor.

Suddenly, glass from the double doors exploded inward, showering them with glittering shards.

Sky screamed. She felt Cal grip her arm and he hauled her off her feet, pushing to the left, down another hallway toward the den.

Gunfire erupted.

"Cover me," Cal told his team quietly. "Taking her out the rear entrance we infilled."

Bullets whistled by Sky's head. The guards had found them and were now attacking the villa. More returning gunfire from the M4 and the Kalashnikov AK-47's roared in return. Sky tripped over her own feet, trying to get to the wall as Cal turned and fired back. She went sprawling, slamming hard onto the stone floor. There was a ripping, stitching pain tearing up from her abdomen. Sky cried out, instantly tucking inward, her hands pressing hard against her belly, the pain nearly making her faint. Bullets were singing up through the hall. The sounds of the rifles hurt her aching ears. She couldn't hear anything. She felt Cal's arms go beneath her shoulders and knees, lifting her into his arms. In moments, he was running down the hall full tilt. Sky clung to him, biting back a cry as the pain increased in her abdomen. *No! Oh, God, no! Don't let me lose our baby! God, please don't do this to us...*

Cal used his boot and crashed open the door leading outside. He heard Sky crying softly, felt her tensing, felt her arm tight around his neck. She was hurt. Wounded? He didn't know. He called Lauren, his voice calm and low, giving her the go to get to the villa ASAP. Carrying Sky quickly around the end of villa toward the parking lot, he heard Alex and Jack picking up the tempo of battle behind them. The clamor between rifles was echoing and ear splitting.

Cal saw a soldier run around the end of the villa, cutting off the path where they were heading.

Sonofabitch! Cal hissed and dove for the ground, keeping his arm around Sky's waist as he drew up his rifle at the same time. He hit the grass, releasing her. She cried out. He focused on the man, lifting his rifle to kill him. He snapped off one shot, taking out the enemy.

How many more soldiers were coming to surround the villa? Cal didn't know. What he did know was the operators were trying to make an end run and surround them. They were like an angry hornet's nest. He pulled Sky next to the wall.

"Stay here!" Cal rasped.

Sobbing, bending over with pain, Sky squeezed her eyes shut. Cal left her side. She couldn't see anything in the night. Everything was black. She was alone. And there was a firefight going on. Sky tried to stop sobbing, knowing the sound could draw attention. She heard gunfire erupt very close to her. It had to be Cal's M4 rifle returning fire. He'd run toward the corner where the other operator had just come from.

She didn't know how much time passed, the night was a mix of lightning and thunder above them intermingled with the roar of rifles below. Sky was looking back toward the den they had escaped though when lightning flashed. Sky gasped. There were two Russian soldiers charging toward her! *Oh, God, Cal!*

Looking towards the corner Cal had disappeared around, she saw him reemerge, gun at the ready. Screaming his name to warn him, she heard gunfire belch loudly from her left. Cal dropped to the lawn, firing quick rounds past where she sat cringing against the wall of the villa.

It started to rain in buckets. Soaked, shaking, Sky saw Cal running toward her, rifle up, as lightning flashed again. She wasn't sure she could stand. Cal knelt at her side and Sky could hear him breathing heavily.

"They're all dead," he rasped. "Lauren's out front with the SUV. I'm going to carry you. Hang on…"

Sky bit back a cry of pain, feeling as if her belly were ripping apart. The pain was stabbing, and she winced, trying not to cry out as Cal gently eased her into his arms. The rain soaked her in an instant, the silk robe clinging to every part of her skin as he ran around the villa corner, toward the parking lot. The firing had suddenly stopped.

Cal halted, opening the rear door to the SUV and gently depositing Sky into the large cargo area. Alex appeared at his side.

"She's injured," Cal growled. "Climb in!"

Alex threw his rifle into the middle seat, tore off his helmet, vest, and balaclava, then reached for his medical ruck. Cal shed his combat gear as well. They both climbed in the rear of the SUV to be with Sky.

Driscoll shut the rear door and then climbed in the passenger side seat. He slammed his door shut.

Lauren gunned the SUV, hauling it around like a race car driver, heading down the rain slick driveway, the lights stabbing through the stormy night.

Cal yelled to Driscoll, "Alert the carrier. Wounded coming on board."

Sky lay on her back between the two panting men. Her hands were pressed tightly against her abdomen, and she brought her knees up because it caused her less pain. She felt Cal place a blanket beneath her head. He was touching her, his roughened, wet hand sliding soothingly down her left arm, his knees pressed into her hip.

"Alex," Cal growled.

Alex handed him a flashlight. "Turn it on and hold it for me?"

Sky winced as the halogen light was turned on, lighting up the entire rear of the SUV as it sped through the rainstorm. She looked up and saw Alex's face. His eyes were slits, his focus completely on her.

"Where are you hurt?" he asked her gently, pushing his hand across her brow in a gesture to calm her.

"My baby," she sobbed. "I tripped and fell in the hall. I-I hit the floor hard. There's pain…"

"Anywhere else?" Alex enquired quietly, nodding, focused. He kept his hand on her shoulder to help stabilize her.

"Nowhere else." Sky cast a quick look up at Cal. His face was sweaty. He had his game face in place. She reached out, finding his hand, gripping it hard. She bit down on her lower lip as Alex gently lifted her hand away from her abdomen.

"I must examine you, Sky. I will be very gentle. I want you to slow your breathing for me. Breath in your nose, out your mouth?"

She gave Cal a desperate look. "I'm sorry…"

Cal leaned down, kissing her wrinkled brow. "Don't be," he told her huskily, holding her hand. "You're alive. That's all that counts."

Alex was incredibly gently as he palpated across her abdomen through her wet silk robe. He checked each quadrant. Only when he pressed his fingers into the lower right did she wince and cry out, jerking her knees upward, hitting Alex in the shoulder.

"It is all right, all right," the medic soothed, placing his large hand against her belly. "Do you have any discharge, Sky? Any fluid coming out of your vagina?"

She shook her head. "I-I don't think so. Why? What does that mean? Am I losing my baby?" Her voice cracked as she stared pleadingly up into the medic's darkly shadowed features.

"No, no, you are stable, Sky. I need you to keep slowing your breathing. Your baby is all right. I think you tore part of the placenta away from the uterine wall. But you are not bleeding, so that is good news." Alex took her blood pressure and then her pulse. He then brought out a blanket and gently enfolded it around her. "Good. You're doing fine, Sky. I need you to lay there, hold Cal's hand, and relax. Relax," and he tenderly moved his hand in slow motions across her belly.

Sky closed her eyes. Alex's large hand nearly covered her belly. It was like a warm blanket, and it was helping the pain recede. "Th-that feels good. The heat… the pain is starting to go away…"

Alex smiled and nodded. He looked over at Cal. "Just keep doing what I just did? She is your wife, married or not. I think she would prefer your hand on her baby, not mine," and he gave Cal a sloppy grin.

Cal followed his instructions. He felt the SUV shift, heard the pounding rain beginning to lessen. They were now on the main highway leading away from the villa. He lifted his head and called forward, "Anyone tailing us?"

"Negative," Jack called back. "How's Sky?"

"She's stable," Alex said. "Everything is okay back here."

Cal looked down at Sky. Her eyes were tightly shut, her hands knotted against her breasts, her nostrils flared, trying to slow her breathing. He moved his hand over her belly and she opened her eyes, meeting his gaze. "How are you doing?"

"Better," she managed, trying to stop the fear soaring through her. "I'm so afraid I'll lose our baby, Cal… After," and her voice cracked, "after we've gone through so much…"

"Hush," Cal ordered her gruffly, leaning over, kissing her brow and cheek. He could feel her tears on her warm flesh. Inhaling her scent, Cal dragged it into his lungs as if breathing for the first time since her kidnapping. This was his Sky. The wonderful, feminine scent that was only hers. Cal studied her eyes. They were shocky and wild looking, as to be expected. She had had no idea they were coming to rescue her. Moving his hand lightly across her belly, he felt her truly begin to relax beneath his light, tender ministrations. Alex continued to take her blood pressure about every ten minutes. He kept her covered with the dry, warm blanket. Cal could see he was worried. He hoped Sky couldn't see it. She had closed her eyes, sunken back, utterly exhausted, her lips slightly parted. He knelt there, a thousand questions in his mind. Had Sky been raped? Tortured?

Cal could see bruise marks around her throat. It sent terror through him.

Sky reached out, placing her hand on top of his. "There. Right there. Just keep your hand laying there. It feels so warm. So good."

Alex nodded to Cal, saying nothing.

"Anything you want," Cal told her quietly, smiling down into her barely opened eyes. Sky was painfully thin. He'd felt her ribs through her robe when he had been carrying her. She was lighter. Twenty pounds if he was correct. Cal knew Sky's body. Knew it intimately. He held on to his rage over what Alexandrov had extracted from her. Cal knew something horrible had happened. He just didn't know what. Now, as they sped toward the GPS coordinates to rendezvous with the incoming Black Hawk, Cal had to shift out of rescue mode and into caring for Sky. She looked worn out, dark smudges beneath her beautiful eyes. Her skin was so tight across the bones of her face, telling Cal about the tension she'd lived under for a month with that bastard, Alexandrov. He tried to not remember what Vlad had done to her. He was the son. This was the father. What had Yerik Alexandrov done to the woman he loved?

Cal knelt there, his hand lightly on her belly, knowing she carried their baby. He was far more comfortable pulling an op, going into a hot firefight, than shifting to face the dark, nightmarish possibilities and the unknown that lay ahead of them. Loving Sky with every breath he took, Cal watched her drift off to sleep after a while. Alex threw him a thumb's up, happy that she was resting. Her breath had returned to normal. Her hand was over his hand. It felt so damn good. Life affirming. Yet as he glanced over at the medic, Cal saw something he couldn't interpret in his eyes. Was Alex lying to Sky? Was she miscarrying their baby even now? Had he told Sky everything was all right to try and save the baby inside her that was perilously close to being lost? Cal didn't know. And he wasn't about to ask Alex in front of Sky.

His heart ached with dread. With unsureness. Sky was here, with him. But what part of her soul had Alexandrov stolen from her? How much had he taken out of the woman he loved? A sense of helplessness overcame Cal. There was no easy fix for a human who had been traumatically injured emotionally and psychologically. Cal was sure Sky had suffered both. The question now was: how bad was it? How damaged had she become from it? He slowly threaded his fingers through her damp, mussed hair, wanting to soothe her. Cal knew she loved having her scalp massaged by him. It always relaxed her. How could one person's touch make such a powerful, positive difference in another person's life? Cal close his eyes for a moment, internally trying to prepare himself for whatever would happen next aboard the Navy carrier floating fifty miles offshore of Costa Rica.

Cal watched Sky carefully once she was taken to the naval dispensary on board the carrier. They placed her in a blue curtained cubical. He remained at her side while Alex waited outside for the doctor. As a combat medic, he had to provide his examination assessment and other information that would be helpful to the physician assigned to her case.

"Doing okay?" Cal asked her, standing near her head, holding her hand. Sky still had her hand over her belly.

"Just... incredibly stressed out... exhausted," Sky whispered.

"You're safe now. That's the biggest step," Cal murmured, giving her a slight smile. He watched her rally beneath his voice and touch. She loved him and he could see it in her dark, fatigued eyes.

A male doctor stepped into the cubical. He didn't stop to talk to Alex at all. Scowling, Alex followed the doctor in, moving protectively to Sky's side opposite of Cal. He automatically placed his hand on her shoulder to keep her calm.

"I'm Dr. Vincent," the fifty-year old man said. He glanced over at Cal.

"I'm staying. She's my fiancee," Cal growled.

Vincent looked over at Alex with a pointed stare.

Alex said, "You need my report on my patient, Doctor. I am the combat medic who cared for her in the field."

Shrugging, Vincent said, "I'll take over now. You're dismissed."

Cal felt Sky tense. Worse, he saw fear come to her eyes.

"Don't touch me!" she cried out, shrinking away from the doctor.

Vincent scowled, staring down at her. "Excuse me?"

Cal watched Sky begin to breath unevenly. What the hell was going on here?

Alex lorded over the shorter physician. "Doctor, do you have a WOMAN physician on board this carrier? She is pregnant and has been through a lot. She is in deep shock. I think it best if a woman examines and treat her. Not you. You are a man. And it is men who have hurt her."

Cal got it. His heart twisted. His gut tightened. My God, had Sky been raped? Men scared her now? Yet, she didn't withdraw from Alex, who had suddenly become a bristling, snarling guard dog on her behalf. Cal nailed Vincent with a glare. "Get a woman physician in here, now. You're not laying a hand on her."

Vincent sniffed and jerked around in a huff, leaving the cubical.

Sky relaxed a little. "Thanks, Alex," she whispered tiredly. "I-I just don't want to be poked and prodded by a man."

"I understand," Alex said, patting her shoulder gently. "Just rest. We will find a woman on this carrier who will be of help to you."

Cal sent Alex a silent but grateful look. The medic was damned intuitive. He, on the other hand, was a mass of unraveling emotions and not thinking clearly at all. And Sky was looking more and more distressed. He couldn't blame her. She'd been through so much. He leaned over, kissing her lips softly. As he raised his head, he rasped, "I'll get you home just as soon as possible, sweetheart. Just hang in there with me…"

CHAPTER 20

July 15

"**S**HE'S SLEEPING NOW," Alex reassured Cal. They stopped just outside the dispensary. "Dr. Cooper was very good with Sky," he added.

Nodding, Cal hesitated. "At least, with rest, she won't lose the baby. That's the best news. Will you go find Lauren? She was filling out paperwork and a report about us on being board this carrier. Let her know Sky's condition?"

"Of course. Where are you going?"

"I'm staying with Sky." He saw Alex smile and give him a sage nod of his head.

"That is the best medicine for healing Sky could have."

Cal gripped Alex's hand, shook it, and turned, making his way back into the dispensary. Dr. Melanie Cooper was just coming out of a private room where they had put Sky. She was a petite brunette with brown eyes, about forty years old. Cal noted she wore a wedding ring. The doctor's hair was short and close cropped. She wore her spotless white lab coat and a pair of dark blue slacks. "Doc?"

"Yes?" She looked up from her paperwork she'd been filling out on her clipboard.

"If it's all right with you, I'm staying with Sky." Cal expected blow back, but the doctor just smiled a little.

"I'm surprised you even left her side at all, Mr. Sinclair."

"I just don't want hassle about it, Doc. Sky has been through hell. I want to be nearby in case she needs anything."

Reaching out, Melanie said, "It's not a problem. You're not military, you are civilians. You're not breaking any rules. She is your fiancé. So, stay with her. I'll give the staff orders not to intrude unless you come out of her room and need something specific for Sky. We have a console in our main office that they can continuously monitor all her stats on."

"I owe you one, Doc," Cal murmured, giving her a brisk nod of thanks, and heading for the door to the private room. There was a soft light coming from the bathroom, otherwise it was nearly dark. Sky was laying on her side, almost in a fetal position, and it tore at Cal. He sat down in a nearby chair to remove his shoes. Dressed now in a bright red polo shirt, jeans, and socks, he moved to the hospital bed and laid down, easing his bulk so he spooned his body around her back and hips. She stirred as Cal quietly slid his arm beneath her pillow and neck, and then gently brought his other hand across her belly. Sky sighed but didn't awaken. Cal was always humbled by her sensory abilities. She might be in an exhausted, deep sleep, but Sky knew he was here. The moment he lay his hand against her belly, she utterly relaxed. He saw the tightness of her skin across her cheekbones soften. Cal swore he saw a hint of blush across them too, but the light was bad, and he couldn't tell for sure.

He felt exhaustion stalking him. He laid his head on her pillow, her blond hair tickling his nose as he nuzzled into it, inhaling her feminine scent. Smiling to himself, Cal closed his eyes. He was keeping her safe. Curving around Sky, he became a physical, protective barrier between her and the rest of the world that had been hunting her ruthlessly all her life. Well, now it would stop, Cal thought, gently moving his hand softly against her belly. With the elder Alexandrov dead, the Russian mafia in New York City would be thrown into chaos. There was sure to be a fight to see who became their new leader. But whoever it was wouldn't care a fig about Sky Lambert. Last night, the predators that had hounded the woman he loved with his life had met their end. As he felt himself sinking into sleep, Cal understood a new chapter in their lives was about to be opened. He had no idea what it was or where it would take them. What he did know was that he'd be at Sky's side. And he wasn't ever going to leave her again.

Sky drowsily awoke, realizing she was in the delicious embrace of Cal's arms. Her mind was sluggish, exhaustion still claiming her as she barely opened her eyes. She inhaled Cal's male scent. She inhaled life and possibilities. His breathing was slow, and Sky knew he had to be as tired as she was, for differ-ent reasons. She remained quiet in his arms, her head on his shoulder, his moist breath flowing across her neck and cheek. Was this all a dream? Something that she manufactured because she so desperately needed Cal? Needed to be held by him? To feel safe once more? Without thinking, Sky moved her fingertips across his large hand that cupped her belly with such protective tenderness. She felt his roughened skin beneath her fingers and smiled, finally resting her palm over his heart. When she'd given up, lost all hope, he had rescued her. Guilt ate at her. She hadn't kept her faith; she'd quit on him. Shame flowed through Sky. Closing her eyes, she replayed the attack and firefight.

At all times, Cal had placed himself between her and the danger. He'd have taken a bullet for her. He would have died for her. As the memories raced across Sky's mind, she felt Cal awaken. It wasn't that his body jerked or suddenly tensed. It was just a sense he was consciously here, with her. He shifted onto his back, lifting his arm, drawing her up beside him. Sky drowned in his gold and brown eyes that were barely open and studying her. Gone was that hard mask he almost always wore, his game face. In its place, she saw his vulnerability, despite the harsh life he'd lived. The feathered lines around his eyes told her of how much he'd been out in the harsh elements. The lines around his mouth spoke of someone who was serious most of the time. Yet, as she studied Cal's full mouth, sculptured and beautiful to her, she saw the corners naturally lifted upward. That told her he laughed a lot. And how she longed to hear him laugh, the way he did in their cabin. She ached to be home right now. To hear the silence that was so calming to her sensitive state. To rock her baby within her body in that old rocking chair Cal had brought at an antique store years earlier. He'd placed it in their master bedroom, and she loved rocking in it. His mouth lazily curved, and he slid his fingers through her hair near her temple.

"What are you doing awake? Don't you know you're sleeping for two now?"

His gruff teasing made her feel better. His fingers made her scalp prickle pleasantly as he massaged the area. Cal knew what she liked. "I just woke up," Sky offered, her voice hoarse and drowsy. The choke hold Alexandrov had placed upon her had bruised her windpipe, Dr. Cooper had told her. It should heal up in less than a week, and she'd have her own tone and voice back.

Cal stirred and stretched like a big cat, his socked feet hanging over the end of the bed. He leaned over, kissing her brow. Propping himself up on his elbow, he allowed Sky more of the bed so she could lay on her back, looking up at him. Cal stroked her cheek, feeling a ton of emotions suddenly churning and boiling up through him. "I never stopped looking for you, Sky," he began, his voice low and unsteady. "Lauren, Jack, Alex, and I, along with a lot of active-duty SEALs, were combing the world to find where you had been taken." He saw her brow wrinkle. "It took us three and a half weeks to piece all the scraps of intel together. And if it weren't for Alex's input, we'd never have considered Costa Rica as a hiding place where Alexandrov had you imprisoned."

Nodding, Sky closed her eyes, simply absorbing Cal's tender touch, his calloused fingers moving from her cheek down to her chin. "I understand," she whispered unsteadily. Looking up at him, she felt his finger move beneath her chin and gently lift her mouth closer to his so he could kiss her. Nothing felt so right as this moment for Sky. She strained upward, wanting desperately to kiss this man who had saved her, who had been her shield. His mouth tenderly bushed her lips. Sky made a soft sound in her throat, wanting more, wanting Cal. She wasn't disappointed as his mouth curved against hers, rocking her lips open, sliding against her, luxuriating in her softness. Sky rested her hand against the stubble of Cal's cheek, fingertips tingling in the wake as she stroked his hard jaw. Everything about him was blatantly male. Hard. Angular. Stubborn. Animal sensual.

Sky felt his mouth leave hers wet and aching for more. Cal smiled down at her, framing her cheek with his palm.

"Welcome home, sweetheart. You're right where you belong."

The words were emotional, vulnerable, and honest. It made Sky reel internally, the power of Cal's love she saw mirrored in his face, heard in his unsteady voice. His eyes were alive with gold and umber, telling her how much he desired her. How much she knew he loved her. "I love you so much, Cal... so much..." and Sky's voice caught, tears blurring his face momentarily.

"I know you love me."

Cal was so confident. Knew himself so well. Knew her equally well. "With my heart. With my soul," she whispered brokenly.

"Now, you're carrying our baby. Loving her or him. When I hold you, I'm holding that little tyke, too."

Sky nodded, overwhelmed with so many emotions, good and bad. "When Yerik told me I was pregnant after Dr. Zapata examined me, I didn't believe him at first. But as I looked at my symptoms, I knew he was right." Sky swallowed hard. "Cal, I was never so happy or so terrified."

"Happy for us? Terrified of what he was going to do to you?" Cal saw pain come to her eyes. "Dr. Zapata told us that he was going to force you to abort your baby," he explained quietly.

"Y-yes. And I lived in a special hell, Cal. I wanted to fight to save our baby."

"Dr. Zapata was put into an untenable position, just like you." Cal told her what Alexandrov had done to force the doctor to do the unthinkable: to abort Sky's baby in order to save her own kidnapped children's lives. He saw instant understanding come to Sky's eyes.

"That poor woman... She must have felt so torn..."

"The good news is the day after Alexandrov threatened her, we walked into her office. She identified your photo and his. We offered her help and protection and she agreed to work with us to free you."

"That's how you found me? Through Dr. Zapata?"

"More or less," he said. "Like I said, there were a lot of people working twenty hours a day sifting through thousands of comms and satellite photos. I don't want to burden you with all that right now. You need to rest."

Nodding, Sky moved slowly to her side, sliding her arm across his waist.

"Hold me? It was the one thing I missed the most," she murmured against Cal's chest, nestling closer to him. "Every night I went to bed, I would imagine you were there, behind me, shaping me against your body, holding me tight. Holding me safe…"

It was so easy to bring Sky into his arms, holding her gently against himself. Cal felt his erection stir, and knew she felt it against her belly. "Just ignore what's going on below," he told her, mirth in his tone as he kissed her hair, feeling her sink deliciously against him.

"For now, I will. Dr. Anderson said two weeks without sex while the placenta tear heals."

Cal smiled. "I'll survive, so don't stress yourself about it." He felt Sky's hand move tentatively across his chest. It was as if she were checking to make sure this wasn't a dream, that he was real. He struggled to keep things light between them right now. Sky didn't need to talk about her captivity. Not now. Desperately, Cal wanted to get her home where he knew Sky would thrive, not just survive. Holding her soft gaze, he added, "I love you so damn much, Sky. There's so many ways to show I love you beside just sex." Cal saw some relief in her eyes. Again, a gnawing ache sat like a hard, sharp rock in his heart. What had Alexandrov done to her? His greatest fear was that he'd raped her. He wasn't about to broach that topic with her right now. He had no wish to continue to tear her up emotionally over the trauma she'd endured with the sick bastard.

"The time I was at the villa, you have no idea how often I ran through our four months we had together." Sky closed her eyes, content to be held by Cal. "Good times…"

"There's going to be a lot more of those to come," he promised her thickly. Cal would do anything in the world to see her smile once again. To see that cloudiness mixed with fear residing deep in her eyes banished. Kissing her closed eyelids, he murmured, "You need to sleep some more…"

July 16

CAL MET HIS team the next morning in a briefing room aboard the huge carrier. They were all dressed in civilian clothes, but Cal had already heard scuttlebutt from the sailors that there was a black ops team on board. They sat in the small room huddled around a gray metal table bolted to the deck. Everyone had a cup of coffee in hand.

"How is Sky doing?" Lauren asked.

Cal knew they all wanted to see her. He'd held off because she was tenuous, and he wasn't sure she was up for any company right now. Even saying hello and thank you to the staff who cared for her seemed to tax her. "She's fragile and completely vulnerable," he warned them. He saw Alex scowl down at the end of the table. His shoulders were so wide and broad, it made the room look even smaller than what it already was.

"Is Dr. Cooper going to see her today?" he demanded.

"Yes, she's taking good care of Sky, and Sky likes her a lot. She trusts this doctor."

"Look," Lauren said, reaching out and touching Cal's arm, "we can visit Sky once she's home and settled in. I'm sure she's in deep shock. She needs us around like a hole in her head right now."

Alex frowned at Lauren. "A hole in the head? As in getting shot in the head?"

Jack rubbed his face, a sour grin snaking its way across his face. "Ohhhhh, here we go again…"

"Slang," Cal quickly injected. "It just means one more bad thing happening on top of another."

"Oh," Alex muttered, taking out his note pad and pen, beginning to write it all down. "Well, Sky is going to need some help. A therapist. Someone she trusts. A woman, for sure."

Lauren eyed him but, said nothing, staring down into the cup of coffee. "How can we help you, Cal?"

He sat back and shook his head. "I'm reeling. That's nothing compared to what is going on inside of Sky. No one except her knows what really happened after the kidnapping. I feel…," and he hesitated, searching for the words to express his sense of things. "I feel Sky is holding on to a lot of shit. I don't think she's anywhere near being able to talk about it."

"You are her best set of ears she has," Alex urged passionately.

Cal gave the Ukrainian a look. "I don't know. She trusts you completely, Alex." And then he looked at Lauren.

"Right now," Lauren said grimly, "we need to leave Sky alone, and let her call the shots. If I were in her shoes, I'd go screaming for home because home is where she was safe. She didn't get kidnapped there, thank God. So home, Cal, for her, is vastly important for Sky to start the healing process. You and your home are mental and emotional stability to her."

Alex cocked his head, admiration in his eyes and his voice. "You are very wise, Lauren. And sensitive to her plight."

Lauren hunched her shoulders, refusing to respond, her lips thinned.

Jack said, "Tomorrow, we're hitching a ride to Barksdale Air Force Base in Louisiana, thanks to Navy generosity. From there, a Gulfstream G700, leased by the military, is flying us into the Reagan International Airport." He turned to Cal. "I've got my people meeting us. You and Sky will be taken to your SUV in the parking lot and you can go straight home."

"Sounds damn good to me," Cal muttered, running his fingers through his hair.

"Well," Lauren said, standing, "I have some more reports to fill out on this mission. I'll see you later."

Jack rose. "Me too."

The door shut, leaving Cal with Alex. The medic shook his head. "I am glad we are alone. I deal with shock all the time out on the battlefield. Sky has been deeply traumatized. I do not know what did it. I only know she is. She has all the signs and symptoms."

Cal stared down the table at him. "That's what I sensed." He sat up rubbing his face. "What the hell should I do, Alex? Should I get her to a hospital? To a psychiatrist?"

"Lauren was right," Alex mused, gesturing the the chair where she sat. "It is sad in a way."

"What's sad?"

"Lauren." Alex's voice softened. "You cannot see or sense trauma unless you have gone through it yourself. Lauren spoke strongly about getting Sky home because she sees you and your home as a refuge. A place to hide. A place to get well. It is her safe house."

Snorting, Cal muttered, "Hell, I know you don't know anything about Lauren's past, but it's about on par with the hellish childhood Sky barely managed to survive."

"You mean physical abuse?"

"Yes."

Nodding thoughtfully, Alex said, "I thought as much when I first met her. The way she acted toward me. I am a big man," and he opened his arms. "And she fears big men. I have figured out that a big man hurt her, and that is why she is afraid of me. She may see me as the man who hurt her so badly."

"Psychologically, it's called a projection," Cal offered. "If that is so, then Lauren sees her abuser, not you. Lauren is tough because she had to be to survive that sick family of hers. As far as I know, it was a foster father who did the damage to Lauren." He saw Alex's eyes grow angry, his mouth turning down, clearly wrestling with his feelings.

"She needs someone who will be gentle with her." Alex rasped, "That is why she likes you so much. Even though you are an operator, you have a kindness running through you. Sky saw it. Lauren recognizes it, too. They both trust you."

"So?" Cal challenged. "You do, too. Sky trusts you. She doesn't cringe when you're around her or when you touch her. Why doesn't Lauren see it in you, then?"

He sipped his coffee. "Because I am a big man. I am a bug-a-boo to Lauren."

Cal grinned. "A what?"

"I was using your American slang," he said proudly. "I'm a bug-a-boo."

Cal cocked his head. "What's that word mean to you?"

"Someone who jumps out of the dark at you and scares you badly."

Rolling his eyes, Cal chuckled. "Bogeyman, Alex. Not bug-a-boo."

"Oh," and he grinned, embarrassed, and shrugged, writing it down on his ever-present slang notebook. "I sometime mix and match things?"

Chuckling, Cal nodded and stood up. "Hey, I give you credit. At least you're in the fight, trying." And then added with a sly grin. "Good thing Lauren wasn't here when you said that. She'd have hysterics over your faux pas. Driscoll would fall out of his chair, howling and rolling all around this deck. You really entertain our boss."

Alex took it all good naturedly and rose. "Maybe Lauren should have been here. She rarely smiles. I've heard her laugh only once. She has a beautiful voice, but I do not think she realizes it."

"Well," Cal said, slapping him on the back, "maybe you're just the guy to reach inside those walls of hers and gain her trust. Hang in there with Lauren. She's a tough nut to crack, but I really think you've slid past some of her defense panels already, my friend."

Shaking his head, Alex muttered, "I see her inner heart and beauty. I see the woman who hides behind walls that she's constructed around herself. There is generosity and kindness in Lauren, but she is afraid to let it out, to be open with others."

"That's called being vulnerable," Cal said, losing his smile. "Lauren doesn't open up to anyone fast, Alex. I think she's less abrasive toward you, now. And, if I don't miss my guess, I think she kinda likes you." Cal saw Alex's head pop up, hope suddenly mirrored in his eyes.

"You are not kidding me, are you?"

"Not about that," Cal said drily, opening the door. "But don't tell Lauren I said that, or she'll come and beat the living shit out of me. Okay?"

"Okay. It is our secret."

Cal saw Alex grinning hugely, like a little boy given some prize he'd been longing for but never gotten. Until now. Shaking his head, he said, "Later, Bro."

Cal met Dr. Cooper out in the waiting room of the medical bay. The place was jumping with sailors needing medical help, all sitting around, waiting for their appointment. Cooper crooked her finger toward him. Cal followed her down a passageway and into another room. The doctor closed the door behind him.

"What's up?" Cal demanded turning on the doctor.

"I had to give Sky an anti-anxiety shot to calm her down, and I didn't want you walking in there not knowing what happened."

Scowling, Cal growled, "What the hell happened, doctor?"

"I heard her screaming," Melanie said. "I went in there. Apparently, she was having a nightmare. And she couldn't stop screaming. I gave her the tranquilizer and finally got her to relax about ten minutes later. After that, Sky fell back asleep."

"Will that medication harm the baby?" Cal growled, flexing his hands into fists and then relaxing them. It was a nervous habit he had when he felt he was out of control. In this case, Sky was out of control. And he had no idea how to fix her or the situation. SEALs didn't like feeling helpless. In this case, there was no solution he could see, and it left him feeling anxious.

"No, I gave her a very, very mild sedative and it will not harm your baby," she said.

"What do I need to do to help her, Doc, after we get home?" Cal felt guilty for leaving Sky to meet with his team just now. He should have been there for her. *Dammit!*

"First, find a woman gynecologist where you live. Get Sky checked out by her. She needs to be on pregnancy vitamins stat. I've given her some to last a week, but she needs to be on them until she gives birth to her baby. Second, she needs a good woman psychiatrist. Preferably someone with PTSD and military experience. And if you get really lucky, a woman vet who has practiced inside the military, working with PTSD."

Cal's eyes narrowed, his hands settling on his hips as he stared at the doctor. "Is that your diagnosis?"

Melanie gave him a bland look. "Mr. Sinclair, I've treated hundreds of cases of PTSD. I know it when I see it. And no, it's not official, but you can have the psychiatrist you choose contact me and I'll send Sky's records and my observations along to her."

"You emphasized a woman," he said. "Why? What do you see?"

"She responds better to woman than men. I heard about her response to Dr. Vincent. She was terrified of him because he was a man."

Cal nodded. "Yeah," was all he managed to mutter, worried. "What's causing it?"

"My best guess is she was recently traumatized by a man."

Cal knew the doctor had no knowledge of Sky's captivity by Alexandrov. That was a need-to-know basis only. "Okay, that's a good piece of info.

Thanks."

"I don't want to keep Sky on any more anti-anxiety meds than necessary. I believe she's falling apart, for lack of a better word, right now. Get her home and she'll have a place to follow the doctor's suggestions, then she can start rebuilding herself afterward."

Cal was getting the same advice from everyone. "Thanks, Doc. We intend to do that tomorrow morning when we fly off this floating city of yours," and he smiled a little at her, grateful for her honesty and care toward Sky.

"One more thing, Mr. Sinclair?"

Cal hesitated at the open door. "Yes?"

"Keep things quiet. Keep her out of crowds. Keep her with low stress activities only. If she has hobbies, try to nudge her gently in that direction. If she wants to talk, sit and listen. DON'T interrupt her. Men tend to run over a woman who is talking or try to 'fix it', interrupting her with a plan that they've concocted. If you do that to Sky in the condition she's in, she'll clam up and maybe never speak about it again. And that could be toxic to her. Do you understand? Learn to be a good listener. You're a SEAL, so you'll understand when I tell you to put duct tape across your mouth in those situations."

"Yes, ma'am, I hear you loud and clear." Cal stepped out into the passageway, taking a deep, shaky breath. Hell, this was ten times worse than that firefight they had yesterday. The task of picking up the shattered pieces of Sky looked like a mountain he could never successfully climb. He wished he had far more psychology training to help her. Rubbing his chest because his heart ached for Sky, Cal felt like a fish out of water. He could handle the enemy jumping down his throat, but he had no experience with a traumatized, pregnant woman. As he slowly walked toward the door that would lead to Sky's private room, Cal decided to do what he'd always done when his mind couldn't figure it out: he would let his intuition guide him instead. He loved her. His heart would be part of that sensing and healing process for her as well.

CHAPTER 21

July 29

CAL STOOD AT the bay window in their bedroom at the cedar home. Sky was down in the meadow, near the winding stream that crossed it. The July afternoon sunlight made her hair glow like someone had placed an eighteen-carat gold crown around her head. He frowned and rubbed his brow. They'd been home two weeks now, and Sky wasn't any better. He'd helped her pick out a very warm and nurturing woman gynecologist from Alexandria. Dr. Anne Simpson was in her late fifties, gray haired with dancing brown eyes, and she was exactly what Sky needed. The woman was a nurturing mother times ten, and Cal was grateful. They'd received good news that the tear in her uterus had healed and she and the baby were fine. Physically, anyway. Mentally and emotionally, Sky continued to be imprisoned by her trauma.

Cal looked around at her easel where she drew with her pastel chalks. Noticing a group of papers turned upside down on the floor, almost hidden, he picked them up. It was the stiff, thick art paper she always drew on. Turning them over, he anchored in shock. Staring down at the first one, it was nothing, but bloody red and black pastel chalk ripped across the paper. His stomach knotted. He slowly looked at the second one. Same thing. Harsh, abstract lines and zigzags, making no real picture. Just angry lines. Cal took them over to the settee and sat down. There were fifteen of them. All the same thing. *Damn.*

Cal was glad Lauren was visiting Sky shortly. He sighed, getting up and putting the paintings back where he'd found them. If only Sky would open up to him. She was like an overfilled helium balloon, ready to burst open and destroy herself with the all-consuming dark emotions from the trauma she had experienced. As he went slowly down the stairs, he tasted hatred for Alexandrov and for what he'd done to Sky. Even from the grave, the bastard was extracting his revenge upon her—and him.

He heard a car pull up, the security monitor beeping and showing activity in the garage area. Moving out through the door, Cal saw Lauren climb out of her Jeep. "Hey," he called, "thanks for coming."

Lauren nodded. Her hair was pulled back in a ponytail. She wore her dark green tee and cargo pants along with her familiar black combat boots. Going over to Cal, she hugged him. "How are you doing?" she asked, searching his face.

"Not very good," Cal admitted. "I wish I had better news."

Lauren pushed the bill of her cap up on her head, frowning. "Has Sky opened up? Let it out yet? Cried?"

Shaking his head, he growled, "No... none of the above."

"Okay," Lauren said, gripping his arm and giving it a gentle squeeze, "let me see if I can get her to start releasing that shit she's carrying." She saw hope creep into Cal's dark eyes. Her heart tore because she saw the grief and a helplessness etched on his face. "Look, I know a little about this. You came out of a dysfunctional family, too?"

"Yeah," Cal rasped, giving her a gentle look, reaching out, squeezing her hand gently, feeling HER pain.

"Sometimes," Lauren said, her voice growing strained, "it takes one to know one. I've been where Sky's at right now. I got thrown into a closet for two or three days at a time. All I got was water." She grimaced. "I hate talking about it, Cal, but I'm telling you, Sky went through severe isolation, maybe a deprivation unit of some sort. She's behaving like it. She's behaving like I did when I was a kid."

Wincing, Cal knew all about deprivation units. His voice became hoarse with shock. "You really think so?"

"Yeah," Lauren muttered, pulling the bill of her baseball cap lower over her eyes to shade them. "Where's she at?"

"In the meadow."

"Okay, I'll go to her. You stay here. Don't come and interrupt us. I'm going to try and spring that hatch open in her, and if you show up, she'll shut back down. This has to be a girl-to-girl talk. You men have no clue about how to communicate. Let me handle this."

Cal placed his hand on her proud, strong shoulder. "Thanks, Lauren. I guess I don't have the tools or the education to fix this one." He saw her give him a sour grin.

"Don't call it education. Call it experience, and that's what the hell it is. It's a bitch and a half." She squeezed his hand. "We'll be back in a while."

"Yeah. Thanks," Cal said, meaning it, feeling his eyes tear up. Lauren turned on her heel and walked confidently out of the garage, made a left turn, and headed down to the meadow below their house. Cal stood there, feeling guilty. Feeling helpless. He hated that feeling more than any other, having grown up with it until age eighteen. He loved Sky. But he couldn't reach her. Slowly, Cal turned and trudged back into the house, praying Lauren could help her.

SKY HEARD LAUREN calling her. She looked up from the book she was reading beneath a pine tree near the creek. Lifting her hand, she felt some of the heaviness leave her as Lauren grinned a hello and jogged down to where she was sitting.

"Hey, Girlfriend," Lauren said, sitting down opposite her after giving Sky a tight, heartfelt hug, "how are you doing?" Lauren pulled off her cap and dropped it beside her, crossing her legs, resting her elbows on her knees, focused in on Sky.

"I should be happy. I'm home, Lauren." Sky shrugged. "I just feel… horrible inside."

"You're pregnant. It's the hormone cocktail from hell."

Sky's mouth pulled slightly upward as she held Lauren's warm green eyes. "You make me laugh. I love your bluntness."

Chuckling, Lauren stretched out on the dried brown pine needle carpet, propping herself up on one elbow, studying Sky. "It's a tough time in any woman's life."

"And you know this how?"

"Uh uh, this is about you, not me."

Frowning, Sky shut the book and set it aside. "I don't mind being pregnant," she admitted quietly, her voice soft. "I love that there's a little one growing inside me."

"Do you sing to her? Rock her? Talk to her?"

Sky blinked. How could Lauren know these things? She saw the look on her friend's face and decided not to go there. "I do. I know it's too early to tell the sex, but I know she's a girl, Lauren."

"Women always know," she said wryly.

"I feel bad for Cal."

"Why? He wasn't kidnapped and tortured for a month. You were."

Her words hit Sky hard. Her blond brows fell, and she looked down at her tightly clasped hands in her lap. "I'm hurting him. I love him, and I don't want to be like this around him. But I can't help it. Now," Sky grimaced, "I'm in a prison once more. Only this time, I'm a prisoner of my own emotions."

"When you get tossed in a dark room for days at a time, Sky, it breaks everyone."

Sky jerked up her head, a gasp escaping her. She stared in shock over at Lauren, who was giving her a cool, steady stare in return. "H-how did you know?"

"Two or three days of deprivation?"

"Y-yes… God, it was horrible, Lauren."

"Did you have a pot to piss in?"

"T-there was a toilet, but I was heaving my guts out two or three times a day. It would hit so fast, and the room was completely dark, I couldn't find my way across to it soon enough." Sky closed her eyes, her voice filled with shame. "The stench smelled horrible. No air… Just that horrid, choking odor… I gagged so much, dry heaved… I couldn't stop…"

Lauren picked up a brown pine needle and chewed on it, all the time her gaze never leaving Sky's anguished gaze. "Well, you were lucky. I didn't have a pot to piss in. When my foster father decided I'd been in the closet long enough, he'd unlock the door. And then he'd beat me again because I'd shit and peed in his closet." She smiled a little. "Then I had to go clean it up."

"How old were you when this happened?" Sky asked hollowly.

"Seven." Lauren took a deep breath and said, "Did you give up wanting to live while you were in there? I know I did. At that age, I was wondering how I could stop the pain I felt, the abandonment, feeling that no one loved me, nor was anyone coming to rescue me." She laughed a little. "Just think at seven I'm contemplating suicide." Throwing the pine needle down, Lauren rasped, "That's got to be some kind of sick Guinness World Record. I should really check that out."

Staring, Sky gulped. Her fingers knotted, grew damp and cold. "Y-you really did think about suicide, Lauren? Killing yourself?"

"Of course, I did. You break a person's spirit and they're hopeless, Sky. I was utterly hopeless. I had no way to get out. I used to sit in that closet and cry myself to sleep. And then I'd dream of this knight on a white horse coming to my rescue, taking me out of the closet, carrying me away from that sucky family of mine forever." She eyed Sky, holding her shamed gaze. "You thought about suicide, didn't you?"

Swallowing hard, Sky nodded. "Not for the same reasons as you did," she whispered, gently moving her hand over her belly. "I knew Dr. Zapato was coming to give me an abortion. I guess… well… I lost hope then. Up until that point, I had faith Cal would find me. I knew he was looking for me. I knew it was just a matter of time and I had to just… hold on…"

"But you gave up because you thought you'd lose your baby? And if you lost your baby, you would die anyway because life was too painful to live? Right?"

Sky nodded. "Exactly. I was actively looking around the room on my hands and knees, trying to find something, anything… to kill myself with."

"Bet you felt horrible about it."

"Horrible doesn't even begin to touch how I felt, Lauren. I love Cal. But I had given up hope. I didn't want to live... God," Sky whispered brokenly, pushing her hands against her face, "I feel so guilty about it all of this..."

"Have you been able to tell Cal any of this yet?"

She sniffed and shook her head. "I-I'm afraid to, Lauren."

"Why?" she growled. "Are you afraid he'll judge you? Call you weak? Be angry that you lost hope and faith he'd come get you?"

Tears drifted down Sky's taut cheeks. "Yes." The word came out as a tortured whisper.

"What else did Alexandrov do to you? Did he rape you?"

"No, thank God, he didn't touch me except once." Sky lifted her head, seeing no judgment in Lauren's eyes. Her husky voice was low and warm with understanding. "After I ran away, he lost it. They had me placed in an interrogation room. He slammed me into the padded wall, grabbed me by the throat. I almost lost consciousness. I tried fighting back, but he had two soldiers there, holding me in place so I couldn't do anything."

"The bastards," Lauren hissed, sitting up. She crossed her legs. "And that was the extent of the physical torture?"

Sky nodded, trying to stem the tide of tears, her fingers wet and trembling. "The rest was mental and emotional torture, day in and day out. I could feel him stalking me, wanting something from me. I had no idea what it was until much later."

"Because the sicko wanted to impregnate you and get a second son to replace the one he lost, Vlad. But he was also a psy ops officer and a chief interrogator in Spetsnaz. He knows exactly how to get inside anyone's defenses and destroy their hope. He broke the spirits of plenty of Russia's enemies." Lauren snorted violently and shook her head. "Sky, you went through hell."

"I just wanted to survive." Sky looked across the meadow at the huge cedar home that Cal had built. "I just wanted to come home to Cal. Come home and heal."

Lauren scooted closer, gripping Sky's hand. "Listen to me. All that can still happen. You have a man in that house who loves you more than life. He proved it in that firefight, Sky. He was your shield. He killed Alexandrov. What makes you think that he'd judge you on any of this? He's been through SERE and so have you. Torture breaks people, pure and simple. You're damned lucky you have someone like Cal who loves you so damn much, he can't see or think straight without you in his life. All he wants Sky, is you. To hold you, help you, listen to you, comfort you when you cry, and laugh with you when you laugh." Lauren dragged in a breath, holding Sky's marred, tear-filled eyes. "Get your ass up and get in there and talk to him, just like you've talked to me. Cal will NOT judge you. You're a warrior. Warriors fight until they realize the truth of the situation. YOU realized the truth of your situation. He can help you heal. Give him a chance?"

Sky nodded, hearing the raw passion and heart in Lauren's rasping words. She released her hand. "Okay," she whispered, looking over at her. "I got it."

"You were afraid Cal would judge you. That's what stopped you. He won't, Sky. I'll swear on a stack of Bibles on that one. I know this guy. We've pulled missions together." Lauren stood up and offered Sky her hand. "Come on. Time to put Cal out of his and your misery. Call the ball."

Sky nodded, gripped her hand, and stood. She picked up the book. 'Call the ball,' was a naval aviator term. When the pilot was flying in to land on a carrier, there was a bright orange ball on one side of the tower, and the pilot could watch it and know if he or she was flying at the correct slope and angle in order to land safely or not. At a certain point, the pilot had to commit. They had to call the ball, take the chance, and land a jet on a carrier deck; one of the most dangerous ways of landing in the world. It was another way of saying one had to have a set of balls to commit to the challenge.

Lauren cut her stride in half and walked with Sky through the meadow. It was late afternoon, and they were surrounded by the buzzing of insects, blue jays calling somewhere nearby, and the heat wafting off the land and embracing them. Lauren saw Sky shift and change. She smiled to herself. *Flip a switch.* Yeah, she did it all the time herself. That's how abuse survivors survived. And if they got lucky, like Sky, they thrived because the man – or woman – or good friends who stepped into their life loved them more than anything else in the world. Lauren didn't scoff at the idea of love healing all. Not after she'd seen the progress in Sky when Cal fell in love with her. It had convinced her it was possible. But she never thought for a moment that love would ever enter her own life.

"Tell Cal I'm leaving," Lauren told her at the steps that led up to the kitchen door. "I'll see him a few days." Lauren leaned over, giving Sky a fierce, gentle hug. "Now," she whispered against her hair, "you put your big girl panties on and get up there and tell Cal what happened. Leave NOTHING out." Lauren released her, giving her a hard, relentless look. "Okay?"

"Okay, I read you loud and clear."

A cock-eyed grin pulled at Lauren's full mouth. "You're stronger than you think, Sky."

Sky watched Lauren turn away, her shoulders squared, head held high, walking proudly. She turned and looked up the stairs. It was time...

Cal was sitting in the living room when he heard the kitchen door open. He stood up, craning and looking toward it. His heart dropped in his chest. It was Sky. He saw her walk in and set the book down on the granite island. Her face was wet with tears. It tore at him.

"I'm over here," he called to her, stepping out so she could see where he was at, so he didn't frighten her.

Sky nodded and walked into the living room. She saw the worry on Cal's face, the grief and helplessness. And she was causing it. Reaching out, she gripped his hand. "Sit with me on the couch?"

Her voice was strained. Cal nodded. "Sure." He felt her fingers, so long and slender, soft and tenuous, grip his own. Sky sat down, leaving enough room in the corner of the couch for Cal. She released his hand and patted the leather. "Sit here? Next to me?"

Cal sat, fear racing through him. He didn't know what to expect. What had Lauren said to her? He held Sky's marred eyes, once so radiant and blue, now looking defeated, dulled, and scared. Cal leaned back, sliding his arm around her shoulders. "Come here," he whispered, urging her gently into his arms. Sky melted against him, as if a part of him. She rested her head on his shoulder, his jaw barely touching the top of her head.

"Talk to me?" he rasped, trying to hold himself calm and centered. He was anything but. His heart was thrashing around like a dying animal in his chest. He ached for Sky, felt the mountain of pain she was carrying. God knew, he wanted to take that load from her, help her carry it. She didn't have to struggle and do this alone. But he understood her actions. As a child growing up, no one had taken the load she carried off her shoulders back then. Those experiences shaped her actions now in adulthood.

Sky closed her eyes, her palm against his heart. "I need to tell you what happened, Cal. And I need you to just listen. Let me finish before you ask me questions?"

"Go for it, sweetheart. I'm a good listener."

His embrace became stronger, more supportive. Sky gulped, and she began to tell him everything, from the first day of capture until the last. At first, her words were halting. As she became trapped within it again, emotions began to flow, and her words quickened. Through it all, Cal silently held her. Sometimes, his arm would tighten around her a little more, and it gave her the reassurance and support to keep talking. Sky absorbed his love, and the courage he gave her to continue. As she told him about the deprivation room, she felt Cal tense. Sky pressed her face against the column of his neck, her voice raw and trembling as she recounted those days. His arm tightened around her. This time, he held her strong.

"I gave up," Sky forced out in a hoarse cry. "I gave up thinking you'd ever come for me, Cal. I-I feel guilty and terrible about it, now. Worse," and Sky reached up, trying to wipe her eyes free of the tears that flowed, "I decided if

Yerik was going to take our baby from me, I was going to kill myself. I-I couldn't... wouldn't... ever let him impregnate me with his sperm." She sobbed against Cal, covering her eyes with her trembling hands.

Cal whispered Sky's name and turned her around, taking her fully into his arms so that she rested across his lap. Sliding his hand gently across her hair, soothing her, his throat was tight with so many emotions that he couldn't speak. Closing his eyes, Cal rested his head against hers and rocked her, knowing that right now, being held was what she needed. She came apart in his arms, her sobs deepening, that vast well of pain and anguish rolling out of her. It was the release she'd needed, and he cried with her, because she'd gone through such a horrific kind of torture. The worst kind. He was no stranger to torture and torture methods. And Alexandrov was a past master at it in the worst sort of ways. He'd broken Sky and then broke her some more. Cal could barely conceive of that kind of insanity in a human being, but he'd seen it before. And Sky had been subjected to it firsthand. By some grace far beyond him to understand, she'd survived it. She was whole, not shattered. A normal human being would have been a thousand of shards of glass on the floor after Alexandrov got done with them. But not her. She might think she was shattered, but Cal knew different. The awe of her strength brought him to his knees.

Finally, Sky stopped weeping. She lay quietly in Cal's arms, sniffing sometimes, continuing to wipe her eyes of tears that never seem to stop pooling in them. He kept the tissues coming, placing them in her trembling hands, knowing that every tear that fell was one less pain she had to carry inside her. Cal knew she had thirty days of tears to work through. There would be other times, he knew, when Sky would break down, needing to be held and carried through that deep wound Alexandrov had scored across her soul.

He couldn't even begin to put himself in her place; what it felt like to be told that her baby was going to be ripped out of her, that she had no control over the process, what a horrific act was going to be done against her. His heart, his soul ached for her. Sky had spent days in deprivation knowing what was coming. The baby created with pure love that they held so intensely for one another, would be killed. If Alexandrov wasn't already dead, Cal would have moved heaven and hell to track down the sick bastard and take him out. A little satisfaction soared through him knowing that he'd killed the sonofabitch already.

The sun was setting, sending a pink color flooding silently across the sky, the shadows deepening as Cal felt Sky stir. He kissed her mussed hair. They hadn't had sex since her rescue. Now, Cal understood why. He eased her away just enough to look down into her wet, marred eyes, seeing the shame and guilt so clearly etched in her waxen expression. "Listen to me," he told her, cupping her cheek, holding her unsure gaze, "there's no shame in anything you felt you had to do, Sky." His voice was thick with emotion. "You've taken SERE and so have I. It's two weeks of hell designed to show you what you can expect when you're captured by the enemy. Both of us know when a human is broken, they give up, Sky."

Cal stopped, pursing his lips, watching her closely now. "ANYONE in your position, given the circumstances you were under, would have lost hope, sweetheart. Anyone. Even me. I can't put myself in your place. I can only imagine and try. I know how much our baby means to you. You're a woman. You're a natural mom whether you know it or not." One corner of Cal's mouth crooked upward, and he gently slid his hand across her belly. "To threaten your baby is the worst kind of torture that I could imagine for you... for any woman. That sure as hell wasn't covered in SERE. And you did the best you could under the circumstances. I don't judge how you felt, or the thoughts you had, Sky. How can I?"

Nodding, she absorbed the feeling of Cal's large hand laying protectively across her abdomen, as if to reassure her and the baby she carried that he loved both of them. There was no judgement on his part as she searched his hard, weathered face. Sky looked into his eyes, realizing how much pain he was experiencing from her kidnapping. She tasted the salt of her spent tears on her lower lip as she licked it, her throat aching from all her weeping.

"I-I was afraid you'd hate me for it. When Lauren put it into black and white terms for me out in the meadow earlier, it sounded silly not to have talked with you, too. Cal," she swallowed hard, her voice wobbling, "Lauren was right. You've loved me since you met me. You NEVER left me, never abandoned me. You were ALWAYS there." Shaking her head, Sky frowned and looked away for a moment. Cal deserved her courage despite her fear, and she lifted her face, meeting his narrowed gaze that held so much anguish. "I was running from the one person I love most in the world, because I was ashamed of myself... of how I'd felt, what I'd almost done... Lauren made me see how dumb that was of me," and Sky managed to quirk one corner of her lips.

Cal kissed her brow and cupped her cheek. "You were afraid to come to me because you thought I'd judge you, Sky?" He gave her a sad look and rasped, "I'll NEVER judge you, sweetheart. Not now. Not ever. We have to give one another that kind of space, that kind of understanding. I know about your childhood, and I understand so much of what you do and why you do it. We can never forget it, but I've watched you change and grow and allowed less of it to run your life than it did before." Cal kissed her wet lips tenderly, feeling her respond, feeling her lips parting to his, no longer so tentative or unsure. He drowned in the warm heat of her mouth, always monitoring himself, never wanting to hurt her or spin her back into the garbage from childhood that she was trying so desperately to extricate herself from. Lifting his mouth from hers, Cal held her gaze that shimmered now with love for him. "I love you, Sky. That's NEVER going to change. You can come to me with anything that's bothering you. Any time. Any place. I'm always here for you. Okay?"

Giving a jerky nod, Sky whispered, "Yes…" She frowned and added, "I'm not proud of the fact I was contemplating suicide, Cal. As much as I've gone through in my life, no matter how depressed and low I was, I NEVER thought of killing myself."

Cal heard the break in her husky voice, saw the humiliation in Sky's eyes. Kissing her cheek, brushing her lips, Cal growled, "Anyone can be pushed into it. You were pushed there. Alexandrov miscalculated with you and didn't realize how strong you really were. I understand your plan to kill yourself if you couldn't find a way to escape and evade him. What choice was left to you? If I'd been in your position, I'd have been thinking the same damn thing, so stop gigging yourself with it. Okay?" and Cal dug hard into her widening eyes.

Sky stared at him, shock rolling through her. She saw the stubborn quality in Cal's narrowed eyes, saw the burning anger and felt it around him. "You would have?" she quavered.

"Hell yes," Cal said, emotion in his tone. "I wouldn't have carried Alexandrov's brat for anything. You tried to escape but got caught. You had no recourse left. If I'd been in your position, I'd done the same damn thing. I couldn't live like that, Sky. And neither could you."

It felt as if someone had removed a dark, heavy weight off her shoulders as she rested her head against Cal's shoulder. Sky closed her eyes. "I wanted to live, I wanted to survive so badly, Cal," she choked. "I wanted to come home to you… to be in our house that means happiness and safety to me…"

Sliding his arms around Sky, Cal held her and pressed small kisses against her hair. "I know that. I was counting on your strength of spirit, Sky, that no matter how long it took, you'd endure. None of us knew what Alexandrov had planned for you." God, if he'd known that, Cal wasn't sure he'd be sane at this point. He loved Sky and it hurt him to his soul that she'd gone through this kind of horrifying torture alone.

"I'm just glad it's over now," Sky admitted hoarsely, sliding her hand across his chest, absorbing his warm, caring arms sliding around her.

"Yes," Cal said, feeling her relax fully against him. He could sense the toxic guilt and shame she'd carried leaving her. "And we have nothing but good things to look forward too. A baby is coming into our lives. You have me.

We'll make it work because we love one another. I want to see the look on your face as you give birth to her or him."

"It's a her. I can feel it, Cal."

He smiled a little. "Far be it for me to question a woman's intuition." He felt her manage a silent laugh. Cal felt as if he'd been dragged through the worst shit in his life in the past month and a half. Now he understood the dark side of loving another person. All the suffering she experienced, he felt it just as vividly, just as deeply as Sky did, because love connected them. That was the price he had to pay, Cal realized. To love another human being was to open himself up to their pain and suffering, too. But Sky was worth the price—at any cost.

As the sun set, the wispy clouds above turning from pink to a bright red and gold, Cal thought how lucky he was to have Sky. She was priceless to him. One day soon, he would show her just how much of a warrior she really was. He wanted to reset her view of what happened down in Costa Rica, but it would take time.

First, Sky needed to start the healing process. This afternoon, the first huge and most important step had been taken, thanks to Lauren's intervention, her wisdom that came from her own tragic experience growing up. A fierce love welled up in him, and he squeezed her gently, kissing her temple. Cal would find a thousand different ways to show Sky his love. She'd opened his heart, allowed light to flood into his dark, miserable life for the first time. She didn't realize how her love for him had given him a reason to live, given him happiness that he'd never known. Cal silently promised Sky he'd show her. Then, with time, she would be able to put this kidnapping behind her. It would become a dark memory, but without the emotional power to wound her again, because he would help heal her wounds and replace them with his love. Sky would look forward, never backwards again.

CHAPTER 22

August 4

FIVE DAYS HAD passed since Sky had talked with Cal about her captivity. She walked the early August meadow, simply absorbing the sunshine and the soft breeze, following the bank of the winding creek. It had been a strange time for her, feeling things she'd never felt before. Maybe it was because of the hormones, the pregnancy. Maybe because she was desperately wanting to heal quickly from the kidnapping. Her heart was raw, but she felt some of her old strength returning to her. If it hadn't been for Cal's support and understanding, Sky knew she wouldn't be where she was today. It bothered her she hadn't been able to make love to Cal since returning home. She wanted too, but there was some kind of internal disconnect within her, and as much as she tried to find it, understand it, she couldn't. At least, not yet. He seemed to sense it and hadn't made any sexual overtures towards her. For that, she was grateful.

She crouched down by the creek, watching several fish swimming beneath the grass bank of the clear mountain stream. They must be rainbow trout, she decided, the sunlight revealing their green, iridescent pink, and silver bodies as they swam languidly through the water. For the first time, Sky felt the desire to try and draw them with her pastel chalks. That was comforting to her. It was another sign that she was slowly beginning to heal. Beginning to hope once more. Before the kidnapping, she was drawing and painting nearly every day. Since her return, all she could do was put angry slashing red and black lines on art paper and then hide them from Cal. She didn't want him to see them, too ashamed of the internal rage that came and went without warning.

She sensed more than heard Cal approaching. Rising to her full height, she turned and smiled up at him. He was carrying a picnic basket to her favorite spot beneath a pine tree near the creek. It was noon, and she found herself famished for the first time she could remember. Since returning home, her appetite had been nonexistent. Daily, Cal fixed her the foods she loved, and little by little, Sky was eating more, regaining a bit of her lost weight back. She loved watching him move. He wore a dark green polo shirt that showed off his magnificent upper body. As always, he sported his black baseball cap, the brim low over his eyes as they held hers. His movements were confident, filled with masculine grace. He met her smile with one of his own.

"Ready to eat?" he called, arriving at the pine tree.

Sky turned from the creek. "I am." She wandered over as he drew the red wool blanket from beneath his arm and spread it out for them to sit on. The pungent scent of evergreen filled the hot afternoon air, and Sky inhaled it deeply, a natural perfume, giving her a sense of calm.

Cal patted the blanket after he sat down, crossing his legs. "I just received a very, very interesting phone call," he said, opening the basket.

"Oh?" Sky sat opposite him, watching as he drew out sandwiches from the basket, a bowl of potato salad he'd made earlier this morning, and bottles of water.

"Yeah," and Cal gave her a wry look, slipping the sandwich into her extended hand. "Now, I don't want you feeling any fear or getting scared when I tell you this. All right?" and he pinned her with a look that made her become suddenly serious. Cal wanted nothing to interfere with Sky's progress. She'd been making slow but steady steps forward in her recovery. He saw it daily in so many small but important ways.

"Okay," Sky mumbled warily, pulling the wrap off her tuna sandwich. "Who called you?"

"A dude by the name of Rolan Pavlovich. He introduced himself as the new leader of the Russian Mafia in New York City." He saw Sky go white, terror in her eyes. *Dammit.* "He called to say that we were no longer of any interest to them. He wished us well in our lives and said that we had nothing to fear insofar as reprisals from them. In fact," and Cal smiled a little, watching her reaction, "Pavlovich was happy when I told him, that Sergeant Mace Killmer, the Special Forces team, had saved us, and had killed Alexandrov. He said it was time for a change of power. I don't think he wanted a war with elder Alexandrov, anyway, and I told him I killed the father. He almost sound jovial about it."

"Oh," Sky gasped, her hand pressed against her pounding heart. "That's good news, isn't it? They'll leave us alone? I was so worried they'd send men after us to get even for Alexandrov being killed."

Cal gave her a wry look. "I was expecting a call like this. And I told him we were happy to hear we're off the mafia's radar. I almost liked the guy. He wasn't anything like Alexandrov. At least, not on the surface. I'm sure he's a sadistic son-of-a-bitch, too. He just hides it better than Alexandrov did."

"Humph," Sky muttered, holding her sandwich, "there's no such thing as a nice Russian mafia person."

"There's Alex," he noted, pushing the bag filled with Fritos toward Sky.

They were her favorite munchies. "He was in the mafia, although he is Ukrainian. When he met you, he decided to turn against his own kind to save your life," Cal reminded her gently.

"Yes…," and Sky sighed. "You're right, Alex is wonderful. I just have a tough time thinking of him running with Vlad's team down in Peru."

"He ran with them for a reason. He was trying to make enough money to get his sister Kira the help and support she needed after being gang raped. Alex and his friend, Nik Morozov, didn't behave like the rest of Alexandrov's team," Cal said, giving her a tender look. "Alex and Nik didn't murder or rape like the rest of them."

Sighing, Sky said, "They were combat medics. They would never condone rape or hurting of another person, friend or enemy." She let out a long, deep breath. "Well, this is good news. It was another silent load I was carrying, and I knew you were too. I was wondering how safe we really were, Cal."

"And you didn't even talk to me about it?" he chided, adding a grin, watching blush sweep across her cheeks. It made Sky that much more beautiful to him. Cal wanted her desperately, wanted to make love to her, but he could feel her sorting out so many things deep within herself. He was finding other, creative ways to love her in return, and in his book, that wasn't a bad thing at all.

"Guilty," Sky admitted, giving him an apologetic look. "But you were thinking about it too, Cal. And you never brought it to me to discuss."

He reached over and caressed her cheek. "Because you're healing. Am I going to keep certain things from you right now because of that? Absolutely. I want your focus on you, Sky. If I felt this news was that important to your healing right now, I sure as hell wouldn't have kept it from you. Lauren counseled me not to overwhelm you with secondary stuff. I want you relaxed, to have some calm in your life. Not uptight like you are right now, with worry."

Cal was right, Sky decided. "Okay," she grouched, nibbling on a salty corn chip, "I'll accept that explanation for now. But later, you'd better come clean when I'm feeling more like my frisky, usual self." She watched a grin come to his face, his hazel eyes dancing with amusement. "I mean it, Cal."

"Oh," he murmured, eating his sandwich, "I know you do. And I promise you, I'll share everything. Just… not yet. You need time to heal, sweetheart. I want to give it to you." *Because I love you.*

Looking around the oval meadow, brightly colored wildflowers waving their heads in the intermittent breeze, Sky nodded. "We're really free now, aren't we Cal?" and Sky turned, holding his somber gaze.

"Yeah, we finally are." Cal knew the information was really sinking in for Sky, taking hold, because he saw sudden hope flare in her incredible blue eyes.

For the first time since returning home, he saw them shine with a radiance that brought him emotionally to his knees. The relaxation in her face was there for anyone to see, the way her full lips parted, that faraway look in her eyes for a moment as she unconsciously rubbed her belly where their baby was growing.

"Are you ready to find out if you're carrying a boy or a girl this afternoon?" he teased her. They had an appointment with Dr. Anne Simpson, Sky's gynecologist, at two p.m. today. He saw Sky smile a little. She was back with him. Here. Now. His ploy had worked.

"Today, after I get the blood test, we find out the gender," Sky responded with a soft smile. "I know it's a girl, Cal. I can feel her."

"Fine with me," he drawled, stealing some Fritos from the sack near her crossed legs. "You have any names in mind, yet?" He saw color rush to her cheeks again, like a kid caught with her fingers in the candy jar.

"Well…," Sky hedged, "I've thought of a few…"

"Like?" he goaded.

"I—just, well," and Sky sighed. "Do you have any favorite names, Cal?"

"No," he said blandly. "I was hoping you'd pick one." He knew how important it was for Sky to do this for herself. For their baby. Cal could live with any name, sensing how important this was for Sky. "What are some you like?"

"The one I really like," Sky admitted, "is Makayla." She gave him an anxious look. "What do you think? Do you like it?"

"I like the name a lot," Cal told her, watching relief come to her expression. Sky could never hide how she felt, and he was glad. She was opening up to him once more, becoming vulnerable and trusting him. Trusting herself. Cal gave her a teasing look. "If it turns out to be a boy, we can call him Mac."

Sky laughed. It was the first time since coming home that she'd laughed. And it felt so good. It felt freeing to her as she watched Cal's expression, that wicked look coming to his brown and gold eyes. Something old and hard dissolved deep within her. She felt lighter but was unsure what it meant. Happiness threaded through her heart as Sky held Cal's amused gaze, that sculpted, strong mouth of his turned up into an unmerciful teasing grin. Her heart flung open, and Sky was drenched with the love she saw in his eyes for her alone. "Okay," she murmured, picking up another corn chip, "if it is a boy, Mac is a good, strong name. I like it."

"So," Cal teased unmercifully, "it's a done deal? Whatever shows up in the test results this afternoon, the baby is either Makayla or Mac?"

She colored and felt heat flying into her face. Sky couldn't explain why the name Makayla was so important to her, but it was. "Yes, it's fine. I'm more than okay with it."

"Well," Dr. Simpson said, looking at the blood test result, it's a little girl!

Congratulations! I'll have the other test results in about four days and will call you with the results.

Sky smiled hugely over at Cal and sat up on the examination table. "See? I told you so." She watched him grin. He reached out and smoothed several strands of hair from her temple.

"So you did. Okay," Cal murmured, "Makayla it will be."

"Pretty name," Anne murmured, handing her the lab results. "And, you're the right weight for being two months old."

"Thank goodness," Sky whispered. She saw the nurse leave and they were alone in the room with the doctor. She hitched up her elastic waist pants across her expanding waistline. Cal slid his arm behind her shoulders and helped her sit up. "She's really okay, Anne?"

"Uh huh," Anne murmured, washing her hands at the sink. "Why wouldn't she be?"

Sky murmured, "Oh... no reason," and she glanced up at Cal by her side, his arm around her shoulders. Anne knew nothing about her kidnapping, and she never would. Sky saw Cal's expression change to one of tenderness as he leaned over, placing a kiss on the top of her head as if to tell her that their baby would not pay the price Sky had for the kidnapping. She felt another load lift, another powerful release flow through her. "It's just that... well... you know, if I'm upset or stressed or something... will affect my baby, Doctor?"

Turning, Anne dried off her hands and tossed the paper towel into a receptacle. "The last time you were here we discussed how you could bond with your baby. Remember? Singing to her. Using that rocking chair you have at home. Talking with her. Massaging your belly gently."

Nodding, Sky said, "Yes, I remember." But she hadn't felt like singing. Not yet. Maybe soon she would. "Would all those things remove stress from her? Even, maybe, very early stress from before?" She felt Cal's fingers move to the nape of her neck, gently massaging the area, as if to calm her real fears about the month of stress after being kidnapped.

"Consistent, daily behavior on your part toward the daughter you're carrying can erase any prior stress, Sky." Anne patted her hand in a motherly fashion. "You're a new mommy and you're going to worry about every little thing." Anne gave her an understanding smile. "Babies are amazingly resilient. It's adults who aren't," and she chuckled, writing some notes on Sky's chart. "So, a follow-up appointment in a month and we'll see how you and little Makayla are getting along. Okay?"

Cal helped Sky off the examination table. "Thank you, Dr. Simpson. We'll be there for the next appointment."

Sky walked over and gave the woman a quick hug. "Thank you," she whispered, suddenly emotional. "For everything." Sky wanted to cry with relief that her baby daughter wasn't going to suffer because of her kidnapping. The relief was so deep, that she felt inwardly shaky. Turning, she saw Cal watching her, concern in his eyes. She gave him a wobbly smile and slid her hand into his, letting him know she was alright. All she wanted to do now was go home with Cal. The house was her home, her safety, her support while she got herself well and strong again.

"Cal?"

"Hmm?" He was at the kitchen counter, preparing steaks, scalloped potatoes, and steamed green beans with slivered almonds and baby onions for their dinner after returning home from the doctor's office.

Sky moved her glass of water between her fingers as she sat on the bar stool at the granite island. She enjoyed watching Cal work. He was so fast with that super sharp knife in his hands. "How do you feel about me giving birth to Makayla here? In our house? Not at the hospital in Alexandria?"

Twisting a look across his shoulder, Cal saw how pensive Sky had become. "I hadn't really thought of it," he admitted. "If it's important to you, I'm fine with it." He turned, wiping his hands on a towel, ambling toward the island, holding her thoughtful gaze. "Women around the world in third world countries have their babies without a hospital all the time."

Nodding, Sky said, "I can't stand the thought of being in a hospital. I want... well... I know I'll be happy having Makayla here, where our love is. You'll be here. I'm not sure how Anne will take it, though."

Shrugging, he leaned his elbows on the island, smiling a little at her. "Doesn't matter what Dr. Simpson wants. But I would think she'd be all with it so long as there are no complications. Don't you?"

"Yes," Sky said, frowning. "I just want harmony from now on. Accord. I want nothing but happiness surrounding Makayla from now on. Hospitals are so stressful. You pick up horrible germs in there, too. I'm afraid of infection."

Cal rose to his full height and walked around the island. He slid his arm around her shoulders and allowed Sky to lean against him. "I think it's fine to birth Makayla here, okay? We can get a midwife or doula to assist us through it," Cal reassured her, because he could see Sky was about to gear up for an argument to get her way. He felt her sag against him in relief, nuzzling his shoulder, pressing a kiss to his chest as her arm slipped around his waist.

"Thank you," she whispered unsteadily. "This means so much to me, Cal."

He pressed kiss to her hair. "Listen, this home is your nest, Mama Bird. Fix it up any way you see fit." Cal leaned away from Sky just enough to catch her glistening gaze. "This is YOUR home. It's a place of safety, love, and happiness for you. I would think that if you're happy, the birth will be quicker and less painful for you. Less stress on the baby, too. Don't you?"

Nodding, Sky sat up and released him. "I have another request. And I'm not sure how you'll feel about it."

"Okay," Cal murmured, leaning his hip against the island, holding her gaze.

"I want Alex and Lauren here when I give birth, Cal. When I was in that hut with malaria and Alex was taking care of me, I remember one time when I came to, he told me…" She chewed on her lip for a moment. Sky lifted her gaze to Cal. "He told me his greatest joy on earth was helping the Peruvian mothers birth their babies. I saw tears in his eyes when he said it. It meant that much to him. And it touched me in ways I can't even begin to put into words."

Cal reached out, grazing her cheek with his fingers. "I'm fine with it, Sky. Have you asked Alex what he thinks, yet?"

"No, I wanted to see how you felt about it first. I'll just feel better if Alex is HERE. I want YOU to be the one to catch our daughter when she's born, Cal. I just want him near because he makes me feel safe. He knows so much about medicine. He's delivered a lot of babies."

"That's fine with me," Cal murmured, watching Sky's eyes shine with joy. "Alex is a part of our family. He saved you. Later, he saved both our hides. I know how much he cares for you, Sky. You're like a little sister to him," and Cal smiled fondly, glad that Alex was another positive male influence in her life. Sky trusted few men. Between himself and Alex, he hoped they would, in time, ease her fears around them. Maybe, and Cal hoped this from the bottom of his heart, he and Alex could restore her faith in males, help her understanding not all of them were out there to harm women.

"And Lauren?"

"Why do you want her here with you?"

"She's my best friend," Sky said with conviction. And then she smiled softly up at Cal. "You're my BEST friend for life, but she's a close second. If it weren't for Lauren caring enough to drive up here and talk to me about my experience down in Costa Rica, I wouldn't be where I am today, Cal."

"I know that. And I'm all for Lauren being with us. Have you asked her yet?"

Shaking her head, Sky said, "No… but I will."

Cal smiled a little. "You know her, and Alex are still at wary odds with one another?"

"Yes, I know that." Sky reached out, stroking his lower arm that was sprinkled with dark hair. "But Alex is good for Lauren, like you are good for me. There's just something rock solid about him, Cal. He's so much like you in that way; an anchor for us in a healing way. I know Lauren doesn't see him that way, but honestly, she is warming up to Alex a little at a time. Don't you think?" and she earnestly searched his gaze, caring deeply for Lauren.

Cal's smile dissolved and he became serious. "Lauren could be your twin sister growing up," he told her quietly. "She's been badly wounded by a man like you were. And yes, she's afraid of Alex because he IS a man."

Worried, Sky said, "Do you think I'm asking too much of Lauren, then? I don't want her to feel stressed out if Alex is here with me, too."

"Listen," Cal said, sliding his fingers through her hair, a gesture that always soothed Sky, "your ideas are sound. They would be coming here because they love you and they want to support you and celebrate the birth of our daughter with us. I think both of them are mature enough to set aside any personal squabbles and focus in on what's important: you and the birth of Makayla."

Reaching out, Sky slid her arms around Cal's neck. "You are so wise," she murmured. "Thanks for supporting my perspective on it. I'll talk to each of them tomorrow..."

CHAPTER 23

August 5

"WHY DO YOU think Sky and Cal are asking us to drive up together for dinner with them?" Alex asked Lauren. He sat in the passenger seat of her red Jeep Wrangler. The ride had been tense, to say the least, much to his chagrin. Every time he tried to start a conversation with beautiful Lauren, she made it clear she wasn't interested in talking to him. She wore a burgundy pant suit with a pale gold tee that glittered in the late afternoon sunlight as they drove toward the cabin. Her red hair was released from her always present ponytail, and he felt like a salivating Ukrainian wolf. She was stunningly beautiful though she wore absolutely no make-up. Her red hair glinted, shades of copper, gold, and darker strands of bronze woven into it. Alex tried to gird himself for her green glare. Instead, he saw her mouth purse, eyes on the highway and traffic ahead of them. Her long fingers moved a bit on the steering wheel. Alex was cataloging all her reactions.

"I don't know," Lauren said, finally. She followed the two-lane highway that would soon have them at Cal and Sky's home. It was a half hour trip from Alexandria to their cabin in the Virginia woods. She was feeling as though she wanted to leap out of her skin, the drive with Kazak had put her at such a high stress level. Lauren was sorry she'd agreed to Sky's pleading request for both to come for a visit and dinner. She should have at least told her they'd drive up separately. Alex Kazak was a huge man. His shoulders were so damn broad, his chest so wide, that she felt scrunched up in the driver's seat of her Jeep. He took up space like the Goodyear blimp in too small a hangar. In this case, her Jeep.

Opening his large hands, Alex murmured, "I think it is important."

"Did Sky say that when she called you?" Lauren refused to look in his direction. Every time she did, she got pulled into his large, intelligent hazel eyes. She swore she could read emotions in them, even though his large, square face remained neutral. And when she met his gaze, her heart did funny things in her chest, making her highly uncomfortable. For whatever damned reason, Kazak affected her. Deeply. Constantly. He was a like a burr under her proverbial saddle.

Alex shook his head. Thrilled Lauren spoke to him in that husky, low voice of hers without anger attached to it, he breathed a sigh of internal relief. "No."

"Then how do you know it's important?"

Alex touched this chest, hand over his heart. "I feel it here." And then he laughed a little awkwardly, allowing his hand to fall to his lap. "I do not think you can be an operator and not have a very finely sharpened intuition. Do you?" and he turned, searching her profile. He knew Lauren avoided looking at him. According to what Cal had said, when she did, Lauren saw the big man in her past who had hurt her, her predator, and not the real him. He'd mulled that conversation over a lot and found that it might be true. That hurt because Alex would never harm Lauren. But she didn't know that she was unable to separate him from her predator. And she wasn't going to give him a chance to show her otherwise, either. Sadness moved through his heart as he realized that he was at an impasse with Lauren.

"You're right," she admitted. Even his voice, always quiet and somehow soothing to her, made her heart respond. It was crazy! Lauren never had a man affect her like this, and it scared the hell out of her. Alex had not touched her or made any move to do so. Yet, when he was around, her heart, her body, wildly responded to him. Nothing like that had ever happened to her before, and Lauren simply didn't know how to handle it. He made her nervous, tense, and uncomfortable.

"I sense it is something good, Lauren. I do not think you need to worry so much about it."

Lauren snapped a glare in his direction and quickly looked back to the road. "Don't EVEN presume that you can sense what I'm thinking or feeling!"

Alex's mouth thinned, his brows drawing downward. Her words were sharp and angry. *Again*. What had he said or done to deserve such a reaction? He'd seen her be open, laughing and joking with other men and women at work. Lauren trusted them. With many of these other employees, she'd been on many missions with them. Perhaps he had to prove himself to her? Surely, three weeks ago when they rescued Sky, she realized he was an operator to be trusted. Someone she could rely on. Someone who had her back. Alex drew in a deep, slow breath, trying to tune into her emotional state. He realized it wasn't anger he felt. It was fear. Fear of him? Just because of his size? That he reminded Lauren of the big man from her past who had harmed her?

"You are right," he murmured, his tone conciliatory. "I have not earned the right to say such things to you. I am sorry."

Great. Now Lauren felt like a heel. She gripped the steering wheel a little more tightly, mouth flattening. Why the HELL did Kazak have to be such a gentleman? It would be so much easier if he was a bastard, an alpha male who hated her as much as she hated him. Lauren suddenly felt guilty. She didn't hate the medic. It was really a battle to stop liking him because he was so damned likable if she was dirt honest with herself.

"Perhaps," Alex offered gently, "as we pull missions with one another, you will come to see I have your back, Lauren. That you could begin to trust me?"

Gritting her teeth, Lauren pulled in the driveway to Sinclair's home, relieved to be getting out of this Jeep and putting some space between them. "If I have ANYTHING to say about missions," she told him coldly, "I'll make damn sure Jack NEVER puts us together on one."

Alex felt like she was throwing knives into his heart. But he knew why, and he tried not to take it personally. The only way Lauren was going to get over his size was to work with him out in the field. There, she would realize very quickly that he was an asset and would have her back. He said nothing as she parked the Jeep near the garage. Climbing out, he saw the sun far in the West, ready to dip behind the evergreens clothing the hills. He appreciated the rugged beauty of this area. Lauren quickly left and moved through the garage to an inner door that led into the home. Dragging in a deep breath, Alex gently put Lauren's issues aside. His heart lifted and he eagerly looked forward to seeing how Sky was doing. And how Cal was handling his own fragile situation with the pregnant woman he loved with his life.

The warmth inside the Sinclair home was infectious to Alex. Cal came forward and they slapped one another on the back in welcome. Sky rushed over after hugging Lauren and threw her arms upward around Alex's wide shoulders.

"Thank you for coming," Sky whispered, emotional, as she hugged the massive medic.

Alex smiled gently, leaned over a bit for her sake, and gave Sky a careful embrace. "You look very, very good," he murmured, releasing her. Sky wore a gossamer cream tunic over a gold tee beneath it. A pair of comfortable white, drapey rayon slacks made her legs look even longer. Alex saw that she and Lauren had, almost telepathically, worn a similar gold tee. He knew Sky was very close to her, and it showed in every way. Even in the colors they chose to wear. They were like twins that had been separated at birth.

"Let's go to the living room for beer and chips," Cal invited them. "For dinner, we're having buffalo roast with all kinds of veggies."

Alex grinned. "Gravy, too?"

Cal handed him a cold beer. "Yeah, for sure." He saw the medic smile broadly. Alex loved gravy. No secret there.

Sky poured Lauren a glass of burgundy wine. She took a glass of water with lime juice in it for herself and walked with her into the living room. She and Cal sat on the couch together. Opposite of them, across the coffee table, Lauren and Alex took two chairs that sat side-by-side. Sky's heart swelled with excitement, hoping they would agree to be with them when she birthed. The wary look Lauren gave Alex spoke volumes.

"You look beautiful, Lauren," Sky said. She touched her gold tee and said, "I think we're reading each other's minds?"

Lauren laughed and nodded. "I noticed. Great minds think alike, right?" and her lips drew away from her even white teeth.

"Right," Sky agreed, grinning.

Cal placed his arm around Sky's waist as she sat forward, eager to talk with them. He could feel her excitement. Her hope. He wasn't sure what would happen. Lauren did not look very comfortable with Alex in such close proximity. The medic, on the other hand, sat relaxed, smiling at Sky with that gleam in his eyes that spoke of how much he loved and adored her.

"Thank you for coming," Sky said, her voice low with excitement. "We asked you two up here for a special reason." She looked over at Cal and then focused on them. "We're having a baby girl. And we've chosen her name. We've decided that I'm going to birth Makayla here, at home."

Alex grinned. "A girl! See, you were right!"

"I love her name," Lauren said, her voice wistful with sudden emotion.

"And is the doctor approving of you having Makayla here?" Alex asked, gesturing around the home.

"Spoken like a true combat medic," Cal teased him. "Yeah, Dr. Simpson is fine with it. There's no issues with Sky's pregnancy. She's healthy and the baby is placed correctly. It will be a straightforward birth."

Alex nodded. "That is good to know." He gave Sky a warm look. "And you look very happy, Sky. Home births are always a good thing. In my country, many women birth at home. It is familiar. Safe. Low stress."

"Exactly," Sky agreed. She rubbed her hands on her pants to wipe off the dampness. "But, there's something else I'd really like to ask from both of you. Cal and I would love you to be present for the birth."

Alex sat up, a smile wreathing his lips.

Lauren did too, her eyes suddenly misty.

Sky directed her gaze to Lauren. "You're my best friend. I WANT you with me, Lauren. Please? It would mean so much to me because you're such a great coach." She smiled nervously. "No one cuts through BS faster than you. You can help me through those contractions."

Lauren smiled softly. "I'd love to be there for you, Sky. But you know in our business, I might be called away on an op. I might not be able to attend."

Nodding, Sky said, "I understand that. But if you're here, would you be with me? With us?" and she looked over at Cal. "We'd love to have you because you're extended family to us." And then, Sky flushed. Her voice grew strained. "I never had a big sister, and you're like that to me, Lauren. You help guide me with all your experiences and wisdom."

Lauren blinked a few times, clearing her throat and looking away, getting control over herself. She swallowed and then swung her gaze to Sky. "You know I'll always have your back. And yeah, if I hadn't been an only child, you'd be the little sister of my dreams."

Sky stood up, walked around the coffee table, and threw her arms around Lauren's shoulders. "Thank you," she muffled, tears in her voice. "Thank you for being who you are. You inspire me so much, Lauren."

Alex traded a warm look with Cal as the two women tearfully hugged one another. He saw Cal's face was open, saw the love he held for Sky in his eyes. Looking away, Alex found himself deeply moved by Sky's request. Even more touching was that Lauren had tears in her beautiful green eyes. Soft green emeralds. He'd watched her game face melt away. The woman beneath it stole his breath away. Lauren had been so vulnerable and open with Sky. Alex found his heart aching to have Lauren one day look at him the same way. It was a dream. But Alex knew dreams could come true if he held the course. And after seeing Lauren's walls dissolve, the real woman emerge, it hardened his resolve to stay the course with her. No matter how angry and defensive she got toward him, he would not take it to his heart. Alex tucked that visual photo of Lauren away in his heart, imprinted it on his soul. It had been an unexpected gift.

Sky sniffed. Cal handed her a tissue from the box sitting on the coffee table as she came and sat back down next to him. He tucked her beside him as she blew her nose and wiped her eyes. His heart was wide open with love for Sky. Cal knew how very much it meant to her that Lauren be present. And judging from Lauren's softened features, her green eyes glistening with unspilled tears, she had been touched profoundly by Sky's request.

Sky smiled apologetically at Alex. "I've become such a sop," she whispered, smiling at him.

"Tears are the heart's way of healing itself," Alex murmured, holding her luminous gaze. "They do not make me uncomfortable."

"That's because you wear your heart on your sleeve," Sky whispered. She saw the confusion spread across Alex's face. Realizing she'd dropped into slang, she shook her head.

"How does one wear their heart on their sleeve?" he wondered, genuinely concerned, while trying to visualize it.

Lauren shook her head. "It means you aren't afraid to show your real feelings," she muttered, giving him a quick glance.

"On my sleeve?" and he held up his arm toward her, now genuinely confused.

Cal chuckled. "Alex, the heart on the sleeve means that you're vulnerable. You aren't afraid to show others how you feel. It's a compliment Sky just gave you. Okay? Not many men are able to do that. God knows, I can't," and he shrugged, giving Sky an apologetic glance.

"Oh," he murmured, "okay. Well? Is this bad, Sky?"

"No, no," Sky said quickly, holding up her hands toward him. "I love you JUST the way you are, Alex. Don't change a thing about yourself!"

Rubbing his sleeve ruefully, Alex nodded. "Okay, I trust you, Sky."

She smiled and said, "I'll try to say this without slang," she promised Alex. "Cal and I very much want you to attend the birth of Makayla, too." Sky's voice dropped. "When I was sick with malaria, you and Nik cared for me. But Alex, you personally protected me from Vlad. You made me feel safe in a very dangerous situation. When I found out you'd delivered lots of baby's, I couldn't think of anyone that I'd want here with me more, other than Cal. Would you come, too? If you're not on an op? I so MUCH want you to be with me! You saved my life, Alex. I want you to see our little girl born. It's the least we can do to thank you for all you've done for us." Sky tilted her head, her voice becoming scratchy. "Please say yes? It would mean the world to us."

Lauren stole a glance to her left. Alex's face dissolved into a tender look as he regarded Sky's passionately fueled request. Her heart twisted in her chest. Alex's eyes were warm with love for Sky. That strong mouth of his that was so mobile, so quick to curve into a smile. She FELT Alex's reaction. Tears drove into her eyes, and surprised by her reaction, Lauren quickly looked away. She would NOT cry! If she ever did, she'd never stop. What was it about Alex's demeanor that just dissolved all her defenses? All her walls? Around him, Lauren felt stripped naked. Far too exposed to those hazel eyes that brimmed with life and hope.

"*Moya zolota*," my golden one," he whispered in his home language, his voice oddly husky, "it would be a great honor and gift to be with you and Cal when your little girl is born. Of course I will come if I am not away on a mission. I would not want to be anywhere but here, with all of you."

Sky gave a cry of joy, leapt to her feet, and hurried around the coffee table. Alex slowly unwound to his full height, giving her a big, sloppy, boyish grin, opening his arms to her. Sky hugged him hard, with all her woman's strength. Alex held her gently, hearing her sob once and then bury her face against his chest. "It's going to be fine, *moya zolota*," and he patted her gently on her shoulder, feeling how much this meant to Sky.

Sniffing, Sky eased out of his arms. She gripped Alex's arm, holding his tender gaze he shared with her. "You saved my life," she quavered. "And now, you are going to see a new life slip from me into this world. If you hadn't done what you did in Peru, Alex, I wouldn't be here now." Sky twisted her head, catching Cal's softened gaze. "None of us would be here."

"Well," Alex said in a mothering tone, low and filled with emotion, "we must welcome Makayla into the world among those who love her. A child birthed with love surrounding her will become as radiant and beautiful as the sun." He gently touched Sky's swelling belly. "I will be here. I am not allowed to use my medical skills here in your country, but I can be a support you."

"I know," Sky whispered, wiping the last of the tears from her cheeks. "I just want you, your beautiful, sharing heart, to be a part of it, Alex. I know Makayla will feel you welcoming her into our world."

Alex removed his hand and grinned. "Oh, I will be here wearing bells," he said proudly.

Cal grinned. "Alex, I think you mean 'with bells on?'"

"Oh," and he gave them all a look of apology. "Your American slang," he side, bashful, "is very tough to remember. Yes, Sky, I will be here with bells on."

"You said something in Ukrainian to me earlier," Sky said, searching his amused hazel eyes. "It sounded so beautiful. Melodic. What does it mean?" She saw ruddiness come to Alex's cheeks and he suddenly became shy, avoiding her glance for a moment.

Opening his hands in apology, he said, "I am sorry, Sky. I slipped into my language. It happens when I'm deeply touched. I always revert to it."

"It was beautiful," Sky sighed. "I never realized Ukrainian could sound so musical, like a poem, maybe a song…"

"Well," Alex confessed, embarrassed. "**Moya zolotaya**, means 'my golden girl or golden one.' You have blond hair, Sky. It is…" and he lifted his chin, thinking of how to explain it in English terminology and understanding. "A father will call his daughter that. A mother will too." His eyes gleamed with sudden teasing. "And if a young man has a woman whom he loves, he will call her that."

"It's an endearment, then," Sky whispered.

"Oh…"

"It's a loving term," Sky explained. "Someone you love, you would call them that. Yes?"

"Of course."

"Okay, in our country, that's known as a term of endearment."

Frowning, Alex pulled out a small notebook from his Levi pocket. "I must write this down, Sky. Otherwise, I will screw the pooch."

Cal burst out laughing. Lauren grinned, rolled her eyes, and then sorrowfully, shook her head.

Alex looked at them for explanation. "Oh no, I did not say it wrong, did I?"

Wiping tears out of his eyes, Cal couldn't stop howling. He held up his hand. "Alex, listen, buddy, you and me? We need to sit down and have some serious head time about when and how to use those terms you've been collecting in that slang notebook of yours. Okay?"

Sky touched Alex's thick, muscular arm and said with a smile, "You wouldn't use a term like that when talking about this conversation, Alex. It would be rude."

Scowling, Alex wrote furiously in his notebook, putting an asterisk by 'screw the pooch.' "Okay, I think I understand now. Thank you for explaining it to me. Please, I apologize to you."

Patting his arm, Sky murmured, "It's okay, Alex. We love you just the way you are. I wouldn't change one hair on your head."

Lauren rolled her eyes and groaned. "You know, I never realized just how much we Americans rely on slang to get something across to another," and she shook her head, grinning broadly over at Cal.

"Alex gives American slang a whole new meaning," Cal agreed, still chuckling. He gave the big medic a mischievous look. "You're one hell of an entertainer, Alex. Thanks for bringing laughter into our house."

Nodding, Alex said, "You are welcome." He turned to Sky. Tapping his notepad, he said, "You just said, 'I wouldn't change one hair on your head.' What does THAT mean? Do I not comb my hair correctly? Is there a special hair on my head that needs to be combed? Does it need help of some kind?"

Sky couldn't stop laughing. She gripped Alex's arm and put her hand over her mouth, trying to stop. The room burst into collective laughs as well.

Finally, Sky got a handle on herself and gave Alex an endearing, patient look. "Are you ready to write this down?" she asked, gesturing to his note pad.

"Of course, *moya zolota*," and he gave her a great, big teasing grin.

"I love my new nickname you've given me," Sky said, meaning it.

"Then you do not mind if I call you that sometimes? Because it is meant with love from my heart to yours. You are like a little sister to me. I want you happy. I want only to always hear you laugh, Sky."

"Thank you," Sky whispered, leaning up and kissing his shaven cheek. "You make me very happy just being here, Alex. Soon, you're going to be an uncle to Makayla." She looked warmly at Lauren. "And you're going to become an aunt."

Lauren smiled a little. "Having family is new to me. I don't know how an aunt behaves."

"Oh," Alex assured her confidently with a smile, "At one time, I had many uncles and aunts. I will help you learn to be a good aunt to little Makayla. I will show you how a loving aunt spoils her niece."

Lauren nodded, unable to defend herself against Alex's broad, genuine smile. Her heart floundered, beat harder in her chest. "Yes, you can teach me how to be a loving aunt. I'd like that." And she would. It was impossible to remain immune to this man. He got under her skin, had taken root in her heart despite everything Lauren had done to drive him away. She saw Alex's smile turn suddenly affectionate, his full attention devoted to her. It felt as if raw, warm sunlight had suddenly embraced her, wrapped itself around her inside and out. The feeling was so startling, so beautiful and poignant to Lauren, that she fell helplessly into Alex's green, sable, and gold eyes that were rich with affection she was afraid to name.

"You know," Alex said, becoming very serious, holding Lauren's vulnerable gaze, "I have a Ukrainian endearment for you, too: malen'kaya.

Lauren heard the melodic words roll off his tongue, felt them wrap securely around her, making her feel so loved that she didn't know how to respond. It was as if there was palpable magic being shared between them. It was raw, alive, passionate. She felt dampness collecting between her thighs. Shaken, Lauren whispered, "What did you just call me?" Because she HAD to know. Her heart was going wild in her breast, opening up, wanting Alex. Wanting his touch. *HIM.* Lauren had never wanted any man in her life. Until right now.

Alex gave her an ardent look, his voice becoming husky, the emotions clearly there. "In English, it means 'Little One.' It is words a man would use for the woman he loves with every breath he takes..."

CHAPTER 24

August 6

"HAPPY?" CAL ASKED Sky, drawing her naked body against his own. It was nearly one a.m. The night had gone swiftly, with Alex and himself playing chess after dinner. Sky and Lauren had gone into the living room and watched a movie with a huge bowl of popcorn. Moonlight shed luminous streams through their master bedroom. He heard that soft musical sound in her throat, his spirit soaring, his heart opening wide.

"Very," Sky whispered, snuggling as close as she could get to him. There was no denying Cal wanted her, his erection pressing tantalizingly against her belly. For the first time since returning home, she felt sexual. And she wanted Cal. His hand smoothed down across her ribcage, flowing across her hip, fingers splaying outward to gently settle against her abdomen. The gesture brought tears to her eyes. He was so incredibly gentle with her. He always had been, but now, since the kidnapping, Sky sensed and felt a new level of tenderness within Cal that he shared openly and willingly with her. He was a complex man of unknown depths, and she was going to spend the rest of her life exploring the many facets of him.

Nuzzling her hair, Cal rasped, "Good thing Alex and Lauren have opposite guest rooms from one another tonight. I wasn't sure what she was going to do after he called her by that Ukrainian endearment."

Sky sighed, moving her hand against his as he cupped her abdomen. "I thought she was going to cry. Did you see it? The tears in her eyes?"

"Yeah. I think his endearment really shook her in an unexpected, but good, way."

"I think Alex finally reached inside her armor and held her very guarded heart in his caring and gentle hands for the first time." Sky leaned over, kissing his thick biceps, feeling the muscles leap and tightened beneath her lips. "You know, Alex comes off as this simple farm boy, but beneath that exterior, there's a man who has exquisite timing. I stood in awe of what he did earlier with Lauren."

"What do you mean?" Cal asked, kissing the nape of her neck, feeling Sky arch suggestively against him.

"Think about this...," and Sky scooted away just enough to study Cal's craggy, shadowed expression. The moonlight moved silently across their bed, chasing away the darkness, replacing it with charcoal grays and luminous white instead. She saw Cal's eyes were hooded, saw the fire in them, the need for her. "He told her in the middle of company. Lauren wasn't going to confront him in front of us. Alex was able to tell her how he really felt, and Lauren had no defense. She couldn't run. She couldn't get angry. I think Alex is very much a fox beneath that good ole farm boy exterior of his."

Chuckling, Cal slid his fingers through Sky's hair, beginning to gently massage her scalp, which she loved. "He'd tell you he was a wolf in disguise. I saw him handle a bad situation in the villa. He's a professional operator. My respect for him is solid."

"Okay, he's a wolf on the prowl, and he's hunting Lauren."

"Good luck to him," Cal murmured, watching Sky's eyes slowly close, her lips parting as he kneaded her scalp, feeling her turn into warm butter in his arms. "I think he's in love with her. Has been from the moment he saw her across the room at Shield."

Sky's eyes flew open. "Really?"

Cal grinned. "What? A guy can't have a hunch about someone when it comes to love. Is it always the woman who knows first?"

Sky smiled and outlined his broad shoulder, trailing her fingers down his upper arm, his flesh tightening, responding to her grazing fingertips. "I happen to agree with you. Lauren will be the last to know it, though."

"Yeah, but she's going to lose the battle and the war," Cal promised her, catching her hand, opening her palm, licking it slowly and then kissing her flesh. He watched a fine tremble go through Sky. She was more than ready to love him. Cal had never felt so grateful. It was as if the old Sky, before the kidnapping, had returned. Tonight, was important to her, having the people she considered her loving family surround her and the baby she carried. And Cal had never more grateful to Lauren and Alex for stepping up to the plate and being there solidly for Sky. He owed them. Big time. Someway, Cal swore he would find a way to pay both of them back. They had helped give Sky the rest of her life back to her, whether they realized it or not.

Sighing, she relinquished her hand to Cal, the tiny electrical jolts flying up her fingers and into her wrist from his slow, sensual assault on her senses. "Lauren has been wounded much worse than me, Cal. I don't know if she can overcome her fear, to reach out to Alex. I hope she does. He's a wonderful man, so kind, patient and gentle."

Cal slowly eased Sky onto her back, allowed her to reclaim her hand. "He's

Ukrainian, sweetheart. They don't give up. Ever. Once he's got an objective, he's going to capture it. Lauren just doesn't realize it yet," and he gave her an amused look. "I'm far more familiar with Spetsnaz operators than she or you are. They draw the kind of man who doesn't quit. He can be filled with bullet holes, but he's still going to come after you until he bleeds out and dies. And Alex is like that, trust me."

"I've never seen that side of him," Sky admitted.

"He strategically blindsided Lauren this afternoon," Cal told her smugly, rather proud of his friend. "That was pure black ops tactics we saw being played out in front of our eyes in our own living room. The man is a third dimensional chess master, trust me. He beat me at chess every time, tonight. And I'm damned good."

"Is that why you looked like you did?" Sky accused, sliding her hand up his jaw, the stubble creating wild tingles through her sensitized palm.

"Yeah. Didn't you feel the shift of energy around him before he spoke?"

"Well," Sky stumbled, thinking back, "I felt something. I guess it felt like a laser sighted in on its quarry if you want to talk in sniper terms."

"Exactly," Cal praised, giving her an admiring look. "You felt it. You iden-tified it. That's how an operator does it: sights in. Focuses. Calculates windage and clicks. Just like a laser. And Lauren happened to be his target." Cal murmured, smiling a little, "Alex was shooting out his love he holds for her. Embracing Lauren with that powerful focus he has at his disposal."

"Ohhhhh," Sky whispered, suddenly realizing something. "Is that why Lauren blushed? I've NEVER seen her blush! Or act so ODD!"

"She acted like a woman who suddenly understood that Alex was silently and invisibly embracing her with his heart and love, wanting her in every possible way."

"You black ops people are spooky!" Sky accused, laughing. She sighed and moved sinuously against Cal, his erection pressing deeply into her belly.

"I've got my sights on YOU," Cal growled, giving her a heated look. "I want you. More importantly? How are you feeling?"

She saw the concern in Cal's eyes, drowning in the sable and gold of them. "Tonight is the first night since we've been back that I'm starving for you, Cal. It's as if someone flipped a switch in me. Before, I felt nothing. I felt dead inside," and Sky gave him apologetic look. "I felt bad… guilty… because I knew you wanted to make love with me, and I didn't want to be touched."

Cal kissed her worried brow. "It was shock, Sky. It turns everything off," he explained, kissing her temple, inhaling her special womanly fragrance. "And as the shock recedes, parts of you start to come back online. You start feeling alive again, wanting to re-engage with life."

"I wished you'd have told me that," Sky grumped, pouting.

"I wish," Cal said, looking down at her pointedly, "you'd have asked me about it. I might have saved you a lot of worry and guilt."

Sky raised her brows and sighed. "I really need to learn to communicate better with you. You're right…"

"Speaking of communicating," and Cal cupped her cheek, holding her lambent gaze, "are you all right with me making love to you tonight? I know you were worried about hurting our baby."

"I'm okay," Sky whispered, grateful for his sensitivity to her concern.

"You sure? There's lots of ways to please you." He saw the hesitation in her eyes, sensed her concern. "Tell you what," Cal murmured, placing a lingering kiss against her slender neck, "let's put you on top tonight? That way, you can decide how much or how little of me you want?" Cal saw the relief come to her large, glistening eyes. Sky had grown up in a family where silence, where never asking questions, kept her from getting hit or yelled at. It wasn't easy for her to suddenly open up and talk to him. It was an ongoing process, and one Cal was sure Sky would improve at over time. For now, he had to watch Sky for subtle signs, slight expressions, or intuitive signals. He was more than grateful to his SEAL training for putting him in touch with that sixth sense within himself.

"Yes, that sounds good," Sky murmured. "Thank you…"

He smiled and brushed her lips, feeling her respond instantly. "Thank me afterward, okay? Because tonight is your night. All I want to do is make you happy. We'll go as far, or as slow, or whatever it is that you need. You're in charge. I'll be happy with whatever you want to share with me, and it will be enough. Okay?"

Sky's heart opened and she felt an unending depth of love for this warrior, this man who had saved her life twice. She moaned softly as Cal trailed a series of kisses down the length of her neck, stopping every now and again, simply inhaling her fragrance. His other hand followed the curve of her taut breast and her breath jammed in her throat. How badly Sky wanted Cal to touch her nipple. She couldn't wait, and she arched into his large, calloused palm, her flesh skittering with the fire of contact. She realized, since becoming pregnant, her whole body was far more sensitive than before. The breath she'd held turned into a guttural moan as his lips suckled that erect, awaiting nipple. Fire arced and dizzied her as it shot straight down to her lower body that ached for so much more from Cal.

Every touch, every sleek movement of his lips across first one breast, and then lavishing across to the other, was tender. Tears were burning behind her eyelids as she was worshipped by Cal. It was impossible to believe a man could be so incredibly tender, barely kissing her, suckling her, moving his large, roughened hand down her hip to her thigh, caressing her, telling her in so many ways how much he loved her.

Something broke inside her and she unexpectedly sobbed. Sky couldn't control it, and deep, animal-like sounds tore out of her throat. She felt Cal gather her up against him, holding her, rocking her, his legs tangled between hers. Her tears wet his chest, her hand opened and closed against his hard, tough flesh. She didn't understand what was happening to her, or why. Hadn't she cried enough? How many more tears were locked away inside her fractured soul? Cal's touch, his kisses, his attentiveness with her, tore open another dark door hidden deep within her.

"I-I'm sorry," Sky wept, pressing her face against him, clinging to him, never wanting to let Cal go.

"It's all right Sky," he rasped near her ear. "Everything's just as it needs to be."

"I-I can't lose you," she sobbed, unable to halt her rampant emotions no matter how hard she tried. Sky heard a rumble through Cal's broad chest. Or maybe it was a low growl of a male animal protecting his mate? She felt so exposed. So incredibly vulnerable. Choking, she sobbed, "I feel like someone has torn my skin off me..."

Cal closed his eyes, jaw against her hair, moving his hand soothingly up and down her long, beautiful back. He hurt for Sky, understanding the shock of the kidnapping was still a vivid, controlling part of her life. "I won't let anyone hurt you ever again." His voice thickened as he held and rocked her. "You're safe Sky. Our baby is safe. I'll NEVER let anyone ever hurt you or Makayla again. Alright?"

Those words sunk deep into her aching heart. She clung to Cal, terror coming out in the form of tears. Sky had never cried so hard, so long, in all her life. Cal's hand smoothing down her back, his soft kisses against her hair and temple, began to calm her. And finally... finally... the tears turned off. Sky lay against him, eyes tightly shut, feeling cleaner. Lighter maybe. Cal afforded her the safe harbor she desperately needed. Wiping her cheek, she muttered, "When is this going end? I've never cried like this in all my life..."

"You have decades of tears stored up inside you," Cal rasped, easing her away to look into Sky's darkened eyes. A corner of his mouth lifted. "When this happens, and it will, I'll be here. I'll hold you. We'll work through this together." There was such raw vulnerability in her eyes, Cal understood what she meant by feeling as if she had no skin to protect herself. He knew the kidnapping trauma was a large part of it. Another part was that she was pregnant. And then, stack her ugly childhood on top of it, and it was the perfect emotional storm for Sky.

Cal kissed her damp brow. "You're going to be okay," he promised her in a deep voice, holding her gaze. "You've gone from running nearly all your life, Sky, to falling in love with me, and then, getting pregnant." His tone turned wry. "And let's just throw in a kidnapping in there for good measure." Cal gave her gentle look. "Is it any wonder your emotions are upside down and turned inside out? You've gone through a lot of sudden evolutions, sweetheart."

"I feel so out of control. The tears… they hit out of nowhere. I was so lost in your loving me…," and her voice died.

"Love opens up," Cal told her quietly, using his thumb to remove the tears across her cheek. "Love makes us both vulnerable in ways we've never, ever experienced before, Sky. It's a helluva scary ride."

"But you seem to be able to handle it a lot better than I do."

He grinned. "I'm not pregnant, though."

Sky muffled a laugh against his chest.

Cal's heart mushroomed as he watched Sky's soft mouth draw into a real smile. Her laughter was music to his soul. "I love you. I need you. And all I want for the rest of my life is you in it."

Sky turned, holding Cal's smoldering gaze, that laser-like focus on her. "I was so filled with love as you touched me," she whispered, "I just can't live without you, Cal. I don't want too…"

He nodded, saying nothing, finding and curving his mouth gently over hers. He tasted the salt of her spent tears. Her hand drifted from his chest, down across his hard belly, her fingers wrapping around his erection. Instantly, he tensed and groaned. It felt so good to be touched by her. He became lost in her heat, her fingers moving suggestively around him, hearing her moan as his tongue tangled with hers. She was so brave. So damned courageous. Cal marveled at her ability to remain open to him, to invite him to her, to celebrate so much. Celebrate life trumping death.

Cal eased her hand from around him and then laid Sky on her back, opening her thighs. Beautiful, creamy, firm curved thighs that he was going to taste and sample. And then, he was going to taste her. Cal rose up, settling his legs inside those beckoning thighs. Sky's eyes were half closed, her breath becoming uneven as he curved his hands around her breasts bathed in moonlight. Two months pregnant and her breasts had grown lush, larger. She was far more sensitive to every touch. When he suckled those nipples, he felt her arch her hips, inviting him into her. He smiled into her druzy, lust filled eyes and leaned over, sampling each nipple, feeling her fingers dig frantically into his biceps, communicating her enjoyment.

It was so easy to trail a series of wet, slow kisses down the center of her body. He paused over her pearlescent abdomen, cupping it with both his hands, kissing her tenderly there, kissing the baby she carried for both of them. Allowing his hands to range down across her hips, feeling the firm velvet of her thighs, he heard Sky moan because she knew what was coming. Cal knew she loved the way he went down upon her. Tonight was for Sky. More than anything, he was driven to pleasure her, give her ecstasy, and chase away those dark, haunting memories. Kissing the inside of each of her thighs, she was so responsive, so hot. His nostrils flared as he caught her sex scent. It made him throb with need of her. He ached to plunge into her depths, knowing she wanted it as much as he did, but that wasn't the plan right now.

Patience was his specialty, and tonight, Cal was going to give Sky all the pleasure she could possibly handle. As he brushed his mouth across those blond curls, she cried out, hips lifting, wanting his mouth upon her. She smelled so good, and he laid down, his wide shoulders easing her thighs apart, giving him full access to her entrance, to her utter sweetness, her strength and womanhood. Moving his tongue slowly around her wet rim, the fluids thick, his primal mind took over. Cal gripped her thighs, holding her captive, and slid this tongue inside her.

Sky bucked and groaned. Her fingers frantically opened and closed upon Cal's tense shoulders. She twisted, sobbed for breath as he found that swollen knot of nerves just pleading to be tasted, nudged, and unmercifully teased it into throbbing, swollen life by his tongue. Cal felt her quiver. Felt how very close Sky was to orgasm. He'd barely started, and she was already there. Somewhere in his mind, he remembered it had been six weeks since they'd last had sex. That was a helluva long time. He slid his hands beneath the small of her back, lifting her more directly to his mouth, and he began a fevered assault upon her that left her sobbing out his name. When she sank her fingers into his bunched shoulder muscles, Cal felt her walls contract and he knew she was coming apart. The orgasm shattered through Sky and her cries became wild, her fingers digging spasmodically into him.

Cal laid down beside her as she orgasmed, slid his hands around her thickening waist, and lifted her over the top of him, her thighs settling on either side of his narrow hips. She was flushed, sobbing for breath, shaking in the wake of the orgasm when he settled her hot, wet, throbbing core against his hard erection. Cal drew her gently forward on him, feeling her begin to lose spatial reality. He kept up the firm pressure, watching Sky lose herself in another orgasm that rolled through her moments after the first one. A pink flush spread across her chest, the moving upward, and Cal smiled, watching the moonlight caress her slender form, watching how the shadows plunged and swelled across the valleys and curves of her body. She was so beautiful.

Unearthly. His.

Cal felt Sky begin to collapse, spent and blown by the two powerful orgasms. He guided her across himself, her brow resting against his jaw, her hands limp across his shoulders. She was quivering, the orgasms still rippling through her, taking her to that other place where only burning, undulating pleasure existed. Cal smoothed his hands down Sky's damp back, feeling the womanly strength of her spine, outlining her flared hips, caressing her cheeks, and then starting from her shoulders and moving downward again. He sensed she needed to rest longer than usual, and he willingly absorbed her like a warm, living blanket laying across him. Feeling the bird-like beat of her heart against his, the warmth of her moist breath feathering across his neck and chest, Cal relished every second of it. He could feel the swell of her belly pressing into his erection. It didn't matter to him right now whether she wanted anything more or not. He'd pleasured her. He'd gifted her with his love, and that's all that mattered. He'd welcomed Sky home to him in the most intimate of ways.

Sky lost track of time. She felt sated. Her body was still throbbing with life, and she marveled at how good she felt. How light. Moving her hand a little, she whispered, "I went away for a while…" She heard a rumble of agreement in Cal's chest, a partial laugh filled with understanding.

"Great sex does that to you," Cal rasped, caressing her hair, sliding his fingers along her nape, massaging her because Cal knew she loved being kneaded by him. It was a small gift, just another way to let Sky know he loved her. "How are you feeling?"

Lifting her head, Sky pushed her hands against his chest and slowly sat up on him. She felt the warm hardness of his erection teasing her wet core, felt the gnawing ache of wanting him inside her. "Good," she whispered, giving him a lazy smile, still half gone, not really all there.

"You look blown," Cal murmured, settling his hands on her hips.

Sky laughed a little. "I am. It's a wonderful feeling…"

"Want off?"

Shaking her head, Sky moved her core firmly against him. His eyes shuttered and narrowed. It thrilled her to be able to affect Cal so quickly. His fingers dug momentarily into her hips. "I want you inside me. Where you belong," she said huskily, a rainbow of emotions winding slowly through her. "I want to love you, Cal…"

He couldn't even get a word out as she lifted herself just enough to draw him slowly into her wet, waiting core. He felt like he couldn't control himself, grunting, clenching his teeth as he easily slid into her silky, hot tunnel, surrounding him, drawing him deeper. And when she eased back and forth, allowing her body to get used to him, to accommodate his length, Cal nearly lost it. Sky's face was soft, her eyes luminous with arousal and love. That smile of hers drove him crazy. She lifted her lips, telling him how much she was enjoying their blazing, building connection with one another.

"Don't...," Cal growled, "be in a... hurry..." because the last thing he wanted was to hurt her or their baby. He wasn't a small man in that particular department, nature or genetics had been very generous to him down there. He gripped her hips to slow her down. Sky was already lost to the boiling heat arcing between them, her eyes closed, her lips parted, her breathing becoming uneven as she lavished in the pleasure of having him within her. The last thing Cal wanted was for her to be in pain, so he gently stopped her from taking any more of him into herself.

Sky moaned, barely opening her eyes. "It's all right," she whispered, her voice wispy, "you're not hurting me or the baby. It just... it all feels so... good, Cal..."

He was only halfway into her. He knew he could touch her deeply, no problem at all. Cal was afraid she'd become so enthralled by the pleasure that burned between them that she'd forget, plunge downward on him, and hurt herself.

Sky stopped moving and opened her eyes. She held Cal's concerned gaze and slowly stretched out across him. "Trust me?" she whispered.

"I don't want you to hurt yourself... or our baby," he rasped, searching her half-closed eyes.

"I would never do that, Cal." Sky gave him a tender look. "Trust me?"

He nodded, feeling her wet, tight walls gripping him until he wanted to groan.

Sky moved slowly down upon Cal, watching him wrestle for control, his teeth gritting, his nostrils flaring as she took more and more of him inside her. She could feel her body burn and then accept. Sucking him deeply into her, watching his eyes grow to slits, his hands tightening around her hips, he was losing the battle to how good it felt between them. And then she lifted her hips, her hands coming to rest on his chest, and brought her full weight down upon him. Oh, the feeling was so vast, so fiery, the pleasure consuming, raw and satisfying. Sky began a campaign to force Cal to stop being concerned, to allow her to love him fully on her terms. She knew her body. She knew how large he was, but she knew where to stop, too. She had almost taken all of him inside her when she began to thrust her hips boldly against his, hearing him groan, watching his face tense, as if in pain. But he wasn't in pain. Instead, Sky knew he was so close to coming, and so was she.

In just a few strokes, Cal felt as if his spine had been split wide open by a bolt of burning-hot lightning. It barreled into his tightened, aching balls and then exploded deep inside her luscious, small body. He felt her contract, felt the fist-like squeeze of her wet walls surrounding him until it was almost painful, and then she orgasmed as he finished his climax. They froze inside one another; neither able to move, just feel and feel some more. The intensity of the orgasms raced through them, rippling, throbbing, alive. It was an incredible celebration of their love for one another. Time ceased. Only pleasure ripped through them, shearing reality away until all that was left was exquisite enjoyment.

Sometime later, Cal felt Sky collapse limply against his sweaty body, felt his heart hammering in time with her own. He could smell her sex, a perfume that he'd never get enough of, the scent of almonds in her hair, that honeyed fragrance of her skin, as he kissed her slender, exposed throat. He would love her forever.

EPILOGUE

O N DECEMBER 1, Sky married Cal at their home, surrounded with good friends from Shield Security. The beautiful, slender wedding dress hung nearby, to remind Sky that she was a very pregnant woman, and that the dress would be used later, in a larger wedding planned for everyone on June 16th, in San Diego, Coronado Island, a year after her kidnapping. Sky had wanted her daughter, who would come at any time now, to have a mother and father who were married. It might be old fashioned, but she had lived with parents who had never gotten married. In her life, that would change, and Cal had agreed fully with her. It was a quiet day spent with the people who loved them, and they loved deeply in return. In September, Lauren had arranged a baby shower for Sky, the women from Shield joining them to celebrate. Cal had a bachelor's party the week before the wedding, filling their home with noise, laughter, and hilarity for the evening.

On March 4th, in the midst of snow falling softly around Cal and Sky's home, Makayla Sinclair was born. Lauren Parker held Sky's hand, coaching her through that one last push that sent blond-haired, seven-pound Makayla into her father's large, awaiting hands. Cal was guided verbally by Alex Kazak, who stood crouched behind him, offering information as the birth quickened. And as Dr. Simpson cut the baby's umbilical cord, saving the blood in a special container, Alex expertly tied off the baby's cord, beaming, thanking the doctor for allowing him to participate.

Sky began to cry after Alex quickly dried off Makayla, made sure her nasal passages were clear and opened. Cal's eyes were dangerously bright as he stared down at the red, wrinkled little baby in his massive, latex gloved hands. He gave his exhausted wife a tender smile.

"She looks just like you," he murmured, a catch in his unsteady voice.

Alex grinned and quickly wrapped Makayla into a special pink blanket that Sky had knitted for her daughter months earlier. "She has your golden hair, Sky. Her eyes are gray blue right now, but I know in a month or so, they are going to turn the color of turquoise." Alex lifted his chin, sliding Sky a proud smile. "Strong genes. She is a beauty."

Cal carried his daughter to his wife's bedside, sliding her into Sky's welcoming, opened arms. Makayla did not cry. She made snuffling sounds, her tiny arms moving energetically as Sky settled her daughter on her belly, guiding her mouth to her swollen, engorge nipple.

Lauren sniffed and wiped her eyes as she sat near Sky's shoulder. "She's so beautiful…"

Alex moved around to the other side of the bed, his hand resting on the headboard, smiling warmly as he watched the baby's mouth latch on to her mother's nipple, starving and hungry and strong. His gaze drifted to Sky, who looked weary, but happy. She couldn't take her eyes off her suckling daughter. And then his gaze moved to Lauren. She was wiping tears of joy and relief away, her expression soft and vulnerable.

Dr. Simpson watched the proceedings. "Makayla is healthy and she's happy. Doesn't get any better than this, Sky. "How are you feeling?"

"Whipped," Sky admitted, "but I don't care. Just getting to hold Makayla makes it all worth it," and she smiled up at the doctor.

"Well, I'm going to shoo everyone out of the room. Your placenta ought to be coming out shortly," and she gestured toward the stairs that led down from the second-floor bedroom.

Lauren and Alex nodded.

"I'm staying," Cal said.

"Yes," Sky said, "you are."

It didn't take long for her afterbirth to expel. The doctor cleaned everything up, checked Makayla out one last time, and left. She promised to return tomorrow and perform a check on them.

Finally, they were alone in their master bedroom. Cal moved to Sky's side, sliding his arm behind his wife's head. He eased his other arm beneath hers to support her as she held their noisy, contented baby daughter. Makayla was opening and closing her tiny fingers against her mother's breast. Cal leaned down, kissing Sky's damp brow. "I love you," he said, giving her and his daughter a gentle squeeze.

Sky wearily leaned her head against Cal's shoulder, so glad he was there, holding both of them with his male strength and gentleness. "I love you so much," she quavered, tears continuing to slip down her cheeks.

"It's over," Cal murmured, kissing her hair. "Makayla is here. And you're okay." Sky had been such a worrywart about the birth. In some ways, Cal understood that her focus was partly about herself. Her drug-addicted mother had never wanted her. Sky's whole life became focused and anchored on her daughter she carried. Cal knew she desperately wanted the baby she carried to know she was loved and welcomed by her family, unlike what her own experience had been. Cal could see the relief in Sky's sparkling eyes, saw the anxiety dissolve. Their perfectly formed baby daughter was healthy, kicking her tiny arms and legs, and noisily drinking at Sky's breast. "You know," Cal warned her with a grin, "this kid of ours is gonna be a hell raiser when she grows up. Look at her."

Sky gazed wearily, her daughter active in her arms. "I wonder if I was like that when I was born?"

The question was spoken so softly that Cal almost didn't hear it, and he had good ears. His heart ached for Sky. "I'll bet you looked just like Makayla when you were born," he rasped, squeezing her shoulder gently. "Beautiful." He could feel Sky's anguish over her own life of being unwanted. "And you're here now with me, sweetheart. And I love you." Cal eased his arm from beneath Sky's and lightly moved his finger down his daughter's plump little cheek. "And so does Makayla." Cal repositioned his arm beneath his wife's arm and held her tearful gaze. "You don't realize how happy you make me. Or her," and he nodded toward his daughter. His voice grew thick with feelings as he held Sky's gaze. "Only today counts, Sky. You, me and Makayla. There's nothing but love between us and in this house of ours. And it will always be that way. It's a new chapter in your life. In all our lives."

"You're right," Sky agreed, her voice quavering with emotion. She leaned upward, meeting Cal's descending mouth, feeling his lips move in adoration across hers. His words, his love for her, gently closed the door on her painful past. Cal was right. It was done and gone. Nothing could be changed about it. She held her wriggling, happy, snuffling, noisy daughter in her arms. And Cal held both of them. Sky silently promised that she would love them with a fierceness that would make her past become a distant memory within her. She'd had nothing. And now, she had so much. It was enough. It would always be enough.

THE BEGINNING

Don't miss Lindsay McKenna's next Shadow Team series novel, *No Quarter*.

Available from Lindsay McKenna and Blue Turtle Publishing and wherever you buy eBooks.

Excerpt from No Quarter

"COME OVER HERE and let me examine you," Alex urged as Lauren walked up to their hut. He pulled out his medical ruck and opened it up.

Lauren stood waiting while he was crouched over the ruck, pulling out what looked like a pen light. "I'm okay, Alex. Just a headache is all."

Rising, he came over and gently took the hat off her head and handed it to her. "Humor me?" and he met her shocky looking eyes.

"I'm not smiling, Kazak."

He grinned and tipped her chin up. "Look at my nose? I want to see if both your pupils are equally responsive to light."

Patiently, Lauren stood. "Thanks for saving my butt in the Blackhawk helicopter. If you hadn't held me, I'm sure I'd be a helluva lot worse shape than I am right now." He moved the small light slowly from one eye and then to the other several times. Alex was so close, and she absorbed his quiet strength. His hand cupped her cheek, not wanting her to move while he performed the pupil check.

"I told you it would be rough."

"You were right."

Alex took the pen light and said, "Good, your pupils are responsive and equal."

"And that means?"

He gently eased his fingers through her hair, moving slowly across her scalp, feeling for a cut or a bump. "That you do not have a bad concussion. Probably just a level one, which gives you a miserable headache, maybe some acute dizziness and feeling tired. But it will not last for usually more than a day or two." The pleasure of getting to touch her silky hair even though damp and flattened by the hat she'd worn, was a personal joy to Alex. Even better, he watched Lauren's eyes droop closed, as if enjoying his examination of her scalp.

"I told you: I'm okay."

"Spoken like a true operator," he teased. Reluctantly, Alex eased his hands from her hair. "You have a nice egg goose above your left eye. That is probably where your helmet struck the door."

"Alex, its a goose egg. You got it turned around." She saw him give her an apologetic grin.

"One day, I will surprise you and I will say all my slang I am collecting, correctly."

He saw her give him a slight smile. It was a gift to him.

"All I need is some Ibuprofen. Do you have any?"

"First," he said, "tell me what other symptoms you have?"

Lauren could hear the spec ops boys puttering around the camp, smelled coffee in the air. She was hungry, her stomach growling. "Headache. Slightly dizzy. I have a bad bruise on my hip, for sure, but no broken bones."

"Dizzy when? How often?"

Shrugging, she muttered, "It's mostly gone, Alex. Worse when I was in the bird."

"You were not walking well after we left the Blackhawk."

"No, because of my bruised hip." Lauren shook her head. "You combat medic types are ALL alike. Such mother hens."

"I am a hen mother," Alex agreed equitably, grinning proudly. "Let me feel where your bruise on your hip is located?

Nodding, she pointed to it. His touch was light and sure enough, it was swollen like a goose egg.

"It is a nasty bruise, but that is all." He crouched and found the bottle he was searching for. Standing, he opened it up and picked up her hand, turning it over and dropping one white capsule into it. "Ibuprofen. Take this with the breakfast they are making for us. I will check with you later today and see how you are doing."

Tingles raced up her as he cupped her hand. Lauren could feel the calluses, and her skin skittered with tiny, pleasurable tingles. "Thanks," she murmured, lifting her gaze to his. The grayish light was disappearing as the world was awakening around them. His face was strong and the stubble gave him a decidedly dangerous look. She was no longer afraid of Alex. "I'm okay with you being a mother hen."

Alex's mouth drew into a wry grin as he released her hand. "Really?"

Lauren popped the capsule in her mouth and sucked on her CamelBak tube, swallowing it. "Don't let it go to your head," she growled in warning, tipping her head back and taking the second capsule.

Chuckling, Alex turned away and pressed the Velcro closed on his large medical pack.

"Hey," Cale called, walking up to them, "you two ready for some fresh eggs? I'm cooking them right now." He grinned at them. "Better than MRE's, for damned sure."

Lauren undid her ponytail, quickly pushed her fingers through her hair, trying to get it tamed into place and said, "I'm more than ready. It's great to have fresh eggs out here in the middle of nowhere. Thanks." She saw Merrill's blue eyes dance with amusement. Taking the rubber band, Lauren quickly remade her hair into a ponytail.

"Come on over to our fire pit," he invited, turning and walking quickly back to where his teammates were sitting on some logs placed around the fire.

"Pity," Alex murmured as he closed the ruck and shoved it inside the hut.

Lauren turned. "What?"

"Your hair is beautiful. It looks nice when it is allowed to go free."

She saw the sudden wishful look in his eyes. "My hair would be in my way, Alex. I can't have that."

Sighing, he nodded. "I know. But someone should tell you how beautiful you look even though we are out here," and he walked with her toward the group.

Lauren felt her lower body simmering. He made her feel good about herself. Maybe even beautiful. Usually, a man complimenting her didn't make a dent in the armor she wore around herself because it was always about wanting sex with her, wanting to take something that didn't belong to the man. Alex was different, Lauren acknowledged. But maybe because she had been around him, gone through a number of experiences with him, and he hadn't made a stupid move like Volkov had, she didn't see him like other men.

Available from
Lindsay McKenna

Blue Turtle Publishing

SHADOW TEAM SERIES
Last Stand
Collateral Damage
No Quarter

NON-SERIES BOOKS
Down Range (Reprint)
Dangerous Prey (Reprint)
Love Me Before Dawn (Reprint)
Point of Departure (Reprint)
Touch the Heavens (Reprint)

WOMEN OF GLORY SERIES
No Quarter Given (Reprint)
The Gauntlet (Reprint)
Under Fire (Reprint)

LOVE & GLORY SERIES
A Question of Honor, Book 1 (Reprint)
No Surrender, Book 2 (Reprint)
Return of a Hero, Book 3 (Reprint)
Dawn of Valor, Book 4 (Reprint)

LOVE & DANGER SERIES
Morgan's Son, Book 5 (Reprint)
Morgan's Wife, Book 6 (Reprint)
Morgan's Rescue, Book 7 (Reprint)
Morgan's Marriage, Book 8 (Reprint)

WARRIORS FOR THE LIGHT
Unforgiven, Book 1 (Reprint)
Dark Truth, Book 2 (Reprint)
The Quest, Book 3 (Reprint)
Reunion, Book 4 (Reprint)
The Adversary, Book 5 (Reprint)
Guardian, Book 6 (Reprint)

DELOS

Last Chance, prologue novella to Nowhere to Hide
Nowhere to Hide, Book 1
Tangled Pursuit, Book 2
Forged in Fire, Book 3
Broken Dreams, Book 4
Blind Sided, BN2
Secret Dream, B1B novella, epilogue to Nowhere to Hide
Hold On, Book 5
Hold Me, 5B1, sequel to Hold On
Unbound Pursuit, 2B1 novella, epilogue to Tangled Pursuit
Secrets, 2B2 novella, sequel to Unbound Pursuit, 2B1
Snowflake's Gift, Book 6
Never Enough, 3B1, novella, sequel to Forged in Fire
Dream of Me, 4B1, novella, sequel to Broken Dreams
Trapped, Book 7
Taking a Chance 7B1, novella, sequel to Trapped
The Hidden Heart, 7B2, novella, sequel to Taking A Chance
Boxcar Christmas, Book 8
Sanctuary, Book 9
Dangerous, Book 10
Redemption, 10B1, novella, sequel to Dangerous

Kensington

SILVER CREEK SERIES

Silver Creek Fire
Courage Under Fire

WIND RIVER VALLEY SERIES

Wind River Wrangler
Wind River Rancher
Wind River Cowboy
Christmas with my Cowboy
Wrangler's Challenge
Lone Rider
Wind River Lawman
Kassie's Cowboy
Home to Wind River
Western Weddings: Wind River Wedding
Wind River Protector
Wind River Undercover

Everything Lindsay McKenna

Lindsay's website is dedicated to all my series at lindsaymckenna.com. There are articles on characters, my publishing schedule, and information about each book written by me. You can also learn more about my newsletter, which covers my upcoming books, publishing schedule, giveaways, exclusive cover peeks and more.

Made in the USA
Monee, IL
28 June 2024

60918938R00142